PEARL HARBOR, 1941

Here is N. Richard Nash's magnificent, bestselling
novel about a time of romance and intrigue, as
Japan steals across the Pacific . . . and three
remarkable people are hurled into a violent,
private war . . .

JOHANNA
A woman ruled by a fervent
lust for revenge.

COMMANDER CLARK
A man burning to possess her
in secret sin.

TOKAN
An aristocrat
who drove them to rapturous depths . . .
and murder.

High on the treacherous slopes of Mauna Loa,
they come together in a jungle of exploding
passions and unspeakable terror just before the
bombs fall . . .

EAST WIND, RAIN

EAST WIND, RAIN

EAST WIND, RAIN

RAIN

N. Richard Nash

BANTAM BOOKS
TORONTO · NEW YORK · LONDON

EAST WIND, RAIN

*A Bantam Book / published by arrangement with
Atheneum Publishers*

PRINTING HISTORY

Atheneum edition published February 1977
2nd printing .... *February 1977*
3rd printing .... *February 1977*
4th printing .... *March 1977*
Bantam edition / January 1978
2nd printing
3rd printing

One

SHE HEARD THE SOUND in the great green ferns. A soft sound, it might have been any animal, a wild goat or a blacktail deer. She was glad it couldn't be a snake—there weren't any in Hawaii, so the legend went, not even in this marshy fen where there were plenty of crawling, lurking places. Maybe it's the boar, she thought, and her hand tightened on the rifle.

It was an antelope. It came out of the dark bracken to try the clearing with one slowly raised foreleg. Hesitant, it kept its small hoof in the air, uncertain whether to set it down inside or outside the darkness. The pronghorns moved a little, a flickering movement like aspen branches. The eyes blinked fast, then didn't blink at all, stone still. They couldn't have been looking *at* anything, Johanna told herself, or they'd have seen her. But the animal gave no sign of seeing anything. It simply stood there, all surprise. Surely, Johanna thought, it can't be surprised by things it knows, the swamp, the jungle, the wild stephanotis, the stumble of creeping spur and thornbush; it must be surprised by its own existence. She envied it.

How beautiful the creature was. And how vulnerable, broadside; one shot would have done it. But she didn't even have the temptation; only the urge to warn the animal against the other hunters: run away, you foolish thing, or you'll be a bloody crumple on the ground. "Go!"

The antelope broke back into the shadow and was gone. Go away, Johanna kept saying, I don't want you.

She didn't want the wild boar either, not really. Nor did she know why she had come on this witless hunt, the only woman among men. Perhaps that was the reason. Being singular. It was a way to keep from getting lost. Increasingly, since her husband had died and her children had grown up, she felt she was bearing witness to a quietly frightening phenomenon. Where's Johanna Winter these days, some faint echo would ask. Where, indeed?

She heard another sound, a crash of undergrowth, and hurried into the brake of brushwood. It was nothing, only a scare of quail, perhaps, or a partridge.

Suddenly she hoped she wouldn't see the boar.

Why had she come? Why had she spent a whole month reconditioning her dead husband's guns, sharpening his hunting knives, quickening her hand and eye on the target range, as if she were twenty-three again and back home simple-mindedly shooting at clay targets on Penobscot Bay? Shoot ahead of the bird, her father would say, *ahead,* you idiot, ahead. Bang, ahead, and the splatter of clay.

Clay, not blood.

Diversion. That's why she was here. She needed distraction from work, from her weekly column on the *News-Telegram.* She was wearing thin. *Quiddities and Oddities*—she had long ago started to pad each item, running to adjectives; she was finding it more difficult to discover trifling niceties she could write distinctions about, and hardly anything seemed eccentric to her any more. Her husband had, in a way, warned her she would come to hate the thing, but then he had a grudge against overdelicate discriminations—he pretended not to know one wine from another; bourbon was his drink, any label at all. She missed him.

She heard a shot. It came from the ridge where the foothills started ascending toward Mauna Loa. Only one shot, but it sounded again, an echo long delayed, mocking the first. She listened for a second shot, a real one, but none came. Someone had gotten the boar, perhaps, on a single firing. She'd know in a moment, if she heard the rattlebox. It would clack louder than the gunfire sound, then the hallooing voices, hunt's over, and someone would have won the year's trophy and, if he wanted it, the boar's head, mounted. Hunt's over; she would be relieved. But she didn't hear the rattlebox, nor the voices.

The damn diversion had to go on. And, to tell her-

self the truth, it had to go on not because the rattlebox
hadn't sounded but because she needed it to continue
until something happened, she *needed* the diversion.
Not from writing the column, that was equivocation.
No matter how hard she worked to pay her weekly
chit of snatches and snippets, she was, she knew in her
gut, idle. Diversion didn't have anything to do with
work. But then it didn't have anything to do with this
hunt, either. Diversion suggested easy, passive pas-
times, comforting and comfortable, demanding no
trials to the breaking point, free of danger. And here
she was, up to her boottops in this sucking quagmire,
bitten by bush wasps and *lepeka* mites, terrified—she
had to admit it—by the potential peril of coming nose
to snout with a hideous killer pig. Yet, despite the
danger . . .

Despite, my foot. She knew it was because of. Something had, in Oscar's words, turned-up-missing in her
life. Risk. Every act she performed, every chore she
dispatched, every obligation she discharged—yes, even
every thought—lacked the single ferment, danger. She
didn't essay any chancy battles any more, she didn't
venture mapless into dark places. If she went to a
dinner party in a wardroom, she agreed to everything.
Barely listening, she would take somebody's disorganized prattle and return it, classified and codified,
having contributed nothing to it but index cards. She
nodded a lot.

"Roosevelt's recklessly pushing us into a war we're
not ready for." At every party somebody would say it.
Yes, she would reply, it appears reckless to us, but it's
quite deliberate, don't you think? . . . "It seems to me
Roosevelt's showing the white feather to the Japs."
Yes, and the yellow one . . . "Need more battle wagons
and fewer flattops." Yes, flattops *are* proliferating! . . .
"Need more flats. Wagons are too fat in the ass for a
fast war." Yes, exactly where they're fat.

Johanna Winter, not only beautiful and charming,
but a good head on her shoulders, thinks about things,
got a good view of the Big Harbor.

Balls. They didn't know her, certainly didn't know

what she believed in because she herself didn't know. What she would risk could be the only measure of her dedication and she didn't see herself risking anything. She had even stopped fighting with her children. No need to any longer; they were, of all outlandish improbibilities, happy. Only yesterday her son had been an ensign; today, a lieutenant, junior grade; tomorrow, perhaps, a full lieutenant; and not many calendars away, a rear admiral like his father. As to Abby, she lived in a persuasion of love with her husband, even if Tad was fifteen years too old for her . . . Johanna wouldn't take issue with felicity.

Stet, she said. There was nothing to cross out, nobody to cross. No dangers, no threats, no shadowy imminences.

One late Saturday afternoon, sitting on the veranda of the Quarterdeck Club, looking down the long sunset to the dazzling fleet in the Harbor, she realized that her three drinking companions, all wives of officers, had slipped away to dinner and she was still drinking martinis and imagining the Filipino waiter naked in her bedroom. She wondered if there was truly a discrepancy between the diminutive stature of Filipinos and the size of their cocks. Trying to rout the speculation, she started to ache all over, then to tremble. She had an urge to scream filth across the veranda and throw potted palms over the white balustrade and run down to where the Buicks and Packards were parked and pee on somebody's running board. Instead, she began to faint.

Somebody came to her with comforts and cluckings and smelling salts. Somebody else pitied her for grieving over her dead husband. Not him, she screamed without uttering a sound, not him; myself.

Loathing her own self-pity, she ran home to the large house where every surface was smooth and washable and there were no nicks in anything, and she took a knife to the impenetrable porcelain of her kitchen table, and ruined the knife. In the middle of the night, when the gin had worn off and she didn't even have a punishment headache, she sat on the edge of the bed, in darkness, and wondered whether she had the courage to go back, alone, to New York. The thought of it set her shaking again: quiddities and oddities against the shrieking assault of the onrushing subway.

If only Hawaii had something to do battle against. She wanted the chance of winning something, but, perversely it seemed to her, she desperately needed a chance to lose. She'd settle for a small battle, a tiny one. But there wasn't even weather to fight.

So she was fighting a pig. What an idiocy, she told herself when she first considered going on the hunt. Then, little by little, as she thought about it, it became more sensible. Something palpable and something ugly. A wild, loathsome pig, the primordial hideousness. She was not like the ordinary hunter who could kill anything in season. She could not, no matter how ruttishly they overmultiplied and starved one another out of existence, have killed a deer or a gazelle. Today, the pronghorn antelope was not for a moment at her mercy; on the contrary, she was at the mercy of the beauty of the beast. She could wage no war against beauty.

She was doing battle against an ugliness, a pig . . . . . . and a prig.

The battlefield had broadened. To include Tad, her son-in-law. She'd always had a formless antipathy to the man and had originally expressed it in a vacuous way: he was too old for her daughter. She knew that was canting nonsense; Oscar had been nearly that much older than Johanna herself and it was not in Oscar's life that numbers counted, only at his death. Her dislike of Tad didn't stay amorphous for long. A week before their wedding, goaded by Abby, her feeling took form: "Because he's a self-righteous bastard!" she said.

"Self-righteous? You're talking about somebody else."

"Him—Commander T. Thaddeus Clarke—him!"

she retorted. "He's rigid. He stands at attention, he sits
with both feet on the floor, he can only walk in one
direction! There's no give to him!"

"No give? He's the kindest man I know!"

"I didn't say unkind—I said rigid. But come to
think of it, it *means* unkind. Even to himself. And you
better sleep with one eye open; a guy who's got it in
for himself—watch out!"

She hadn't exactly known what she was trying to
say to her daughter, certainly she hadn't any evidence
to go on, and she disliked the chapel echoes in her
own voice. Compunctious, she wanted desperately to
be proven wrong, but she was amazed when it happened.

He voted for Roosevelt. The Republican, without
any noticeable twinge of conscience, voted the
straight Democratic ticket. One night, in a mellow
mood, when she applauded his unexpected humane-
ness, his long-sightedness, his emancipation from
bigotry, he stopped her before her speech had wound
down. "You've got it wrong," he said flatly. "I voted
for him because he was right." . . . Self-righteous,
precisionist prig.

When it had come up in the Club, whether she
would be allowed to compete in the boar hunt, three
men had been vocal against it. Two of them mouthed
hypocrisies about the danger to a slim-wristed, weak-
bladdered woman. A boar was a brutal, ferocious
animal; only two years ago, one of them had gored
a club steward and left him in a canebrake, disem-
boweled and devoured. Commander Clarke, however,
had risen quietly and spoken without the slightest taint
of imposture—not about protecting helpless females,
but about protecting privilege.

"I'm very selfish," he said. "I don't want to give
anybody any rights that are important to me. The fact
that she's a woman doesn't bring out the gentleman in
me—I think that's sentimental. The fact that she's my
wife's mother doesn't bring out any family feeling—I
think that's even more sentimental." He was not a
good speaker; he certainly had no talent for demagogu-

cry. But he so deeply believed what he was saying that he didn't need eloquence. "It seems to me that tradition keeps things going properly," he said. "You break with tradition only when things go wrong. It's a good club—I don't see anything particularly wrong with it. I hope we won't allow her to join us."

They allowed her. When she had first raised the question, it had never occurred to her that they wouldn't allow her. She had a full membership in the Club, a lifetime membership. True, it was not solely her own; it included the whole family, each of them by name. But she never questioned her right to it. No need to. As the widow of one of the founders of the Club, she was certainly the woman most welcome to its members and, in her own right, possibly the most appreciated. Since Oscar's death she had come to need the Club more than ever before, and certainly they couldn't think she would do anything to overburden the ballast of the place. She expected her request to join the hunt would be amusing to them, nothing more. When it became an issue, she thought of withdrawing, then got stubborn about it. She didn't count it as a tribute to herself that they had allowed her to join them, but to Oscar, whom everybody loved. Suffer me because of the dead, she thought wryly; so in the end it was a victory for tradition after all.

She saw a streak of black. Brown-black, a blur of it, scurrying across a wet gully and into a thicket of scale moss and bamboo. She raised her gun a little and stared into the brush. It was dense and dark in there. She could have been mistaken, she told herself; an axis deer, perhaps, or a feral sheep—some of the wild ones were known to be almost jet in color.

Yet, it might have been a boar.

Go in for it, she said, go in and see. She didn't. She remembered her son's admonishing finger and the irritable edge in his voice. "If you're stupid enough to go, don't be a *complete* jackass. Stay in the open, understand? If he goes into the brush, don't go in after him—he's waiting for you. You go in and he'll gore your guts."

Not *my* guts, she thought, I'll wait him out.

And she started into the brush.

As if I can help myself, she thought, as if an admonishing finger can point me to common sense. Common sense has nothing to do with it. Warnings don't tell me anything I don't already know; it's not ignorance that has to be vanquished, it's fright. Deep terror, some depth of which I've come to look at for a moment, here in this wet place, some ugliness . . .

Step by wary step, she moved across the scrub grass toward the thicket of bamboo. Even before she stepped into the dense wildness, she could smell the damp from dark and hidden places. She imagined, too, that she could smell the animal, whatever it might be, smell the frightened life of him, without knowing what life it was—sheep, goat, deer, wild hog.

If she took one more step, she would have to part the stalks of bamboo. She would be making the challenge to the beast: here's light, here's sound and here am I.

She started to raise her hand to the bamboo. She couldn't do it. She wouldn't force her folly quite that far, she reassured herself, she still had *some* prudence about survival. How harebrainedly could a woman act, close to forty-five, and still bear witness to her own sanity? Suddenly it was all too senseless. Her gun was too heavy in her hand; her husband's gun, not meant for a woman—a .30/30 would have been light enough. Her clothes were also too heavy and her boots made her legs feel like steel posts anchored in concrete. She couldn't move.

She couldn't run back, she couldn't edge forward. She was—if the beast only knew it—as captive to it as carrion might be. Christ, she thought, that's what immobility leads to; you get consumed by the beast, whatever the beast might be.

She moved. Only one hand, her left. With it she parted two stalks of the bamboo. She heard the faint whisper of the leaves. The canes were tough and woody; it was difficult keeping them apart with only one hand. But all she needed was room enough to step into the brake. Step in . . . where the creature was.

She let her rifle slip downward on her right arm so that she could swing it up quickly. Then, shoving hard at the cane, she raised one foot and moved it forward into the thicket.

The ground was soggy; she might fall. Quickly, the other foot, and she was in the density of undergrowth. Letting the bamboo stalk fall behind her, she touched her left hand to the barrel of the gun.

She didn't see anything. But she knew it was there, the animal, whatever kind it might be, watching her, perhaps, from a low vantage point, ready to spring. She wanted to believe: deer—that was the wild thing she had glimpsed. But she looked down at the ground and the spoor was not little black pellets but dun-colored manure.

The crash.

It went shattering through the brush, tusks down, charging through stalks and canes, breaking out into the clear.

She didn't think. The gun was up. She didn't know she was sighting, taking aim, she had no sense the gun was heavy any more, the trigger didn't seem too tight as she squeezed it off. Only yesterday the recoil had been painful, today she didn't feel it at all. The shot was thunderous, but no louder than she wanted it to be.

The boar rose as if it had leaped into the air. It fell, rolled over, then suddenly was on its legs again. It ran into the clear a few feet, then, as though maddened to desperation, turned right angles, then right angles again, and ran into the brush, a hundred yards away. And was gone.

Johanna started back into the clearing. Where the sump of water had come from she couldn't tell; she hadn't seen it before. Nor the matted vine across it. She fell. The gun in the outstretched arm fell with her, into the tangle and wetness. She struggled to get up and couldn't. Swamp, she thought, oh God, one of those *piholo* bogs, a deadmarsh, and she'd never come out of it. She heard the squish of morass under her; the oozing earth was swallowing, taking mouthfuls of itself. She couldn't move and was certain she never would, when suddenly, using her muddy gun as a lever against the drier land, she found herself free.

She wiped her rifle on her hunting pants, then shoved her way into the clear. Having lost her sense of direction, she went toward the clearing, then edged back again, and couldn't come upon any sign of the beast's blood or bone. Even in the open space where she was certain she had seen him stop and turn, there was nothing to show she had ever pulled a trigger on the animal.

Then the glob of blood, a great wallow of it exactly where she thought she had already looked, and from it, clear as a painted line, the blood spill pointed down the hill. She followed it.

It took her down into a ravine, then into another thicket. Again she suffered immobility. But this time, with all her senses alive and all reason alert, she didn't question it: she would have to go in; she knew that. She prayed the beast was dead. If he was wounded and alive, the danger now was self-murder compared to what it had been in the other copse. The animal, before, had had to hide; now he had to kill.

But she told herself, as she stood at the edge of the canebrake: if he's more dangerous now, so am I. This time—taking courage—she was ready for the brute. If he had tusks, she had a rifle; he was bleeding, she had an unpunctured skin. She didn't know how her reasoning brain could match up to his shrewd underbrush instinct, but she knew one thing: her wits were no longer hobbled by panic. The weighing scales inside her head were balancing again, a caution against a danger, a danger against a reward. She knew what she was doing. She was going in to fetch her trophy.

Slowly she parted the canes. Everything seemed easier this time; even the canes gave way more tractably. And there he was.

He was a milling mass of blood. Demented, he twisted in circles, beating down the undergrowth as a dog does before lying in it. Blood everywhere, spilling in the circles the hog made with his contortions. Moving fast too, as quick as madness, and it didn't look as if he would ever lie down and stop his writhings. He paid no attention to the hunter.

Then he saw her. His motion stopped.

Johanna raised her rifle.

The boar moved forward, tusks low, a noise coming from somewhere inside the animal, ugly and death-meant.

Johanna squeezed the trigger.

Nothing happened. The gun was wet.

She had an errant thought: how ugly, how ugly and enormous he is.

The great hog moved and she veered away from him. He went crashing into canes, fell, pulled himself up again, wheeled toward her once more.

She pulled at her hunting knife and couldn't get it free. Turning the rifle, she had the butt ready for him when it happened. The boar stopped suddenly, quivered, and fell. On the ground, he shook, pulled his front legs toward his hind ones, then was still.

Johanna waited. Give him a moment, she warned herself, don't trust his death.

Suddenly—the canes behind her—she heard a noise. She twisted, again with her gun raised.

The man made a gesture. "Are you all right?"

It was Tad. She had seen him only an hour ago; now, somehow, he seemed different—changed from any way she had ever known him. Cleaner than his accustomed cleanliness, taller than he was tall. And surer than he'd ever been before, surer than any man had a right to be, about anything.

"Was it your shot?" he asked.

How could he have missed seeing the beast? She pointed. He gazed at the bloody heap, not going closer to the animal.

"You sure he's dead?"

She nodded and started toward the mass.

"Wait," he said. "If there's a breath in him, he'll kill you."

She didn't listen to him, but walked closer. To show her disdain for his caution, she got close enough to prod the animal with the barrel of her rifle. The beast surged. He made a grunt of rage. Starting to rise, his forefeet pawed and scraped in the muddy ground; he raised his tusks and opened his mouth to moan his fury at the woman. But he couldn't pull himself to his feet.

Tad pointed to her rifle. "Give him one," he said.

"It's jammed," she replied. "Wet. You do it."

Tad didn't raise his gun, just looked at Johanna, then at the suffering animal, then back to her again.

"Shoot him," she said.

"He's your kill." Without emphasis.

"Shoot him—he's in agony—shoot him!"

"If I do, I'll claim him," he said quietly. "The trophy's for the kill."

"You bastard," she said. "Lend me your gun."

"No." There was no contention in his voice. "I don't like women hunting. Use your knife."

Without another look at the dying animal, he walked out of the underbrush and into the clearing.

Her eyes followed him, then turned to the animal. If there were a choice of monsters, she thought, she felt more akin to the beast than to the man.

The boar was making strange sounds—heavy breaths, then a small cough, then the breaths again. She couldn't bear to look at him. His blood was spreading all over everything and would soon be under her feet. He started to quiver. Suddenly all her hunter's courage was gone and she felt the animal's tremblings as if they were her own. Kill him, she urged herself, kill him.

She reached to her waist and this time had no difficulty freeing the knife from its sheath. It was an old knife and had, she was sure, seen much blood. She wasn't confident she knew the best way to use it, wasn't certain the beast would let her use it.

Slowly she circled the animal so as to come upon him from behind. When she got close, his shaking seemed abruptly to become more acute, as if he had caught her scent. She wondered whether she smelled as vile to the pig as he did to her; a fetor almost unendurable to her as she stood arm's length away from him.

Somewhere she had heard: behind the ear. She plunged the knife deep into the beast and a fountain of blood spurted out onto her hand, onto her clothes, across her face. At once, as if exploding, the beast emptied itself of its excrement, a simultaneous emission of gore and feces and all the rank wetnesses of obscene death.

From somewhere in the distance she heard someone call her name, then someone else with the cry of halloo and congratulation. In a moment, she heard the rattlebox and soon the men came running.

Two

THE STENCH OF THE dead pig on the floor behind Tad was disgusting to him. It lay on a tarpaulin that was not large enough, and whenever the airplane banked to the left, another rivulet of blood spilled across the aisle. An hour after it was shot, it was still bleeding, not only from the gunshot and knife wounds, but from its snout. With everybody already a few drinks to the wind, somebody had done a bungling job of cleaning the animal's ordures. True, it had not been an easy task. The bullet had inauspiciously pierced the bowels. Cleaning the viscera of the animal and stuffing it with greenery had, if possible, made things worse; now the greenery itself was a stench and a brown ugliness oozed from the beast's mouth and anus. Tad thought he would be sick.

He considered moving to another seat, but the way the old utility transport plane had been converted, Johanna's seat was facing his, halfway down the aisle, and he was disinclined to let her notice how disturbed he was by her dead prey. He could, of course, have insisted on having the beast moved. It was, after all, blocking an emergency exit, and even on a civilian plane that was forbidden; on a naval aircraft it was an actionable offense. But there was a more flagrant breach, he speculated, in the use of the service aircraft for private, sportive purposes. Even if nearly all the members were Navy officers, the Club had no charter from the Navy, no certificates or articles, a Quarterdeck Club without quarterdeck rights, as old Admiral Kley once warned them. And to exercise any privileges that had not been granted—a plane for a pig —was, to put it in the euphemism of the officers' mess, unauthorized.

Except by custom. Well, custom was not to be derogated, not in Tad's mind; custom was the essence. It

14

made the written law, which I'ad respected to the iota, manageable. Custom was the gist of things.

Goddamn it. Stop thinking salutes and ceremonies, he told himself, when what you're really thinking is: why didn't you shoot?

All she asked you to do was shoot the goddamn gun and dispatch the goddamn wounded pig, and what you gave her was hogwash, no pun intended, about the trophy not belonging to her if you killed the animal. When what you really meant was: go in close to the bloody thrashing thing and knife it. Face the danger of being a man.

But, pushing himself one step further: if it had been a *man* who had asked you for the shot, your finger would have pulled the trigger, bang. Custom, my ass, Mr. Clarke, you exposed her to a danger to which you would never have exposed one of your men. Why?

Don't think about it. Men hate their mothers-in-law; it's a hatred hallowed by tradition. There it goes again. "Tradition," a young man had said in a midshipman writing exercise, "is brackish bilge. Saluting the quarterdeck and drawing a dead horse and swords-up-and-swords-down and letting fly the sheets—they save the worthless ship and scuttle the mind." Of course he stopped short of handing the paper in; he'd never have been third in his class if he had. Instead: "Tradition is the Navy's peace of mind."

And he had come to believe it was his peace of mind, too. It was hard won, every silver whistle of it. Sweat and heart's blood, for he wasn't a Navy junior or the junior of a junior, not the way the Winters were. Johanna, the daughter of a rear admiral and the wife of one; her two children going generations back to—Christ, to sailing ships.

But Thaddeus Clarke—only his name sounded like old Navy. And even his name, long ago, had to be revised and reassembled a little. Tom T. Clark had become T. Thaddeus Clarke, and suddenly the stammering orphan from an impecunious part of Philadelphia had acquired a nominal pedigree. He told himself at the time that he had to call himself Thaddeus rather than Tom because the letter he stammered on most painfully was *t,* and his tongue became swollen every time he said his name. But he soon found he was calling himself Tad, not Thaddeus, without stammering at all—and he got to wondering whether he was entirely telling himself the t-t-truth.

Anyway, it was tradition that pulled him out of misery. The tradition of the Stephen Girard Fund, for the care and betterment of orphans, the application said. For the care and betterment of tongue-impeded, acne-skinned Tommy Clark. For speech classes and cleansing his skin and cutting his hair and getting him to "understand his chronic constipation," for tempering his terrifying dreams and his wet-handed guilts in the darknesses of night. And for, finally, nine laudatory letters, including one from a state senator, which ceremoniously launched him into the swim of the Naval Academy.

Because he had no family nor even any friends by whom he could measure himself, he had to find other gauges. The one he came to rely on most confidently was usage. He made himself acutely perceptive of the common practice of people he admired. But he was not only the pragmatic achiever; he had an instinctive love of the art of process; in fact, he often found himself sacrificing the material end if the means had no form he could admire. The canons of custom became precious to him. And ultimately he found he couldn't easily free himself of them.

It was only in the most recent years, when he had freshly come to Honolulu, that he had been able to relax a little; only when he had finally come to realize he was a successful man, and a loved one. Certainly by Abby and her brother, loved. But he always had a distrust of relaxation; always, in his mind, it suggested the diversionary tactic of an unknown enemy. He knew that the release of one tension almost invariably meant the constriction of another. And in the happiest time of his life, he was developing an ulcer.

That goddamn shot. The failure to *make* the shot. Two years ago he'd have had no qualm over it. Right was right; when could right ever be wrong? If she was going to be a man, let her be a man.

But, again, the stammering truth: if she had been a man, he'd have shot the animal.

Screw off, Johanna Winter, I hate your guts.

Five, six, seven seats down, on the other side of the aisle, she was asleep. Or pretending to be asleep, he suspected, so as to avoid the Victrola record conversations that had been worn in the grooves. Good-bye, Singapore, Captain Hewlett had been saying, burbling in his beer glass; they're scared to hell of us but not scared of the British, so it's Singapore-for-nevermore. Or Commander Sladen: no battleships tomorrow, no subs, nothing but floating palaces of planes, quadruple deckers of them, ready "to launch aloft a thousand million shining wings" and blast the bejesus out of the jaundice-bastards. Or old Rear Admiral Kley, normally the canniest of them all, but now tipsily adrift, telling the lesson of Scapa Flow, not quite remembering what the lesson was or if we had anything to do with it, not even sure of the slogans any more: if a victory is to be gained, I'll gain it, all hands to bury the dead, life is not so short but that there is time for victory.

Even more than the boredom, Tad suspected, she was trying to escape the lewdness. He couldn't quite put together how it had happened. Admittedly, nearly everybody was a bit boozy, but he had seen most of them that way before, and a few prime drunk, yet none of them as gamy as this. Obscenity eructed as if from a burst sewer pipe. It started blandly, more a slip of the tongue than anything else, when Lieutenant McEwen had asked to heft Johanna's gun and wondered if she'd like to heft his. Somebody snickered. Then Captain Embry, more sozzled than the rest, told Johanna he wanted to point out something to her, a point at issue that had to be pointed out more pointedly than all the other points, and he pointed at her breast, his weaving finger triangulating to find her nipple. Somebody playfully struck his hand down and there was another laugh. Athletic supporters got into the conversation and it was all cock talk and Captain John Cotter-Hayes, who was en route to the head, took out his penis before he got there. The cordon they formed around him was the biggest howl of all, and Johanna drifted as far away from the men as she could, sat down and closed her eyes.

It puzzled Tad. Did her presence lure the men into obscenity, or defy them to it? Were they trying to say exactly what he himself had said: I don't like women hunting. I don't like one of them here, especially if she's a trophy winner, but if she is here, this is what it's about. But he knew it wasn't about that—their bawdry wasn't usually a mode of warfare—and he hated them for showing it that way. It was a victory for Johanna; she had seen them all as she had seen that fool Cotter-Hayes, exposed. And Tad realized she'd seen him that way too . . . Use your knife . . .

He saw her stir in her sleep. He wondered if she was dreaming. She looked more like her daughter, he thought, than like her son, but she had Ben's high forehead and the faint flush that suggested perennial embarrassment. Asleep, her face had a blank-paper innocence, guiltless of any inscription. How different the face seemed to him when she was awake. How wised up the woman was, he thought, how shrewdly she maneuvered herself, how amiably she suffered impostors when he knew she wanted to spit into both faces of hypocrisy. Right now, when she was asleep, was the only time he could stand her, when she looked vulnerable.

She was, he had to admit, more beautiful than Abby. Worn, a bit, but more exciting, more sensual, fuller of breast, more lush of mouth. He often thought, watching her move across a room, that her walk was calculated to tantalize. He wasn't quite sure of that; wasn't, in fact, sure what else about Johanna was calculated. It bothered him sometimes.

She opened her eyes. She was staring right at him. She was smiling.

For an instant he thought: she's Abby. The smile is her daughter, the look of deep gentleness, Abby.

Especially the friendliness—no, the *need* for friendliness. It was, of all things, a forgiving smile, saying how foolish to be hostile, how did we ever get lost in that unfriendly neighborhood, does anybody know the way back? A smile, a flickering eyelash couldn't say all that, he told himself; in fact, it might not be saying anything. He had imagined it.

Her eyes were shut now; she was asleep again.

No, he hadn't imagined the smile, only its meaning. There was no friendliness in it, only contempt. It said as plainly as if it had been typed and notarized: I got the boar. With the shot and with the knife. Without you, without your help. The trophy.

It was precisely what he would have expected the smile to say. Yet, perversely—almost obsessively—he went back to his original instinct of it: friendly. He had caught her, in a half-asleep, unguarded moment, thinking pleasantly of him, even warmly, perhaps.

"What are you all twisted up about?" the voice said.

Tad turned. It was Ben. The young man pointed questioningly at the unoccupied seat; Tad's hunting cap lay on it.

"Sure," Tad said. He picked up the cap and with it waved Ben to sit beside him.

He looks so perfect in his clothes, Tad thought, as trim in bush rags as in his lieutenant's uniform; what a waste for him to spend so much money in custom tailoring, he'd look debonair in hand-me-downs. And young; he'd always look as young as right this minute, always graduation day, tossing his white cap in the air. Yet, somehow, he didn't envy the boy, he liked him too much. Brushing imaginary dust off the young man's trousers, "Benny," he said.

Ben returned the affection but pretended not to. "Don't be too friendly," he said. "I'm going to ask you the same thing."

"No," Tad said quietly. "I told you no last week."

"It's another week."

"Same answer. I'll stencil it."

"Why, for God's sake?"

"Because I need you."

"You've stenciled that too. It doesn't mean a thing."

"I do, Ben."

"Bullshit."

"No, I do. There's nobody in Intelligence—not in my section anyway—who can manage the language."

"Herbstmann can. He lived in Tokyo longer than I did."

"*Schick dahng* means 'airport,' not 'electric razor.' "

"Anybody could have made that mistake. It wasn't Japanese, it was Korean."

"You knew it was Korean, why didn't he?"

"The cipher was wrong."

"That's what *he* said. Why didn't you?"

"All right, I'm smart. Why do you want to penalize me for it?"

Tad felt the cut. And was surprised by Ben's insensitivity. Their association a penalty? He had imagined the young man had shared the pleasure of it. Perhaps he was wrong, he thought defensively, in believing the boy liked him; perhaps he had his mother's guile. No, he must stop—one of these days he *had* to stop—being so suspicious of affection. He'd seen too many signs of the boy's gratitude: when Tad had stayed up with him, nights, teaching him ciphers, when he'd shown him how to use an ordinary ruler and a logarithmic scale to decode a seemingly impossible V-Schema, when he'd pushed the boy toward early promotion. More than gratitude. The day Ben inherited one-third of his father's estate, he went directly to Tad—not to his mother, not to his sister—and asked him to be his executor. In case somebody starts shooting somewhere, the young man said. In case somebody starts shooting at *you,* Tad asked himself, who would your executor be? What man would you love enough—and trust enough? . . . Not even Ben . . . He'd thought of it often, and often it made him hurt . . . What right had he to distrust the boy's affection?

Still . . . "Why do you call it a penalty?" he asked.

"Somebody buggering you, sir?"

"I asked you a question."

Quietly, "You know damn well I didn't mean 'penalty.' I only meant a code room isn't where it happens—not for me. I don't want to be in an office, I want to be on a quarterdeck." He paused a moment. "And I want to ship out."

"Leave Pearl?"

"Yes."

"Why?"

"Oh, reasons." Too casually.

"Like what?"

Ben didn't answer for a moment. When he did, Tad suspected it was an evasion. "I want to go to Manila."

"What the hell for?"

"That's where it's going to start."

"Horsham says Singapore. So does Hewlett."

"They're feeble-minded. Manila."

"Everybody's got his favorite. You say Manila, Horsham says Singapore, Rudy Deak says Kra, Blackburn says Vladivostok."

"Kley says Scapa Flow."

They both laughed.

"Stay here," Tad said, more a question than a command.

Neither spoke for a moment. Then: "Tad . . . I've already put in for it."

It was a shock. The commander tried to remain expressionless and as still as possible. He had known that the turn was inevitable, but he had expected the conversations to go on for weeks, maybe months. And it had never occurred to him that the young man would ever take the step without permission.

"I won't allow it," he said quietly.

"It'll still go through."

"No, it won't. I'll write you down as incompetent, untrustworthy, cowardly and—and . . ."

Smiling. "And what?"

". . . and a little mother-crudding bastard who wets the bed and betrays his best friend."

"Be my best friend, Tad—please." Then, with the simplicity of someone who has finally come upon the essence, "I want the sea."

It would be hard to say, and Tad didn't know whether he could say it today; later, perhaps. But he managed it. "Okay, Benny."

Ben nodded his gratitude and touched Tad with a tentative hand. "I'm glad it wasn't easy for you." He looked down the aisle, at his mother. "It'll be just as tough, telling Johanna." He got up.

"She's asleep," Tad said.

"Playing possum, I think."

"Is she?"

"Can't you tell?"

"No."

The young man hesitated, seeming to debate whether to pursue it. "What *can* you tell about her?"

"Not very much." Trying to make light of it, "It's not all that important, is it?"

"Whether she's asleep or awake? It's earthshaking."

It was only a small pleasantry, Tad thought, only this side of being a joke. Suddenly it wasn't a joke, it was as dead serious as Ben could be. And too burdensome to hold.

"She's out to kill you, I think."

The boy said it so completely without inflection that it sounded cruel. Tad tried to smile. "Don't be a jackass," he said.

Ben didn't respond. Simply walked away, down the aisle, toward his mother.

Tad's eyes followed him. As Ben got to Johanna, he paused, then seemed to change his mind about telling her. She didn't open her eyes until after her son passed beyond her seat.

Again, she caught Tad's glance. Again, the smile.

It was taking him forever, he thought, to drive from the hangar, upward on the winding road, to the foothills of Aiea Heights. But it always took forever, since he was always impatient to get there; he loved

the mountainside. It was lush and not too cultivated
—in places there was still an occasional cane field
—and the view as one ascended became, as Abby put
it, unhurriedly spectacular. All of Pearl Harbor was
down below, Ford Island, the lochs, the shipyard, the
channel opening to blue-green sea, and all were sur-
rounded by a tracery of white surf and the unlikeliest
arabesque of palms. Nothing was so close that the
boiler-scrape-and-barnacles were visible, but close
enough that, nighttimes, the lights of every ship were
separate and each gangway had its name.

And he loved the house. It was a small one, rented,
of course, and tucked into a niche in the hillside. Half
the lower level was garage and the other half his
study. The terrace was the roof of the garage and ran
the length of the cottage, every room having access to
the exhilarating vista.

He got out of his car and walked up the pathway to
the front door. Coming by way of the fern path and
under the clean, cool bougainvillaea arbor didn't make
him feel any cleaner. He was dirty and wanted a
shower, wanted to wash away the hunt, and his impatience to get clean seemed, for some reason, like
an extra layer of uncleanliness.

It was still Sunday afternoon and Abby would be
home, not teaching today. He'd come out of the bathroom, bathed and smelling of *kukane* soap, and lie
naked on the bed. She'd be reading, perhaps, or sun-
ning on the terrace, with nothing on. She'd make
chatter from the outer sunlight to the darker bedroom
and he'd say what, I can't hear you, what? She'd step
onto the threshold, as beautiful as her breasts, and
repeat what she had said, pretending she hadn't caught
the hint. Then he'd say what again, you've got to
speak more clearly, what, what? She'd come closer,
talking softer and softer all the time until, at last,
whispering, she'd stop making words, only murmurs
in his ear, then he'd kiss her mouth altogether quiet,
then her breasts, then he'd be inside her and quiet, so
quiet, until the sounds again, the loud ones, the won-

derful screaming sounds that stayed alive in the air.
And then, when it was over, what–what would mean
something else again, and they would laugh.

But she wasn't home. There was a note, instead, on
a legal-sized pad propped against the backsplash of the
bathroom sink: *The films arrived unexpectedly and
I promised the kids. So, off to school. Please be an
angel and pick me up. Say, four? If you're not there
by 4:15, I'll come by Liloa's Taxi, and it'll cost a
fortune and I'll sulk. I love you. What?*

He didn't understand a word of it. What films, and
what had she promised the kids, and why did it have
to be Sunday afternoon, and what the hell did it all
have to do with her teaching English to Japs and
Filipinos?

He didn't want to understand. He hated her going
into that part of town. Last month there had been a
rape in an incense parlor three blocks down from
where the school was. And only this past Thursday,
in the very alley that bordered the north side of the
school building, a middle-aged woman had been, with
surgical precision, dismembered. The supposition was
that it was Filipinos who had done it. It was always
convenient, blaming the Flips, for they rarely de-
fended themselves. The men blamed them routinely,
without thinking; the officers at mess—during nuts
and brandied peaches—did it more reasoningly. "It
has to be the Flips," old Kley would say. "Sex
jumps, that's what it is, sex jumps every time. The
Chink and Jap girls can't stand 'em, Hawaiians won't
give 'em a wiggle, and they're too little for white wom-
en. So what do they do? They go prowling for
Minnie Yank, they board 'er and cornhole 'er. That's
their method—always doing *something* behind your
back. And when she lets out a little scream—gizzard!
These cashews taste like dog do."

Tad didn't think it was the Filipinos. If it had been,
it would have gotten into the papers. A Filipino
crime was always good for a headline. But nobody
printed it. That meant, by cipher, keep it quiet; which
meant, by interior cipher, don't stir up the Japs. And

the provocations were becoming more and more frequent.

Why the hell couldn't Abby teach in a safe place? He looked at his watch. It was a little after three. He wondered if he'd have time for a shower before picking her up. No, dammit, he might be late, and she'd be gone and then she *would* sulk, and he'd be irritable and she'd say she didn't want to go to the damn luau tonight and watch him glowering in his white suit, and he'd say he didn't damn well want to go either but he couldn't *not* go because people would say he was pouting because his mother-in-law had stuck a pig and won the trophy.

Still filthy and smelling the pig on himself even though he hadn't touched the beast, he went outdoors again, descended the path to the garage, dented the rear fender of the brand-new Hudson against the post, cursed, and drove southeast toward Chinatown.

His antipathy to the Oriental section was at its worst today. He used to like going there, four years ago when he first came to Honolulu, but in the last year it had undergone a change that bothered him. Even the name had changed. He recalled that people customarily made a distinction; there was the Chinese section, the Japanese, the fish and produce area, the wharves. But now, by some illogic of anxiety, it was all lumped together in one pejorative term—Japtown —as if it were a slum in Tokyo, and every street, a lurking place. Abby said she saw no alteration in anything, that war jitters were making people suspicious of their oldest friends, but it seemed to Tad that the area had indeed changed. He felt certain that when he went into a Japanese grocery store these days, despite the fact the shelves seemed as bounteously stocked as ever, the storekeeper had just run out of the one item without which the recipe wouldn't work. Oh, very sorry, sir. Polite, always polite. In fact, did they used to make the smiling bow and the serpentine hiss quite so often as they did these days?

What gave him his uneasiest misgivings was that the streets were getting emptier. Oh, come on, Abby would say, you're getting impossible, you and your suspicions; nobody's following you, the streets are no narrower than they always were, and the alleys no darker. However, despite the fact the Japanese consulate was importing more and more colleagues, as the visas dubbed them, the rest of the Japanese population, he felt sure, was diminishing. The streets seemed emptier than usual, even if Abby pointed out that her classes were no smaller than before. That's kids, he would say, not adults in the streets.

"All right, Thaddeus," she said, to put an end to the argument, "they're slipping away."

Slipping away. Why had she used the very words he'd had on his mind? She must have noticed without noticing she noticed: the Japanese ebbing away like quiet water, drifting from the shores, silently disappearing.

Two months ago, when his botheration became most acute, he had written an order for a watch-and-count. It was turned over to Communications. They spent three weeks on it and came up with not one single case of unusual departure or defection. Specific men who had vanished—a Japanese automobile mechanic, a chiropodist, a newspaperman on the *Nisei Courier*—hadn't vanished at all. One had moved to Waikiki, another had gone to Seattle to visit his brother and sister-in-law, the third was in a Hilo hospital with kidney stones. When he read the Communications report, he had a new worry. It troubled him that Abby might be right: his job was making him paranoid . . . Paranoid or not, there were those mutilations.

He drove up to the school buildings, two of them, prefabricated, joined at right angles to each other, one structure for classrooms, the other for offices. They looked like barracks except that they were hemmed in closely by stores and a sidewalk café and, beyond, a run-down warehouse now used as a secondhand furniture mart.

The street was quiet and he found a parking place right outside the schoolhouse door. He locked the car and tried both handles before walking away, up the steps to the main entrance.

The door was locked. He tried the smaller door, the one at right angles, in the alcove. That too was locked. Noticing the small wooden sign NIGHT AND EMERGENCY and the bell under it, he rang. Nobody answered. He rang again and could hear the loud clangor echoing down the corridor. There'd be no question of somebody hearing it, if anyone was there.

He looked at his watch. Still not yet four o'clock—3:57, to be exact. Perhaps she'd dismissed them earlier. Walking down the steps, he paused on the bottom one, glanced toward Beretania Street, then *makai,* to the docks. There was no sign of her.

Had he gotten her note wrong? He was certain he hadn't.

A dart of anxiety. Stop it, he told himself, nothing's happened, not a thing. Take a pill. He reached inside his coat pocket; he kept them loose in there these days, so that he could get at them quickly, secretly. Snapping open tin boxes or unscrewing bottles was too conspicuous—he hated it when anybody caught him popping a stomach tablet in his mouth. How ignominious it was to be chewing this shameful, minted chalk. And it didn't help right now. The anxiety was still there; soon the gut would ache.

He hurried down the length of the building, glancing through the windows, seeing no sign of anybody, no one. As he hastened to the alleyway, he told himself nothing would have happened here, nothing could, not in the sunny innocence of a crystal Sunday afternoon. Nothing; the alley was empty.

Then he saw the open doorway of the office wing. He hurried toward it.

Inside, the corridor was pitch black, with small rooms on both sides, all doors closed, nobody in sight. He tried the first door, marked OFFICE—PRINCIPAL. It was locked. The next door, marked FACULTY—that too was locked. LIBRARY, MANUAL TRAINING, STOREROOM —all locked.

He heard a sound and didn't know where it came from. Outdoors, he thought at first, then clearly indoors. A familiar sound, yet strange because it was in the wrong place; it should have come from one of his Intelligence cubicles rather than inside a school building. A code scramble, like the voice on the office record player when the gears are modified.

He stopped moving. He debated a moment, even more worried than before. A while ago, he had had a single problem, now double. One had to do with his wife, the other with his work. He had an inchoate dread they might be connected.

Punctiliously he again consulted his watch; it might be useful, later, to know exactly when things had happened. There was the nervous possibility he might be studying the time in the hope of freezing it, to prevent the dreaded next minute from happening. It was 4:01.

The scrambled sound was louder for an instant. He thought he heard voices.

Hurrying back to the door, he looked at the lock to see if it was a double-click latch that might lock him in. It was an ordinary Yale; he could let himself out.

He started back along the corridor in the direction of the scramble noise. Abruptly he stopped, alerted by another sound; more accurately, the absence of it. The playback device, whatever they were using, had ceased. The building was silent.

He wondered if it meant they suspected someone was there. They might have heard his footsteps. He stopped walking. He waited.

The ache that he was afraid would come, came. The anxiety sharpened. Abby, where are you?

He couldn't just stand there forever, he thought, stand posed in the middle of a dark hallway, waiting for a door to open, for a gun to go off.

The scramble sound started again. It came from the end of the hallway. Walk quickly, he said, while the sound is loud. But walk narrowly, think thin, think small, think as tiny as the fear is great.

Toward the end of the hallway, as he approached the door, he prayed it would be ajar. It wasn't. But it wasn't locked. Softly, as soft as the turning of a page, he turned the knob.

The room was in darkness except for the shaft of brilliant, flickering white light. They all sat looking at the screen, perhaps forty of them, all children, gazing hypnotized at the flashing movie, at the silly Donald Duck, his voice quacking unintelligibly, scrambling everything, clucking his consonants, squashing his vowels, while Abby stood beside the screen and translated the animal's American mush-mouth gibberish into tongue-delicate Japanese.

The small Oriental faces were even rounder than usual, in wonder. The children didn't laugh at the animal; it was as if they didn't want to insult him. A puff of chatter suddenly; then, like smoke, gone.

As Abby saw him in the open doorway, he hoped she didn't see how foolish he felt. Scrambled ciphers, codes of danger . . . Donald Duck.

"Hello, darling," she said blithely. "We're not laughing yet, we haven't entirely caught on."

The teacherish we-talk; she sounded, somehow, too young for it. She flipped the switch and the room lighted up. "But they loved Porky Pig," she said.

The children were getting out of their seats. One of them said, "Th-th-that's orr, folks."

As the others giggled, Abby whispered, "That kid got the best laugh of the day. I wonder how they can love it and still take it so seriously."

Tad made a sinister face. "It's ominous."

She liked his self-mockery and squeezed his arm. "Hello, darling," she said again. "How was the hunt?"

But as he started to tell her, he could see she wasn't listening, for the elders were coming in—parents, an older sister or two—to shepherd the children home. One of them, a middle-aged man in a shiny silk suit, lovingly gathered his beautiful five-year-old son to himself as if the child were part of his clothing. Then he turned to Abby and bowed his gratitude in a number of Japanese expressions, and somebody else concluded with the English epitome, "We multiply thank you, excuse me."

When the other parents and children had gone, the silk-suited man was still there, still reiterating his obligation. Abby packed the four movie shorts into their metal boxes, checked the projector and all its appurtenances, and when she was entirely finished, ready to leave, the man was still there. Not knowing how she could politely get free of him, she looked at Tad who was smiling but unhelpful. It was only when she started to turn off the lights that the Japanese man took the hint and departed.

But not entirely. He was on the front steps, waiting for them.

The elaborate lingering resumed again; the man simply wouldn't go away, but stood there, a gush of giggles and good humor.

"My husband, Commander Clarke," Abby said with a slightly Oriental deference. "This is Saburo's father, Goru Nishi."

"How do you do?" Tad said respectfully. The man nearly choked himself with merriment. "Ah yes, ah yes," he kept repeating, "ah very good indeed yes." It was all the English he could manage.

That should have finished it, but didn't. An inconclusive silence, then Mr. Nishi wasn't smiling any more, simply staring. He was focusing on Tad as tightly as if his eyes were taking a time exposure. Uncomfortable under the hypnotic scrutiny, Tad gave the man his broadest smile and said "Hi."

It was, to Mr. Nishi, the cue to renewed hilarity. "Hi," he said, "hi-hi-hi-hi!"

Giggling, he ran down the steps. His son, serious and sober-faced, trailed him down the street. At the corner, Nishi turned to show he was still in stitches, waved a final hi and was gone.

"You didn't know I was that comical, did you?" Tad asked.

Abby smiled, but with reservation. She didn't find Nishi amusing. "He's strange." She was preoccupied. "The kid comes in with black-and-blue marks."

"He beats him?"

"Pinches him."

She was more upset than Tad thought she ought to have been. She was always more upset; never seemed to be prepared for an unkindness, as if cruelty were breaking a precedent.

He took the film boxes from her and put them in the back of the car. When they were riding homeward, it occurred to him. "Why'd you have to show the movies on Sunday?"

"They're commercial films—it's the only time they wouldn't be in use."

"You mean those kids have never seen Donald Duck?"

"Oh, yes," she said, "they've seen Donald Duck."

"Then why the big treat?"

"Well . . ." She seemed puzzled by the question. "Why not?"

Of course, he thought, why not? . . . But, niggling, why?

She saw him going over it. Her hand reached out and touched his on the wheel. Her voice always had a gentleness, a softness in it as if she were lying in eiderdown. "Don't worry everything, darling," she said. "Some questions don't need answers."

He knew she was right and said, as inconsequentially as he could, "That man still puzzles me."

". . . Yes."

They rode in silence for a while, then talked about the hunt. When he told her about Johanna's bagging the animal, she didn't seem nearly as surprised as he had assumed she would be. Abby thought a moment, then said, almost to herself, "I'm never surprised that she gets what she goes for. What surprises me is what she goes for."

She closed her window and he realized the heat of the day was over. The wind had shifted, gusty now; there was sea in the air.

When they got close to their house she asked to be let out at the front entrance so she could pick up the mail; she had forgotten it this morning. It was only after he had dropped her off and was descending the driveway to the garage that it occurred to him it was Sunday and there would be no mail today.

Going up the path and through the arbor he had a restive sense: I never seem to conclude conversations with Abby; there's always something to dispose of at a later time. And somehow the later time never arrives and there are always new tag ends. He wondered if he'd ever be able to tie things together; he wondered why he had to.

When he got to the front steps, Abby was waiting for him at the doorway.

"Why didn't you go in?" he asked.

Her bag was open and she pointed down at it. She looked a bit unnerved. "I've lost my keys."

"Really?"

"Maybe I didn't bring them out with me."

He turned the knob. The door was locked. "You must have had them when you left. You apparently locked the door."

"Oh, yes," she said vaguely.

He had the uncomfortable sense that she didn't feel as vague as she sounded.

"Any mail?" he asked.

She smiled sheepishly. "I forgot it was Sunday."

He unlocked the door and they went in.

Three

JOHANNA WOULD rather not have gone to the luau at the Quarterdeck Club, and she was particularly reluctant to be present at an early stage of the *imu* when they would be preparing the boar. It was a Polynesian custom, not a naval one, that the trophy killer had to watch the beast being lowered into the pit. The animal shrinks in the cooking, Sammy Hanaha said, and there had been occasions when a hunter would make the unwarranted charge that a smaller pig had been substituted for a larger one. When Sammy called her late in the afternoon to remind Johanna to come early, she said she wouldn't, she trusted him not to palm off a piglet for a hog, but the head steward seemed hurt by her lack of interest.

As Johanna drove up, crowds of young Hawaiian scullery boys and steward's assistants were rushing back and forth across the triangular gravel yard that was bordered by the club kitchen, the greensward and the swimming pool. Sammy was gleefully waddling around in a state of obese blessedness, bare to the waist, his amber skin awash with sweat that glistened on every roll of fat.

The hog was already on the singeing spit.

"A big one," Sammy said, pointing giddily at the animal. "A fat one, almost da kine like me."

He slapped the dead beast playfully; then, as the fire boys waited for the signal, made his final inspection. He examined the iron spit, which went straight through, snout to anus, and turned the handle slowly, one full revolution. "Look a l'inside," he said proudly to Johanna as he pulled back a huge flap of belly flesh. "Look how is good clean up." Which indeed it was, all eviscerated, every bit of waste cut away and the rib cage rubbed with soy sauce and rock salt and minced lime rinds. Outside, however, the pelt

was as she remembered it except that the blood had
now dried black, glazing the coarse matted hair of the
animal. She hadn't noticed how mangy the pig's skin
had looked, and malignancies took over her mind,
scabies and pustules and distempers, and she had to
turn her head away.

"Make fire," Sammy said, and one of the boys
lighted the oil-soaked hickory chips while the other two
started turning the spit.

The smell of burning hair was a vengeance upon her;
she felt green. I'll have to go away, she thought, or
I'll add something to the other vile outscourings.
Abruptly they were spraying vinegar on the burning
pelt, and while the second stench was sharper, it
seemed somehow to dispel the poisonous fetors of the
first.

The spit stopped turning, the singeing was over,
the animal was on a canvas drop cloth, and they were
treating it in a way she had never seen an *imu* pig
prepared, rolling it in a paste of ginger and fermented
pineapple juice, sticking it with cloves and garlic and
dill seeds, then throwing cayenne all over it.

"This one not fill with red-hot stone," Sammy
bragged. "Fill him with red hot *makana*."

Sammy's *makana* was his annual present; it arrived in a wheelbarrow. It was his own recipe, a stuffing of peppered poi and sweet guava paste, of fennel
and the gentle Maui onions, tiny green Puna tan-
gerines, seaweed and *kelaki* seed, and nuts, thousands
of nuts, ground ones and whole ones—hazels, peeled
litchis, coconut. By the bare handfuls, they shoved
the conglomerate mess into the animal, both ends,
mouth and maw, until it swelled into an enormous
sphere, then they stuck it closed with a complicated
contrivance of palm thogs and bamboo slivers. Finally the skin again, more ginger, more pineapple juice,
garlic, dill, cayenne.

Sammy ran a few feet from the trussed animal and
looked down into the pit where the hot stones were
glowing. He clapped his hands and the tallest of the
boys started to rake the embers. Flames leaped up,

but Sammy didn't want that to happen, so they threw corn husks on the fire and layered the hot stones with banana leaves. The smoke smell was sweet until somebody threw a handful of pods on the fire and there was a strange scent in the air, woody and savory, like carnations.

They trussed the boar's legs with baling wire, then four of the boys lifted the massive, slippery animal. Grunting and giggling and making lascivious noises at one another, they lowered the slimy creature into the pit. One of the boys kicked at the boar's tusks, again and again, and shouted something that sounded like a curse. Another boy did the same. It was a ritual. Then somebody pretended to spit at it and another boy imitated him.

She thought: how sweet they generally are, how smiling, how kind to one another, how gentle to strangers, how lovingly they touch their flowers and finger a bit of seaweed . . . and how vindictive they are to a dead beast, the kill. As if the slaying process was not ended by the death of the animal but had to continue until it was consumed. The mouth, she thought, as the ultimate murderer.

They were putting more corn husks and banana leaves into the pit. Now, a layer of sweet potatoes, then plantains and great slabs of pork and dolphin meat and small *koa'e* snappers; a whole burlap sack full of clams in pearly shells, dumped into every empty space; then taro shoots and Filipino peanuts and fat chunks of Portuguese sausage. The final layer of corn husks and banana leaves—and, at last, earth on top of everything. They stamped it and dampened it and . . .

The horns sounded. That is, she thought they were horns—and a few of them were, indoors, in the clubhouse; but most of the noise was the blowing of conch shells, all raucous except for the one closest to her, which had a sad summons in it, lonely, like a loon on a faraway lake, somewhere in her memory of New England.

She didn't notice nightfall happening and suddenly

it was a fact. The guests were arriving. The men in their Navy white—not quite full dress, she realized—dinner regalia; and the women, eschewing muumuus and *holokus,* gowned and jeweled and even stockinged. They would all feel like Mainlanders tonight. Trophy night. The night of Johanna Winter, the first woman winner, and she wished she weren't there.

She had an impulse to quit, not fully certain what it was she would be quitting, to run home, lock the door of her house, hole up in some small room, some encompassable place, in a closet, perhaps, sitting on the floor with a book in her lap. No, that was years ago, back in boarding school, alone and lonely. Not today—today she was nearly forty-five, a woman with a family, not alone, not alone, not . . .

Somebody was waving to her from the veranda. She pretended not to notice. She wasn't ready for people, not yet, wasn't ready to accept the congratulations or to relate the thrills and perils of this idiotic Nimrod day. She turned her back to the veranda and walked toward the golf links.

Would this be a three- or four-martini night, she wondered. If she could have an old-time talk with Abby, she'd settle for a small vermouth. Or a talk with Ben, him teasing her about some bygone skirmish they had settled long ago. But her daughter and Tad wouldn't arrive until they had to, and Ben mightn't arrive at all if he had a date in town.

She wondered if he had one; she was seeing less and less of Ben these days, and hearing less too. He had become so silent about his girls, and never any need to be—they all had such open, friendly faces—she'd think he'd be happy to talk about them. There was one angel creature last year, a dear one, fresh out of Goucher; Johanna had gotten her a job on the *Honolulu Advertiser.* What was her name? A nice homemade name like Sarah Cooper or Becky Something.

Wouldn't it be good if Oscar were alive to see what great kids they had turned out to be? Yes, wouldn't it be good if Oscar were alive . . . or dead. Die, dear Oscar, please die . . .

She walked closer to the clubhouse. She would hardly be able to force herself indoors tonight. She was making it, scarcely, by smaller and smaller perimeters, encircling the building. She could hear the first sounds of glassware and ukuleles and guitars, the first tinkling of tentative laughter.

"I caught you," she heard the man say.

She turned. It was old Kley with one of his sickeningly sweet pineapple rum drinks in his hand. Old Kley. She wondered why she persisted in calling him old, he couldn't have been that ancient or he'd have been retired. She had a suspicion he was playing at the role of dotard, that he had some enigmatic reason for doing so, and she wondered what it might be.

"Caught you, caught you," he kept repeating.

"How are you, Burkie?" His name was Burkington Kley. Nobody had ever called him Burkie except Oscar and, latterly by inheritance, Johanna. She thought he considered it an endearment; perhaps it was.

He was coughing now, that shallow little fake cough of his, and apologizing for snoring on the plane and boring everybody with talking in his sleep.

"Well, you won it again," she said, referring to Scapa Flow.

He wasn't the least bit embarrassed. "I'll never understand it." He shook his head quizzically. "I've never even been there. And I keep winning a battle that never happened. Win it every time—never lose —when I'm asleep, of course. I wonder what the hell that *is?*"

"It's called a dream, I think."

"Yes," he said wanly. Then, twinkling too deliberately, "I have them about you, too."

Well, here it goes again, she thought, he's going to dole out his semiannual lubricity.

"You're very bad on my bed linen," he said.

"I'm sorry, Burkie," she rejoined gently. "Send me your laundry bill."

"I'll send you me."

"No, I can't launder you, Burkie, hard as I've tried."

"You haven't tried *me,* Johanna." He bubbled with enthusiasm. "I promise you, Jo, you try me once and you'll sail straight home! Just put your hand on the tiller!"

She smiled affectionately at him, patted one of his cheeks and kissed the other. "You're a darling to keep trying."

He flushed a bit, then gave her a confidential little wink. "And you're a darling to turn me down."

Oddly, she realized she had meant it: his ridiculous passes didn't disturb her at all, she almost liked them; he *was* a darling to keep trying. Besides warming her, his advances amused her. It was another role Burkie was playing, lecher; the companion role to dotard. With Oscar he had always played still another role —garrulous fool. None of those costumes, Johanna was convinced, was the real habiliment of the man. Yet, she was never able to imagine what he really was, this man who had filled every commission with brilliance—mariner, security officer, head of public relations, and now in an undefined and unlisted liaison position between Intelligence and Communications. She had only one disquiet about Kley: if all those fatuous parts he played were protective coloration, perhaps they were all betraying their purpose —too vivid, the colors calling attention to themselves.

She put her arm through his and gave it an amiable squeeze. "Shall we go in together?" she asked.

"Yes, and pretend we've been in the bushes."

"They'll think it the minute they lay eyes on us." She smiled.

That pleased him. "Will they?" He looked at her with unconcealed fondness and his face turned serious. "You think anybody suspects that we talk this oatmeal?"

"No," she reassured him. "We don't even suspect it ourselves."

Then he said quietly, almost to himself, "Strange how much we can get away with."

She wasn't sure what he meant and was about to ask him, but she realized the subject was over for him and he was guiding her toward the main entrance.

The foyer and the bar, even the room they called the junior salon, were all lighted by candlelight when Johanna and Kley entered, and she thought there had been a power failure. But she remembered it was a new thing—lighting the large Molokai tapers on Christmas Eve and luau nights—and she preferred this mellow glow to the hysterical white lights in the unremitting white-walled rooms. Remembering her mother's pronouncement that anything's endurable in candlelight, Johanna thought the evening might not turn out so bad.

Somebody grabbed her. It was a man, behind her—strong arms around her waist, tight—and a cold breath down the back of her neck.

"Benny, stop it!" she said, without seeing him. "Stop, you cretin—stop!"

He let her go and she turned. He stood there, grinning and showing more teeth than he had, certainly more than he had any right to have.

"Been in the bushes with the admiral?" he asked. "Oh, sorry, sir."

"Punky insubordinate," Kley said. "I'll have you cut to ensign. Remind me."

"I'll send you a note, sir," Ben said.

There weren't, as yet, too many people at the bar, and the hush in the semidarkness was still polite. Everybody who needed a drink already had one; none of the faces were anxious. It wouldn't be long, she thought, before the members and their guests would be layered between the stools, and the women's voices would be shrill with laughter, unstoppered with the corks. Johanna wanted a martini and wondered if anybody would notice if she asked for a double. Yes, Kley would notice and pretend not to, and Ben would notice and do a front page on the subject. She had just had her first sip of her single martini when she heard the well-known voice down the bar.

"One sloe gin and soda, one sweet vermouth."

He's still at that sugar-tit of vermouth, she thought, still nursing one small wineglass through a lifetime of sobriety.

"Oh, Tad," she heard her daughter say, "for once, put a little rye in it."

He pretended not to understand. "Put some rye in her sloe gin, please," he said, and she laughingly countermanded the order.

Johanna wondered why Abby hadn't joined them, then realized, as the girl's face lighted, that she hadn't seen her mother. "Hey, hunter-lady," she called with pleasure. Then there were small jokes and large congratulations and people seemed to remember this was no ordinary Sunday night, a woman had won the trophy and there would be a tangle of reasons to drink a little more than usual.

Abby moved a step closer to her mother and pointed to Ben. "Did you hear about cheesehead?" she said to Johanna.

"What's he done?"

"Ask him," Abby said.

Johanna turned to her son. "Did you put your finger in her Pablum?"

Abby said, "No—in yours." She was upset; smiling too hard. "He's put in for transfer."

Go slow, Johanna told herself; no mother stuff—it might not mean a thing. Have an easy little sip of your martini, then the response, whatever it may be, flip if possible.

"Did you hear me, Mother?" Abby said.

"Yes, she heard you, loosemouth," Ben said. "Couldn't you wait to let me tell her?"

Abby retorted, "There's going to be a war, you lunatic!"

"Do you always have to play the end of the second act?" he said irritably. "I'm wearing a uniform—what do you think it's for? Your husband's wearing one too —what do you think *that's* for?"

Tad touched her gently. "She pretends it's tweed."

"So do we all," Johanna said, with as little significance as possible. She was grateful for the opportunity to make it a general concern, not hers alone. If they could only stick to generalities for a few minutes more, her pulse would settle down.

But she knew Abby saw right through her. She felt the girl's hand secretly groping for hers and realized how cold both hands were. She gave her daughter's hand a quick squeeze, then let it go. Damn, she thought, you're Navy and you're grown up; don't reach for mama—mama's more scared than you are.

"Well, if you're going," she said, grinning at her son, "shove ass."

Kley laughed louder than the others and hugged her. Ben disengaged her from the admiral and danced her out into the junior salon. There were already a number of couples slipping around, trying to keep step with the busy ukuleles and the whining guitars. Johanna hoped her son wouldn't put her through the whole number, pretending she could dance to the whimpering music.

"Lady, you're great."

"Yes, I am," she said. "I shot me a boar this day."

"Anybody I know?"

She forgave him.

He was giving her credit for more courage than she had. She had to set him straight. On the other hand, she mustn't make too much of this. She was, as she might have reminded Abby, Navy. Nobody courted war, not even Navy people; she was no exception. At least it was bad form to cheer about guns going off. It was still worse form, considering one's military persuasion, to air your pacifism with other than a postured passion. But this was her son.

"I don't want you to give me badges for bravery, Ben."

He smiled; he understood. "Well, no demerits, certainly."

"Abby's right. It's going to happen dirty."

The instant she said it she realized it was asinine; when did war ever happen clean?

"Oh, I don't think so," he said. "Those yella-fellas will run."

"You mean yella-coward or yella-Japanese?" She knew very well what he meant. She hoped to embarrass him a little. But she didn't.

"Both," he said.

"That's what I mean—a dirty one."

"Come on, Mom—what do you expect? It's going to be a yellow-white war."

"Just like the other one's a Christian-kike one?"

"Well, I wouldn't put it that way."

"But you would call it Jew and Gentile, wouldn't you?"

"That's what it is, isn't it?"

"No, I don't think so," she said quietly. "Hitler's everybody's boar, I think."

She hadn't meant to say boar, was surprised when she heard it said. She thought the word would come out "evil." Boar wasn't even an approximation of what she had in mind; she didn't think of the animal as having any morality; he wasn't everybody's evil or devil or . . . She wished she had carried her drink onto the dance floor.

"You've got to promise," she said.

He knows what I mean, she thought, and he's itching to get it over with, but she had to continue, had to say what every war-muddled mother ever said, as if she had never eaten off naval silverware, never heard gun gossip in a wardroom.

"Promise that if you get a command you'll sail your ship only on safe water."

"The Monongahela—how's that?"

"Excellent . . . And you won't get hit."

"I'll duck."

"I wish you could duck it altogether," she said, then forced herself to brighten. "Now that I've begat all those idiocies, where would you like to go?"

"Manila."

"You monster."

"Come on, Mother, what makes you think Manila will be so dangerous?"

"Because your father said—"

"Christ, that was two years ago." He didn't hide his annoyance. "If you think any island in the Pacific is going to be safer than any other island—"

"Then why can't you stay *here?*"

Abruptly, disliking every sound she heard herself make, she left him in the middle of the floor and went back for her drink. He followed her with a rueful smile and got himself a bourbon with a splash of soda, and they stood, back against the bar, not saying anything. In a little while, his glass empty, he said something about having to drive into town to pick up Ellie Carter. (That was the girl's name, the one from Goucher, not Sarah Cooper but Ellie Carter. What difference did it make?)

When Ben was gone, she ordered a double martini and decided the hell with it. She resolved not to move ten paces away from here, where all the shiny bottles were; the bar would be her night's commitment. She must be careful, however, not to drink too quickly or too much; she might fall down. So she took tiny sips, the tiniest possible, but didn't stop sipping. From time to time, someone would come to her with a puffy compliment about the pig or with a shaking head that waggled how amazing she was or, as Abby put it, with a giggle-and-gush. Twice during the evening, Sammy came in to report that the boar roast was progressing apace, once to say it was beginning to smell—da kine nice—and the second time to say they had uncovered it a bit, just for inspection, and it would be ready well before midnight.

Well before midnight, the ukuleles stopped and the drums began. Then those damn conch shells again, followed by the old bosun's pipe. As the two goldenly beautiful Hawaiian boys led her up onto the little platform in front of the band, she thought: I'm the newly crowned varsity girl, I'm the head cheerleader with bare thighs and pompons on my ass and these Hawaiian lads are going to stand me up on that platform and kiss me all over. But a middle-aged Club Coordinator chewed a cud of words about Club Spirit and Club Bravery, and he gave her a small gold cup and everybody was yelling speech, speech.

She started to say things but all she could think of was the boar's shit when she struck him with the knife, more shit than would fill this gilded silver cup, but not as much as overran this platform on this sweet Polynesian night. What she found herself saying— jelly and marshmallow—was a giddy ambiguity. "Oh, what I'd like to fill this lovely loving cup with, what I'd like to fill it with!"

Everybody clapped and thought her charming. And she fled.

She found herself outdoors, in the balm of soft moonlight, not knowing where she was walking, but trying somehow to get to water. Once, years ago, she had heard that in the old shipboard days, when they put poison out for the vermin, the first sign of success was the rats rushing to ports and hatches, to drown themselves in the sea. Homing toward water as she was, she wondered: where's the bilge hole?

Only a few hundred yards from the clubhouse she was in a lushness of night-black greenery, heavily tropical with the humid torpor of the jungle. There were orchids everywhere, wild and cultivated ones, and trees that entwined with one another and rankly overgrew the footway, so that she couldn't be sure she was on the right path to the lagoon.

When she first thought she heard the footsteps behind her, she felt certain she was mistaken. They were simply underbrush sounds: growth by night and the stealth of creatures. Besides, if someone were really following her, she told herself, he certainly would have caught up by now; she wasn't walking fast. Why did she say following and why did she say he? If there was anybody behind her, it might have been someone haphazardly out walking like herself, and a woman. Even an animal, a deer. No, she was no longer back in the real jungle; this was a garden here, a man-made Eden, carefully cultivated to cast an illusion of woodland wildness. She had walked it many times before, she knew every step of it, how it wandered in a damp mystery, then suddenly opened up to a bridge that spanned a lagoon, thence downward, twisting toward the Harbor. She felt a sense of privacy about this path, for she had walked it so frequently alone. And she was alone again tonight; mistaken about the footsteps.

She heard them again. The rise and fall, the moving, then the silence.

She decided not to move for a moment. I'm not really drunk, she assured herself, but she knew she wasn't entirely sober; they might have been her own footsteps she was hearing. She waited, then added another moment of waiting time, to make sure. There was no sound.

She resumed her walk. Even though there was nobody behind her, she would be glad to get out of the woods and into the clearing, near the bridge.

The footsteps again. Midmovement, she stopped to listen. This time, even while she was motionless, she heard the soft crunch, then the sound of treading, soggy this time, in wet ground.

She turned and looked, walked back a pace or two and squinted into the darkness. She saw nobody. Frightened now, afraid to go forward, more afraid to go back, she turned on the footway and continued in the direction she had been going, toward the lagoon.

The instant she got out of the woods, with her first glimpse of the little bridge and the quiet lagoon, her apprehensions vanished. She had come out of a darkness that had seemed to strangle her; any imagined terrors were possible in it. Here, standing over the water, everything was brilliantly illuminated, the moon was so full and bright that all the sky was whitened by it. But the major difference was stillness. In the undergrowth, unknown things were moving: the small beasts of the night, the devouring insects, the outrageous vines, rampant even in darkness. But out here, in the revealing light, there was the motionlessness of the mown lawn, the stability of the sturdy little bridge and the utterly placid water, becalmed.

She stood on the summit of the bridge and looked down at the glazed surface. She wondered how the dark pond could be so still and remain so clean. Stillness meant stagnation, someone had said to her. She tried to remember who had said it. Not that the thought went very deep; ah, yes, she was quoting herself.

She wished she were altogether sober, not half. The water would be half again lovelier if she were half again clearer in her mind. The moon might seem smaller, true, but then it would be better contained, it wouldn't spill itself so prodigally across the sky.

Something glittered in her hand. The gold loving cup; she had forgotten it. Without another glance, she tossed it into the lagoon.

"My God," the voice said, "that's gold!"

He was a tall man, as tall as a pillar, she thought nonsensically, if the pillar is a tall one. A civilian in dark clothes, he walked out of the shadow of the wood and came hurrying toward her.

"Did you *mean* to do that?" he asked. "Crikey—gold!"

"Plate," she said. "Over silver."

"Even so."

He was handsomer than anyone need be, even if his eyes were too bright and his hair too shiny. But there was nothing else excessive about him: all the rest was right. He had precisely the right amount of gray at his temples and was the right age for a man to be, forty, she would say. But she wasn't too sure of the accent; there might be too much Oxford.

"You've been following me," she said.

"A little."

"What does a little following mean?"

"It's a lie. It means following a lot."

She thought: he knows how disarming it is to confess to a tiny lie. She wondered if he'd confess to larger ones.

"Why didn't you just come right out on the pathway?"

He smiled sheepishly. "I couldn't find it. I got stuck." He pointed down. His patent-leather shoes were muddy; so were his satin-striped trousers. His embarrassment was charming.

"Why were you following me?" she asked.

He didn't answer directly. "You don't remember me, do you?"

Of course she didn't remember him, she had never seen him before, not a glimpse. But, studying him more closely, "Should I?"

"Yes, I think so. We met on a number of occasions —tangentially, of course."

"How tangentially, what occasions?"

"When your husband was stationed in Tokyo."

Something, she didn't know what, made her pull back a little. "When was that?" she asked.

"When did we meet or when was he stationed? He was there from—let me see now—June, 1930, to April, '35, as an attaché—then from '35 to "

"We left in '35," she said.

His smile had mercury in it. "I know that. I was testing you."

"To avoid being tested?"

"No. Simply to avoid being accused of finding the data in a book."

"Is that where you found it?"

He smiled abashedly again, and she realized he knew exactly how to smile that way. "Yes," he confessed.

"Why did you look for it?"

"I wanted to meet you—so I prepared all the appropriate facts so I could manage all the appropriate lies."

"When do the lies stop?"

"This instant. I didn't really want to meet you—I wanted to meet your son-in-law."

Her mind had been flirting with the word "effete" as a description of the man; now she discarded it. Not effete, just too elaborately English, the inflection ostentatiously displayed, the energy cautiously hidden. She would be more guarded than she had started to be. "It shouldn't be difficult to meet him. You're a guest, aren't you?"

"Well," he said, "a kind of party-crashing guest."

Her smile was as spurious as his. "If you're going to tell lies and immediately confess they're lies, how will I ever catch you?"

"When I tell the truth."

"Will I know it when I hear it?"

"Yes. Right now. My name is Hugh Jerrold."

"Have I caught you at something?"

"Yes—at being who I am. Sorry. I won't let that happen again."

"Come along," she said.

She found herself walking a little ahead of him, she didn't know why, possibly as an act of faith that he could be trusted behind her back. She wondered why she was impelled to make such an affirmation unless it was bravado. It had been a long time since she had felt the need to be wary of a man. It was evocative; it aroused her a little. In this lift of excitement, she found herself doing an odd thing. She could have taken a quick, open pathway back to the clubhouse; only fifty paces this side of the bridge there was a well-lighted gravel walk. Instead, she led him back the way she had come, through the mystery of twisting vines and darkness.

Indoors, the candles had burned out and nobody had replaced them. The electric lights blazed and the junior salon was as bright as a clinic. All the Navy men in their spotless white uniforms seemed suddenly to be interns dancing their ladies straight into the operating room. They needn't wear their damn war regalia, she thought, we're not fighting yet. She wished they didn't all look so horrifyingly beautiful.

And there stood the man, Tad Clarke, who was to her the most beautiful and horrifying of all, and she was at a loss to know what chilled her about him. Jerrold was no longer laggard behind her but at her side. She pointed to her son-in-law and they made their way around the apron of the dance floor to the group of middle-aged men just the other side of the French doors, on the terrace. For an instant, she couldn't catch Tad's eye. At last she did and he seemed puzzled when she beckoned to him. She saw him murmur something, then disengage himself from the others.

"This man wants to meet you," she said to him. "His name is Hugh Jerrold." An instant, then she said Tad's name.

Jerrold nodded ingratiatingly and Tad gave the stranger a neutral glance. The Englishman hastened to fill the hesitant moment. "I'm sorry to take you away from your friends," he said.

"Not important," Tad replied. "We were talking about launchings. There was some difference of opinion about how the old Hawaiians used to christen their boats. Captain Crowley says they used to smash somebody's head against the bow."

"Wasn't that the Tahitians?" Jerrold said.

"That's what I thought," Tad replied. "There was also some question about the Greeks. Did they break an amphora of oil or of wine?"

"I'm not even sure about the Americans," Johanna said. "I know it's wine—but does it have to be champagne?"

"Oh, I don't think so," Jerrold said evenly. "Sometimes they piss on it."

She couldn't believe she had heard him. What was less believable was the utterly casual expression on Tad's face.

"Is that what you've heard?" Tad said relaxedly. Then only his eyes changed, narrowing. "What do you want, Tompkins?"

"I wish you wouldn't call me that," Jerrold said.

"Nagy? You like that better? Or the German name —I've forgotten what it was."

They had both concealed it so well she couldn't be sure they had known each other; it seemed an antic of some sort. "If you already are acquainted," she said to Jerrold, "why did you need me to . . . ?"

Her unfinished sentence left a vacuum that the Englishman didn't fill.

"It's a good question," Tad said.

The man looked at her son-in-law quite directly. If he was playing at being earnest, he was doing it well; there wasn't a trace of subterfuge in his face. "I wanted to start all over with you, Thaddeus," he said quietly. Then, half apologetically, "And well referred." His humiliation started to go deeper. "And suddenly I knew I couldn't put it over—and had to muck all over everything."

She was just this side of feeling sorry for him, but the man was too clever; she wouldn't get caught in *that* trap. Nor, certainly, would Tad.

"What do you want?" he repeated flatly.

"I want to sell you something."

"Not buying."

"You'll want it when you hear what it's about," Jerrold said.

"I don't want to hear."

Johanna started to edge away. "Since I introduced you two, I'm glad you get along so well."

"No, don't go." Jerrold took a step after her. "He'll be civil as long as you're here." As she continued away, his voice entreated. "Please don't go. Secrets aren't really secrets, you know. Everybody's got everything. It's all barter. Open market. Please."

She did feel sorry for him, she couldn't help it. His brittleness was gone; he'd sullied himself and he was ashamed. She thought she was starting to peg him: he was a bright, impulsive man, a clever idiot charlatan, a fool. Human. More human than her son-in-law, more vulnerable. Of the three of them standing there, she had the strange sensation: this cheap-john betrayer— she liked him the best.

"I need money, Thaddeus," he said. It was as if he were reporting a constantly open, unhealable wound. "I'm in very low estate. I can't sell anything to anybody."

"That's because you've sold everything to everybody."

"That's not true. I sold Hans Roethe what Berlin already knew, only he didn't know they knew it," he said. "And this is different. Nobody knows this."

"No, thanks," Tad said. As crisply as a right face, he turned away.

Jerrold grabbed his arm. "Wait. You can buy this on approval, Thaddeus."

"No."

"Approval, you nit. If the goods aren't satisfactory, return them—without charge." As he thought he saw Tad hesitate, he had a quick recovery of his former airiness. "No charge—don't even pay the shipping." He put a special emphasis on the last word.

Now she saw the reason for Tad's hesitation. He hadn't had an instant of temptation about whether he would engage the Englishman. What had given him pause was how to disengage. He found a way. "Jerrold, I'm going to give you something for nothing. This club, technically speaking, isn't government property. But if I do catch you on Navy premises—anywhere—I'm going to lock you up. If I catch you somewhere at night—off premises—with nobody around—I'm going to beat the hell out of you."

Anomalously, the threat seemed to increase Jerrold's composure. "In your job, Thaddeus, you should be more opportunistic than you are. It wouldn't have hurt to take advantage of me, you know. But since you're giving me something for nothing, I'll reciprocate. This hasn't anything to do with what I want to sell. This is quite minor. A bit of scuttlebutt I give away as a free sample." He paused, then resumed as offhandedly as possible. "Somebody very close to you is going to get violated."

Saying which, he slid softly away. Too perplexed to apprehend the warning, Johanna's eyes followed him. It was only when she turned back to look at Tad that her alarm quickened.

His face was ashen. His head moved quickly, not entirely under control, his eyes darted about the room in a hasty, unquiet search. Then he saw her, Abby, in a small clot of people at the far end of the veranda.

She was sitting on the balustrade, her head back, laughing, her hair as green-silver as moonlight could make it. Without a word to Johanna, barely giving her a glance, he hurried to his wife.

Violated . . .

Johanna wouldn't let herself be shaken as Tad's dread had shaken him. She didn't share his apprehensions about Abby in the incense section of the city. The rapes and mutilations—they had nothing to do with quiet, gentle Abby; they had to do with a dark and furtive spite that rioted in a neighborhood none of them could quite understand. Johanna had no doubt of it: they were outlanders, she and her family would always be outlanders, and that meant alien to the native viciousness and violence. There had to be, after all, *some* compensation in the fact that, as service people, they were strangers everywhere they went; they were not at home here. And not at home, certainly, to the local malevolences and revenges . . . certainly not Abby. Nobody Johanna had ever met—and she was confident nobody Abby had ever met—had harbored an unkind thought about her daughter. As a matter of fact, Johanna remembered a family conversation. It had begun with Ben saying, not altogether without envy, that nobody could think a mean thought about Abby; it would be as impossible as thinking a mean thought about Christ. And Oscar had reminded: somebody did.

Somebody will.

The thought was freezing to Johanna.

One day—no, one night—my daughter, my good daughter, my gentle daughter, will walk down a back street of Honolulu and she will be damaged.

Stop it. She must quit scarifying herself with these macabre images of sons at war and daughters bloody in alleyways. She had to go somewhere, to do something, to find some work more demanding than quiddities and oddities, she had to *leave* . . .

There was a clang of bells and a clatter of wood blocks. Conchs were blown and the guitar players strummed their highest notes. The boar was being lifted out of the hot earth.

The air was full of the smell and sizzle of wind-cooled coals, the succulence of hot dolphin meat and aromatic snapper, the delicate enticements of fennel and thyme and dill, the strong savory assaults of broiled clams and hot, peppery pork. The guests ate decorously seated at tables and indecorously milling about with slabs of dripping seafood and steaming meat speared on long bamboo skewers. There was a gayer, livelier vibrato in the air, not only because the guitars and ukuleles were strumming faster, but because the food and the ingenerate grapple for it, no matter how ceremonious, were quickening the pulse of the party.

And how soon it happened, when the carcass of the hog was nearly bare and the bones were a mangle of skin flaps and bone scraps and tattered ligaments, that the party was taken over by an enormous quiet. The animals were digesting. No, Johanna corrected herself, it wasn't the quiet of digesting beasts; there was some other stillness she hadn't accounted for—it was as if the guests had already departed. Or *wanted* to depart, that was the essence of it, they wanted to escape from the very environment where the boar had been devoured, wanted to wash their hands of its juices. That was a difference between men and beasts, she thought: we have such a guilty need to run from the scene . . . Looking at the carcass, she was glad she hadn't had a morsel of it; yet she felt as overstuffed as if she had gorged herself on the whole animal.

Somebody came in screaming.

Johanna didn't know whether it was a woman or a child who screamed; it sounded like a frail voice suddenly grown clamorous with terror.

Everybody ran out onto the lawn behind the club-house. There was nothing there. Then somebody said the thing had happened in the parking lot, but there was nothing there either. When they heard the sirens of the ambulance and motorcycles, they knew it had happened along the roadway, just inside the club grounds, near the palmettos.

It was a lovely grove, the Club was proud of it. The palmettos had been carefully selected and carefully tended. They grew out of a ground covering of white stone chips, tiny flints of marble as white as snow. Two frosted light bulbs were hidden in the palm fronds so as to cast subtle lights on the fern palms and the palmettos from Niihau and the paper palms that had been imported from Japan. The light from one of the frosted bulbs shone through the latticework of palm leaves onto the man's body.

He lay on the clean white stone chips in his clean white uniform. The only uncleanliness was the blood. It was on his abdomen and on his legs. Mostly, it was at the juncture where his legs became his belly. The penis was intact, albeit bloody, but the scrotum had been cut away. It lay, both testicles encased in it, on his coat, right over the breast pocket, below his naval insignia, in the place where ribbons and awards are customarily worn. Had it not bled, it might not immediately have been noticed. But the blood ran down into the pocket and below it and made a streak on the white twill.

The young man was unconscious but not dead. It was Ben Winter and, despite the mutilation, he seemed serenely asleep.

Four

THE INTERNS FROM the Naval Hospital lifted the wounded man onto the stretcher, then loaded him inside the ambulance and shut the doors. Nobody, they said, was permitted inside the emergency vehicle, but at the last minute they made an exception and allowed Tad to accompany Ben to Hospital Point.

He sat between the two young doctors and in the darkness tried to see Ben's face. The boy was still out, totally unconscious, breathing with a profound evenness, and the doctors agreed it was lucky he was senseless. But when the ambulance turned onto the shortcut that connected the two main avenues, the road was badly paved, the stretcher jounced on its frame and Ben awakened and started screaming.

Tad begged the senior of the two interns to give Ben something to relieve him but the man said they'd soon be there, so all Tad could do was grab Ben's hand and try to hurt it. But the shrieking didn't stop.

Nor did it stop until well after they wheeled him into the operating room. By that time, Johanna and Abby had arrived. Unfortunately, there were two cars to take care of, so they drove up separately, without the comfort of one another's presence. Yet, when all three of them began their vigil in the corridor outside the operating room, separateness was still all they could manage, for they had no solace for one another. It was as if, by discussing it as little as necessary, they were spared too close, or too early, a look at their common catastrophe. Abby and Tad paced isolated pathways along the dark corridor, passing one another in silence. Johanna leaned against a wall of the corridor, smoking quietly. From time to time, the glow of her cigarette lighted up her tautened face. Casting a furtive glance at her, Tad marveled at the ritual bravery of an officer's mother, and felt certain she could not keep it up; he didn't want to be there when the outbreak came. Yet . . . there might be none.

He wondered whether Johanna was thinking his thought: there had been a warning. Jerrold, explicitly: *Somebody very close to you is going to get violated.* But Tad had never associated it with Ben; only as a dreaded atrocity against Abby. For a reason that had misled him—all the ravages had been perpetrated against women, in downtown Honolulu, in the tenderloin district of Japtown. And it had never occurred to him, in the posh purlieu of the Quarterdeck Club . . .

It puzzled him that Johanna had not referred to the Englishman's prophecy. Just as he was about to mention it to her, she approached him and murmured the man's name.

"Yes, I was just thinking of him," Tad said.

"Do you know where to find him?"

"I think so," he replied. "I probably have some stuff on him in my files."

She nodded; that was all. And they resumed their vigil.

Toward three in the morning, the surgeon came out of the operating room accompanied by a nurse and an orderly. He spoke more to Tad than to the women. "We've sewn him up. There probably was some hemorrhaging—quite a good deal, I suspect. But I think it's over—he'll be all right."

He'll be all right. What a way to dismiss the gelding of a twenty-three-year-old boy. Tad's thought was apparently Abby's too; she began to cry. The doctor drifted away and whispered something to the nurse. In a moment she approached the visitors. "You'll have to leave," she murmured.

Before the situation could become embarrassing to the nurse, Tad hastened after the surgeon. "I'd like to stay, if it's all right. In case he awakens in the night and doesn't know what's happened."

The doctor had a doubtful instant, then glanced at the stripes on Tad's sleeve. "Just you," he said.

Tad nodded and turned to the others. Abby asked, "Shall I leave the car? Mother can drive me?"

"No, take it."

"How will you get home?"

"I'll pick up a service car." Then, unaccountably annoyed, "Don't fuss, Abby—take it."

Johanna was simply standing there, remote and abstracted, concentrated yet eerily vague, like someone doing a crossword puzzle, trying to find a word. It was inexplicable, the distance in her eyes. Abby took her gently by the arm and led her away; Johanna didn't seem to notice.

Not long after they were gone, a nurse wheeled Ben out of the operating room. Tad hastened to his side and looked down at the unconscious young man. His face had a high flush and he was breathing roughly through his mouth.

In the recovery room, the plumpish nurse sat in a creaking wicker chair on the window side of Ben's bed and invited Tad to sit on a similar chair in the corner. Shortly the woman fell asleep, a quiet sleep, and soon the noise of Ben's breathing subsided and he too was breathing almost silently. The room, the entire hospital, the outdoors; everything was still.

Tad sat in the semidarkness envying their sleep. He ached. He felt the harm to the boy as if it were his own. He hadn't realized how much of his deepest self he had hazarded on the boy. He loved him.

He couldn't believe, now, how much he had disliked Ben when they had first met. It was a disaffection that had promised to be unalterable. And by no feat of his imagination could he ever picture himself meeting anybody in Ben's family whom he could like, much less marry.

"You really want me to do this?" the boy had said on the first day of their meeting. He had given Ben a chore too menial for the boy's talents. The ensign had executed it perfectly and in half the time it should have taken, but had chafed, feeling that Tad had given him a useless drill, to cut him down to size. Toward the end of the day, to reassure the boy in a friendly way, Tad had called him by what he had assumed was the ensign's name. "Don't call me Benjamin," the young man had said. He was snide, but not insubordinate. "One syllable will do. But if you need three, try Benedict." For a time Tad didn't try anything. He called him You.

They had to detest each other. All their differences were abrasive and irreconcilable. Tad had worked hard, he had been a moiling grind, nothing had come easily to him. A stammerer to whom language was an enemy, he had gone through a whole cycle of contest with words. He started by being in terror of them. Then awe, then an arm's-length truce with them, by way of print. Finally, too belatedly, he thought, a deep affection. He was now, by choice and deep necessity, an addicted reader.

Ben was glib. He didn't even have to read. He had unquestioning trust in his own verbality, and in his intelligence. If a problem was an old one, he never studied to find out how it had been previously solved. He treated all problems, old and new, as if they had just this instant arisen, for the very first time, and he was the one selected to find the first solution. His disregard for the written experience of the ages didn't seem to slow Ben down a bit. He found it quicker to consult his wits than the card catalog of the library. But the problem was he didn't have all the information he needed, and he was arrogant about claiming it was unnecessary. That's what caused their first violent argument.

Ben bungled a code. It was a German-Japanese one and it should have been easy. The compromising trick of it was in knowing that one of the key words was Goethe. Ben didn't know the name, he had never heard of the poet. That didn't seem possible to Tad and, in a flare of impatience, he had called Ben an illiterate. To which Ben had retorted, "Listen, Clarke, I come from a smart family. We don't have to *grind* our brains sharp—they're born sharp. How about yours?"

Derisive, but not punishable. Therefore, the more maddening. Tad was on the verge of retaliating, not officer to officer but man to man, when he realized it wasn't necessary. The boy was punishing himself. He was ashamed; his eyes dropped, his face was flushed. Tad turned away from him, and when he turned back Ben was gone. He was gone for two days. On the morning of the third, Tad got a note of apology.

For a while they worked together neutrally. Ben allowed Tad to teach him things, foot by measured foot; occasionally Tad allowed Ben to leap an unmeasured mile.

They found themselves in a new siege. They wanted desperately to continue disliking each other and were frustratedly embattled against their encroaching affection. And one day—it happened so obscurely that neither of them noticed—they discovered they had joined forces, everybody had won, and they were friends.

But Tad, close as he was to the boy, never got over being envious. He had to confess, when confronted, that he was not contemptuous of Ben's brain but envious of it. "You don't have to remember *anything*, do you?" he asked. "Christ, you don't save a single synapse."

"No, I don't. What's a synapse?"

But Tad envied other things too. Ben's style, his effortless warmth, so available to himself; his grace with women. But most of all—how could he phrase this to himself without seeming soft to the core?—he envied Ben his father.

It was an old envy, born long before Ben was, sometimes as dim as the void it came from, sometimes quickened by a triviality, say the sight of a child holding the hand of a full-grown man. Such a vision, even as he sat here in a hospital chair, brought back memories of old pangs he thought he'd never have to think about again. For example, fireworks on the Fourth of July.

It had happened when Tad was seven, perhaps eight. He had lived with a number of families by that time, at least a half dozen. He'd stopped believing what he was told: this will be "your new home." He had learned that a new home was a contradiction. Not newness but oldness was what counted; he quit expecting to realize a familiar dream in a strange bedroom.

It was the father part that always disappointed him the most. He always hoped he would stay long enough for the father of the house to teach him something that took some time to learn—how to hunt or fish or how to use a bench saw. It never happened, but he never gave up hope. He kept waiting for a father as if his turn to have one hadn't yet arrived, but any day now . . .

While waiting, he wandered the city streets, he selected houses he'd like to live in with fathers he'd like to adopt. On rainy days, he tried to pick one out of books. There weren't any in Dumas, but Dickens had a lot of them. When a book had no father he could be a son to, he tried to find another comfort, a magic sentence, an alchemical word, an open sesame to unlock the prison of his loneliness.

One day, on the Fourth of July, he went to watch the fireworks. The display was a free one, in Fairmount Park, but it was presumed that children barely of school age would be accompanied by their parents. Tad did not, of course, consider himself accountable to such presumptions and wandered, freely and alone, among the crowd. As the throng thickened, he realized there were advantages in being alone. You could worm yourself in and out of places, wriggling into the smallest space crawling between people's legs, unfettered by the restraining grip of a parent's hand. But as the crowd became denser and denser, and as people began to get uncomfortable with their confinement and even somewhat panicky, he thought he might like to give up a little of his freedom from a parent's hand in return for some of its comfort.

He had never witnessed fireworks before, and a terrible thing happened. The first explosion came, unseen and without warning. It was so close it was deafening. He began to quake. On the second explosion, terrified, he reached for someone's hand. His own hand didn't know what it was doing. He felt the man struggle, felt the pocket, still had no comprehension what he had done or what he had meant to do, felt the man grabbing him.

"Pickpocket! Goddamn little pickpocket!"

There was a skirmish, a tussle, the crowd opening, making a circle as if a viper were in the center of it. Somebody started to shake him, then somebody else, a slap; in a little while, he was taken in hand by a policeman. Not actually arrested but escorted to the small house on Callowhill Street where he was living.

"Take care of this kid," the policeman said. "Clean him up."

The way the woman of the household took care of him was to push his head against the handrail of the stairs. "You're getting us all in trouble, you dirty thing," she screamed. "So you better stop puttin' on airs. You better get it in your head—you got no father, no parents of no kind at all. And you hardly got a home and won't have if you don't do like I been tellin' you. You go down there tomorrow, you dirty thing, you go to that Bureau of Welfare and tell them sonsabitches, if they keep me waitin', month after month, for my lousy couple dollars, you won't have a home, you won't have a meal, and you won't have a bed to piss in!"

He went down to the Bureau of Welfare the following day. En route, he promised himself faithfully, he vowed with all his quivering soul, that he would never again search for any parent. But when he spoke to the gentle-voiced young man who actually listened to him, he wondered if the man might not be just the right age . . .

Tad could not recall when it was that he stopped searching. It was not something that happened, it was something that ceased happening. Years after that Fourth of July, one evening, toward nightfall—he was already a full lieutenant, on a visit to the Philadelphia Navy Yard—he realized he was back in the city where he had grown up, and he wasn't looking for any hand to hold. How had the need gone, into what studious night at the Naval Academy had it vanished? What had happened to the agonized energy of the quest itself? Where had he been when it had so unobservedly ceased? Where were those years?

Recently, here at Pearl Harbor, long after the quest was over, he had found the father . . . in himself. He discovered that it was easier to be one—to Ben—than to find one. He wondered whether that was true of an ordinary, fully familied, fully parented man. When he gives up searching for the dream father, does he then endeavor to become one? Not that he, Thaddeus Clarke, would ever achieve that ideal, but was that what he'd be going for if he and Abby ever had a child? As soon as they were married a bit longer, he'd want to start asking that question.

Meanwhile, there was Ben to look to, maybe now more than ever. And if empathic pain was in large degree a measure of a man's father feeling, then this boy was his son. What's more, his agony for Ben was intensified by one terrible thing. A small canker ate at his conscience.

Mightn't he himself have done something to cause this attack? Didn't the assault inescapably have something to do with their work? They were trafficking in illicit information, dangerous merchandise. He himself, on numerous occasions, had sent Ben into Japtown, and the young officer had never come back without something that had peril in it. He had uncovered a shipyard leak in a basket-weaving studio on a side street, near the Honolulu docks. With his knowledge of Japanese he had cut into a message line between an offshore sampan and a crippled old man named Rokura Shiba who made mattresses out of goat hair. He knew a hundred shadowy people on the dark side of legality, desperate people, some of them, who pretended to respond to his friendliness and easy charm, and were not to be trusted. Could it be there were secrets in his head that he had never entrusted to the code room? But, then, why wasn't he killed?

He couldn't follow the question through, possibly because the room was heavy with the fumes of anesthesia, and he was dozing. Unaware that he was falling asleep, he had the impression he was drifting only a short distance away, not too far from Ben, always available. Then he heard someone awakening him.

There was nobody there, only Ben and himself. The nurse's chair was empty. Yet, it couldn't have been Ben who was calling him—the light on the night table shone on the young man's face and he was still asleep.

Tad could have sworn he had heard a voice, distinctly saying his name. But the sound didn't recur.

Ben stirred. His lips seemed cracked and dry, and when he moved them Tad thought he might be wanting water. He was murmuring something. He lapsed into silence, then murmured again. "Moon."

It was just that much, hardly a stirring of the air. It might have been some other word. Then, more distinctly this time, "Moon."

His lips stopped moving. He was asleep again, and still. For a long while Tad leaned forward, readying himself, listening closely in case the young man spoke again. But he didn't repeat the sound, nor any other, seeming to have fallen into a quieter, more restful slumber.

The room was getting hotter, Tad thought, the anesthesia fumes heavier. When the nurse returned, he got out of his chair and, muttering about the need for fresh air, tiptoed into the corridor. Except for the night supervisor reading at the half-lighted desk at the far end, the hallway was deserted. Avoiding the lighted area where he might have to speak to the attendant nurse, he drifted toward the dark end of the hallway. The medicinal vapors had made him dizzy. With each step along the corridor, everything seemed to get more and more out of focus. The entryway he was approaching, the dimly illuminated back door, the wide windows opening onto the moonlit parking area, the balusters of the staircase, all vibrated in a precarious tremor. His ears were buzzing, he was hearing a sound as indeterminate as Ben's murmuring.

The sound, like Ben's single word, was real. An insistent whispering, harsh and spasmodic, rippling through a membrane. But, except for the night supervisor who was practically out of sight and certainly out

of earshot, there was nobody in the corridor. And all
the doors were closed. He walked a bit faster, toward
the end of the hall; there might be someone on the
stairway. Looking upward, then downward, he didn't
see a soul. Abruptly, he heard the sound more clearly.
He turned. It came from the corridor, from the telephone booth. Hurrying to it, he pulled the door open.

It was Johanna. She was not using the phone. The
booth was apparently a hiding place. To avoid being
ejected from the hospital, she had taken this refuge,
he assumed, until such a time as Ben would come to
consciousness. The sounds, the convulsive ones, were
coming from Johanna.

She was not crying. It was more terrible. She was
gasping, choking for breath. Whatever she was experi-
encing, whether heartbreak or rage or shock, or all of
them, was too tumultuous for her. She had bit her lip
savagely, there was a gash across it; her mouth was
running with blood. And she was inhaling hoarsely, as
if in panic that the next breath might not come.

"Johanna."

As though strangling, "Go away."

"Come out—let me help you."

"Go *away!*" The fury was maniacal.

He shut the door as softly as he could and stood
outside the phone booth for an indecisive moment,
then walked toward the rear door.

Johanna. She had never learned to weep . . . or had
been taught how not to. Navy manners, in the Spartan
way; salt seas without salt tears, the old commodore's
poem went. How lucky Abby was that she could weep;
it occurred to him. Johanna had let her weep, had perhaps encouraged the freedom to do so. He wondered
at what cost to the mother . . .

There was a flash of light outdoors, in the driveway.
A car came roaring in, faster and noisier than it should
have in a hospital area, and rocking to a stop. The
lights went dark and three men got out.

Tad watched them approach the building. The first
was Admiral Kley, his gray head bent forward, charging the darkness. Behind him was someone whose walk

Tad recognized, the tilted gait of a man pacing a listing deck. Walter Blackburn, one of Kley's liaison men, a captain in the Security Division of the Office of Naval Communications. Behind them, a spare man, shorter than the others, hurrying, taking more strides than they did, yet actually losing ground.

As they opened the door, Kley saw Tad. He's annoyed that I'm here, was Tad's quick impression; the old man didn't pretend otherwise.

"It's late for you, isn't it, Commander?" Kley said.

"Early for you, sir," Tad said evenly.

It was meaningless. The old man seemed, lately, to go out of his way to be pettily vexatious with him. Or, simply, crotchety.

"This is Commander Clarke," the admiral was saying. Then, to Tad, "You know Wally, of course. And this is Howard Young—Lieutenant Young, Police Department."

The detective smiled and nodded amiably, then spelled it. Until the man stressed the extra letter, it hadn't occurred to Tad that the name might originally have been Yung. There was nothing particularly Chinese about the policeman's face except for a smoothness of skin; it was cleaner of beard than the faces of most middle-aged men.

Kley, as if he knew precisely where Ben could be found, was on his way to the recovery room. Halfway down the corridor he stopped and turned around. "Where is he?" he asked.

Tad pointed two doors down, then looked at the police lieutenant. "You're not going to try to question him, are you?" he asked. "He's not conscious."

The detective's good nature didn't change. "Well then, we certainly won't get much out of him, will we?" More soberly, "The doctor said he should be out of it soon, so . . . I don't mind waiting."

Kley wasn't listening. He was already on the threshold of the recovery room. As Tad was wondering whether decorum required that they knock on the door, the admiral was summarily opening it.

By this time, in a fluster of alarm, the night at-

tendant had come hurrying from her desk and Ben's
nurse had entered the corridor. There was a flurry of
badges and identification cards and Kley, with courtly
deference and a firm hand, informed both nurses that
they needn't stand watch.

All four men entered the recovery room. Tad looked
at Ben and was amazed. The young man was sitting up,
fully awake. His eyes were wide open, his body re-
posed, his hands quietly resting outside the white cover-
let. It couldn't be possible. Then Tad realized that
what he had taken as an expression of total consciousness was, in fact, a comatose glaze. The patient was
barely aware that visitors had entered the room. All
he gave them by way of recognition was a quick blinking of the eyes, then the stuporous stillness again.

Young approached the bed without any hint of pro-
fessionalism in his smile, his friendliness genuine. But
when Ben gave no response either to his introduction
of himself or his expression of sympathy, neither the
man's smile nor his intention to question the patient
altered in the slightest.

Tad said, "Can't this wait until morning?"

Blackburn nodded. "He's clearly not conscious yet."

The detective, not ruffled, looked from one officer to
the other. "Oh, I think he is."

"He's right." Ben's voice said quietly. "I am."

Kley walked quickly to Ben's side. His words were
a low whisper, to prevent the others from hearing.
"You don't have to tell them anything you don't want
to, Ben."

Tad knew the hint was unnecessary. Ben, if he possessed even a glimmer of consciousness, would be
smart enough not to reveal a single letter of indexed
information.

"I have nothing to tell," Ben said.

While it was precisely what he expected the boy to
say, what astonished Tad was the calm. There was not
the faintest quaver in Ben's voice. No disturbance. His
eyes were unclouded, his mouth firmly set, his hands as
relaxed as if he were asleep. Tad returned to his
original assumption: he's under heavy sedation, he's

asleep with his eyes open. Then the appalling thought: he doesn't remember anything, doesn't know what's happened to him.

But it wasn't true. Ben said, still without raising his voice, almost as if he had rehearsed every word: "I was walking to my car. I heard someone behind me. As I turned, I felt something terrible at the back of my neck. I don't remember anything else. The first time I was aware of anything was in the ambulance. I was in pain."

Starting to lift his right hand as if he were going to move it to his groin, he resisted the movement.

Still ingratiating himself, Young asked, "Are you in pain now?"

Ben seemed to debate whether to answer. "No."

"Is there somebody who would want to hurt you?"

"No." Without emphasis.

"Are you sure?" Young persisted. "You are, after all, in the position of having . . . information."

Ben simply looked at him. The boy's mastery of himself was uncanny.

Young was undeterred. He was about to pursue the questioning when Kley stepped in. "Now come on, Howard," he said. "He's told you what he knows. I admit it's not very much, but what's he going to do? Let's leave him alone, shall we?"

The detective's head nodded in total agreement, but his body made no movement away from the bed. "Well, we all want to find out who did this, don't we?" Then, quickly, like a trick, turning to Ben, "Could you make some kind of wild guess—was there any warning?"

"None."

Tad stepped out of the darkness and took one step into the light between them. Jerrold's name was on the tip of his tongue; yes, there was a warning, he was about to say. But just as Young looked up at him, as he met the detective's eyes, something as yet unresolved told him: don't. He glanced at Ben. No signal passed between them, yet he knew to be cautious. Say nothing about the warning, he told himself, until you've questioned Jerrold.

Ben's head was turned and he squinted upward, past the light, at Tad, and the moment was over. There was a milling stir in the room and, presently, the visitors were out in the hallway again, making the kind of provisional half-talk of men who do not know how to resolve themselves to inconclusion. As Tad watched them going toward the police lieutenant's car, he observed that they walked more slowly than on their arrival at the hospital, with less resolution.

He himself didn't feel very resolved—not about anything. The scant praise he gave himself for not having blabbered Jerrold's warning was overweighed by his self-blame for having considered it too narrowly. What particularly threw him off balance was Ben's disassociated, unearthly behavior. Clearly the boy knew what had happened to him, yet he was behaving like a coolly impersonal spectator. If he was going to have a delayed reaction, as Johanna had had, it might be more horrifying than Tad could imagine. Yet, that was precisely why he had stayed on at the hospital; to be there if Ben should need him. He turned around and made his way back to the recovery room.

Ben was asleep. Not drowsing, fast asleep. For an instant, Tad thought he might be faking it. But when he mentioned his bewilderment to the nurse, she said it was not unusual, that patients often, after operations, go in and out for a while. They can't help the anesthetic, she said ponderously, and they can't help themselves. He drew enough solace from the woman to decide it would be all right if he went home.

He didn't go home. Outdoors, with the cool wind coming from the sea, he now felt wide awake and restive. Jerrold was on his mind, and what the man might know, what tool of information he had and how he had honed it to the sharp edge of warning. Tad scoured his brain to remember what he himself knew about Jerrold. Not much; he regretted that now. Too soon he had spotted the man as a total impostor, not the part impostor that an operative had to be if he was to be valuable; worse, untrustworthy not only as to his loyalty but even as to his judgment.

He had better reappraise the man. Question him. Then the worry: he might not be able to find him. He used to have a dossier on the Englishman, not a fat one but certainly an address or, as a Chinese merchant mariner once labeled it, the number of a number. It would be in his office, he hoped, and he would go for it.

He didn't regret not having the car. He needed to walk, needed the darkness to conceal from himself some of his ache about Ben; he could almost literally feel the fresh air blowing the anesthetic fumes out of his head.

The Harbor was a comfort to him. He would never get over the deep sense of quiet, yet the quickened pulse of new discovery, every time he walked here in the night. It was always the first time for him, always the views of the yard and the dry docks and Tin Can Alley and the submarine base were an experience nobody had had before, certainly not Tom Clark. And Ford Island, across the narrow channel with all the capital ships in the Row—they mesmerized him, every battlewagon of them, from the old *Utah*, the dowager queen, to Kimmel's flagship, the *Pennsylvania*, the bright and brazen courtesan. He knew how drab they appeared by daylight, the nullity color, the cheerless, disappearing gray, and how gracelessly heavy-bottomed they looked, with all their sweats and swabbings showing. But it was a measure of the magic of the Harbor how the moonlight whitened them. Nighttime, all the deck toil was beyond remembrance, and they were mysterious seafaring argosies on an ancient, spell-weaving sea.

What a difference there was between the Harbor and his office. As he came out through a northeastern gate and started up the hill to the squat little building, he played with the idea that moonlight bewitches everything and tonight it too would shine with enchantment. But seeing it, a quarter mile away, he realized that no sorcery could ever make it seem other than a cheaply stuccoed bungalow, tin-roofed, temporary and ugly. It didn't even have the dignity or protection of being within the high-security district, the Navy side of the gates. It was, as one of his younger assistants described it, like a dormitory off campus. That, he had to face, was the gist of Tad's disaffection: it was out of things. And so was he.

No matter how much Kley, his superior, reassured him to the contrary, he knew it was true. You're an important liaison between Communications and Intelligence, the admiral had said; to Tad it meant working in the most dismal of places, "the brack," neither salt water nor sweet, nameless in a nameless job. And it didn't help when they gave his work a new classification. It had been called a "desk," the most minuscule atom in the Navy's molecular structure. Overnight and arbitrarily, to throw a sop to Commander Clarke, it had been raised to a "subsection." The Auxiliary Desk that had been the catchall file tray of every miscellaneous chore acquired a loftier title, Special Section. But it still functioned as a file tray.

Approaching the front door, he had the exasperating thought: he wouldn't be able to get in, the door would be locked. Damn Abby—did she have to lose her keys? Back at the Club, before getting into the ambulance, he had given her his whole bunch of keys so that she could drive the car. Why hadn't he thought to slip the car key off the ring? Why hadn't he thought . . . with white-coated men loading Ben into the ambulance . . .

This long walk from the hospital, miles of it, and he was going to be locked out.

The door was open. Not just unlocked: ajar—open. His old vexation, anew. It hadn't been the first time he had come upon an open door. Nobody, not a soul in his office, ever gave a second thought to security. Not Schotley, not Herbstmann, not even Ben. True, there was nothing to steal. Whenever there was anything classifiable, anything that had to be routed through Intelligence, anything off the Red Code, it had to go, immediately, to Radio, North, a safety building, or directly to Kley's office. Within the security borders of the Harbor. That the men could go about leaving doors and files open—it gratingly quantified, in Tad's mind, what little value was placed on the work they were doing. No Jap would want to snoop in here; even the enemy didn't consider their work important. It rankled. They were, after all, in a confidential department of the service; at least a *discipline* of secrecy should be maintained. And he himself needed the discipline to support an illusion.

He entered the vestibule and, in a fit of pique, slammed the door shut behind him. As he opened the inner door, he saw a light. It shone out of Schotley's office, a sharp golden triangle of it, across the dark corridor floor. He heard the youngish voice, Schotley's, talking quietly on the telephone. And it was after three in the morning.

Tad started to move, then halted. Attention, he told himself. Kley's cynical precepts flashed through his mind; if there's something you shouldn't hear, listen. If there's someone you shouldn't know, meet him. If there's something you shouldn't see, photograph it. And don't trust your goddamn mother. Kley's Law: Be Paranoid. Don't fight the sickness of the job, the old man cautioned; the disease of the oyster—a punditry—is also its pearl. Be paranoid and listen.

He couldn't make out Schotley's words. All he could tell was the tone, an affectedly warm laugh now and then, chatty and gossipy. The cheap, pilfering bastard. He was sneaking a free telephone call on the transpacific. To his girl friend, no doubt, in the middle of the night, early morning in Los Angeles. Working his cheesy little corruption.

He didn't really dislike the lieutenant. The young man was personable and hard-working. Tad wasn't so much bothered by the filching of loose-leaf binders and the padding of expense accounts as he was by the stupid man's naked, wet-mouthed ambition, by his squeezing credit from the cracking of codes that were written in plain English, by his writing heavy and pompously worded reports on obsolete ciphers.

Tad took a few steps closer to the light. There was

something awry about the phone conversation. If Schotley was talking to his girl friend, there wasn't enough molasses in it.

"I was about to hang up when your brother said you were just coming in from the movies," he was saying. "Was it a good show?"

Coming in from the movies? At this hour? Tad looked at his watch. In Los Angeles it was barely 5:30. In the morning.

Tad tightened. If it was not morning but nighttime, the call was going the other direction. Not eastward to the Mainland. Westward. Asia.

"Oh, yes, we're all very well—how's *your* family?" Schotley said cozily. "They are, huh? I'm glad to hear it. Not the big boys, you mean—just the three girls? Well, I'm sure you miss them, don't you—absence makes the heart grow fonder . . . Yes . . . Okay, then —let me know how they all make out, will you? . . . Yes, thanks . . . I'll give everybody your best."

A few more friendly vacuities, click, then silence. Tad paused a few seconds, undecided whether to let Schotley know he had heard him. The phone call was not innocuous, he felt no uncertainty on that point. The conversation was synthetic, compounded of overfriendly tones of voice, carefully selected cues, all meticulously edited. And Tad couldn't break any of it. He could watch and wait, he thought, and start to monitor. But then, if Schotley was getting nighttime information, he might be giving it as well.

Tad stepped into the doorway.

Schotley looked up from his desk and didn't disguise his shock. "Hey," he said with a smile too broad to hide his agitation. "Hey, you caught me!"

"Yes." Watching. "Doing what?"

"A little overtime." The lieutenant was a bit too hearty. "Do I get time and a half for it?"

"You may get time. What was the call, Schotley?"

The heartiness was gone. "Rory Boyle—you remember Rory Boyle."

He remembered Rory Boyle. A bright, darting man who had been court-martialed out of the Navy for being an alcoholic. Later, when he had dried himself to a cadaverous thinness, he turned his boozehound reputation to good use. Pretending to remain a drunken derelict, he was always good for a job that suggested available venality and a shrewdly trained eye. Tad had never hired Boyle, had not kept track of him.

He asked carefully, "Where's Rory now?"

"Manila."

"What've you got going?"

Schotley flushed. His dilemma was evident. He didn't want to surrender his information and, possibly, lose credit for it. On the other hand, he didn't want to face a charge of having done something unauthorized. He evaded. "Rory was here about two weeks ago."

"Here—in this office?"

"Oh, no—in Honolulu. He—uh—called me."

"Why didn't he call me?"

"Well . . ." He was hedging. But subtlety was difficult for Schotley. "He said you were . . . incorruptible."

"Yes, I see why he called you." Schotley didn't show any injury. "What was your deal with him?"

"Well, not really a deal, Thaddeus, not what you'd call—"

"What was it?"

"If he gives us anything we can use, we pay him— no fixed amount and no arguments—whatever we think it's worth."

"But that *is* a deal, Schotley."

"Well, I guess in a way—I guess yes, you could call it that, yes."

Schotley was starting to sweat. Tad pointed to the telephone. "Have you got a code going with him?"

Quickly, openly frightened now, Schotley said, "Oh, it's a private code. " Private codes were expressly proscribed. The instant Schotley mentioned it he knew he was getting deeper in trouble. "But I didn't give him one of ours—honest to God I didn't!"

Tad decided to let that ride for a moment and get to the main point. "What's he giving you?"

"Position of the Jap fleet!" He was relieved not to be talking about the code, and proud of his accomplishment. "Everything! He's keeping track of every movement—carriers, battleships, everything!"

"How's he doing it?"

"Monitoring their radio—he won't tell us any more than that."

"What code are you using?"

"No—I told you—honest—we made it up!"

"All right, you made it up, but you *are* using a code. What is it?"

Again, a touch of pride. "Well, it's beautifully simple. When he talks about his 'family,' it stands for the Jap Navy. 'Children' means ships—all classes. 'Boys' are aircraft carriers. 'Girls' are battleships. 'Babies' are the rest—tin cans, sweepers, tenders, et cetera."

"I heard you say something about three girls?"

Schotley's voice was excited. "That's it, Tad—they're missing!"

"What do you mean, missing?"

"Missing—gone—Rory can't locate them. They've gone off the air."

"Which ones are they?"

"He only knows the name of one of them—the *Huso*. He thinks it's the flagship of one of their fleets."

"A flagship—and he can't track it?"

Schotley raised his arms in a bewildered, helpless gesture.

It was naïve. It simply meant that Rory's private monitoring resources, whatever they could be, were inadequate. Even if it meant that the three battleships were off on some mysterious errand, according to Rory, the man's tip would be suspect: difficult information too easily acquired. However, Tad had no inclination to discount anything prematurely. Yet, it wouldn't do to encourage Schotley. "Don't worry about the wagons. They may be in dry dock."

Schotley didn't smile. "Or out of it." Since Tad didn't deny the possibility, the lieutenant thought he saw his superior coming his way. He pursued the advantage. "May I go on with Boyle?"

"Absolutely not."

"You mean we just throw this information away?"

"No, I'll pass it on to Kley."

In a panic: "You won't tell him where you got it, will you?"

"I'll try not to."

"Thaddeus, let me go on with it. I'll be careful."

"I said no."

"Why not, for God's sake?"

Tad kept his temper in check. "How many children does Boyle actually have? I mean real kids—in his own actual family—how many?"

Schotley looked mystified. "I don't know—I think a son and a daughter."

"So if anybody intercepts your phone conversations about the Jap fleet, they hear Rory talking about his hundreds of kids—God knows how many babies, maybe a dozen sons, a dozen daughters. Is he putting them all through college?"

Schotley's face went red.

Stupid numskull, Tad thought. A code man, paid to be one, promoted to the third rank upward in the echelon of officers, lulling himself with simplistic solutions, forgetting a primary principle, a cardinal rule, that the idiosyncrasy is the first betrayal of the secret message.

"Go home," he said. "And this time, for Christ sake, shut the door."

He didn't wait for the younger man to leave but continued to his office at the end of the hall. He unlocked the door, turned on the lights and went immediately through the connecting doorway into the code room. Unlike his office, which was always in order, the code room was a jumble. It was an enclosed place, without a window, too small to contain what it did and cluttered by the excesses. But it had an atmosphere that pleased Tad: it suggested cobwebby old libraries and wizards' workrooms. On shelves and on tables there were stacks and stacks of indexed sheets, a miscellany of cipher pieces made of cardboard and celluloid, reams of double-sided carbon paper for backward writing, a special typewriter with a double bank of keys, resonators, sounders, clackers, dictionaries, atlases, maps in piles and rolls, blackboards, encoding and decoding machines, and a whole set of what Tad called his crazy mirrors, which pictured things backward and forward and upside down and in distorted shapes.

And, of course, the files. He went to the wooden one and opened it. There was neither a folder nor an envelope with Hugh Jerrold's name on it. But there was one typewritten sheet of paper, no more than that, headed by the name William Jocelyn Tompkins.

He took it back to his office, switched the desk light on and read. The information looked like a practical joke. It was full of inconsistencies that were not only incredible but supercilious. The man had three "real" names. He attended Oxford and Cambridge simultaneously. While stationed in New Delhi as a cultural attaché, he was in Los Angeles as a technical adviser on a film based on the life of Lord Kitchener. He was the author of five books, two on linguistics and one each on lithography, stamp collecting and faïence; the titles of the books were not known, nor the publishers. Three years ago, when the biography of the man had been compiled, he had three addresses, one in London, one in Dorset and one in Manila. No Honolulu address was given.

But there was a Honolulu phone number. Tad dialed it. He thought: wouldn't it be a miracle if, out of all the incoherent, unreliable drivel, one thing was accurate, his phone number? The phone stopped ringing and the operator came on the line. She asked what number Tad had called. A few moments later, she reported that no such number existed.

He put the receiver back in its cradle. As he was setting the phone down on the desk, something caught his attention. It was in the black agate ashtray on the visitors' side of the desk.

A bunch of keys with Abby's initials on the round gold tag he had given her. He looked at them: three keys—house key, car key, postbox key, all intact. Beside them, on a calling card with Hugh Jerrold's name on it, was the message: *Can you meet me on Monday at Karli's restaurant? Say, five o'clock?*

Tad put the keys in his pocket and, making a wad

out of Jerrold's card, started to throw it in the waste-basket. He resisted the impulse and smiled; there was no enjoyment in it. He'd have bawled hell out of an ensign for throwing the card away.

He felt a heaviness in his gut. Senseless; he must rout these formless, shapeless forebodings. If Abby said she lost her keys, then Abby lost her keys; their reappearance in this way didn't mean anything to the contrary. He must dismiss from his mind this ridiculously portentous foreboding.

No, he couldn't dismiss anything. Kley's Law: Be Paranoid.

Five

JOHANNA SAT IN THE phone booth, in darkness, and tried to make herself cry, and couldn't. Tried to make herself scream, and couldn't. Yet, she was screaming, wasn't she? Did it matter if nobody heard, if she herself didn't hear; a scream was a scream. Wasn't it? Even a silent one, wasn't it, wasn't it?

There were other questions. What to do for her son? What to do for his pain? Now, tomorrow, whenever the pain came, forever, what to do for it? What to do for her own?

Whom could she kill was a good question. Whom could she butcher for having done this to her son; a very good question.

Scream; but, no, only silence.

How about humor? There was perhaps some comforting irony she could summon. Once, as editor of her college paper, she had written there was no possible subject that, at heart, did not have a jest in it. An acrimonious one, perhaps, but always something to remind you that life was a practical joke, the practical part being its way of balancing things. The scales of jesting justice. She had been scoffed at—Johanna of the Jesting Justice—but she had really meant it: irony, the leveler. Where was the leveler now?

Was there any moral principle, jesting or otherwise, that could make sense of the castration of her beloved Ben? What crime could he have committed, what crime could any man commit, that should be punished with male death? Not just death alone, which was without sexual partiality, but the cruel vindictive death sentence: exist, but do not increase your kind.

It must have been done with a knife, and she wished she had one. But whom would she slash? Years ago, when she was in her teens, she had lifted a pair of scissors to her nagging, bedeviling mother. "Go on!" her

mother had challenged. "And *then* whom will you kill!"
To which preposterous question she had shrieked preposterously, "I'll find *somebody!*"

Find somebody now. She would, somebody, she
would . . . but whom? That man would know, that
shifty man—Jerrold—he had said that word with a
terrible doubtlessness, violated; an augury. Tad would
know where to find the Englishman, and through him
there would be some way to lay hands on the mutilator
. . . lay claws on him . . .

Opening the door, she looked out into the corridor.
There was dawnlight, coming in the windows, silver-
gray. She would go to his room again. A number of
times she had slipped down the hallway, holding close
to the walls, hoping not to be seen by the night attendant, and certain at last that she had been seen and been
suffered. The first time, right after Kley and the other
men had left, she had stood there at the partly open
door, gazing through the dim light at her son. He was
sitting up; his eyes were open, but he made no sign he
saw her. He had been talking, the nurse said, but now
he was comatose again. The second and third times he
was asleep.

She got out of the phone booth and straightened up.
Her neck was stiff and she ached all over. She wondered
if that might be an excuse for going home. She had
never used illness to obtain a remission from anything,
perhaps she had one remission coming to her. So sorry,
Benedict, I can't visit you in the hospital, not this time,
I have an important headache to attend, you won't
mind, will you?

What if he really had to answer the question, whether
he minded or not? It struck her with painful clarity:
he might be relieved not to see her. Whom would a
castrated young man rather not see than his mother? His
wife, perhaps, but he need see her only once; then they
could flee from each other. His mother, however . . .
no matter how far across the world he removed himself,
he could never escape his mother's pity.

As she moved slowly down the corridor to the
recovery room, she had the deathly premonition that

this time he would be awake and they would have to talk to one another. If only there were some alternative to this visit. Why couldn't she, feeling as empty as she did, fall into a faint and have to be carried away? No, consciousness was a knife at her throat, too sharp for fainting. It all came back to screaming, didn't it? . . . Too late now.

Forward, she walked quietly forward. And prepared an endurable meeting in her mind: I enter the room and he opens his eyes. He says nothing and I say nothing. No questions, no motherly straightening of bedclothes and patting of pillows, no can-I-get-anything-or-do-any-thing-for-you. We maintain the silence. It is not a burden but a balm. If there's a magazine, I sit and read it. If he wants to talk, we talk. If he doesn't, we don't. Then I go away.

Excellent. She was there now. At the door to the room, the night nurse was coming out. She was slinging a navy-blue cape over her white uniform and preparing to depart.

"Slept well," she said tersely, and Johanna wondered whether she was talking about Ben or herself. Ben, of course; if he hadn't slept well, she wouldn't have, either. "They'll be moving him to his own room in a little while," the nurse said.

Johanna nodded and entered. Ben was sitting up. His face, this Monday morning, looked not one bit different than it had on Sunday night. He seemed well rested and his hair was combed. Yet, there was something errone-ous about him, wrong tone, out of focus. She hadn't known what to expect of him, but what she was seeing was nothing she could have imagined. He seemed ab-stracted, that was all, not with anything particularly importunate, more as if he were assembling a number of minor details, like a schedule of his chores for the day. She had been agonizingly preparing herself for a larger moment; she couldn't handle the smaller one.

"How do you feel?" The question was rubber stamp, of course; she could find no other kind.

"All right."

"You—uh . . . ?"

"No—no pain."

He was overcoming her difficulty for her, doing it too easily. She had thought he was not quite out of shock; perhaps he was too soon out of it; too soon adjusted to what he knows. Yet, his eyes did not seem to converge upon her properly, there was something wrong; perhaps there was still some part of him that hadn't emerged from the narcotic. She had come too early, she told herself, or too late. But how could she know, she had nothing to go on, nothing but the things she had resolved not to resort to. "Is there anything—can I get you anything?"

"No," he said uninflectedly. "I'm sure the hospital will take care of everything."

His voice was so matter-of-fact it stunned her. He was talking exactly the way she had hoped they might talk, and she couldn't stand it. Addressing her across an insulating distance, as if she were a nurse, a stranger. There is something we have to suffer together, she wanted to say to him, either in words or in silence, but together. She wanted to touch him, touch his hand, caress his face. But she didn't dare; he was closed against a touch; he wouldn't let her. And perhaps he was right not to, knowing she couldn't keep the pity out of it. Oh, Benny, she ached to say, let me do it for a little, let's both let it hurt for a moment. Let me reach you, if I can, let me hold you, rock you . . . She stopped herself. Beware of pity. Don't burden him, the poor damaged one; pity only the strong.

"Do you have any idea . . . ?" No, that was the wrong thing, she realized; how did that ever get into it?

"Who did it?" he asked unblinkingly. "No, I don't."

She tried to pick something out of the air. She couldn't. "If there *is* anything I can get for you . . ."

His voice tightened a little. "Nothing, Mother. Thank you." Hearing his own inflexibility, he pretended to smile. "Don't worry now."

Only those three gentle words and she realized, with an access of shame, that she had entered the room not

to comfort but to be comforted. She was begging him
to tell her that tragedy was not tragic, that he would
learn to live with this catastrophe, that it would ultimately turn out to be not as terrible as it had once
threatened to be. Assure me you will be happy, the
eternal mother cry, the maddeningly pathetic silliness,
promise me never to weep. Well, he wasn't weeping.
And he was, if only in a meager way, trying to comfort
her. And it made her sick of herself.

"They'll be moving me soon," he said.

The hint was plain. "Yes, I'll go," she said. "I'll call
you later."

She left the room and on her way outdoors caught
sight of the hospital office. Returning, she entered and
approached the clerk behind the desk. Was there anything she could do, she asked him, sign a paper or
something? The young man smiled pleasantly and informed her that since it was a service hospital, the Navy
was in charge, she didn't have to do a thing, not a jot.
The Navy was always so willing to do everything for
you, Johanna thought, she wondered if she could get it
to weep for her.

In the car and driving fast, she wished there were
another way home than the road that took her past the
Club. Yet, irrationally, when she came to the front
entrance where the attack had taken place, she slowed
down. Some compulsive necessity, perhaps the need to
bring her inchoate soreness into one clear blain that
she could manage, made her stop the car.

A policeman was stationed there, parading the pal-
metto grove. She couldn't imagine why. Nothing was
likely to happen there again, certainly not in this morning daylight, and nothing was changed since last night.
The blood was still on the white stones. She thought
waywardly: let me wash it away, that's *something*
I can do. It was too morbid a thought and she made
herself stay until the sickness passed.

What returned her to common sense was the recollection that here was where Ben had come for his car
when he was on his way to pick up Ellie Carter.

Ellie Carter. Somewhere, wherever the girl lived, she had been stood up. Johanna reflected without amusement that people who are stood up go through stages of annoyance, anger and, finally, worry: did a terrible thing happen? Yes, Ellie, it did . . . Somebody had to tell her.

Johanna's house was one hill over from Aiea, where Abby and Tad lived. They used the same road for part of the way and had somewhat the same view of the Harbor. When she pulled up into her driveway, Ryozo, the elderly Japanese gardener, was already at work, pruning the eugenia hedges. He mumbled a question that she didn't understand. But she said yes and it seemed to please him tremendously; she didn't try to imagine what she had said yes to.

The house was too big. No matter how much extra furniture she had jammed into it since the rest of the family had moved elsewhere, it didn't seem to get any smaller. Worse, it was so goddamn neat these days. She had let the house cleaning woman go, she didn't need one any longer. She considered hiring somebody to make things look disorderly again.

It was just after nine o'clock and she really ought to call Ellie Carter. How are you, Ellie, how've you been, how do you like your job on the *Advertiser,* by the way, my son's been castrated. No, stop theatricalizing, goddamn it, it needn't be said in such melodramatic understatement. What way, then? Was there an acceptable form for it? How about silence? Perhaps if you don't mention it to anybody, you yourself won't get to hear about it.

She phoned the *Advertiser* and asked for the research department, which was where she'd gotten Ellie the job. "May I speak to Miss Carter, please?"

"Who?" The man's voice was brusque.

"Ellen Carter."

"Oh, yes—Ellie," he said. "She doesn't work here any more."

"She doesn't?" she asked. "You mean she's in another department?"

"No—she left the paper."

That was strange. She hadn't heard that Ellie had changed jobs. "You wouldn't know where she's working now, would you?"

"Chicago, I think."

"Chicago?"

"Oh, yes. Long time."

"How long?"

"Well, let me see." She heard him ask somebody else. Their voices were indistinct. Then, clearly, "Two or three months."

She thanked him and hung up.

No conclusions, she warned herself. Don't jump the wall, her father used to say, unless you see the other side.

Whatever nameless dread was on the other side, one thing was certainly lurking there: Ben had lied.

Her mind was jumping again and she had to stop it. Not necessarily a lie, maybe only a petty fabrication. It could mean something as inoffensive as a trivial foolishness. On the other hand, it might mean something as culpable as . . .

It occurred to her: he wanted desperately to leave Pearl Harbor. Why had she said desperately, why was she loading it that way? There was no desperation, no last extremity in his urge to get into action, to take to the sea. It was simply an act of courage, a yearning to get into the arena.

Or out of it. Was there something here he was afraid of? Had he had a warning?

The Englishman's warning came to mind again. Could Jerrold have known that her son had betrayed . . .

Whom?

Stop jumping, she told herself, stop, stop.

She couldn't stand all the possibilities in her mind, all the contingencies, all the dangerous surmises. Nor did she want to arrive at clarity; chaos might be better.

Sleep might be the best. She had been awake all

night; she would go to bed. But she knew she couldn't sleep; yet, how could she face the day?

She started to cry. But it was only a wetness of the eyes, the tears had nothing to do with her; they did no good. The scream was still inside her.

Six

HE SMELLED THE COFFEE and heard Abby in the kitchen. She was doing things too silently. There was no deliberately accidental clatter that would normally be followed, when he entered, with abject apology: "Oh, did my noise wake you? I'm so sorry, darling." None of that. He wished there were.

She had slipped silently out of bed, trying not to disturb him. It was quid pro quo—he had tried not to disturb her when, in the early dawn, he got into it, but she had been awake, waiting for him. She had moved close, murmuring about being cold, which she never was, and she had the shivers, saying Ben's name a few times. Except for holding her, he had no comfort to give; there was nothing he could say about Ben except the fact, which wasn't interpretable in consoling ways.

Out of the shower and dressed, he wondered if she had seen the keys. He knew she couldn't have; he had stowed them away too carefully. But he was long past taking anything for granted. Opening the dresser drawer, he reached under the pile of socks and found the gray pair at the bottom. He unrolled the ball. The keys were there, of course, why had he imagined otherwise? He put them in his pocket and thought: I won't discuss them. If there's a worry in them—she's got enough to handle right now. And there could be a worry, worse than she might dream of . . . The keys had been returned by the very man who had sounded the warning that someone would get violated . . . No, he must not tie them together too soon—wait for his meeting with Jerrold . . .

When he entered the kitchen, Abby's quiet somberness had lifted; she had gone to work at routing it, he felt sure, and she was now cheerier than necessary. "Hey, when did *you* get home?"

"You heard me," he replied. "Dawn's early light."

"How'd you get here?"

"Walked."

She whistled. "Murder. Got any feet left?"

"Two feet, three blisters."

She actually *did* seem cheery; he wondered how she managed it. She didn't wait long to tell him. "While you were in the shower, I called the hospital," she said. "He's amazing. He had a huge breakfast and they'll be moving him out of the recovery room. He should be up and about by the end of the week."

She was doing it well, the Navy brat, courage before breakfast surrender be damned, I have not yet begun to fight. "Good," he said quietly.

He sat down to the papaya but, having no appetite for it, started to suck the lime. "What's in the newspaper?" he asked.

"Nothing. Just another warning from Japan."

She knew what he meant and was avoiding it. As she handed the paper to him, "Nothing about Ben," she said.

She was right. Only tidings of the war plague that wasn't raging right now; small swellings and festerings, and, here and there, an erupting boil. The big news was in the diplomatic negotiations and, within two articles in the same newspaper, they were proceeding nicely, and falling apart. One of the headlines said, *Japan Press Warns U.S. to Quit Pushing*. Another, to keep anxiety teeter-tottering, said, *Progress Seen in Japan Talks*. If there was a ray of hope, there was none in Europe. Every country had been pulverized. Like iron filings, they clung trembling to the steel Axis. Hitler looked to Moscow and wondered if he could stay warm through the winter; Mussolini looked to Africa and wondered if he could stay cool. Churchill looked to Roosevelt and wondered if he could bring him to the boiling point; Roosevelt looked to his fellow citizens and wondered the same. The war was in hiatus. The world was waiting for the next movement, expecting it to be American; meanwhile, it was suffering from the war, but not, at the moment, waging it. It was Monday, November 24, 1941; war was hell, but not a hell of a lot of it was happening.

Nowhere in the paper was there any mention of the attack on Ben. Perhaps, Tad thought, it had occurred too late at night for the morning edition. Still, since there had been a police report immediately after the assault, there should have been time to cover the assault. The *Star Bulletin,* this afternoon, would be bound to carry the whole damn thing.

"Are you going to eat with only one hand?" she asked.

He hadn't been aware of it. He was eating with his left hand, his right one in his pocket, clinging to her keys. With a discomfited smile, he raised his right hand to the table and reached for another slice of lime.

"You'd better have some toast," she said, "before you eat any more of that acidy stuff."

"Yes." He started to butter a piece.

He wanted to get out of the house as quickly as possible. It disturbed him to be here, concealing something from her and muddling as to why it was important to do so. He couldn't, by any repatterning of his thoughts, imagine how she could have had anything to do with Jerrold or his warning, certainly not with the atrocity upon her brother. Then what was bothering him? Did he suspect Jerrold had known her in Japan? Did Tad see them, in some figment, crossing diminutive bridges, studying stunted evergreens, reading haiku together? But it was impossible, she was only a child at that time. Maybe *that* was his botheration: she was still only a child. Barely twenty-one—with a husband nearly twice her age. It was easy to have such botherations. Nameless, baseless, floating ones, in and out of nightmare, in and out of reality. Inexplicable keys in his pocket.

Then why didn't he simply tear them out of his pocket, toss them on the table and say, "How about it?" Not because he didn't want to add to her worries today —he'd better be honest about it—but because there would be an accusation implicit in the question and he was not ready to charge her with anything. And because there might be no basis for a charge. And because, if there *was* anything slightly uneven about the situation, Abby might be tempted to lie, and he would be giving her no alternative. And because—most important—that was not the way to do it. It wasn't good technique to settle for raw information. It must be carefully refined, without a taint on it; even the method of acquiring it must be immaculate. Because information, the purest kind, had the most puissant fire power. It was the invincible ordnance. There wasn't, finally, any other kind of knowing. And before acting, he must know.

The major problem was that such meticulousness demanded phenomenal patience. How could he wait for his five o'clock meeting with Jerrold? How would he ever pass the day?

Testily. He again rebuked Schotley for leaving doors and files open. He reprimanded Herbstmann for not keeping visa reports up to date and for temporarily mislaying a radio traffic analysis. And when he called Blackburn's office to ask for a code man who could replace Ben, he irritably turned down two suggestions and accepted the third ungraciously. A bad day.

It was worse when Kley arrived. He hadn't expected the admiral; the old man rarely visited. If he wanted you, he summoned. It was only when he was going to saddle you with a particularly unpleasant chore that he came calling, hearty and sociable, so that you couldn't beat a retreat. Here comes Sweet Old Ironass, Ben once observed, bearing fruits and flowers; watch out, don't bite the peach, there's a dumdum in it.

He appeared in the middle of the afternoon and remarked that Tad's tin-roofed office was too damn hot and it was disgraceful to make a Navy commander sweat his brains-and-balls in a hellish incinerator. As if he couldn't, by a finger snap, have transferred Tad to better quarters.

Tad was too busy and much too fractious to pander to the flimflam. He tried not to sound too ruffled. "Is there anything I can do for you, sir?"

"No, nothing really, Thaddeus," he said. "I just got to feeling terrible about young Ben and I came over for a word, that's all. Or to give one."

He meant a word of comfort, of course, and Tad was abashed at having misjudged him. "I wish I had one to give," he replied.

"No idea why, huh?" the admiral asked. "Why, who, wherefore?"

"None."

"Awful," he said heavily. "Awful and unimaginable." He cleared his throat a number of times, forcing himself to cough. Then he slapped his palms against his thighs. He was embarrassed about something. "Hey— Jesus Christ—tell me something. We all walk around thinking we know certain things and then something happens and suddenly we realize we don't know what we *thought* we knew. Now take this matter of—you know—castration and eunuchs and that kind of thing. I always thought I knew what the hell that was and suddenly . . . What I mean is, I know he won't be able to—uh—rise and shine with a woman. But how about the rest? I mean . . . his voice won't change, will it?"

"No, it won't."

"Well, Christ, that's a relief, isn't it?" He tried to lighten things. "Can't have a soprano on the captain's bridge, can we?" When Tad didn't deal with the question, he went on. "How about his beard and stuff? He'll still have to shave, won't he?"

"Yes."

"It's a goddamn cheat, isn't it—he loses a joy and keeps a nuisance." Then, having ridden himself of the paltry humor, he became weightily serious. "Well, if there aren't going to be any outward signs of it, his career needn't suffer. It's a good thing he'll be transferred—nobody has to know a damn thing about it. If we can keep it out of the papers."

"Well, that won't be so easy, will it?"

Quickly, "Why do you say that—have they been after you?"

"The newspapers? No."

"Then maybe they won't." Suddenly he wasn't the sweet, fumbling man, comfort questing and abashed about his sex ignorance. He was a suspicious, crafty ferret. "You sure they didn't reach you?"

Annoyed, "Of course I'm sure."

"Well, if they do, don't answer them," he said sharply. "It's not a Navy matter except that Ben's one of ours. It didn't happen on Navy property—we've got nothing to do with it."

True, it wasn't a Navy matter. Tad wondered why Kley had to make so elaborate a disclaimer. "Is somebody saying it's a Navy matter?"

"Oh, no, not at all. And let's keep it that way. If the papers call me, I don't know anything." Then, the finger pointing, "Neither do you."

"Well, I *don't* know anything."

"Good." He started to go. Then, easing a little, "Did the newspapers call Abby?"

"Not that I know of."

"Johanna?"

"I wouldn't know that."

"If they do—same thing—clam 'em up."

Tad felt a restless disquiet. "I don't see how I can direct them any way at all—since it's *not a* Navy matter."

"We don't want it to become one, do we?"

Tad nodded, not certain whether he was nodding in comprehension or agreement. Kley apparently saw the irresolution. He came back into the room and his voice was more direct, more genuine. "I didn't mean to worry you, Tad. The thing is terrible in itself and we all know it. It won't make it any better to have it spill all over—on you, on the Winters, on the Navy. Let's shove away from it." He smiled with the kindliest intimacy. "Let's put out to sea. The sooner to sail, the sooner to sleep."

Whatever seaman's gibberish that was, the old man's intent was warm; he was more engaging than Tad had ever seen him. What's more, he was right. This time Tad's nod was without reservation.

Before going, Kley glanced down at Tad's desk.

There was a pile of mess and a pile of neatly stacked memoranda. He pointed to the memoranda. "Anything I can take back?"

"Yes, there is, as a matter of fact," Tad replied. "But I haven't written it up—we've lost three Jap battle-ships."

"Track, you mean?"

"Yes—one of them's the *Huso*."

"You're not tracking actual ships, are you?"

"Oh no—only reports on them."

"Whose reports?"

Well, here goes Schotley, he thought. But, as he had promised, he would try to protect him. Just one hand's worth. He said carefully, "We're monitoring."

"Jap reports, of course."

"Yes."

Schotley was safe—Kley was darting ahead. He was grinning, getting a mischievous pleasure out of something. "That's delicious," he said.

Tad didn't know where the joke was. "Is it?"

"Of course." He was enjoying it more and more. "*You* haven't lost 'em—*they* have. The dumb little yellow bastards can't keep track of their own ships—not even their capital ships!"

"I wouldn't be sure of that."

"You wouldn't? Well, let me tell you something. They're lousy mariners, Thaddeus, they're *historically* lousy mariners. Ever hear of Mihonoseki? It's not a person, it's a place. They staged a great big war game there—the whole damn Combined Fleet—to train the crews for night action. Know what happened? Two destroyers collided with two cruisers—bang, in the dark! Two hundred men drowned and one commanding officer killed himself. They're stupid, Thaddeus."

"That was in 1927, Admiral."

"Their Navy got bigger, Thaddeus, it didn't get brighter." He started to laugh. "They're stupid—and thank God they're stupid. Here they are—see?—same old stupidity. They can't keep track of their movements, they can't keep track of their goddamn bowel movements. And, boy, if they can't, they'll shit all over themselves."

He continued laughing for a bit, but when he saw that Tad didn't, he sobered. "Laugh, Thaddeus." Then, with affection, he gripped Tad's shoulder. His voice was painstakingly paternal. "There are too many serious things—this is something to laugh about. Laugh, boy!"

"Will a small smile do, sir?"

Kley heard the irony but didn't stop smiling. Their smiles were matched now, with good humor in neither of them. Tad's sarcasm had been too abrasive.

Then something altered, subtly. The anger in the old man's face became quite another thing; the breach in his expression was no clearer than a hairline crack in an eggshell. But it was there, a look of injury, wounded. He was at pain to conceal that he was hurt by the rejection; he made another effort, aborted, to smile. Then he quickly departed.

Old glooms came back to Tad, too vague to localize in time and place. From childhood, surely . . .

The old man, for all his fatuousness and deviousness, had tried to show a fatherly affection. There had been other fathers who had *seemed* to offer affection, but had never raised a hand to prevent a parting, and had said good-bye with hearts intact, except his own. Beware of fathers. Pickpocket, they all cried. Fathers can be dangerous.

And yet . . .

Karli Karli was a multibreed Islander, as thin as his long brown cigarette. He ran a restaurant in which he didn't eat. The doctor had forbidden him all spicy food since he had asthma, so he sat in a corner, smoked his forbidden cigarettes, and fanned himself with a sandalwood branch. The leaves stirred air into his sick lungs, and if he pricked the stem with his fingernail, the fragrance of the wood slightly counteracted the stench of tobacco.

Seeing Karli, Tad had an impulse to talk to him. The man had worked for him when the commander's

Special Section was no more than a Desk, and the stringer had done a dozen men's work at once, with octopal tentacles everywhere. About to greet the restaurant owner, Tad thought better of it. And Karli Karli was pointedly looking in another direction, with no hint of recognition.

If you asked Karli what sort of food his restaurant specialized in, he would say Hawaiian, Chinese and Kansas City Beef. What it really specialized in was not food but a startlingly crimson drink called *chi doku*. Nobody ever saw the drink made. It was prepared at night, after hours, in gallon-sized earthenware jugs, and doled out by the bartender into tall glasses half filled with ice. Some guessed it was a combination of absinthe and various kinds of rum, some said absinthe and various kinds of *sake*, some said absinthe and absinthe. While no two people could agree about how the drink was made, there was unanimity about what the name of the drink meant. *Chi doku*, in Japanese, meant blood poison.

Hugh Jerrold was halfway through his third *chi doku* when Tad arrived and ordered a glass of white vermouth. As the Englishman was coming to the end of his drink, Tad thought: he doesn't show any signs of three snakebites, but any minute he may stiffen and not be able to tell me anything.

He had asked the Englishman only about the keys, putting off until later his question about the atrocity warning. He was now convinced, on hunch alone, that the returned keys and the warning were two faces of the same coin, but he wasn't ready to let Jerrold know his suspicion. Something might slip out in the course of conversation, he hoped, if he could lay back for a while; meanwhile, stupidity was a better mask than cleverness.

Although the drinks had made nothing blur in Jerrold's mind, he was relaxed about tangential interests in the restaurant, the polyglot nature of the customers, the chow mein—ham-and-eggs food, the bedroom availability of the waitress.

Tad was losing patience. "We were talking about the keys," he said.

"Oh, I remember. I haven't forgotten," Jerrold replied equably. "It's like a loss leader. I'm going to give you that information gratis if you buy something else."

"I told you no."

"You also told me the first chance you got you'd punch me up." He winked. "If you can change your mind on one point, why not on another?"

"I haven't changed my mind. There's still time."

"Would you like to know where the first Japanese attack is going to be?"

"Not from you."

"What difference where you get it?"

"I've bought three things from you, Jerrold. The first one we already had—not your fault. The second you sold to us—then immediately sold *them* the warning that you'd already sold the information to us. The third was an outright fake."

"*Caveat emptor.*"

"That's what I'm doing."

"Don't really want to know where the Jap attack will be?"

"No."

"Don't leave the shop. I've got lots of pretty things. Look around."

"How much are the keys?"

"You've already got them. You mean how did *I* get them?"

"Yes   how much?"

"How much cash have you got?"

"With me?"

"Yes. Shell it out."

It would be a prank of some sort, Tad knew, an easing of the tension so that later he could be taken unaware. He reached into his pocket, pulled out his wallet, and opened it. Sixty-five dollars.

Jerrold counted it. "I'll take fifty." And he did so.

The man certainly wouldn't settle for so little, Tad

thought, unless he was even more desperate than he had said he was.

"Yes, I'm as bugger-beggared as that," Jerrold said.

"The keys?"

"It's simpler than fifty dollars' worth. I stole them."

"Why?"

"Two reasons. I wanted to shock you into paying some attention to me. What I had to sell didn't do it. I fancied that your wife *would*. And I was right. My second reason—I wanted to have a go at your house."

"Did you find anything?"

"Not a bloody jot." He made a rueful grimace. "The hell of it is, you people don't have anything that's marketable, not a damn thing. Not in your house, not in your files. And I'll tell you a secret—nobody's got anything that's worth a dollar. Not Layton, not Rochefort. You want to hear a shocker? Not even Kimmel! Every ruddy thing you've got the Japs already know. If somebody could come up with one fresh little flyspeck of information—a doodle on a scratch pad—the Japanese would buy it. Even from me. So here I am, reduced to a fifty-dollar set of keys."

"You're a liar."

"Yes. I'm a liar."

"Who stole them?"

"Nobody. They were found."

"By whom?"

"Japanese man named Nishi. Giggling little fellow. His small boy is in your wife's class. She was showing Donald Duck—she left the keys near the movie projector. Simply forgot them."

"You miserable crud."

"Yes, rather."

Yet . . . could it be as innocent as that? Or was it what Jerrold wanted him to think? But he had to believe, where Abby was concerned, that things were as uncomplicatedly innocent as the Englishman said they were. She had simply forgotten her keys; nothing more than that. The suspicious excuse about going to look for the mail on a Sunday was simply that she had forgotten what day it was; also nothing more than that.

And the fact that it was Jerrold who returned the keys —as well as giving the atrocity warning—was a coincidence; again and again, nothing more than that.

Or was there more?

"By the way," Tad said, "there's something else I might buy from you. You warned us that somebody might get hurt."

"Oh, yes." Unconcernedly. " 'Violated,' I think I said."

"Where'd you get that information?"

"Same fellow."

"Nishi?"

"Yes."

Then there *was* a connection. Tad took another sip of his vermouth.

Jerrold took a sip of his crimson-colored drink. "Matter of fact, he was on his way to the Club last night. To return the keys. Actually that was only a silly pretext. What he was going for was to warn Abby that her brother was going to have, as he put it, 'a misfortune.' He was too late to warn . . . but in time to see."

Tad's hand went unsteady. He put his glass down. "He saw it happen?"

"So he says."

Tacitly, knowing nothing else was necessary, Jerrold picked up the fifty dollars, left part of it to pay the bill, and got up. Tad knew he was meant to follow him. They threaded their way among the tables and past Karli at the front door.

In absolute silence, they walked along King Street, skirted Aala Park, crossed the Stream and entered Chinatown. He wasn't sure whether the turning, twisting alley route was the only way to get there or whether Jerrold was trying to confuse all sense of direction. Presently, however, Tad realized there was nothing to hide. Although the place was on a narrow back street, it was not only unconcealed, it was public. A camera shop. FOTO EQUIPMENT, the sign said, G. NISHI, IMPORTER.

How ludicrous it was, Tad mused, how ridiculously

obvious and pat. All over Oahu, smiling Japanese were snapping pictures, clicking Honolulu and Hickam Field and Pearl Harbor into their little black boxes. They were shooting millions of picturesque photos of battleships and airplanes and dry docks and oil dumps and sub bases. They were making black-and-whites, tints and mezzotints, luminescent transparencies of Hawaii's mountains and valleys, its waters and reefs. Nothing sneaky about it, they were candid shots, candidly confessing open surveillance. There was no need for confession, really—whatever photographs the Japanese could not easily acquire the Americans enterprisingly sold them. Every drugstore, every five-and-ten, every department store displayed magnificent aerial vistas, postcards and albums and twistouts and fold-ins, in miniature and enlargement, of every square foot of the city, from Kahala to Kahili. But the Americans did not keep track of daily changes and movements and revisions, so the Japanese clicked and clicked, and kept their albums up to the minute. They smiled and smiled, and the Americans were hospitable, also smiling, saying cheese.

While Nishi sold the cameras. More than that, Tad would have bet. The man must be processing the pictures, sifting their information, authenticating and labeling them, blowing them up under microscope and reducing them to microfilm, assembling them into panoramas and dioramas. And filing everything with the *joho kyoku*, Tokyo's Third Bureau, for Intelligence. Or, like Jerrold, selling it to them.

Nishi was waiting. Without any sign that he recognized either of them, he stopped labeling the small packages of lenses on the counter in front of him, assembled them neatly into stacks, unlocked the wall cabinet, stowed the lenses on a shelf, and locked the cabinet again. He walked toward the end of the counter where a young Japanese clerk was waiting on two customers at once. He whispered in the young man's ear, went past him, turned a corner and disappeared.

Jerrold glanced at Tad and they went to the end of the counter, following Nishi through an arched doorway into a long, narrow corridor. The light was dim and there was a mildewy damp; through it, sharp as a paper cut, the odor of hypo and acetic acid. They couldn't discern Nishi at the far end of the corridor until the door opened ahead of him. He waited for them and silently beckoned them into the darkroom. Turning on an orange safety light, he went to the wall over the enlarging counter and pulled a chain that gave a little more illumination, not much. Neat as the developing room was, the smell of the place was spiteful.

The instant the door was shut behind him, the grave Nishi was his giggling self again. He was bowing and talking very fast; the mushy sounds he made seemed to come through soft noodles.

"Do I have to translate that?" Jerrold asked. "How's your Japanese?"

"Nil," Tad said, "but I get the point—he's pleased to see us."

"Actually, he wants to know if you are *truly here*," the Englishman explained. "It's tactful Japanese for will you do business?"

"Will he identify the man?"

Jerrold reported to Nishi, then reported back. "He says the man who committed the most despicable depravity—for which Nishi apologizes in the name of all the islands of his country—is a very fine man."

"Very fine man commits despicable depravity— I'll file that. Ask him who and why."

Jerrold said a few words and Nishi stopped his inane giggling. He looked at each of them but didn't respond immediately. When he did, his Japanese words were no longer addressed to Jerrold but directly to Tad. Then he waited.

"He says . . ." Jerrold paused to handle a difficulty. "He says his Japanese friend and your American brother-in-law had a business arrangement. And there was a misunderstanding."

"Tell him he's a goddamn liar."

"I can't say that in Japanese."

"If he's implying Ben's been selling information, tell him I'll kick his teeth in."

"That also is untranslatable."

"I want the man's name."

"Look here, Thaddeus, you've got to do this tactfully. There's a certain decorum. One respectful step at a time. And if, at any point, you insult this chap—or suggest you don't believe him—the whole thing breaks down."

"Say it any way you like. I just want to know who the man is."

Jerrold turned to Nishi, gave him his most affable expression, and even bowed a trifle. The Japanese man heard him out most deferentially—no nervous titterings—and replied solemnly. He spoke with the studious reflection of a man who is measuring his own gravity.

"He says he's in a painfully difficult situation," Jerrold translated. "The person whose name you want is, as he says, an old friend. But more than that, he's a man to whom Nishi owes a *giri*." Jerrold paused, searching for the concept. "I don't know exactly how to translate that—it's a loyalty, it's a covenant. But it's not that simple. It's worldly and mystical at the same time. Anyway, it's a most profound obligation."

"Ask him if he recognizes any other obligation. To plain decency. A boy's life has been wrecked."

"Well, I can't put it to him like that. It's not done that way."

"How the hell is it done?"

Jerrold pondered, then spoke tentatively to Nishi. Shortly, they seemed to be reasoning closely, each of them deeply courteous, allowing the other to complete the total thought, to the conclusion of every periodic sentence. Then, a great show of cogitation, there was no more to say and they nodded accommodatingly to each other.

Jerrold looked worried. "He says the only way he can overcome his *giri* is if his friend should, in some way, do him an unkindness or an injustice. In such a case, Nishi would be quit of his obligation."

"What sort of injustice?"

"Well, if his friend were selfishly to stand in the way of Nishi's good fortune."

"How much?"

"Five thousand dollars."

"Tell him to go to hell."

"He isn't suggesting that amount. I am." Then he added, so loosely that the threat was hardly discernible, "That's not such an exorbitant figure considering he'll be giving you compromising information . . . And silence."

A staggering prospect: yesterday's horror would continue. The assault on Ben had not been a finite thing; it was the start of an infinite series, one of the integers of which could be blackmail. The threat of pain in public, and in perpetuity. Whatever traffic Ben was involved in, keeping it quiet was going to be expensive. And what made it most unnerving was not so much whether he should try to keep it quiet but whether, in the end, he could. Blackmail: its classic dilemma, he thought ruefully.

There was too much unresolved about it, too much to question and investigate, especially alternatives. Guardedly, starting to hoard hours and minutes, he said, "I don't have that kind of money."

"It's data, Thaddeus—think of it only as data. Your section is buying it all the time."

The anger was surging. He turned it into wryness. "Christ, man, I can't use government money to pay for the sellout of the government."

The Englishman twinkled. "Why not? It's . . . procedural." As he saw his insult was a blunder, he continued hastily. "However, I will admit you've made a delicate point. So . . . may I suggest . . . Johanna."

Tad bridled. "What about her?"

"Get the money from her. The Winters are well larded, I'm quite sure."

Tad's stomach hurt. "I don't take money from my mother-in-law."

"It's her own son we're talking about. But if there's a nicety there, you can get it from your wife." His voice changed timbre. It was ugly. "I warned you about the boy. Any minute you could be warned about her."

Tad didn't know he was going to hit the man. But after the first blow, the second was deliberate. Then he couldn't stop.

The Japanese was between them, pulling them apart, spluttering, "Stop it—stop it, both of you—you want to bring people in here?"

Nothing could have stopped him except the sound of Nishi speaking English. He broke away as if the language had been a blow. He felt it more than anything Jerrold had done to defend himself.

Hurrying away, through the corridor, then outdoors, he still felt the punishment of his own stupidity. How mindless he had been to assume the Jap knew no English. The man had been in business here, possibly a long time; he was bound to know *some* of the language, maybe not enough to be fluent, but certainly enough to understand. Stupid, stupid. It didn't matter whether it was important or unimportant, it didn't matter that nothing in the meeting had been affected by Nishi's pretense, what mattered was that he had entered the encounter without remembering the basic tenet of his business: everything is a lie. In commerce with the enemy—and everybody is conceivably an enemy—there is no truth, not in word, deed, glance. There isn't even a language of truth. Every meeting has a new tongue, and every tongue, double—as Nishi's was. It was all a lie.

If it was all a lie, then it could have been a lie about Ben.

Of course.

He felt better, he walked faster.

Yes, of course. Ben couldn't have been guilty of a betrayal. There wasn't a cell in the boy's body that couldn't be trusted. His loyalty was bred in the bone. They could do anything to him—they could keelhaul the boy—and they wouldn't get a word out of Ben Winter.

The realization that this was so and that Tad wholemindedly believed it to be so—it was like the lifting of a drag anchor. He was sailing.

And a wonderful thought occurred to him. He need

no longer think of this whole matter as being secret. Since Ben had done nothing shameful, Tad could immediately go to the police. He could call that lieutenant —what was his name, Howard Young—and simply say: there's a man who knows something about the mutilation. His name is Nishi. He owns a camera shop. Pick him up.

Tad's pace quickened. He went down one street, then another, looking for a phone booth. On Bishop Street, in a drugstore, he found a telephone. He put the coin in, asked for Information and got the number. Dialing it, he listened as it rang, and thanked Ben for the inculpability that allowed Tad to make the call. Let them investigate every word of the boy's dossier, let them study under a hundred microscopes every whorl of his fingerprints, they would never find anything to incriminate him.

As he heard the man's voice at the other end of the wire, Tad had an unaccountable chill. It froze every nerve. He didn't answer. He hung up.

He would have to find the man on his own. And he hadn't the vaguest intimation where to start.

Once, when he was a novice at Intelligence work, an old-timer who went back to the covert days of Room 2646 of the bygone Navy Building advised him: if nobody will tell you anything, commune with the ambience. It was the first time he had heard the word, and the man explained that some of his best leads, inspirations that had seemed to spring from nowhere, had actually eventualized out of *atmosphere*. Environment —if you steep yourself in it, if you invite its friendliness —will suddenly whisper confidences in your ear. It will offer hints and allusions, it will illuminate obscure meanings, it will simplify motives, identify strangers.

Tad couldn't imagine himself being as friendly with the Japanese quarter as he used to be; it had darkened and receded in the last few years. Moreover, he had deputized nearly all his Japtown work to civilian operatives. Now he would have to do some of it himself.

He called Abby on the phone, told her he would

not be home for dinner, and started to walk the streets of the Oriental section. Concentrating on what had changed about the neighborhood, he went into a couple of new importing stores, bought some litchis in a new herb shop, had a bowl of delicious kelpy noodle soup at a *saimin* stand he had never seen before. A store that originally had been a pool hall and had become an incense parlor was now blatantly a whorehouse; a spice shop that had once smelled of enticing teas and exotic condiments, making a tantalizing bitterness in the air, now smelled too sweetly of cheap perfume and cannabis. He had the dejected feeling that the neighborhood was being furtively abandoned to unknowable decays. Other than this, the ambience was telling him nothing.

Then it did tell him something. Return, it said, to the old quarter, as you saw it when you first came to the city, and to the first man you hired here.

It was dark when he got back to Karli Karli's restaurant. He found the owner in his usual place, an alcove away from everything, breathing as heavily as usual, fanning his asthma with the sandalwood branch.

"Anything new on the menu, Karli?" he asked.

"Not a thing," the owner replied.

He hadn't changed much in the last few years, Tad thought. Thinner, perhaps, although he had never imagined Karli could get thinner; his cheekbones were nearly through his skin. But everything else, the same, everything carefully nondescript as ever, nothing classifiable. His clothes, vague and of no precise design, were chosen to obscure; his hair was brown and blond and gray and therefore colorless. Not even his speech was descriptive of anything; he spoke a number of languages and none of them seemed native. Like his name, Karli Karli was unidentifiable.

"Nothing new to eat?" Tad persisted. "No new specialties?"

Karli wheezed, every breath painful. "No specialties on the menu any more."

"Nothing cooked to order?"

"No more, Tad."

"I came all the way."

"Only tourist trade, Tad, that's all. No more specialties. Just what's on the bill of fare. No specialties."

"I'm paying more these days."

"I don't need it—business is good—don't need it."

"But I need you, Karli."

He thought the man would respond to the urgency—a plea, almost—with at least a hint of sympathy. Instead, a flash of anger. "No."

"Daytimes, Karli."

The word was a keynote they had had between them. In the early days, when Karli had first begun to help him, the man's unconcealed alarms were a new experience to Tad. He had never seen anyone expose his terrors so nakedly. There was always some peril stalking him, and no matter how fast he ran he could not outpace it. His hands always shook and his lips were cracked not only from the mouth-breathings of asthma but from the gaspings of fright. None of Karli's terrors, to Tad's knowledge, ever materialized. Once, when the commander indicated that a particular dread had turned out to be a succubus of the man's own making, Karli got angry, swore at him, and shouted that the thing was real.

"Then what is it?"

"The night air!"

And he meant it. His asthma had led him to the conviction that the night air was full of insidious microbes and suffocating moistures. Bad things. But Tad was convinced that there weren't only bad *things* in Karli's night but bad spirits, nameless and insubstantial as the air. From that realization onward, Tad gave him only daytime work.

But now, it appeared, even the daytime was frightening to him. So he sat in this alcove in a crepuscular light that was neither day nor night. And Tad speculated, now that it was dark outdoors, how Karli would manage to get home.

He himself would have to manage to get home, and he tried to remember where he had left the car. Recalling the street, he started toward it. On his way, he bought the *Star Bulletin*. Anxiously, under a street lamp, he opened the newspaper to see what it had to say about the attack. Nothing on the front page. Good, they had buried it. He pored over the other pages, one by one, quickly at first, then scouring every column.

Not a word. He couldn't believe there hadn't been time to cover it for the afternoon paper; he couldn't believe they had considered it too insignificant a happening. Perhaps no such happening had occurred.

It was 10:00 P.M. The foyer was dark. Nor could he see any light beyond it, in the kitchen or living room. The bedroom door was open; no lamp was lit. The house was empty. Yet, somebody had been there, he was sure of it, for there was the smell of cigarettes, and neither he nor Abby smoked. And possibly still there, it might be, waiting in the darkness.

He questioned whether he had entered quietly enough; if he had been heard. He decided not to move too soon, or too quickly. He waited.

Somebody was whispering. Speaking in such a hush that he couldn't hear a word, certainly couldn't identify the voice. Another voice, also undefined. He started to walk softly. He was glad the foyer floor was carpeted.

At the archway into the living room, he paused. They were not in the room, they were outdoors, on the terrace.

Abby's voice. He wished she would speak just a few decibels louder so he could hear her words, at least her mood. Her visitor sat in the fanbacked rattan chair, smoking a cigarette; Tad could see only the smoke. Then the long inhalation and the glow. Johanna.

"Hello," he called.

Abby's voice: "That you, darling?"

He joined them on the terrace. "Why are you sitting in the dark?"

"Look," his wife said, pointing down to the Harbor.

It was right to sit in the dark. The display in the port below made beauty an effrontery, too bold. Everything was there, or seemed to be, every battleship, destroyer, every tiny tugboat that ever boasted a light boasted one now, glittered, sparkled against the blue-blackness of sky and sea.

But Johanna's chair was faced away from it; she apparently didn't want to be distracted by irrelevant beauty. She was quiet. She barely greeted him but sat there altogether contained—compacted, almost—as if an artist had painted her to be totally confined by the wickerwork of the chair.

Abby said, "Have you had anything to eat?"

It had been a long time since the soup and litchis, but he wasn't hungry. "Yes, I have."

He felt her keys in his pocket. He took them out. "Your keys were returned."

"Yes, I know," she said quietly.

Not trying to conceal his surprise. "How did you know?"

"Ask Johanna."

He didn't ask immediately, didn't even look at Johanna. Abby was turning on the terrace lights; Johanna continued smoking. She took one last puff of her cigarette, snuffed it out.

"Aren't you curious?" Abby said. "Ask Johanna."

He turned to Abby's mother and looked at her inquiringly. Johanna gripped the arms of the chair slowly, released them slowly, gripped them again. "Jerrold called me," she said.

"Today?"

"Yes. I saw him an hour after you left him."

"Did you meet Nishi?"

"Yes."

"They asked you for money?"

"Yes."

"Did you give them any?"

"Well, I wasn't carrying five thousand dollars around in a purse, but I did give them something."

"How much?"

"Not money. A bracelet. Not an expensive one."

He would have preferred not to show his anger, but it got away from him. "As earnest money?"

She gave no sign that his censure bothered her. "Yes, as earnest money."

"Christ."

"Yes, you are, a bit," Johanna said.

"You're letting them blackmail us," he snapped.

She was calmer than he was. "The only other course was to call the police. I didn't feel I was quite up to that." Then, point blank, "Were you?"

Queasy, he wished he didn't have to admit it. "No."

Without a hint of criticism: "Then we're both letting them blackmail us, one way or another."

Their voices had been polite, restrained. Not Abby's. She was enraged. "I think you're both toads. The two of you—that's what you are—you're toads!" She stopped and he thought she was going to control herself, but she got more furious. "Why do you both assume—why doesn't either of you ask—how can you both take it for granted that Ben's done something he has to be ashamed of? How can you both go sneaking around, paying your dirty little tributes, and not even *ask* him if he's done something wrong?"

"Ben will lie."

Johanna said it so quietly, so flatly, that Abby was shocked. Even Tad couldn't believe how coolly detached the woman was.

Abby recovered. "Ben doesn't lie."

"He's been lying," Johanna said with continued quiet. "Ellie Carter left Honolulu three months ago. He hasn't been seeing Ellie Carter—he's been having meetings in Japtown."

There it was then, Tad thought grimly. Another impossibility turned true, another vicious impertinence to torture the mind. Ben, his protégé. Ben, his friend. Ben, his family. Peddling a code book, perhaps, or a whole cipher, getting into what Jerrold called "the mercantile end." But why?

Abby was saying it too. "Why? I don't believe it." But he could see she was already starting to believe it. "Why? He doesn't need money. Was he gambling?"

"Not that I know of," Johanna said. "But he is a gambler."

Doing it for the thrill, was what Johanna was imply-

ing. Tad couldn't make sense of it. But then, no matter
how many Jerrolds he had known, and Karlis and consulate secretaries who weren't consulate secretaries—the
hired marks and custom informers, the professional and
amateur stringers—he could never tell what it was that
had turned them into traitors; certainly it wasn't always money. And here was Ben, caught in it, trying
to get out, trying to slip away to Manila . . . and do
what? Continue betraying information? In a more stra-
tegic place?

They were quiet now, all three. Tad turned to Johanna. "Did Nishi tell you who the man is?"

"Yes."

"Well?"

She waited too long to answer. He suspected she
wasn't going to tell him, he couldn't imagine why. When
he heard the reason, he couldn't believe it. "I can't trust
you," she said.

Abby, reflexively, "Johanna, you don't mean that."

"Yes, she does," Tad said. Then, to Johanna, "You
don't think I'd hurt Ben, do you?"

"I don't know what your loyalties are, except—
you're Navy."

"So are you."

"Not really. He's my son. He's been hurt—and I'm
going to protect him. It's not one of the most dignified
things I can think of, paying blackmail. But if it's
money we're talking about, that isn't so dignified
either."

"It's not money we're talking about," Abby said,
"and you know it."

"Do you suggest I not pay it?"

Tad said quietly, "Yes, I do suggest it."

"That's what I thought you'd say." Johanna nodded.

"Then why did you tell us anything—if you won't
tell us the important thing?" Abby said. "Why didn't
you keep it to yourself?"

She had struck something deep. Johanna raised her
hand to her breast, tried to arrest the gesture and
realized she had already revealed how unsteady she

was. "Because I was . . . scared. I didn't know whether I could handle this alone. I still don't know. I simply have to."

She went indoors. Abby followed her. After a moment, when the lights went on in the living room, Tad too went in. Johanna was covering herself with a white woolen stole and on her way to the front door when the phone rang. Tad answered it.

The voice that asked if it was Commander Clarke's residence didn't sound at all Japanese. It was meticulous speech, strong and slowly articulated. Foreign, yes, but it could have been English. It was only an instant later, when he asked for Mrs. Winter—specifically Mrs. Johanna Winter—that the rhythm of deference suggested Oriental.

Tad put the phone down and said to Johanna, "It's for you."

She looked surprised, but only for a moment. Coming back from the front door, she took the phone, acknowledged who she was, then listened intently. For a long time, she took little part in the conversation, saying yes occasionally, nothing more. At last she said, "Yes, I'll be there."

When she hung up the phone, she barely glanced at the other two. She scarcely said good night, didn't say she would call or see them, or let them know any more than she had already told them.

Seven

A LL THROUGH THE next morning, nothing stayed where Johanna put it. She set a coffee cup on the kitchen counter and, without moving it, it turned up on the mantel in the living room. She lit a cigarette, placed it carefully in the groove of an ashtray, couldn't find the ashtray and discovered the lighted cigarette perched on the edge of the dining room table. Well before noon she gave up looking for her reading glasses and wrote her weekly column without spectacles, straining at every word.

She had totally forgotten that the column was due yesterday. It was the first time in the three years she'd been working for the *Day-Telegram* that she had had such a lapse. Phoning Andy Wescott, the editor and publisher of the small paper, she apologized and said she would send the article down by messenger. When the boy arrived to pick it up, she had forgotten where she had put it, and it took her twenty minutes to find the envelope—in a place where she was positive she hadn't left it.

She couldn't get that Japanese voice out of her mind. Last night, after putting down the telephone and leaving Abby and Tad, she kept hearing something wrong with the timbre of it. If Nishi and Jerrold hadn't told her that he would be Japanese, she would have said that the sound coming through the telephone receiver was not at all Oriental. Maybe he wasn't. His last name, Tokan, that was not at all typical. Every last name she had ever seen in Tokyo ended in a vowel, *ara* or *iru* or *ima,* something like that. Perhaps Tokan was his first name and Kano was his last, as it was still done in Japan, last name first. Yes, that was it. But there was still something wrong: he didn't sound like an educated Japanese trying to speak English faultlessly, but like an

Englishman trying a Japanese accent. For an instant, last night, she had thought it was Jerrold.

"Kano Tokan here," the voice had said. Then, "Would you kindly say your name?"

The request had struck her as odd, since he had asked for her by name, and the phrasing seemed false, too precise, too precious. "My name is Johanna Winter."

"Mr. Nishi told you who I am?"

"Yes."

"You will come to me?"

"Yes."

"My house. It is not far from Nuuanu Avenue. But you will not find it unless you listen to me with great care."

He gave directions as painstakingly as if she were the foreigner, not he, and when he was through, he repeated them. "You understand me?" His voice was punctilious. "Fully?"

"Yes."

"You will come to me?"

"Yes, I'll be there."

"Nine o'clock—tomorrow night."

Without waiting for her to agree to the time, he had hung up. It was that, more than anything else, that had given her doubts about the man. The abruptness of the hang-up. Un-Japanese. Too often it was difficult to get Japanese people off the phone; the ceremony of farewell was long and courtly; there were innumerable obeisances to the mouthpiece.

What finally did convince her he was Japanese was her recollection of the single sentence. *You will come to me?* He had said it twice and there was no mistaking the remembrance. A lovely poem she had heard Mitsu read. The girl's voice came back to Johanna with the same purling sensuousness as the man on the phone. *You will come to me . . .*

Well, then, he *was* one of them. For the two days since Ben had been hurt, she had been hoping—praying, in fact—that it would not be a Japanese. Another drop of gall to add to the public bitterness against "the yellow bastards."

As to herself, she couldn't find one caustic word to say against them. Her five years in Tokyo had been the best, the sweetest, the most tranquil years of her life. She had found her *heikin*. It was a word that meant more than "equilibrium"; it signified not only the discovery of the fulcrum of her life but the levers that made her turn and move. And, mostly, feel.

She had never, for example, been able to feel the great surges of emotion one was supposed to feel about monumental works of art. She could never respond to the great rolling cadences, to the movement of mountains, to all she was expected to feel about Beethoven and Shakespeare and Michelangelo. Suddenly, in Japan, she realized she didn't have to. The tiny brown gnarl on the branch of the cherry blossom might be as beautiful as the pink blossom itself, as beautiful as the tree, as beautiful as the lustrous assault of a thousand trees. Not everything of beauty needed the illimitable sky in it; a single bud might do it. Beauty, Mitsu showed her, was a matter of balance. And really much simpler than Johanna had imagined. Even more playful. Like being on a seesaw. If the object of beauty was too heavy, it lifted you too high, too frighteningly in the air; if too light, it couldn't elevate you from the earth. Beauty, to Mitsu, was the perfect balance between heaven and earth. It was all so pleasingly oversimplified, so sweetly naïve, that Johanna couldn't, at first, accept any of it. She felt as if a thief were offering her beauty, free, and it was stolen goods; she was too discerning to think it ever came gratis, there was always a headache to pay for it. But at last, with a sigh that went to her depths, she succumbed and embraced it. And the part that was a surprise to Johanna, the outcome she would never have hoped for, was that ultimately she was able to balance more than the gnarl on a cherry branch. Even, except for the chronicles, Shakespeare. Without aspirin. And all of it—well, nearly all—she owed to Mitsu, her dearest friend, the most deeply aesthetic human being she had ever met.

And Mitsu was a whore. Oh, hardly that, Oscar, you can hardly call a geisha a whore. Well, he answered, when you're talking specifically about Mitsu, you can't say a geisha is necessarily *not* a whore. No, Oscar, and you can't say a professor of chemistry is necessarily not a whore, nor a rear admiral, nor his wife . . . and so the nonsense went . . .

Johanna never knew Mitsu's real name. One morning, the girl simply showed up at the embassy auxiliary cottage, as the Japanese called it, and said her name was Mitsu Tekisetsu and immediately informed Johanna that her last name was made up, but it meant suitability-and-happiness, and didn't Johanna think that was a wonderful name to have? Johanna said yes, she thought it was, what can I do for you?

Mitsu didn't reply immediately. If her hesitation seemed at first to be a lack of English, Johanna soon realized she was mistaken. The young woman expressed herself fluently, especially her emanations of delight and amusement and enchantment. Such moods she could articulate with great coherence, even subtly, and with an amazing understanding of the English language. It was only when she was troubled that she was suddenly tongue-tied and her accent was almost unintelligible. Right now she had reached the nadir; she was silent. At last she found her voice.

"I am geisha in House of White Ginger," she said. Then, another silence. "Where your husband is frequent guest."

"Yes, I know he is a guest there." Johanna's voice grated with belligerence.

Mitsu blinked. She was puzzled by the hostility. She wasn't here to tell tales on the American woman's husband. It had never occurred to her that Johanna might *not* know her husband was a guest there. All of which she said haltingly, and concluded, "Is good thing for husband come to geisha house."

"Yes, sometimes I think that's true," Johanna conceded. She was annoyed at her own starchiness.

"I come to ask large question," Mitsu said.

"Yes?"

She held back. "Your husband is kind man, fine man, most generous man."

"Thank you."

"But . . ."

Johanna was a trace apprehensive. "Yes?"

"What is matter with your husband? He is not good health? He is sick? He not have pennis?"

Rhyming as it did with tennis, the word went too fast. When Johanna caught up with it, she felt a confusion of alarm and relief. From as high an elevation as she could hold herself, she answered that her husband was not, to her knowledge, inadequately endowed.

Mitsu raised and lowered her head quickly, in lieu of a bow. "I am so glad, I am so indeed very glad," she said. At last, when her head stopped bobbing, she leaned forward confidentially. "Then why he does not use it?"

"At the geisha house?"

"Not with anyone. Never," Mitsu said. "Why? He does not have the usefulness of it?"

Johanna was amused. It was as if the girl was saying Oscar possessed a property but not a franchise. "Oh, he uses it."

"*Sssss.*" Sheer ecstasy. More than a revelation to Mitsu, an epiphany. It was precisely the divination of truth she had come for.

"Then you will please to tell me," she said to Johanna, "what custom, what method, what practice-and-habit you are using."

Johanna felt disarranged. "You're asking me to tell you . . . ?" She was unable to continue.

Mitsu couldn't conceive of Johanna's being so ungenerous as not to tell her. As a Japanese, she had taken an impossible position by offering to put herself under obligation to a stranger. It was incredible that she would be turned down. Certainly if she herself had been asked, she would gladly have shared her practice-and-habits. She assumed, therefore, that the American woman did not understand her request; they were having a language problem; she would have to make herself clearer.

"You use perhaps some device of tantalizing nature?"

"No." With asperity.

"Perhaps you do not use device *before*. Some time if you use device *after,* it become device *before*. In this case, *after* is as good as *before*. You use *after?*"

A bit umbrageously, "Neither before, after, nor during!'"

Mitsu was shocked at the "during." "Oh, no, not during—never not during—no, not during, no."

Johanna wasn't sure, but rather suspected, she had had enough of the geisha. With scarcely controlled dudgeon, she was on the verge of dismissing her when —and she would be grateful for it always—a ray of illumination struck her. The girl was not only not trying to offend Johanna, she was in dead earnest, and truly perturbed. She was not a corrupted prostitute in search of an extra American dollar, nor was she here to affront respectability. She herself was respectable. She was a student doing research, a dedicated artist intent on improving her craft, trying to discover a new technique that would aid her in giving greater pleasures of sense and sensibility. She had come distressfully upon her first failure, and was asking for help.

Johanna said quietly, "I don't use any devices."

It seemed to sadden Mitsu. She was hoping for an easy answer, a new apparatus she had never heard of, a delicious new wine with aphrodisiacal properties, a bit of silk, a special feather. But it wasn't a quick and easy gadget she was going to get from the American woman, no labor-saving technology the Americans were famous for—no, nothing new, only the old certainty, the diligent application of her craft. Art was indeed long.

Johanna saw the disappointment. "I'm sorry, Miss Tekisetsu."

"Please call Mitsu. You are nice woman. I like you. Mitsu."

Johanna spoke her own first name and Mitsu arose

and bowed. Surprised at herself, Johanna found that she too was standing and bowing. They both saw the incongruity and laughed and sat down again.

Johanna would rather be with Mitsu than with any other person she met in Japan. The girl delighted in all things. Unlike most Japanese, she was not moody, she was never bored or depressed. And she found beauty in unlikely places. Once, as she and Johanna were walking through a covered passageway in the Asakusa section, Mitsu saw a little boy defecating in the darkness. She stopped and gazed at the process.

"Mitsu, come on," said Johanna.

"No—is not finish."

"Mitsu—please."

As they were walking along, Mitsu saw how uncomfortable she had made Johanna. "You think is not miracle?" she asked.

"What—shit?"

Mitsu was shocked. "Oh, was not shit—was shitting. All opening which are for let dirty out are for let beauty in."

Johanna, out of patience, said that when all the orifices were considered, even the technology of such a principle was ridiculous, and there had to be an end to Mitsu's erotic poesy.

But Mitsu was serious. "This little boy, when he is man and come to woman, she will wash him and touch him everywhere, even there—and will be great beauty." Seeing she had not won her argument, she pursued it. "You think pennis are beautiful?"

"Certainly, in a way."

"Not 'in a way,' but in all way, everything."

"Oh, come on, Mitsu."

Passionately, "Pennis are most beautiful thing in world," she said "You come to geisha house. I will put you in viewing room and you will see how beautiful are pennis!"

Johanna had never heard of a geisha house viewing room, much less would she go to one. She couldn't see herself as a voyeuse. Mitsu begged her to come, not once, but on a number of occasions, and each time was rejected. But she didn't give up; it seemed a matter of deep urgency to her, for she needed her American friend to see that nothing she did for a living was even faintly tainted with sordidness. But at last, forlornly, the geisha stopped issuing the invitation.

One lovely spring evening, when Oscar was in Hong Kong on official business and Johanna was feeling lonely, Mitsu arrived with a present. It was a cruet, a beautifully decorated one, tiny clown faces peering out of reeds and rushes, deeply lacquered. A *rikyurushu* cruet, Mitsu said, and since that's what it was, she had filled it with a sweet liqueur. Johanna had never tasted *rikyurushu*, certainly nothing by that name, and she found it exquisite. It was less a drink than it was an essence, an attar from petals and leaves of fruit rather than from the fruit itself. It seemed to her she had barely sipped a thimbleful and she was drunk. Not drunk in any way she had ever been. She still possessed all her faculties, heightened, it seemed, and all her senses. Indeed, nothing about her became qualitatively different except: all things were now possible.

Even going to the geisha house. Mitsu had arranged everything with the utmost finesse, especially getting the permission—an invitation, in fact—from her client whom she called "my most-affection-friend." Johanna sat in the dark room, all by herself, looking through a narrow glass, seeing but unseen, not one blush embarrassed. And that evening she had no experience even remotely related to depravity; quite the contrary, a sense of wonder.

It was a revelation of sheer exquisiteness. It couldn't have been that way anywhere else in the world, she thought, and it couldn't have appeared such an enchantment if it had been performed by a lesser artist than Mitsu. It began with music and a quiet conversation between Mitsu and her most-affection-friend. Johanna could hear none of it. Then started the ritual of undressing, step by discovering step, as if every button and zipper of the middle-aged Japanese man's clothing was a new surprise and a new delight to the girl; behind each closure something precious had been hidden, every opening revealed an unexpected treasure. Then the washings and soapings and rinsings, the soothing benignity when the water was warm, the excitement when it steamed of heat or ice. Water, in the Japanese girl's hands, was a purifier and a lubricant, a beverage and a healing broth, a sacramental aphrodisiac.

The playthings were next. Not toys, Mitsu insisted, nothing to belittle the manhood of her most-affectionfriend, this was not a game of mother and child, and his giggling tears of happiness were not to be misinterpreted as mewling infantility. This was no puerile creature trying to escape the pains of maturity, Mitsu interrupted everything to explain, this was a grown man enjoying the culminating pleasure of it. Not nursery play but passion. The acacia branch did not tickle the man, it exhilarated him; the gossamer sheaths she put on him, one after another, were always a trace too small, so that as he grew, the sheath would break and show him how large he was, what a vast manhood was in him; the nipple he sucked on, by virtue of the fact it gave no milk, reminded him he had long since given up the need for it, and was now old enough to repay the woman with liquid of his own. When at last, sheathless and enlarged, he moved into her, she cried out how mountainously heavy and airily light he was, how he gave her pain and pleasure, but the pleasure was deeper inside her, and how he was no longer a child, yet always young. Always young was the whisper of the aftermath, always young, always young.

Even when it was over, it was not over. As he lay on his back, seeing infinite sky through a finite roof, she stroked his penis and stroked it, as if it needed comforting, and she hummed sweetly and softly, and only occasionally would Johanna hear a faint drift of words: ". . . it is my lute . . . it is my samisen . . ."

So it ended, as many things ended for Mitsu, in gentle music.

There was one special time when Mitsu made music.

It was in a darkness Johanna would always remember. They had gone on a jitney bus, along with a whole party of Tokyo people, to a hilltop a number of miles outside the city. They were going to dine in what Mitsu called a classical restaurant and, shortly after midnight, they would witness an eclipse of the moon.

Johanna had seen a number of eclipses but Mitsu, none. While the moon was bright and full, the guests chattered and twittered so giddily that Mitsu said they were all guinea fowls that had accidentally broken their eggs. But as the sky darkened and the moon started to dim, the gabble abated, then ceased, and they all became hooded. Soon the silence had apprehension in it. The looming dread of darkness seemed to have something terminal about it. As the hovering dimness went to black, as the eclipse became total, the people gradually receded from sight; then they completely vanished. Nobody was there. No sound was heard, no wind, no stir of clothing, not a human breath.

Slowly, shade by shade, the moon began to reveal itself. Lagging, the light returned. At last the moon was again a white fullness in the sky. Even then, nobody spoke. The awe was too pervasive, nobody could find anything simple or quiet or true enough for utterance, nobody could find the *shibui* word to say.

Mitsu wasn't aware she started to hum. The tears coursed down her cheeks and she murmured a music she had no notion she was making. Slowly, head after head turned in her direction. A woman smiled. Two elderly men nodded. Then, as they started down the hill, as they passed Mitsu, the elderly men bowed to her. Others did the same. They silently wanted her to know they admired her and they were grateful. She had found for herself, and for them, an appropriate—that was the significant word—an appropriate way to celebrate the going and coming of the moon.

It was largely through Mitsu's eyes that she came to see such beauties in Japan, in life itself. If Mitsu helped her to love the Japanese, it was not because they were Japanese, but because the girl loved everybody in the world and they all happened to live in Japan. Still, it was not, to Johanna, merely a coincidence of place. Even when Mitsu died of the tuberculosis that was endemic to the island of Skikoku where she was born, Johanna continued to love the Japanese.

Not that she had any illusions about them. Not all Japanese were as loving and gentle as Mitsu. She had seen a boy, hardly seven years old, driven from his home by his parents because he had failed an examination and lost face. She had been told of a village carpenter shunned into poverty because, in an evening of too much *sake,* he had boasted that his youngest son had more courage than a samurai. She had read about a fifteen-year-old girl, desperate because her brothers would not allow her to utter a single word for a period of two months, who had scrounged for a cat in an alleyway and had beheaded the animal with a shard of window glass.

She had heard the cultivated voice of a quiet-spoken man who had castrated her son.

Johanna drove her car to the edge of Japtown. She parked and locked it. The rest, she knew, would be walking in the dark.

She would have preferred going to see Tokan by daylight. But, although she had had no opportunity to ask why he had set the appointment for nine o'clock at night, she could guess what he would say: it is better that you not be seen coming to my house. Reasonable, yes, but not necessarily what he meant. There might be some dismay in the man. And the educated Japanese, more than any people she knew, were not prone to gaze at their misgivings too openly in the sun.

Rather than pleasing her that the man might be worried, it frightened her the more. An anxious Japanese, Oscar used to say glibly, was not to be comforted but avoided; such men are dangerous. And she knew that the neighborhood she was walking in—these days, that too was dangerous.

The moment she got out of the car, she suspected he

had tricked her into coming a circuitous way, so that repeating the route, at some later date, might be too difficult to recollect. No, that didn't make sense; he must surely have surmised she would jot down the directions, which was what she had done. Yet, something was wrong. There was no need, it seemed to her, to leave Nuuanu Avenue and go through alleyways—she was sure she was doubling back toward Chinatown. There was something else about the route that unnerved her. Not the darkness. It was the sense that the alleys were not as narrow as they seemed, that they bellied out into huge voids toward the center of which she would be drawn and never heard from again, and that the darkness was not truly dark but a cyclorama of false blackness behind which eyes, gazing through peepholes, were watching her every movement.

So she must do nothing oblique. She kept her movement straight, walked as steadfastly forward on the cobblestoned passageways as if she knew precisely where she was going. Actually, at the last turning, half a mile back, she had stopped having the slightest sense of where she was going. There weren't any more stores to use as landmarks, no *saimin* counters, no houses; even the street lamps were getting farther and farther apart. Abruptly the pavement stopped. She was in the countryside somewhere, going upward—or was she imagining upward? And now, in a wooded place, and certain she had made a wrong turning, she was lost.

She saw the lantern.

It couldn't simply have materialized that way. It had to shine dimly at first, at a distance, then more and more brightly; it was illogical for it not to have been there, and then, all at once, a bright presence.

And the person holding it. Too still. Too quiet. She knew that whatever held the lantern was a living thing, for there was the faintest movement. But not enough. Too quiet, too quiet. Not a human being, a human being couldn't be so quiet. An animal holding a lantern.

She was frightened.

The thing started toward her. Slowly. As it came,

the lantern caught a glint of something with a shine to it, like silk. Then the kimono, and the woman's face.

Unhurried, the woman kept moving closer. It wasn't comforting. Not too close, Johanna wanted to say; far is close enough. Perhaps a hundred feet away, the woman stopped. The lantern showed her face. Don't be afraid of it, Johanna told herself, it is a quiet face. Middle-aged, perhaps a servant; but, no, too much certainty in the expression, too much infallibility for a servant; this woman has never made an error, never mistaken a name. Perhaps his wife. Then the woman's aspect changed, in a constrained way, and there was trouble in it. She made no beckoning sign, yet, when their eyes met and she turned, Johanna knew to follow her.

Why there was a doorway here, in the midst of this seeming woodland, Johanna couldn't tell, until she was on the other side of it. And she felt herself stepping over a threshold into Japan. It was as she remembered a hundred gardens, all different yet all the same, and this one was, by some assiduous feat of design and embellishment, typical of all of them. Although it was a garden that could only recently have been arrived at by some master artisan, it had all the traditional elements: the gently curving path illuminated by stone lanterns, their oil wicks giving off a tentative, flickering light; the low embankments of coddlingly arrested greenery; the stretch of gray sand, only sand, with the few rocks so serenely placed as to defy any motion of the mind; the pool of golden carp, still and still and suddenly darting in and out of the darkness; the watchful iron crane, perilously poised as if at any moment it might break out of its metal constraint and come to life among its prey.

All there, and all leading to the house, meticulously placed and meticulously symmetrical, two lighted windows to the left of the entrance, two lighted windows to the right. As they approached it, the gravel path made a subtle turning toward the front door so that they had to pass a window, and be watched.

She saw him through the glass. He wasn't sitting

cross-legged on the floor but on a high-backed chair that gleamed of Oriental mahogany. He was reading. She couldn't believe he could be reading so profoundly at a time so full of preoccupation; the man must be pretending. But as they approached the door, it struck Johanna that he might not be dissembling anything, and the thought was chilling to her.

The woman opened the door and stepped back so that, for the first time, the guest could take precedence. When Johanna heard the door click closed behind her and looked back, the woman was gone. She had forgotten how soundlessly and into what subtle hiding places Japanese wives could disappear.

In the dark entryway she paused before daring to go into the room. At last she moved. He sat there, in a wide place unlike any Oriental room she had ever seen, yet not altogether Western. The room was too high-ceilinged to be Japanese, but one of the walls was utterly white and bare with one overpowering brown-black burl of twisted, tortured wood mounted on it; only in Tokyo could she have imagined it. With such a wall, the opposite one was irreconcilable. It was a clinically precise treatment of a Western library: shelves of textbooks, bound periodicals, encyclopedias, dictionaries, with bracket lights illuminating everything, and metal-encased labels on each shelf.

"Please come in," she heard him say.

When she entered, he lay his book down and rose. He didn't bow as she sensed he wanted to, and she wondered what rigor of restraint he had put upon himself to prevent it. Nor did he affect the inevitable smile. Watching her with level eyes, almost unblinking, his gravity seemed to say, paradoxically, that they already shared some sober comprehension of each other. He was her own age, she would have guessed—younger, older—a mask of agelessness about him.

Once he had welcomed her into his study, he didn't say a word. Nor shall I, she decided, for silence, the special silence when the word is there and consciously withheld, was the advantage the Japanese always seemed to have, and she envied it.

But not only couldn't she maintain it, she had no control on how to break it. "Why did you do it?" she blurted.

She knew what would happen even before he replied. The pretense. That damnable courteous disquisition on other concerns so that he could come circuitously upon the crux of the matter and take her by surprise.

"I wish you had said something not totally related," he said, with a display of candor. "You could talk about the room—I wish you would. Some say it is beautiful, but it isn't really—not to me. It troubles me. Perhaps I should not have tried to do two things at once. Bringing two things together—it's wearying, isn't it? How banal the effort gets to be. Perhaps there will never be equanimity." He had been making talk, to nobody, not even to himself. Abruptly, however, he turned his eyes on her. It was an intimate question. "Do you know what equanimity is?"

"No."

She wasn't replying to his question—she had a workable sense of what the Japanese meant by equanimity—but to his pursuit of the unrelated. Did she have to go through this smiling, tea-ceremonied, mat-squatting charade?

She couldn't believe what he was doing now. He was illustrating—physically illustrating—equanimity. It was ridiculous. Walking to the opposite corner of the room, he indicated a stack of books that was piled up, one upon another, into a slim and precarious pillar about waist-high from the floor. Carefully, without haste, he carried a short library ladder from the corner of the room and spread its legs athwart the pillar of books. Slowly, making each step of the ladder an event, he mounted it. When he got to the top, he stepped from its summit onto the pile of books. As he did, he barely seemed to be glancing at them. There was no instant of uncertitude, no tremor of unsteadiness, no breath any shallower than any other breath. He stood on the pile of books and didn't stir. Nor did the books. They didn't topple, sway, didn't move a hair. He stood there silently, totally without expression, as if he had forgotten she was there.

She wanted to laugh, wanted to embarrass him, but she couldn't. And when the instant was over when she *might* have laughed spontaneously, she realized he had won something, she couldn't tell what, except that the demonstration he had given was not ridiculous any more.

"Equanimity is the elimination of the critical observer—oh, not *you,* Mrs. Winter—I am the critical observer," he said. "I am the most captious of them." As he continued talking, she barely noticed that he came down from the pile and approached her again. "I used to think of equanimity as one's relationship to the world. To the earth, in fact. We are constantly falling onto it, losing our balance—or into it, losing everything. But that is mere equilibrium—it has nothing to do with the greater thing. Equanimity describes the deeper balance—with one's self." Then he paused and, for the first time, attempted a smile. "I am, Mrs. Winter, in a state of equanimity."

"You have no imbalance with yourself?"

"None."

"Nothing that you've done—"

"Nothing," he interrupted.

"My son is . . ."

This time he didn't interrupt. He allowed her as much time as she might need to finish the sentence, if she could. She couldn't. He did it for her. ". . . without his manhood. He was unworthy of it."

"And you could be the judge of that?"

"Oh, yes. I knew."

"Knew what?"

"He was a betrayer." This time his smile came with even more difficulty. "He betrayed his country, then he betrayed those to whom he had betrayed his country. When a man gets caught in such a confusion of fidelities, he has already lost his principal fidelity—to his manhood."

The controlled quality of his voice was helping her

control herself. "You wouldn't care to tell me exactly how he betrayed everybody?"

"He worked for us. Then he had—so he said—an access of conscience. I think it was fear. At any rate, we could not let him run away, knowing what he did."

"Then why didn't you kill him?"

"He was still valuable—we still needed him. In fact, we still do."

"I don't believe a word of it."

"I think you do, Mrs. Winter. I think you believed it even before you came here—or you wouldn't have come."

"I don't think you'd have *asked* me to come if there weren't some lie in this."

"Lie?"

"Yes—something you're afraid of being caught at."

" 'Caught' is precisely the word. You are quite right —I don't want to be arrested." With the open face of a man speaking the obvious, "And if I am arrested, I don't want you to press charges."

How simple it was. He needed her to help keep him out of jail—that's why he had called her. Nobody was free of the danger of what all the others knew. Blackmail was canceling itself out; everybody was blackmailing everybody. If she wanted silence, so did he. Silence was the most valuable commodity and it could be shared, he was saying, by all the participants. Noise would reveal they were all in the same business, mercantile men in the traitor trade, her son like the others, all guilty.

He was putting it even more bluntly now. "We all blackmail one another, Mrs. Winter. I pay you, you pay me, we both pay Nishi, Nishi pays Jerrold. Blackmail hangs over all of us. It is one of the expenses of the business—it is 'overhead,' a very apt word."

She felt blood in her throat. "I won't pay it. I won't have you over my head. I will pay you nothing."

"It's little enough—only silence."

"It's a great deal to me."

"I cannot believe you would tell the world your son is a traitor."

She couldn't believe it either. She felt such a bleakness that she wasn't sure she could manage to leave with any show of self-respect. But that was gone anyway, too late to cry about.

But she did hear a cry. It came from the other side of the library wall. Muffled by books, it wasn't clearly a cry at all. More the stifling of a labored breath, or the moan of someone coming out of nightmare. It was the voice of the woman who had guided her here, Johanna thought, it was Tokan's wife. But suddenly the door opened and the girl came in.

Not a woman, a girl. She couldn't have been older than twenty, Johanna thought, a tall creature, taller than the average Japanese, and frailer than most. She had a curiously inclined posture that gave her a touching aspect, like a flower cracked in the stem. Her hair was not totally black but seemed to be lighted by the faint glow of an amber lamp. She was unutterably beautiful.

As she entered the room, weeping, Johanna heard Tokan command her, in Japanese, to go back. But the girl didn't seem to hear him; she turned all her attention to Johanna.

"My wife," he said, introducing. Then, unexpectedly at a loss, not knowing what to say, "She is not supposed—I told her—she is wrong to be here."

The soft weeping stopped for just an instant. "How is he?" A grief, a choked breath. "Ben—how is he?"

Here was the whole lie.

The spoken lie by Tokan to save himself the ultimate shame; the silent lie by Ben to protect whatever there was left of his relationship with the girl. Yes, her son had committed a betrayal, but of an easier kind, betrayal of the mind to favor the heart, the betrayal that a romantic Westerner might forgive but an equally romantic Oriental never could. And castration the hideously poetic punishment.

He was murmuring to his wife. There was no longer any command in his voice, certainly no cruelty; he was begging her to leave the room.

Her weeping ceased. She turned to go back through the doorway by which she had entered. She stopped. She couldn't move, not that direction. She let out a sound that was all pain. Then she wheeled and ran, not into the other part of the house, but altogether out of it.

"Muna!" he called.

Johanna didn't think, she ran. Past Tokan, out into the entryway, outdoors, across the garden where she saw the wraithlike figure running.

"Muna!" she cried. "Muna!"

Johanna ran to the end of the garden, then through the doorway. She heard a sound behind her, a rustle in greenery; she turned, she rushed toward something heard but unseen. She couldn't have disappeared so swiftly; Johanna was not that far behind her. The girl was gone.

Johanna ran, simply choosing a direction, any direction that gave her running space, and suddenly she stopped, realizing she had been running more from the sheer animal release than in pursuit of anyone.

The girl was lost and her son, found.

That was the upsurge in her, like a wave cresting and breaking and giving her the joy of it. Betrayal of the heart, of the bed, of the fidelities of marriage, those were the common manageable things, they happened every day, and there was pain in them, pain for everybody, but manageable. That was the expedient thing, manageable. Not like treason.

Suddenly she realized that here she was, in woodlands, in darkness, not knowing where she was going. And not afraid. Not the least bit apprehensive. If she was lost, she would find her way. Somehow or other, she would get out of this woodland and onto a hard, paved street.

And it was exactly as she had said it. On Nuuanu Avenue, she hurried to her car. She couldn't wait to get away, to get somewhere, a drugstore, a hotel, the railway station, any place where she could find a phone.

She found one at the junction of the railway and trolley line. She hurried into it and telephoned the police.

As the phone rang, she thought of the last time she had been in a phone booth, down the hall from Ben. The pang returned, sharp, agonizing. Would she ever get over it? She could think of no analgesic that would ever free her of the ache. Except, possibly, one. Revenge might be a painkiller.

The ringing stopped and somebody in the police department answered the telephone.

Eight

A<small>BBY WAS STILL</small> asleep and made no sign that she heard the disturbance, so he would have to do something about it. It was getting-up time anyway, he thought, with daylight pushing through the loose weave of the monk's cloth. He hoped the doorbell wouldn't ring again or she would awaken; he'd better hurry out of bed to prevent it. Out and tiptoeing, he carefully closed the bedroom door behind him. Illogically, he was certain it would be Johanna, even if it was barely seven and Johanna would never come at that hour and never unannounced. Dammit, she could have telephoned. It didn't portend too well. He opened the door.

It was Jerrold. "I'm sorry to be so ruddy early," he said, "but I wanted to catch you before you left."

Vexed, without thinking, Tad started to shut the door on him. Jerrold pretended to find it amusing, shoved forward and showed him what he had in his hands. "If you lock me out, I'll run off with your milk and newspaper. I'll leave the cream—I don't use it."

It wasn't his nauseating charm that prompted Tad to let him in, it was the newspaper. Jerrold clutched it tightly until he got past Tad, then ceremoniously handed it to him in the living room. "You got the worst of that trade." Grinning, he pointed at the paper. "There's nothing in it."

He was right, there wasn't. Not even news of Moscow falling to the Nazis, word of which Tad had heard on the radio last night. And nothing about any arrest.

"Only interesting thing about the paper," Jerrold teased, "is the date."

Right again. It was Friday the twenty-eighth. On Tuesday night, Johanna had phoned Abby and told her she had called the police. Nearly three days, and the man had not been arrested; certainly no mention of

131

it in the papers. No mention of anything, the attack, the notification of the police, nothing.

Jerrold was chuckling, relishing it; he had a taste for the preposterous. "Maybe he's done a bunk. Off to Tokyo. Booked passage on a sampan. Very romantic. Silver sails in the moonlight."

"Maybe he has."

"You wouldn't *know* that he has, would you?"

It was his tone rather than the question itself that surprised him. Jerrold had turned serious. "How would I know? Is it true?"

"I'm asking *you*," Jerrold said.

The man's sudden solemnity bothered him. He had been trying to tell himself there was nothing suspicious about the absence of newspaper coverage. The attacker had been arrested and the police were trying, for their own reasons, to keep it undisclosed. "You think he hasn't been arrested?" Tad asked.

"I know he hasn't."

"How can you be so sure? Maybe they've put a lid on it."

The Englishman looked at him squarely. "Is that what you think?"

". . . No." He hated to agree with the man, on anything. Irritably, "What are you here for?"

"Just rooting for truffles."

"Hogs."

"I'm not snobbish." Then, sociably, "So glad to hear about your brother-in-law. Quite the little love boy, isn't he? Or should I say, wasn't he?"

"Get out."

"Oh, come now, Thaddeus—I'm congratulating you. It must have been a relief to know he wasn't filching Yankee secrets—filching Jap wives is quite all right, isn't it?" He saw the threat gathering in Tad's face and added quickly, "Don't heat up, old man, I'm not here to get, I'm here to give." Before Tad could reject any offer of free samples, he rushed ahead. "Commander in Chief, Pacific Fleet—want to know what happened to him?"

The question was too compelling; Tad halted.

Jerrold saw he had him and could take his time. "He was put on war warning."

"Well, that's not exactly big news, is it? We've been on one alert or another for over a year."

"I didn't say 'alert,' old fellow, I said 'war warning.' "

"Are you lying?"

Jerrold simply pointed to the telephone.

"Since when?"

"Yesterday."

"Who did it?"

"Washington, of course."

"Who in Washington?"

"Who else?" Jerrold shrugged. "CNO—Stark."

"To Kimmel, you say?"

"That's right."

Tad felt the war clutch. Things tightening with a suddenness now. But he mustn't start believing the man. "When yesterday?"

"Afternoon."

He had caught him. It couldn't have happened yesterday afternoon; there would have been time for him to be informed. He had been in his office until dark. Just before leaving, he had twice been on the telephone to Layton and once to Mayfield. On his way to his car, he had run into Rochefort. Not one of them had mentioned a war warning. Nor had the radio last night.

"Thank you for the news," Tad said quietly. "Now it's getting late and I'll have to dress. Would you please go?"

"You don't believe me, do you?"

"No, I don't."

Jerrold reached into his pocket and carefully extracted a three-by-five file card. "I just copied out the important part. Would you care to read it?"

Tad took the card. It read:

This dispatch is to be considered a war warning. Negotiations with Japan looking toward stabilization of conditions in the Pacific have ceased and an aggressive move by Japan is expected within the next few days. The number and equipment of Japanese

troops and the organization of naval task forces indi-
cates an amphibious expedition against either the
Philippines, Thai or Kra Peninsula or possibly Borneo.
Execute an appropriate defensive preparatory to car-
rying out tasks assigned in WPL46. Inform district
and Army authorities.

"Kimmel got this?" Tad asked.

"Yes." Then, confidentially, "Only problem with it is that Admiral Stark has really pulled a couple of gaffes there."

"About what?"

"Well, grammar, for one thing. Really, now—an admiral and doesn't know his bloody singulars from his plurals? 'Indicates'? No *s* wanted, old man, none whatever."

Impatiently, "Come on."

"The big mistake—he says Thai, Kra, Philippines, Borneo. What silly rubbish. None of them."

Clearly, the man was crystal gazing again. Where actual information was concerned, sometimes he came up with it, more often he didn't. As to prediction and prophecy—never to be trusted. Caustically, "You know, of course, where the first attack *will* happen, don't you?"

"Yes, I do."

The cliché: "And you've gotten it from an unimpeachable source."

Jerrold heard the mockery. "Don't be sweetcock, old boy. I do have it from a good source. There's a Buddhist monk—"

"Yes, he's on Maui. We've got him. What else?"

"A fellow who makes mattresses out of goat hair."

"Rokura Shiba. What else?"

Exasperated, Jerrold lashed back, "What the hell difference about the source as long as the *fact* is right. The *fact* is I know where it will be!"

"Where?"

"Here!"

"Here—in Hawaii?"

"Pearl Harbor!"

"Jerrold, there's no limit to what you'll say to get yourself some attention."

"You bloody condescending sod! You know what's going to happen to this bloody island? It's going to get wiped out because your piddling little alert isn't worth a damn. It doesn't man a single bloody gun that's got any fire power in it. And it bunches all the Army planes together where a single fart will blow 'em all up. If a couple of Zeros come spitting out of the bloody sky—"

"The Navy planes will just sit there and let it all happen. Is that what you think?"

"What Navy planes? They'll be gone! Some of 'em are already gone!"

"What the hell does that mean?"

"The *Enterprise!*"

"What about the *Enterprise?*"

"The whole damn carrier division—it shipped out."

"Shipped out? When?"

"In the night."

"Last night?"

"Yes—with Halsey."

"For where?"

"Wake."

The Englishman named the island without a flicker of hesitation. As he said it, his expression changed. The anxiety was gone, he was crowing now, having come up with something he was sure of, incontrovertible, and shocking. Tad had heard no report on Halsey's departure with the carrier division, not even a rumor. He was stunned.

Hurrying to the glass doors that led out onto the terrace, Tad tore them open. Quickly, a bit hectic, he hastened to the railing and looked down at the harbor.

"Jerrold!"

The Englishman was not far behind him. As Tad pointed toward the ships, he heard the man's quick intake of breath. Turning, he saw Jerrold go pale. There was no anger in Tad's voice, hardly even any contempt. "You stupid jerk."

The man's voice was an outcry. "I'm not! I got it from two sources!"

"And you didn't have the competence—you didn't have the simple common sense—to get up on a hill somewhere and check whether it was gone!"

"I did! I came up here to Aiea. It was still dark—I couldn't see!'"

"Why didn't you wait?"

"Because—God, I was so certain. And I wanted to catch you before you left the house—to *use* it on you while it still had some surprise in it!"

The man was more than frustrated, some mooring in him was starting to give way. His eyes had a desperate, forlorn look, he couldn't keep them still. Right there, in front of Tad, he was about to come apart. But he didn't. He made the huge effort and, in his public school fashion, accomplished it: he pulled his socks up. It was in the moment of the Englishman's courage that Tad felt sorriest for him.

"Jerrold," he said not unkindly, "why don't you give it up?"

"And do what?"

"Christ, you've got an education. You're a charming enough bastard—there must be something you can do. In business or somewhere."

Jerrold had hold of himself again, the supercilious grin was back on his face. "I don't have the bum for it, Thaddeus," he said. "I can't keep my thingama-gummy in a chair. No bloody discipline. Unless . . ." The supercilious covering was like voile, too thin, and it blew away; he was naked again. The plea was clear. "Put me on the payroll, Thaddeus." Before Tad could demur, Jerrold was pursuing it in a spate of entreaty. "Make me an auxiliary, Tad. I don't care how subordinate the job is. Make me your cheapest little stringer for a start, but put me on. Any assignment at all—whatever you ask me to get, I'll get it. I'll never sell you a pig in a poke—only specifically what you ask for."

Tad was about to interrupt him, felt the necessity to halt the supplication so the man wouldn't regret it later, but Jerrold was unstoppable. "I can't *go* anywhere, Tad—nobody trusts me! If I go back to London, I'll get narked and Whitehall will grab me. They hounded me out of Singapore. If I go to Tokyo, nobody'll ever hear of me again. Christ, even in Berlin——!" It was an outcry in the confessional. Then he said, more quietly, "Now, you take my word, Tad. In one week, two at the most—you'll be at war. No avoiding it. Roosevelt wants it, and it's going to happen. Right here. And the minute it starts, every goddamn one of us questionable characters will get thrown in the choky-poky. But if you give me a job, I may be able to avoid it. In return for which—*because* everybody knows I'm not to be trusted—you'll have the most trustworthy stringer on the street."

Tad had no impulse to hire the man. Still, he found himself sorry for the Englishman, forgetting the conniver's unscrupulousness, letting himself get infected by a purulent sentimentality. He needed an antiseptic, and he himself had to supply it. "You've got it wrong, Jerrold. Trustworthiness isn't the star qualification where an operative is concerned. There's hardly a stringer on our payroll who won't sell, both directions. Everybody has to be checked against everybody, five times. Why not? If a guy's honest, what's he doing in the business? So it's not honesty that counts—it's brain."

Brain, the spy's most vulnerable vanity, and he had lampooned it. But Jerrold took it without flinching. He was back now, fully recovered, to his head-tilted frivolousness. He made an elaborately debonair salute with his right hand, threw Tad a kiss with his left, and swaggered his way out the front door.

Slipshod spy that he was, Jerrold had forgotten to take his handwritten three-by-five card with him. Tad studied it. Between the departure of the *Enterprise* and the war warning, one piece of information was visibly inaccurate, but how about the other, the warning? That too might be a piece of Jerrold's botchery, yet there was something naggingly probable about it. And if it was true, he would have work to do, delays that would have to be shortened, people to call in.

He wondered if it was too early in the morning to phone Kley. The man was an early riser, but it was still not eight o'clock. So as not to awaken Abby, he went through the spare bedroom to the other bath. He showered, shaved and dressed. He brewed some coffee and made some toast. Sitting on the terrace, he started to read the newspaper while eating breakfast, when he realized it was eight o'clock.

He called Kley. "Oh, no, I've been up for hours," the admiral said. "Matter of fact, I was about to dial your number. I wanted a meeting with *you*. What's yours about?"

"Well, I'd rather not mention it on the phone."

Touchily, "Just give me a label."

"War warning." He heard no response. "Is it true?"

"Yes. You'd be hearing about it later. How'd you get it so soon?"

"Jerrold."

"Well, *that* happens to be true—but, Christ, I hope you're not listening to that man . . . What else did he try to sell you—attack on Pearl Harbor?"

"Yes, he did."

"He's been peddling it everywhere. Don't buy a thing from him—he's a goddamn nuisance. I've been thinking of having him picked up."

"On what charge?"

"Never mind. Don't bother your little head about it."

Tad winced. Don't bother your little head. The patronization. It occurred to him that Kley was treating him as Tad was treating Jerrold: short on brains.

Kley's voice: "How's eleven o'clock for you?"

"I'll be there."

He was about to hang up when the admiral said hastily, "Wait a minute—not at my office. I'll meet you at the hospital—Ben's room, second floor."

"The hospital?"

The admiral heard the puzzlement in Tad's voice and laughed. "Oh, that's right, I forgot—you don't know, do you? The police picked Tokan up at three in the morning."

"My God! Where?"

"At the Jap consulate."

"How'd it happen?"

"No problem at all. It was routine. The consulate

made no difficulty whatsoever. Simply handed him right over. Well, why not? He wasn't registered with them—and they don't want trouble any more than we do."

"Have they charged him?"

"You bet. With everything. Aggravated assault and battery. Mayhem. And since he left the boy to bleed, they've even got him on attempted murder. If they can make it all stick, he'll get twenty or thirty years." His voice had self-satisfied amusement in it, as though he had just won a ten-dollar bet. "Eleven o'clock—the hospital," he said, and summarily hung up.

Tad remained near the telephone, not moving, toying with the puzzlements like a plateful of food he wasn't hungry for, poking at this, at that, everything getting messier. Oh, that's right, I forgot, Kley had said, you don't know, do you, they arrested Tokan. Did he really think Tad would believe he had simply forgotten to tell him? Why was he being so elaborately casual? Why the meeting? And why at the hospital? If Tokan was arrested, why not just let the law take its course?

Well, he wouldn't worry it. He'd pour himself another cup of coffee, take it on the terrace and finish reading the morning paper.

As he put his coffee cup down on the terrace table, he thought he saw a motion down below. He walked to the railing and looked down at the Harbor. A number of ships were repositioning. The carrier division was in movement. The *Enterprise* was putting out to sea.

Fretful, he drove his car recklessly to the office. Jerrold finally had something, he was tapping a leak. It could be coming from anywhere, from an officers' mess, from Cincpacflt, even from Kimmel's flagship. Or it could be one of those pestiferous trivial things, the hardest kind to track: somebody sends a telegram and writes too firmly on the Western Union pad; a boatswain lays in a larger than usual supply of his special pipe tobacco; an executive officer rushes his Chinese laundryman. Everything was too gapingly open. Last year, a smart-aleck Intelligence ensign, to prove access, had broken into Vice-Admiral Colbey's private quarters and come away with the man's Bible, bifocals and suppositories. Kley made the comment that Colbey's ass was tighter than his security.

But that didn't tighten security. Certainly not at Tad's office. When he arrived, early morning, the door was again unlocked. Hurrying back to the code room, he found that neither deciphering machine was equipped with a lock, and he had ordered a half dozen of them. Hearing Schotley arrive, he called to him, and the lieutenant appeared on the threshold. "The door—last night," Tad said, trying for as little emphasis as possible.

"Not me." Defensively. "I locked it when I left."

"Were you the last one out?"

"I think so. Yes, I was."

Somebody picking a lock; there was no sense to it. So useless, they would get nothing here. Then, come to think of it, why was he making a fuss? "How about the locks for the machines?"

"They haven't arrived."

"Get them today. If you have to go for them yourself—get them."

He dismissed Schotley and stewed unproductively for two hours. He tried, without success, to read an illegible report from a Korean news vendor; he called the radio shack and was unable to cadge any information from Rochefort; he couldn't mend the broken Coca-Cola machine.

At 10:45 he got into his car and drove to the hospital. He knew where Ben's room was. On Wednesday, when he had visited the hospital, he'd had a disturbing few minutes. The boy had pretended to be on sedatives, too dopey for conversation. There had been silences. Johanna and his wife had had the same experience. Abby, sensible as always, had said: we're asking *him* to comfort *us;* he has tougher things to do. Johanna had said, almost inaudibly, that she had had the same thought.

When Tad reached the second floor, he saw a confusion of nurses outside Ben's room. Excitement, on the edge of panic. One of the nurses streaked toward, then past, him. He tried to stop her, but she had no time for questions, she was gone. He hurried toward the room.

"What's happened?" he asked.

The nurses looked at one another, not certain how to answer. One of them, a wintry woman older than the others, said, "You're not supposed to be here, sir. Visiting hours—"

He didn't let her finish. Hurrying through, he made his way into the room. There was nothing to see. Nobody in it. Empty. The senior nurse flurried in after him. "Really, sir, you're not allowed."

"Where is he?"

She started to splutter, and her face got as tight as if she were pulling drawstrings. He tried to mollify. "Please, I'm his superior officer—and his brother-in-law. I assumed that he knew we were coming. Where is he?"

"I don't know—I just don't know." Her voice was rising. "One of the nurses came in to get him ready for lunch and he was gone. They've looked everywhere. He's gone!"

"How? He can't even walk."

"Oh, yes. Yesterday afternoon—and last night—he was doing very well."

"Did he get dressed by himself?"

"He had no clothes. The police—they came and took them on Monday morning. They were all bloody—they said evidence—they needed them for evidence."

"Did anybody bring him any fresh clothes?"

"No, sir. I'm quite sure of it."

"You mean he left in his night clothes?"

She hurried to the closet. It was empty. "And a bathrobe, yes."

In case Ben might have left a note, he looked all over the bedside table and on the floor under it. He straightened up the bedcovers to see if there might be even a scrap of a message. There wasn't a word. Reaching for the phone on the night table, he called the BOQ and asked who was currently in charge of the officers' quarters. A few minutes later, a man's voice, just as young as the previous one and equally out of breath, said, "Yes, sir—he was here this morning. He didn't have his key so I let him in. All he wanted was some clothes. He wasn't wearing much more'n a bathrobe."

"Did he say where he was going?"

"No, sir, he didn't."

It had to be the beach, there was no other place. It was only a shack that Ben had rented in early spring, a few miles from Kailua, windward, on the sea. He used it, as he said, for swimming, much, and for surfing, little. That hadn't anything to do with it. What it was for Ben was the great vast deep, the challenger. He would go to it to test himself, to match his solitariness against its magnitude, go there alone—he rarely invited anybody—to see how forsaken he could dare to be in so wide and forsaken a place. And Tad always saw a change in him, tenuous, almost imperceptible, whenever he returned from that long strand of beach between the mountain and the sea. Serene and more self-certain, always; the return from a retreat.

The retreat again. The refuge from the hospital bed and from the court trial looming over him, and from whatever official bedevilment Kley had in store for him . . . and from his pitying family. Well, he couldn't retreat forever; sooner or later—and the world's importunities would make it sooner—he would have to come back to life. And Tad knew, without knowing how he could be so deeply convinced, that he could help the young man return, if Ben would only let him. So he decided to drive out to Kailua.

For no longer than a breath, he was tempted to leave a message for Kley and tell him where he was going. He desisted. He simply got into his car and went.

The trip was a lengthy one, over the mountain, and the road was gutted, narrow, winding. Never safe when the wind was high, it was especially dangerous if the day was bright and clear, for then the view from the Pali—the vista of crag and canyon and sea—was a bewitchment that made the driver forget the road, and suddenly there was another car twisted, somewhere, on an escarpment. Descending, the downward drift was rapid, exhilarating, the car seemed wheelless, he was on a glider sailing on a gust. Then suddenly there was the sea.

Ben's house, like his hospital bedroom, was empty. Tad had been wrong, the young man hadn't come here at all. The wooden shack, no different from any other place Tad knew these days, was unlocked, open, windows wide, available. The room was immaculate, as Ben always was; the kitchen and bedroom were more than tidy, they were lintless; the refrigerator was shipshape—crackers in a tin box, the remnants of a Brie and Gorgonzola wrapped in tin foil, green mangoes covered with many layers of newspapers so that they would ripen slowly.

Tad went indoors and stood inconclusively on the front porch, not knowing whether to go or wait; perhaps Ben would, after all, appear. He watched the waves, then mounted the steps to the slightly higher deck—Ben called it his forecastle—under which he kept a rowboat, a surfing board, a fishing reel.

The sea was calm. Usually, huge breakers came roaring and stampeding in, the white manes of a thousand white horses, and magically went to silence on the beach. Today, however, nothing roared, the rollers came in on a quiet surge, softly vanishing. Such stillness.

Then he heard the car. His pulse quickened at the sound of it and, hurrying down from the deck, he turned the corner of the house. It wasn't Ben, it was Kley, in his huge blue Packard, and he wasn't the only one in it. Johanna and Abby.

"Is he here?" The admiral opened the door and strode possessively toward the house.

"No, he isn't," Tad said.

"Well, then, we'll wait a bit." The admiral was granting time, a largesse. "Something tells me he'll be here."

Johanna was the something that had told him, of course, or Abby—and it looked as though they would all, including himself, turn out to be wrong. The women were withdrawn, a bit awkward, as if they felt they shouldn't be here and weren't certain why they were. Well, he wasn't certain either, now that Kley was there. The admiral seemed to sense everybody's discomfiture, and to take pleasure in it. Tad's surprise at seeing them apparently gave him a mischievous delight. "Didn't know it was kith-and-kin time, did you?" The old man twinkled.

"No, I didn't."

Tad's eyes were suddenly drawn to Johanna. He had the unbuttoned sense that she had been staring at him. As he turned, he saw her focus change and go inward; odd, he thought, she imagines *I've* been staring. Now, wouldn't it be peculiar if Abby were staring at both of us? She wasn't, she was gazing out to sea. He had an impulse to touch her. Moving to her side, he leaned and pressed his lips lightly to her cheek. Abstractedly, she patted him. How distant the three of us are this moment, it seemed to him, like cousins-twice-removed who assemble only on calamity days.

Kley was louder than usual. "I'll be missing my lunch. Has he got anything to eat?"

He hadn't really asked it as a question, nor did he wait for an answer. Without a glance at the others, he rumbled up the wooden steps and into the house. How exasperating the old bastard was. He had seen Kley, at the Club, for example, the acme of gentlemanly consideration, scurrying to open doors for women, pulling chairs out, offering napkins to rout imaginary spills of water, bowing like a Japanese *maître d'*, knock-kneed with courtesy. And here he was, loudly commandeering the place, an aggressive boor. It hadn't anything to do with the fact that those were convivial occasions and this was a business meeting of some mysterious sort. What it had to do with, Tad was convinced, was keeping people off balance. Kley's caprices were seldom, if ever, careless; his playful and impromptu mischiefs were coolly deliberate.

When they got indoors, the old man was already standing in the archway between the kitchen and living room, eating crackers and cheese. "Better have some of this," Kley said to Tad, "or your belly will act up."

He wondered how the old man knew about his stomach malaise. He'd never told him, nor, he was sure, had Abby, and he couldn't recall ever chewing a chalk pill in the admiral's presence. It was getting crookedly comical, he thought, how his secrets were dwindling, how increasingly difficult it was to lock doors, files, machines; now, even the hugger-muggers of his digestion. And Johanna was staring at him again, what the hell secret did *she* know?

He turned to Kley. "What's this meeting about?"

"Soon enough." The admiral didn't stop munching. "When Ben gets here—if he does."

Abby, tentatively: "If it's Navy business, why am I here? Or Johanna, for that matter?"

"It's family business," Kley replied.

Johanna pretended to be joking. "Then why are you here?"

Abby saw Ben first. She was looking out the window and put her hand to her throat. Tad moved quickly to her side and saw Ben's car glide slowly to a stop. The young man got out and paused, indecisively gazing at the other two vehicles; a man quietly facing what he has dreaded. For an instant, it was by no means certain that he wouldn't turn and get back into his car, but at last he started toward the house.

Tad wondered if he had seen them watching him through the window. If he did, he gave no sign. He looked terrible. His face was drawn and his eyes had a brightly darting light in them, an unaccustomed one; they were frightened. He walked weakly in a way that was somehow too unsteady, even considering his infirmity; he seemed almost, by his gait, to be mocking his ignominy. And over the whole picture of his pain, a worn bewilderment.

As he entered, Johanna arose from her chair. But not a flutter; she took no step in his direction. Abby, on the other hand, hid nothing. "Oh, Benny," she cried, and flurried toward him; she had no guile for hiding sympathy. "Are you all right? Where were you?"

He tried to be flippant, falling back on family banter, but it rang hollow. "Hello, chicken," he said, "are you flapping or flying?"

"Where did you go?" she insisted.

It was clear how hard he was working to keep himself steady; why, Tad reflected, wasn't it clear to Abby? Even physically steady. He wished Ben would sit down. But he needed to remain upright, apparently, stiffening himself against other, worse collapses.

Abby's question still hung in the air and the boy seemed to set himself the challenge of answering it. "I've been trying to reach Muna," he said. "I was worried about her. He—Tokan—he's a vengeful man and —as we all know—violent—and—" He couldn't make it. He had been speaking in a monotone, like a reader trying to decipher illegible handwriting. Now something came clear to him, a cry, "I love her and if she gets hurt . . ."

Nobody stirred. Kley stifled a cough. Ben, more evenly now, resumed. "I finally reached her this morning—after they arrested him. I thought, she'll need something—money, at least—and I wanted to see her. So we made an appointment to meet somewhere and I went there and she—I waited and—a long time . . . She stood me up." He smiled, as if he were looking for a joke, however bitter, and he found a cheap one. "Stood me up in the only way she could."

It was all he had to say. He looked around, not at anyone in particular. He didn't know what to do with himself. He was gray.

"If she didn't show up," Kley said quietly, "maybe it's just as well."

Tad slowly turned to the older man. The insipidity of the comment didn't anger him; he simply couldn't comprehend how the man could arrive at such vacuous comfort.

Kley moved to the fireplace and stood in front of it, facing the others. He was taking the classic position, on the hearth, where paternal pieties are spoken, except, Tad mused wryly, there was no fire to give the sanctimonious old man the aureole he needed.

"I know you all think that's an easy answer," Kley said. "But it will be better for everybody—especially that young woman herself—if this passes as quickly as possible. And if, in the meantime, we don't—any of us—do anything injudicious."

Tad had a nameless apprehension. He looked at the others. Abby seemed puzzled, but no more than that. Ben, still standing in precisely the same place as before, was miles away. Johanna folded her arms across her breast as if a cold draft had blown through the room.

Kley was continuing. He was talking not to Ben but about him. "Whatever generous impulse he feels about the young woman—I respect that, but it's totally unnecessary. She doesn't need any financial help—her husband is quite well off—and one way or another, she'll get along all right. As to the rest of us, I think it would be best if we allow the court to do its own work without offering any interference or . . ." He paused a long time, either because he was reluctant to say the word, or because he wanted to underscore it. ". . . help."

The word hung in the air like a hornet's nest. Only Johanna had the courage to challenge whatever acrimonies might come stinging out of it. "What help are we not to offer?"

Kley was moving cautiously. "Nothing in this is exactly what it seems, Johanna. Take this man, Kano Tokan, for example. He's listed in the phone book as an importer. Well, we all know—nine chances out of ten—importer means spy. But he *is* an importer. Imports art work, Japanese books, scientific equipment, whatever. And he's got all his proper papers—nothing out of order. But periodically he goes on these strange trips—strange, I mean, because we can't track him. He's got a Japanese government job of some sort. We're sure of that. Then why did the Japanese consulate disclaim him? Who the hell is he?"

He paused as if his questions were, in themselves, conclusions; nothing more need be said. But Johanna, trying to rein herself in, did speak. "I don't understand, Burkie. Are you suggesting that because Tokan is somebody you want to keep your eye on, we shouldn't help get him convicted?"

"No, I'm not saying that, Johanna." He was hedging. "What I mean is we don't really know how important this man is."

Tad said, "To get away with this, how important does he need to be?"

Kley heard the irony. His mouth got a bit thinner. Slowly he turned to Tad. "I'm not treating this impudently, Thaddeus. I don't think any of us should," he said frigidly. "I told you nothing in this is exactly as it seems. We're Americans, and while we're not exactly apathetic about infidelity, we don't go around avenging it with surgical cruelty. But the fact of the matter is, Ben did have an illicit affair with the wife of a resident alien—and the Navy can't condone that."

Abby said hotly, "It goes on in the Navy all the time."

"Among ourselves," Kley rejoined. "And the Navy doesn't sanction it—it barely tolerates it."

"That's beside the point, Burkie, and you know it," Johanna said. "Is what Tokan did to Ben any just measure of—"

Kley interrupted. "No, it's not! It's not to *us!* But Tokan's a Jap—and it may be perfect justice to a Jap!"

"We're not in Japan, Admiral," Tad said.

"In a sense we are. Right now—when we're trying to avoid a war—when we're trying to come to terms with those little bastards—we have to be both places at once. We've got to try to understand what's going on in their minds. We've got to see everything two ways. We've got to double-think—"

"And double-talk," Johanna said.

It stopped him momentarily. He reached into his pocket and pulled out the front page of the *Shimbun,* one of the two local Japanese newspapers. He held it up. Across six columns there was a banner headline; under it, the pictures of Ben, Muna and Tokan. Handing the paper to Johanna, Kley said, "Here—you know Japanese—read it."

She reached for it and, as she studied the item, murmured something about not reading well enough. It was evident, however, that she had caught the gist of the article and her eyes began to swim. Abby took it from her. For a while she said nothing. At last, haltingly, "They say—it was a noble act. Tokan performed it with courage and . . ." She searched for the translation and, giving up, spoke the original, ". . . *tekito* . . . I don't know what that means."

The translation came from Den. "Fitness," he said astringently. "What else does it say?"

"Never mind," Abby replied.

"Go on—read it," he insisted.

"No." She dropped the paper and started to cry.

Ben crossed the room and picked up the newspaper. With an unshaking voice, as if the words were causing no suffering at all, he translated: ". . . that the arrogant, treacherous American got less than he deserved. His death would perhaps have been more equitable than his castration. However, there is something to be said for the nicety that keeps him alive in the world, childless and joyless, a eunuch growing corpulent with the years, his man's voice turning to a querulous treble . . ."

He laid the paper down. The corners of his mouth were turned up as if he were reporting a pleasantry. "You wouldn't know they used to write with soft brushes, would you?"

Kley was trying to ameliorate. He crumpled the newspaper. "Of course the man's an idiot—all that stupidity about querulous treble and stuff. But that's not the point. What I thought you ought to see was that the Japanese—here—and possibly everywhere—may soon be thinking of Tokan as something of an avenged hero."

"And we're not to interfere with that," Johanna said.

He didn't answer immediately. The glint of shrewdness seemed to go out of his eyes. He appeared suddenly uncovered, a man available to her if she wanted to wound him. "Johanna, we're still *talking* to those people. There's still a chance we can keep the peace."

"Oh, Christ," she said. "Are you going to hang the war on *us*? Are you going to say that if we send that monster to jail, we incited the Japanese?"

"I'm not saying he shouldn't go to jail," he answered.

"Then what the hell are you saying?"

"I'm saying that the police can call Nishi as a witness. Nishi saw the attack—and that's all the court needs. Let the Japanese condemn the Japanese—let the yellow bastards kill each other—and the Americans stay out of it."

"What do you mean, 'stay out of it'?" Johanna asked. "Just disappear?"

"Almost literally, yes."

"My God, you don't mean that!"

"Yes, I do." The admiral's voice was reasoning and reasonable. "Ben wants to be transferred—we'll transfer him. Thaddeus and Abby actually know nothing about the case—not firsthand anyway—so all they have to do is keep quiet. As to you, Johanna, I think you ought to have a vacation on the Mainland."

Johanna looked at him steadily. "Like Abby and Thaddeus, I also 'know nothing about the case—not firsthand anyway.' Why do you suggest that *I* go away?"

"Because you'll make trouble if you stay."

"And I won't?" Tad asked.

It was the quietest of questions, and a challenge. It had no deliberation behind it; it was pure impulse. Nor did it demand an answer. He had no sense where it had come from, nor where he himself was going.

Abruptly he was aware of the others, staring at him.

Kley broke the silence. His voice was gentle, even paternal. "Well, Thaddeus, I hope—I certainly hope you won't get into something you don't actually know about. I'm not going to allow you to get hurt in this, Tad."

There it was, that damn fatherly thing again, the loving-hating authority, the threatening kiss, the outstretched hand that had the slap in it . . . but could not yet be rejected. Momentarily immobilized, he could neither accept it nor refuse it. Kley's voice sharpened. "You're not exactly a meddlesome fool, are you?"

He could say yes, I am, and *be* a meddlesome fool; or no, I'm not, and be something of a coward. He said nothing, merely turned away. He could almost feel an issuance from the admiral, of gloating accomplishment. The old man shrewdly by-passed Johanna for the moment. "Ben," he said, "I hope you can see the wisdom of my advice."

It was a dead voice. "I don't care."

"Well, you've got to care about this, Benny." He was even more fatherly than before, wanting more than agreement, needing his family to love him. "It's for everybody's good, you know."

"I don't care."

Kley turned to Abby. "Honey, I better talk to you. You're the most sensible one of all of us—always have been. Please tell them I'm not a cruel tyrant, making them do something they don't want to do. It's for the family's good as well as everybody's."

She was incoherent and a bit shaky, but she believed every word she was saying. "I think that's true. I think the more quickly and quietly it's over—why should we want to make it more public than it already is? I don't think it's to Ben's advantage to have the whole world know that he's . . ."

She saw where she was going and it was too awful, and she couldn't go there. Kley walked quickly to her, commiserating, and touched her. "Exactly, honey."

He had gotten all of them, one way or another, except Johanna. At a loss for a moment, he approached her. He was his old courtly self again, but none of it was pretension. Deeply fond of her, he didn't want to lose whatever affection she might have for him. "Johanna, please reconcile yourself to this. There's nothing you can do anyway. You're not an eligible witness. If you're around, the reporters will be after you, your picture will be all over the trial, the papers will want to make a carnival of it. So please—get away from it, as quietly, as quickly as you can. And don't you worry —the Jap will get it."

Her voice broke. "I don't believe it!"

"He will, Johanna—he will!"

She was out of control. "No, I don't believe it! Something tells me he won't! He won't! He'll get away with murder!"

Tad thought: I hope she didn't hear herself say that. But she did, and her face went white.

And Kley didn't let it alone. "It's not murder, Johanna," he said softly.

Without a word, Ben left the room.

Nine

I T WASN'T A DREAM; Johanna was fully awake. And clearly, in the middle of the night, lying in bed, she heard somebody repeating *a Babel of tongues, a Babel of tongues, a Babel* . . . It was a frightening discord of murmurings, blathering at her, mouthing at the darkness. Sitting up, with a cold wind gusting from somewhere, she tried to remember the whole quotation, whether it was Old or New Testament, or whether it was a quotation at all; something about the tongue being an unruly evil. There was no sleep at all, her eyes were big, and she knew clearly what unruly evil it was; she remembered it and Ben's face when she said it, and she heard other Biblical quotations, curses mostly, Old Testament where the curses had more spleen in them, about her tongue cleaving to the roof of her mouth, or torn by its iniquity. *I didn't mean it, Ben, I didn't mean it, the tongue should tear before it slips.*

She got up, impatient for daylight. Kley had been so incontrovertibly right about it all, prophetic almost: she had to leave Honolulu, her and her tongue, had to take herself out of harm's way.

She called the Pan American office even before it was open. She kept on calling, and suddenly they were there and asking if she wanted to reserve her return trip as well and if so, when.

"I don't know when I'm coming back. If ever."

How did those words get said, *if ever*, and by what slip of the tongue *this* time? Of course she was coming back . . . Coming back to whom, to what? Ben would be transferred. It was not altogether unlikely, if war happened, that Tad and Abby would also go elsewhere; the truce between Tad and Kley was attenuating to a thinner and thinner thread. She would be coming back to an empty city, her family gone, her friends at the

153

Club not so many as they used to be and the new ones hazier, as if her eyes were weakening. Even the house didn't belong to her. There was a lease somewhere, with something left on it, not much. Navy people don't buy, Oscar said, they rent, they have new jobs, new friends, they buy new address books, often. But if she didn't come back, where would she go?

The reverie again: Is there an opening for a—well, what am I?—a writer of sorts. It's San Francisco, Chicago, New York. I'm Johanna Winter. I'm a—well, I can hardly call myself anything as estimable as a journalist—I used to write a column, oddities and such. And I arrange things—I've done a *lot of that*. Charities, a half dozen benefits for charities, oh, a lot. And I do things with schools. When my children were young, a foreign land, no kindergarten, no nurseries to speak of, I started one, quite an experience, a play group in an alien tongue . . .

. . .. *alien enough, Ben, I might have found another tongue, to say it better, I couldn't have said it worse* . . .

No, Mrs. Winter, so sorry, there's no opening, not if you don't know precisely what you want, or what you *can*. Better stay where you are, the hills in San Francisco are somewhat steep, Chicago gets windy and cold, and you don't like the subway bearing down, you're quite afraid of it.

When did all the fears come, she pondered; she didn't used to have so many. It began first with Abby's marriage, then with Oscar's illness—leukemia—and the overhanging doom of an empty life. It was in the early stages of his sickness, in the first pallors and fevers of it. To fight her own night terrors, she had decided to get a job—a small job that wouldn't take her too far away from her husband's needs.

Andy Wescott, who owned the *Day-Telegram*, a newspaper just starting, was an old friend of Oscar's. He was gangling and spare, as Maine farmers are spare, and he moved his mouth in a ruminating way, chewing an imaginary tobacco cud. She said to him, "I was a journalism major at college—and I edited the paper."

He had a dry smile. "Yes . . . well . . . let's start with your merits first. Can you write?"

"I . . . yes . . . I've got this idea for a column. I brought a sample along with me."

It had been insultingly easy; sometimes she wondered if he ever read it. She was always sure he gave her the job to please Oscar, for no other reason. Once, when she had the flu, he told her, "Don't stew over the column, Jo. Won't matter if you miss a couple."

He said it didn't even matter to the makeup of the page. It simply didn't matter—except to herself. Mail them in, Andy would say, no rush, you don't have to bother coming into the office. But I *want* to come in, she would say, I want to be a part of the newspaper, part of my job. After a while, however, her pride bruised at being unnecessary in the newspaper office, she started mailing them in.

The job didn't drive the fears away; she simply learned how to store them out of sight, in dark closets. But now, as she opened her closets to pack, her old dreads came out of the shadows, frightening her so that she couldn't decide what clothes to wear or carry, what books to take for reading on the plane. The closets—how did it become so terrifying to open them and see all the stuff she had jammed into them over the years, and see them all so empty, full of darkness?

She had plenty of time to pack; she had days, in fact. But she knew that, as Clipper time approached, it wouldn't get easier; hour by hour she would slowly petrify with fear and then, at the last minute, when she was totally turned to stone . . . It used to be so easy. No choices—take everybody, take everything. Two children, two dogs, one cat, two yellow finches, an incomplete erector set, a blanket that would never get clean, Old Gold cigarettes, library paste you could only buy at Woolworth's, *Me and My Shadow* and *Always* and *Bye Bye Blackbird* and a bit of dough for sourdough bread. How impossible it used to be to make room for all the junk and make it all fit and pull together; and yet how easy, how sweetly simple and easy it was; no choices—take everybody, take everything.

The main difference, those days, was in knowing that the arrival would always be happier than the departure. The last arrival, Honolulu. She remembered it with such a longing. The old *Lurline* pulling into the Harbor. All that sick-sweet pageantry—the brown bodies swimming to meet the liner, the frangipani, the plumeria, the orchids on the water, the embrace of leis, aloha, we love you, aloha, aloha, the cloying, treacly heartaching friendliness of it, love, love. Love was something you smeared all over yourself that made you fragrant and sweet. The faces of love, the Hawaiian, the Japanese, the Chinese, love, love—and the exquisite Eurasians, everybody mating with everybody, oh love. How awful and aweful it was. That was '36, the year the first Clipper flew across.

There was talk of more Clippers nowadays and fewer steamers. The boats were getting older; they would be retiring them, one by one. The crowds were getting thinner too; love wasn't in such close quarters any more; you could walk through and not get jostled by it, not touched, in fact. There was an unsubstantiated rumor that people were being paid, these times, to go down to the wharf, paid quietly, of course. Some of them, it was said, were complaining that the few dollars were not enough. Aloha didn't come cheap any longer. The Filipinos had stopped coming altogether; love was getting dangerous. The Japanese, even when a *maru* came in, were getting fewer all the time. No Japanese women and children, hardly any at all; mostly men in heavy spectacles and dark suits; and the *maru*s had stopped coming. It was all passing; if there was a war, it might never happen again.

If only she could decide on one book, one book she could read on the plane . . .

The telephone rang. It startled her. She picked it up and shouted into it, louder than she had meant to. She had never heard the man's voice before and, although he spoke clearly enough, what he was asking didn't make sense.

"Right away?" he said.

"Right away what? Who *is* this?"

He repeated his name. "Young," he said. "Lieutenant Young of the Honolulu police. May I come over and see you right away?"

"No," she said. Then, trying not to understand, "What for?"

"I have a few questions to ask."

"About what?"

"The arrest of Kano Tokan."

Alerting herself, she dutifully mouthed what Kley might want her to tell him. "I have nothing to say about it."

He was so ready for her response he hardly let her finish. "You certainly must have something to say, Mrs. Winter. It was you who reported him to the police."

He said it flatly, the fact itself needing no resonance of voice; it reverberated as if in an echo chamber. "How soon can you get here?" she asked.

"I'll be there before you put the phone down."

It wasn't much of an exaggeration. The bell rang and he stood on the threshold, an ascetic-looking man, more a monk than a detective, wasting no time, his identification poised in the air, a white card in a celluloid case. "Howard Young," he said, and he spelled his last name.

He had barely accepted the chair she offered than he made a confession openly designed to inveigle her trust. "I want you to know," he confided, "that I am not as unprejudiced about this case as I should be. My mother came from Detroit, but my father's name didn't have an *o* in it. His family—those the Japanese didn't kill —they are still in Mukden."

Kley would have been pleased to hear it, she thought. Another variation on his theme: let the yellow bastards murder each other.

"So you see," he confessed, "whatever you tell me I will use or not use—" he searched for a wary expression—"so that the wrong people don't get hurt."

"I've told the police—"

"Everything you know," he said, with an ingratiating

nod. He had heard it many times but was not disapproving the banality. "Now tell me what you do not know."

"You mean you want me to make things up?"

He was wounded. "Oh, no. I want you to remember what you think you do not remember."

"Like what?"

"How did you find out it was Tokan?"

She was apprehensive. He was too friendly, too readily her ally. She said carefully, "I don't understand. A crime was quite clearly committed—and Tokan was quite open about having committed it. Nishi was an eyewitness. That's that, isn't it?"

"Well, that is not necessarily that, no."

"But it *is*—exactly."

"Not *exactly* exactly." The same annoying repeat of wordage. "The Japanese do not consider it was exactly a crime—and Tokan didn't exactly confess."

She was stunned. "But he did confess."

"To you, perhaps."

"Apparently to the police as well. The Japanese newspaper indicates he's quite proud of having done it."

"The newspapers, as you know, aren't always given the facts. Tokan claims the police were somewhat impolite to him. He has bruises on his arm."

"He's a liar."

"How do you know? Were you there?"

"I mean he's just generally a liar—about the whole thing."

"He may be a liar—generally. But his black-and-blue marks are specific."

"They could have been self-inflicted. You don't know what cruelties they can submit themselves to."

"I know about Japanese cruelties," he said quietly.

"This is all beside the point, isn't it?" Things were slipping away and she was trying to hold on. "Nishi was there. He was outside the Club the night it happened. He saw it."

"Tokan says Nishi is a liar." Then, without stressing

the statement, "He claims Nishi will say anything for money."

She slowly folded her hands in her lap, and waited.

Young continued. "You gave Nishi a bracelet?" As she didn't answer, "It was garnets, I think."

She faced him as openly as she could. "That was not in payment for a lie, it was payment for the truth. I wanted to know who had hurt my son, and he told me."

"I believe you, Mrs. Winter." He added, with extreme care, "But there is a tendency, when injury has been done to both sides, for one claim to balance another."

"I have a witness. When I gave Nishi my bracelet, someone else was there."

"Mr. Jerrold."

"Yes."

"Unfortunately what Tokan says about Nishi, we can all say about Mr. Jerrold. His hand is out to anybody."

He saw her frustration and made a small humming noise that was meant to be sympathetic. "Mrs. Winter, we have very few grand jury cases in the Territory of Hawaii, but, as you can imagine, nobody wants to skip any steps in this case. So a grand jury has been called and an indictment is being written. Whether they can arrive at a true bill and what it'll be, who knows? If you can help, if you can think of anything . . ."

"Think of what, for God's sake?" she cried. "I've told you what I know. You think if I had more to say against this man, I wouldn't say it?"

He nodded and got up. "You won't mind if I go and see your son-in-law, will you?"

Obviously he wasn't asking for permission; it was an obscure threat.

"Does it matter if I mind? Of course I don't—but he's not likely to know any more than I do."

He nodded vaguely, but still did not depart. Delaying at the door, the knob in his hand, he debated, troubled, then turned back toward her. Sententiously,

"Mrs. Winter, I haven't been entirely honest with you. I have left something out. I dabble a little bit in painting, and if I do a good picture and I leave a space, a truth fills it. But in the law, if you leave a space, it is generally a lie." He paused briefly. "This mess is worse than I told you. You want to know how Nishi got into it? Well, he started it all. He brought the whole thing to Tokan's attention. You see, Nishi—he's a camera importer. But he's something else too—a very good photographer. He takes very sharp, clean pictures . . . of very dirty things."

"Dirty?"

"Well, your son used to take her—Muna—to his house at the beach. They swam naked, they did everything naked."

"I don't call that dirty—and anyway, I don't care about that."

"Wait a minute. I think you have to understand what this can add up to—in court, I mean. I'm sure you're an experienced woman—you've been around, you've traveled. And I think I understand you, Mrs. Winter. I may be of Chinese descent, but I'm an American—and I see things American. And I think you do too. What I'm getting at—where love is concerned—making love, I mean—there are American ways and there are Japanese ways."

"Never mind," she said quietly.

He misunderstood. What she intended was for him to stop driveling, there was no necessity for him to edify her on the subject, she had some acquaintance of it; what he construed was that she didn't want her proprieties offended.

"I'm sorry if this is embarrassing," he said, "but you see that girl knows more ways to bang the drum, excuse the expression, than most of the girls down on Maunakea Street. She can make big men out of little men." He saw his blunder and said quickly, "Not that your son is little, understand." Deeper and deeper, the bathos worsened. Trying to extricate himself from his own tactlessness, he blurted, "Mrs. Winter, that girl, she not only uses her body, she uses things—

objects—she uses ways that would make you vomit! Those picures—they're filthy, they're obscene!"

Without raising her voice, "Would you please go now."

"What I mean—that Jap's *got* us, one way or another—and if there's anything you can do . . ."

The quiet exploded. "What the hell can I do?" Hearing herself shout, she drew back. "If you please . . ."

He said no more. He left.

Johanna hastened to the telephone and called Kley's office. She got no answer—it was Saturday—so she called the Makalapa house where he lived, then the Club. She didn't reach him and her skin began to tighten. She couldn't put it off, she had to get to him, had to tell him: shrewder though you may be than all of us, you're wrong about this. I can't leave now, I can't turn my back on this trial, I can't leave my son alone, to face the charge of having created a loathsome obscenity when all he was guilty of was falling into a foolish, ill-fated love affair.

The doorbell rang. It would be Young again, she supposed, come to pick up something he'd forgotten, a dirty fig leaf perhaps.

It wasn't Young, it was the newsboy. He was collecting for the month of November, nearly gone, and belatedly bringing her the morning *Advertiser*. When she had paid him, she hurriedly shut the door and with anxious eyes scanned the front page. No news of Tokan's arrest, nor had there been yesterday, in either the *Day-Telegram* or the *Star Bulletin*. The largest headline said, *Russ Capital Fall Nears As Nazis Crack Through;* a smaller one, *Japan Moves South From Central Asia,* headed an account of thirty thousand Japanese troops en route southward toward either Haiphong or Saigon. Nothing about Tokan and Ben. Not anywhere, not even in the back pages.

There was something wrong with that. There had to be news—why wasn't there? Specific events had occurred—an atrocity attack—the arrest of the perpetrator—why had they been dramatized in the Japanese paper, yet not even mentioned in the American one? Something too disturbingly twisted about it . . .

She telephoned the *Day-Telegram* and asked for Andy Wescott. She had always thought of him as craggy, no-nonsense, New England honest, not good at ducking and dodging, but today his manner was all evasion. "Well, Johanna, we don't have any real information—not confirmed, I mean. We don't want things backfiring, do we? A libel action—something like that. Do we, now?"

"But there are certain *facts,* Andy . . . It just seems strange."

"You're the one who's strange, Johanna. Do you *want* coverage on this?"

"No, of course not!"

"Well, then . . ."

When she hung up, she realized how awry it all was, and how foolish she had been. She *didn't* want to see it in print—and she had been relieved not to find even one little midden of filth in the papers. Then why had she made the call?

Filth. Suddenly, within less than an hour, she had come to label it filth. Yesterday, romantic that she was, it was a tragic love affair, today she thought of middens. And was relieved that no sign or stench of them was in the wind. Yes, relieved because the whole occurrence might easily have turned into a public orgy—it might still do that—but so far, thank God, it hadn't.

Kley was right. Yes, she had to confess it: she had experienced an enormous sense of deliverance from not seeing her son's face smeared across the public pages. She had no inkling how the uncanny feat of concealment had been accomplished, nor was she going to pry and poke at it; her pain over the catastrophe was palliated by the fact that the whole world wasn't leering at her son's lurid pictures, not pointing the filthy finger at the fair-haired American eunuch. And possibly, if Kley's strategy was right, and Johanna did nothing to interfere with it, the public would never get its prurient opportunity.

Yesterday, in the car coming home from Ben's, the

admiral had spoken shrewdly: you've got a choice, Johanna. You can make it somewhat easier on your son and on everybody else, including yourself—or you can indulge your own need for revenge, make it tough on everybody, and maybe not even get the revenge, in the end. But I beg you, Johanna—let the yellows betray the yellows, and the whites well away from it. Let the filth disintegrate and disappear. Don't raise a world-wide tempest, don't roil the seas. Let the Pacific remain pacific. Go away.

A long-headed choice. Get packing.

She would have to get back to it now, take it up where she left off, the exodus. She looked around the living room to see how far she had progressed before Young's arrival. Nowhere, really. She would have to start with a suitcase. Opening the hallway closet, she ferreted into the interior darkness and came out with a large gray three-suiter. Something rattled inside it and, shaking the thing, she had a capricious hope that whatever the object was it would please her, it would be a happy memento of an earlier time. It was nothing, just a loose packing strap; the bag had no remembrance in it, it was empty. Recalling how there was never room enough in all their luggage—every bag was overfull —she had the deadening sense that this time no matter how much she put in the suitcase, it would remain empty.

It was still empty in the afternoon. A packing chore that should have taken an hour or two had taken all day. Like someone who had never packed a bag before, she had no notion what she needed, where she was going or why, how long she would be there, or if she would return. And she couldn't bring herself to care.

Her back ached as if she had been carrying coals. Something took over, some deep infection overpowered her mind and muscles, it marauded her feelings and left nothing.

Apathy. No, don't let it in, it's a quiet enemy, shut it out.

Only yesterday, it seemed, she had had a great emotion. Was it rage? Yes, and some use for it, revenge. But now it was all being felt for her, all done for her. Kley was managing everything. She needn't bother her head with it or her heart or her will; nothing. She no longer had anything to do with yesterday's fury, it was hardly her own any longer. And whatever might be left of the scream she had stifled by sheer will power she was now stupefying with lassitude. Relieved, that was the word, wasn't it, when she had seen no mention in the papers? Relieved to be free of the scream; it had been frightening. She was well rid of it. She didn't need it any more. She didn't need anything.

Johanna drank all evening, by herself, and went to bed thinking she was drunk, and wasn't. She had dreams, she had nightmares, she had bedlams of them. Some started quietly enough. Her father was putting up the Christmas tree—erecting it, he insisted. Don't call them ornaments, he advised her, use *les noms propres, les boules,* and he was naked, not naked without clothes, but naked without his pipe, he had mislaid his pipe. The other person was reminding her: however pressed you are, you must never say spit, a lady doesn't use that word. But Daddy uses it. Spit is a man's word, do you understand that it's a man's word? Yes, Mother, but what word may I use? Expectorate is acceptable. May I expectorate? No, dear, you may *say* the word, but you may not *do* it; you must promise me you will never do it. No, Mother, never. You must never expectorate anywhere, never, not in public or private places, not on your shoes or face to remove smudges, certainly not on the faces of others, or their necks or backsides or organs, not on their floors or decks or deserts. Never on the desert, no, the Bible says so, do not expectorate on the desert, nor on men when they are big, and refer the question to Mitsu, who will explain everything aesthetically. The man will do the same, will take you through the passageway, open wider, please, spread more, my darling, spread, there are other things to touch, to get the taste of, the mouth must suck stronger, the pheasant neck is stuffed tightly with hot rice, if the *sake* is warm enough, and the monkey flowers should be set at a distance, the syringes ooze first, then they spurt, sometimes the cords are not necessary, sometimes the thongs, the laces, do not chase the good animal, we will love it as we make love, see how warm and wet its things are, the scented wetnesses, spread more, do not cut the skin, do not bruise it, see as deeply, look as deeply as the need to see, do not refer to anything you cannot taste, kiss, eat, tell, finger everything with a variety of tongues, the animal may go, the thong is wetter than it need be, the thing has come, the all of everything, paint everything with soft brushes, with wetness and soft brushes, how the liquids run, and the sounds are bloods, and the doorbell rings, it rings, answer the doorbell, Tad, wake up, Thaddeus, answer the doorbell . . .

It wasn't early. The sun was full up. She went to the door and it was nobody.

She would spend her day like that, with nobody, and her night would be too damn impossible with such miserable drunken dreams, when she wasn't drunk. She must stay dry all day, she must keep things neat and dry, dustless and spotless, never cleaning with a damp cloth again, take a feather duster to her life.

Awake now, fully awake. As soon as it was late enough in the morning, she would call Ben. Was he all right, was there anything she could do for him, she would ask. But ask it carefully, so he wouldn't sense any moist breath of pity in it. Careful everything from now on, no commonplace discourses, no easy utterances. All future conversations to be outlined in advance, cautiously spelled out, typewritten if possible, clearly titled. Never stray from the title: a guidepost.

She got him on the phone. No, he said, everything was fine, he needed nothing, he was going to be quite busy now, going to do a lot of reading he had been meaning to catch up on, it's an ill wind, you know, yes, quite busy. He had his guidepost too, his titles. This one was The Sensible Thing.

The sensible thing for her to do, she told herself, was to go away, let him alone while he worked things out.

"Work what did you say, Mother?"

"Did I say?"

"It's a terrible connection."

"What? I can't quite make it out."

"No, not anywhere. Did you?"

"It'll really be quite all right, won't it?"

"I have plenty of them. If I need more, I'll ask."

"That's all right, then."

"Oh, it's perfect."

When they hung up, she had the shakes. She hadn't understood a word he had said except the title, and that was a lie. Too soon. He was writing sensible titles without knowing what the rest was all about. Too soon, oh too soon, what can I do for him, what can I do?

She phoned Abby.

"Mother, what's the matter with you? Are you all right? . . . Mother?"

Abby was saying "Mother," not "Johanna." That meant there was trouble, more trouble; she wondered who it was this time.

"Mother?"

It's me, I guess, the trouble's me.

"Abby, honey, listen to me," she said quietly. "I am perfectly all right. It's Ben. I just spoke to him on the phone. I could say that it was a bad connection, but that's not what did it. It doesn't matter that I didn't understand a word he said. It matters that he sounded sensible. He has no right to sound sensible, not yet—because there is nothing he could possibly see in his life right now that could be called sensible. So I am worried . . . to death."

"Mother, I don't understand a word you're saying."

Johanna was suddenly weary. "I thought . . ." And she couldn't finish the sentence.

"Thought what, Mother?"

"Well, we might ride over to the beach . . ."

"Oh, Mother."

"I just don't know what to do."

"Do nothing, Mother."

"Yes . . . You're right . . . How ridiculous I am . . . I'm sorry . . . Did I wake you?"

"Oh, no, we've been up."

Johanna hung up. She reminded herself: how lucky I am to have a level-headed daughter. Do nothing, Mother. How rational. Oracular wisdom. It must indeed be the wise thing; everyone was advising it. *That,* then, would be what she would do with herself from now on. She had at last found her vocation, heaven-sent, as if she had asked, What is my calling, Father? Nothing, my child, do nothing.

Abby arrived just before noon. "Let's go," she said briskly.

"What?"

"Come on—it's what you want to do—come on."

"What's happened?"

"Nothing, Mother. It's just that you got me worried, so I called Ben. I called and I called and he didn't answer."

"He's swimming, probably."

"Oh, I'm sure it's something like that, but if you're going to stew all day—come on, hurry up, Tad's in the car."

They drove quickly and almost in silence. Clearly Tad was opposed to the waywardness of the trip, but he shunted his irritation onto the wheel, scanting the curves and pushing the precipices. Neither of the women betrayed any alarm. Johanna, in fact, welcomed the risk as if it were a pleasurable assault, somebody slapping her back to life. When they got to the top of the Pali, the sun was already westering; as they descended, the sea was golden.

Ben wasn't there. And not a thing was wrong. His car was parked outside the house; even locked. Indoors, on the kitchen counter, there was fresh coffee in a can that had been opened, apparently, this morn-

ing; hot coffee in a percolator on the kitchen table.
The refrigerator was newly stocked with milk, butter, bread and bacon. The bacon package was intact,
but two eggs were missing; he had had breakfast. The
dishes were washed and drying on the drainboard of
the sink. The radio was playing, somebody recount-
ing the two football events of yesterday, the Bears
versus Na Alii and Army versus Navy. With football,
everything was all right.

Outdoors again, on the other side of the house,
things were also exactly as they should have been.
Under the lean-to, Ben's rowboat was propped carefully against the board-and-batten of the building, the
oars neatly hung across the wooden pegs; his fishnets
were heedfully stretched across the rafters, and the
housing around the butane gas cyclinder was latched
and locked.

Johanna, having gone indoors, outdoors, then indoors again, felt sheepish. Ben had spent a quiet Sunday morning, had breakfasted, had listened to the
radio, then gone swimming in another cove, or walking to the boulders. Their whole trip had been an in-
dulgence, a poultice to her maternal aches and pains,
her frets and follies. She opened the cupboard where he
kept his liquor. Even that showed the signs of careful
husbandry; new bottles of gin, Scotch, bourbon, not the
best brands, not the worst; good buys, all of them.
Somebody who normally doesn't encourage visitors,
yet lays in a store of liquors other than the kind he
himself drinks, is thinking sociability . . . and futures.
His toughest problem might be his mother.

"Anybody like a drink?" she asked.

"Have one, Johanna," Abby said.

Everything easing back to normal; she's calling me
Johanna. She poured herself a third of a tumbler of
gin and saw Tad's eyes glancing at the glass. "Would
you like some?" she teased. "I'm afraid he doesn't
have any vermouth."

"No, thanks."

They talked of distances and how misleading they
were in ocean vistas, they talked of varying sands, the

white of Waikiki, the black of Kalapana, the barking
sands of Kauai. They said the barking sands didn't
really bark, they grunted as they scrunched, mostly;
yes, mostly. They worked away at all the last little
edges of conversation long ago rubbed smooth by
island boredom. Only half the sun was left in the sky,
and it was splattered across the western horizon when
the door opened and Ben stood there. He was stark
naked and wet all over. He had a towel in his hand
and was scrubbing his sopping head with it. He didn't
enter the room, simply stood on the porch, in the open
doorway, unconcerned about his nakedness, smiling.

"Great swimming," he said. "Some day I'll swim to
San Francisco."

"In case you hadn't noticed," Abby said casually,
"you're buff."

"I noticed," he said.

He didn't move, just continued to stand there,
leisurely rubbing his head with his towel, still smiling. His smile had a high gleam to it, as if it had been
made by the sunlight, euphoric. Then, matter-of-fact-
ly, without laying stress on anything, without affirm-
ing or denying, he proceeded to dry the rest of his
body, his neck, his shoulders, his arms, his armpits,
his chest, his back, his belly, his buttocks, his penis,
his thighs, his legs, his feet. He did not linger over the
drying of his penis, nor did he hasten past it. He paid no
particular attention to the raw, bloody scar where his
scrotum used to be, not did he do anything to draw the
attention of the others.

Johanna could not see the whole slash, only a hint
of it, but she hurt for all of it, the same slash, deep,
searing. Yet, this is his declaration, she thought, he
wants us to see him. Wants us to see all of him, all that
is left, wants us to know his body is enough, or will
have to be enough; he will make do with it; wants *us*
to make do with it . . . And she would have to.

"You care for a drink?" she said, inviting him indoors as naked as he chose to be.

She felt Tad's stare. He was gazing, not at Ben or at
his wife, but at her. It was an enigmatic stare. She

wanted, poignantly for an instant, to know what it meant.

"You still on bourbon?" she said to Ben.

"Yes." He came indoors.

"Soda?"

"No—water."

"I think I'll have one too," Abby said. "With soda —not too strong."

Johanna poured it and handed the drink to her daughter. Abby had a sip or two, then Tad borrowed her glass, tasted it and gave it back. They talked about the sea and Ben swimming in it and how smooth it was in the other cove compared to this one, where the breakers were working out a grudge today. Before long, nobody seemed to be wearing more clothes than anybody else.

Johanna had a surge of unbelievable happiness. She was proud of herself for having so quickly understood what the boy was saying by his nakedness, and of him for saying it. She had had no glimmer of hope that she would be capable of seeing the world so differently so soon. It was because of Ben—what a wonder the boy was to her—it was Ben who had shown her she could do it, would have to do it, because he demanded it of her. How proud she was of him—and of Abby, and even Tad. A family acceptance of a family wound. They had suffered it together and understood, today, that it could never again torment them as it had already done.

Ben finished his drink and, without announcing what he was going to do, drifted into the bedroom. He was in there dressing; she could hear the closet door opening and closing and the screak of bureau drawers warped by sea damp. It brought up the subject of oceanside humidity and what salt does to bicycles and cars, and how fast you can run on wet sand and how slowly on dry. World-shaking subjects, these, Johanna thought, and how delicious it felt to scale such eminences on such toy-sized vehicles. Abby laughed more lushly than she used to, a woman's laugh, it had darkness in it, midnight. She wondered if they laughed in bed, before or after. No, he wouldn't be a laugher, that one; he would be giving away too much; he had a secret. She tried to unriddle what his glance had meant, a moment ago.

Ben was a long time coming back. She didn't hear him in the bedroom any more; hadn't, indeed, for quite a while. She called to ask him if he wanted another drink. He didn't answer.

Abby giggled. "He's gone to sleep, I bet."

Johanna was looking toward Ben's room. She didn't notice Tad going out onto the porch. She barely heard him: "Oh, Christ," he said.

Abby was running.

"What's the matter?" Johanna called.

"Oh, Christ," he said again.

Then all of them were running. Down, down, harder to run in dry sand, down to the water's edge.

"Oh, God!"

He was a head bobbing in the golden sea, a head and golden arm, up and down, catching the sun, swimming eastward.

Tad, out into the water, knee-deep: "Come back! Come back!"

Then, out of it, toward the lean-to next to the house. Abby got there first. She started to tug at the boat. "Help me," she cried. "Christ, help me!"

He shoved her away, she was tugging at the wrong end. He pulled at it and did no better. Johanna, at the other end. They didn't bother to hoist it over their heads, but lugged, by anxiety and awkwardness, to where the surf came. Abby, carrying oars, running, stumbling in sand.

"Hurry," he yelled to her.

He was in the boat now, pushing out, and Johanna was trying to get in.

"No—stay back. No!" he shouted.

"I'll help you row," she cried.

"No—no!"

There was no sense, not to any of it.

"If you have to pull him in—" Abby shouted. "Let her!"

Johanna was already in the boat.

"Ben!" Abby screamed. "Benny!"

Tad pushed out into the sea.

"Come back!"

He gave his whole body to the oars, gave all his ache, gave his hatred of the slowness of the sea, gave more than he had, rowing, calling the boy's name, rowing.

Johanna was still. Stillness, now that it was happening, was all she had to give.

When they came abreast of him, he was no longer swimming. He was floating face downward, as if he had sunk and risen a number of times. When Tad pulled him into the boat, there was no life in the swimmer. He didn't look dead. He wouldn't, she supposed, not for a while. At least he would not be bloated, she told herself; they had come in time to find him, as he was. In a little while, he would have been completely taken into the deep, to rise again, in a few days perhaps, an ugly object, unrecognizable as Ben, recognizable only as an incidental drowning in the sea.

Dead on Sunday, buried on Monday; it was a nursery rhyme. It wasn't easy, Kley had told her, to arrange a funeral so fast, but he thought it wise to get it over and done with and, for a little extra consideration, speed could be arranged.

Oddly, it was only Tad who had made a fuss: I want him buried at sea, he said. Kley was annoyed. He made the point, regretfully, that there was no occasion for it. To which Tad replied that the occasion was a sailor's death.

"He wanted the sea," he said.

"He got it."

The surprise of the statement was not its coldness but its source. Not Kley. Abby said it. And that was the end of it. Ben was buried, in a moderate-priced casket, and laid into the earth of a sunny cemetery, on the outskirts, somewhere.

She would never go to visit him there; Johanna set

her mind to that. She would make a point of forgetting the route the limousine had taken; she would not remember the name of the cemetery. She would never put flowers on his grave. She would never allow herself any emotion about him; if she did, she knew she would never make the next day, and the next.

Apathy was, after all, the best.

She hadn't cried. Not all Sunday afternoon or night, not the following morning, at the mortuary, not at the grave, not coming home from it. Nor would she cry, this Monday morning, now that she was back at home. In a little while, she would resume her packing. Not quite yet. For the moment, she would take her clothes off—mourner's weeds, heavy—and wear something lightweight, the lightest nightgown she owned. She would make herself some tea, hot, boiling hot, so it would scald her tongue . . . It didn't scald. Nothing could pain her.

She sat in the window alcove of the dining room, her cup of tea and the *Day-Telegram* on the table. The newspaper had just arrived. She must remember to cancel everything; she should have told the boy on Saturday.

The headlines were always the same and always going to be. Hull and Kurusu were, as usual, in a crucial meeting. Roosevelt, because of the crisis in the Orient, was hurrying back from his Georgia vacation. Tokan was free. She turned the page.

Had she read it and passed it by, or had she imagined it? She went back to the front page.

It was there. Not a large article, no headline to speak of, but on page 1. The first time she had seen any reference to it in any English-language newspaper:

JAP IMPORTER FREE

The Territorial grand jury, after a weekend of deliberation, has brought in a finding of "no true bill" against Japanese importer Kano Tokan. Charged with, among other things, an attack on Lieutenant Benedict O. Winter, USN, the Japanese was exonerated without trial for want of evidence. No witnesses appeared to substantiate any of the police charges. Kano's wife, Muna, did appear, however, on behalf of her husband. According to Tokan's attorney, Karu Hidemada, Mrs. Kano would be willing to testify that, on the night of the attack on the Navy officer, she and her husband spent the entire evening at home. The search for the attacker continues.

Quietly she put aside the paper and finished her tea. She sat at the table, scarcely moving at all and not thinking very much. Detachedly observing herself, she was vaguely interested in the minimal level at which her whole person was operating. There were no upward surges in the graph. Nothing in her seemed to be surmounting the lowest thresholds, not of thought, of feeling, of will; even her blood seemed to be coursing at the slowest rate possible.

At last she arose and went to the telephone. She called Pan American and canceled her airplane reservation.

Then she went to the window. She looked up into the afternoon sky, right into the blazing brilliance of the sun. Then she screamed. She screamed the sun to splinters. She didn't stop screaming. Nobody could make her stop. Nobody could take the rage away from her, nor the revenge she would make of it. Not Kley, not the Navy, not anybody. It was hers. The scream was her own.

Ten

"**N**o, I'LL GET OUT here and walk," Tad said. "Don't bother going up the hill."

He really wanted to walk, wanted to get away from the look of black, the mourning clothes that didn't become his wife and her mother. It was a puzzle to him how they had managed to find the costumes, two women who never wore dark clothes in the tropics, and suddenly they had them without purchasing so much as a stocking. Women have black tucked away somewhere, they're always ready.

He wasn't. As he trudged slowly up the hill to his office, he considered how he could rid himself of the image of the straps loosening as the graveyard attendants lowered the box into the ground. Goddamn Kley anyway. If he could have done the whole thing so expeditiously with a few phone calls, he could have made an extra call or two and arranged the burial at sea.

Yet, perhaps it had been a mistaken notion, a false, romantic picture about what the ocean meant to Ben. No question that Tad had been wrong about the cottage. It was not, as Tad had imaginatively projected it, a place where Ben was always solitary, where he tested himself against the loneliness of the sea. According to the police detective, he had brought the Japanese woman there, often, and made love. And, perhaps, if he had lived, considering he had laid in a store of liquor, there would have been other guests. Why should it surprise him that the sea was different for a Winter boy than it had been for Thomas Clark? For them the ocean was a festive, social place, a great aquatic ballroom. They went on yachting cruises, they shot at skeets, they luffed their sailing boats into the winds, they had their bootleggers bring old wines and foreign spirits to them in the safe distance of unprohibited waters, they gambled at far, untroubled anchorages. The sea was the playground of the Winters; one did not mourn in it.

He had been thinking of himself. The lonely seascape, with the flight of crying gulls and the desolate wind rack, and the twilit gray that mourned of loss, that was a setting not for Ben but for himself. For himself, at the very beginning, when he saw the ocean for the first time. He was fifteen and wouldn't have seen it even then if he hadn't gotten a job as busboy in an Atlantic City restaurant. Nor did he, in those working days, see much of it. A glance in the morning, before work, a glance in the evening, after it. Never when the bathers were there, with the umbrellas up and the beach mats and beach balls, and the screaming, falling, feeling, touching, hugging, kissing, never any of that. Only when the light was gray, mostly at dusk, the tide coming in, the strand a wetness, deserted. A time to let the tight clutch of his solitariness loosen to the far horizon.

How desolate he was then, mourning a loss so general, so indeterminate that he never knew what he mourned; it was the climate of his life. And now that his loss was distinct, was the mourning any more bearable? Was it easier to know he would always grieve for Ben?

I want the sea, the boy had said. And Tad knew he himself wanted it too, desperately. The sea should have given meaning to his belonging to the Navy; without it, what did it mean that he belonged? Was he still, aged thirty-eight, still so desperate to belong? And why did he feel it now, so deeply, when he lamented Ben?

He made his way through the corridor and hoped he could get to his own office without meeting anybody. Luckily, they were both busy: Herbstmann loudly giving someone directions on the telephone, Schotley training the new boy who was to take Ben's place. He had met the kid briefly on Friday; an ensign, Fellows was his name, who seemed no older than sixteen although he had to be past twenty. He was myopic but didn't wear glasses. Whether it was out of vanity or concern that spectacles would go on his report, he pretended his vision was twenty-twenty, yet could barely read the mirror-writing made by the double-faced carbon. Tad felt sure he secretly took the sheets into the john and read them in the looking glass. But he was ingenious at codes, a real codehead, except for his ignorance of Japanese, worse than Herbstmann, with a little dog-eared tourists' phrase book on his desk. He'd be all right, though; a good boy . . . He wasn't Ben.

When he got to his office, he saw the newspaper on his desk with the little article encircled in red crayon and the legend, in Schotley's writing, *They let the bastard go!*

He read it through twice. He couldn't believe it. It was impossible. No matter what extenuation could be pleaded, Oriental or otherwise, no matter what justification by reason of jealousy run to madness, that was all moot for a jury, not a grand jury. The man had, in fact, drawn the knife, he had committed the deed; had been seen doing it by Nishi and had admitted it to Johanna. No true bill? What sleight of hand had been practiced?

None, perhaps. They were all at fault: Kley, Johanna, Abby, Ben, himself—all of them. They had all acted as if justice were automatic, it had a self-regulating tiller, its own gyroscope that would resist all inequities and rotate steadily around its own honorable axis. They should have known there was nothing automatic about it; it all had to be done by hand; people had to be present, doing it. And not one of them had been present, not one. Such complacency, such moral laziness. A boy mutilated and, in effect, murdered—and unavenged by wrath or justice . . . And now it was all over . . . Too late. Something to be forgotten—the crime, the criminal, the victim. Let it all die, as Ben was dead. Let it pass. And, maybe, just as well.

There was a sallow face at the door: Herbstmann. He looked, as always, put upon. A complaining young man, convinced that his superiors mumbled in order to confuse him, nobody ever made directions plain. "Isn't your phone working?" he asked.

Tad lifted the receiver, heard the appropriate buzz. "Yes. Why?"

"Mrs. Winter's trying to reach you. On three."

He expected Abby's voice. It was Johanna. A first time: she had never called him at the office, not on any provocation. Her voice sounded too tightly tuned; wrong notes were playing.

"Can you come over?" she asked.

That too would be a first time. He had never visited her house unless in Abby's company, had never been invited there alone. "Is something wrong?" He heard himself: how imbecilic the question was—earth still fresh on a young man's grave—yes, something's wrong.

"Have you read the papers?"

He had a vision of her shaking the front page at the telephone. "Yes, I have," he replied.

"They've let him go." Then, out of breath, "I have to talk to you."

Not only the tightness of the voice, but something in its undertones . . . Once, in New York, coming out of a movie theater, a woman, too young to have what seemed like an older person's madness, wearing a paper bag on her head and a coil of clothesline around her neck, standing motionless, humming a monotone, a tremolo . . .

He was about to give her an excuse. "Johanna . . ."

"Please—I need you."

Not only need in her voice. Ferocity.

The road to the right would have taken him home; the one to the left, to Johanna's house. As he turned left at the division, he realized his memory had been wrong; he *had* been to her house alone—once before, at Oscar's invitation.

He had met Abby's father on the day of his arrival in Honolulu; Oscar had, in fact, come to the pier to

meet Tad's boat and had driven him from the wharf to
the Bachelor Officers' Quarters, where they had a few
drinks while Tad was unpacking; one of the last times
Tad had drunk bourbon. Then they had walked together, not altogether steady on their feet, and the
older man had pointed out the sights of the Harbor.

Oscar was easy to like and Tad liked him immediately. The rear admiral was Kley's associate, on the Communications side of the liaison, but he did nothing
the way Kley did; the latter's lines were deliberately
twisting and unsettling; Oscar's were secure and un-
wavering, point to point. He was a man never as tough
as he sounded, with an exuberant boisterousness
that would have seemed vulgar in anybody but Oscar
Winter.

If Tad was reticent about showing his fondness for
the older man, Oscar had no such reticence. The way
he invited Tad to his house the first time was a case in
point. "Come over tonight," he said. "I want you to
marry my daughter."

It was one of Oscar's jokes, except he meant it. A
little over a year later, Tad and Abby were married.
It was on their first wedding anniversary that they
heard, quite by accident, that Oscar was dying of
leukemia.

How strange that he rarely thought of Oscar any
more, after having been so deeply attached to him . . .
Lost fathers, better forgotten . . .

He turned the corner of Johanna's street, drove to the
dead end and parked the car. As he walked down the
aisle of eugenia bushes toward her front door, he
thought: Johanna is central to three people whom I
have loved; why is she the only one that I don't?

The door opened and, as he entered Johanna's house,
he didn't see her. She was behind the door, huddled
back, trying to be invisible. "I'm not dressed," she
said.

She was wearing a nightgown, a sheer one, as thin as
gauze. Lurking in the darkness of the foyer, she
murmured something, a confusion of things, about

putting some clothes on. Then she hurried past, barely brushing against him, out of the dim entryway. Suddenly she was a silhouette against the window in the blaze of the setting sun, and he saw her naked through the cloud of nightgown, all of her naked, her breasts in contour, her body slimmer than he had imagined, yet somehow more opulent. Then she was gone.

He heard the bedroom door open and close, he heard no other sound. She was more beautiful than he had pictured her, more beautiful than the last time. What a strange phrase, "the last time," as if he had ever seen her unclothed before; why had such a curious expression struck his mind? Oddly, he couldn't rout the fantasy that he had indeed seen her totally naked at some time in the past, he couldn't remember when or where. How ridiculous the illusion was: if he had ever seen her that way, the when and where could never have slipped his mind. The boar hunt. That was it, the boar hunt, she was naked then, with all her clothes on, as naked as he had seen her a moment ago. Absolutely unclothed, a fearful Johanna, a self-horrified one, saying help me, shoot the beast, help me, I need you. That was the nudity. And here it was again: I need you.

She came back. Wearing a skirt and a loose sweater, she was thicker now than he knew she was. He would never see her again, he realized, without remembering her body, its teasing contrariety, slim and voluptuous, a nakedness against sunlight.

"I hope you'll help me," she said.

"To do what?"

She didn't answer coherently. "I don't know how to go about it—what to do—I don't know what it entails. I have a feeling—danger—I'm sure there's some— and I'm quite sure I won't be able to handle it myself."

"Handle what, Johanna?"

"Terrible things! I want to see him—terrible things happening to him!"

She stopped. Her face was contorted; not her face at

all; the ferocity again, terrible and cruel. Bringing herself under constraint, at last, she spoke more evenly. "I want to see him tried. I want to go to Nishi and make him tell them what he saw." She was rushing ahead too fast; she seemed to need a retard, and he could see her make an effort. "I know that if he never appeared, it won't be easy to *make* him appear."

"No . . . it won't be easy."

"Nothing is. I have to do it."

Her face was flushed. She looked feverish. "Are you sure you do?"

He saw alarm. She was afraid he would talk her out of it. She didn't dare let him. "Please, if you tell me reasons—I have to stay a little insane—I don't want you to be rational with me. I don't think I can stand—I mean—*I have to do it!*" Then, trying to control the frenzy without losing the urgency, "Will you help me?"

"No."

"Please."

"It's not a good idea, Johanna."

"Please—spare me the Kley! I can't take any more Poppa Kley!"

"It's not Kley. I feel that way myself."

"He makes us think we do. He makes weasels of us."

He felt sure she didn't mean the epithet against herself; she meant him. Even if she didn't, he mustn't let her self-confessed insanity shake him off balance. "Whatever Kley made of us—that was some days ago. It doesn't matter now. Ben is dead."

"Thank you. I must put that on my calendar—it slips my mind."

"Let it, for God's sake!"

"Oh, please—I can do without your placebos."

"What can't you do without, Johanna?"

He was surprised: the question put a brake on her. She was trying to think of its meaning, trying to find an answer. It was the first carefully advised thing she said: "Revenge, I think."

She was reasonable now, partly at least.

"Can you afford it?"

She laughed grimly. "It's like the yacht. If you have to ask the running cost . . ."

"But can you, Johanna? You're right—it can be dangerous. To yourself, to others. Even to Ben."

"I may not have heard correctly—didn't you say 'dead'?"

"Yes." He tried not to retaliate against her rancor. "Why don't you let him alone?"

"It's as the man said when we were choosing the casket: 'It's not for him—it's for yourself.' "

"What'll you get for yourself, Johanna—except a continuation of pain?"

"Oh, no! The end of pain—that's what revenge is."

"It won't hurt you to drag Ben's name through all the dirt?" He saw it was useless. The ferocity had returned. She had a hunger for havoc. "Why don't you let him alone, for God's sake?"

"If you won't help me, I'll do it myself!"

"Johanna—don't!" Then, pleading, "The detective came to see me on Saturday. They've got pictures—they say they've got dirty pictures!"

"No! I can't imagine dirty pictures! Those people were in love. I don't give a damn how they expressed their love for each other! I don't care how naked they were with one another—I don't care what they did with one another or how they did it—to them it must have been beautiful! I can't imagine them thinking it was anything else! If there was anything dirty about it, it wasn't the people making love, it was the Peeping Tom who took the pictures!"

"That may be what you think, it may be what I think—"

"Are you sure it's what you think?"

"It doesn't matter what I think—that's my point! Nor even what you think! It matters what people will see when they read the papers. And what they say about it!"

"What can they possibly say that could be true?"

"Even *that* doesn't matter! What they'll say is that your son was perverted!"

"You prude!"

"That's what *they'll* say! Not me—they!"

"You dirty prude! It's you who are talking—you! How can you bear to look at yourself? Do you sleep naked? How can you bear to *see* yourself? You prude —you dirty prude!"

There was nothing he could say. He didn't know what defense there could be against such a charge. And if he could find a defense, he doubted that she could hear it. She had a rage to devastate.

He started to go, hoping that some counteractive madness—like poison fighting poison—would bring her back to reason, and she would stop him at the door. She didn't.

Driving home, he tried to make the exigencies of traffic steady him, but he remained unnerved. Everything about his meeting with Johanna had upset him. And the view of her, naked against sunlight—that too was no longer a pleasurable excitement but an uneasy trespass. Once, in a Woolworth's in Philadelphia, at the age of ten, he had stolen an imitation leather watchband for a watch he didn't have. He hated possessing it but couldn't bring himself to return it; he wanted, for some reason he couldn't articulate, to possess the thing. This, too, this image of her, was a guilty possession, a piece of mental booty he coveted, it made a stir in him, and he wasn't sure he wanted to rout the image from his mind. Like the watchband, it was something he had acquired by stealth, but could neither use nor get free of.

Yet . . . perhaps he hadn't acquired it by stealth. Perhaps the view of her, naked, had been *given* to him, a gratuity from Johanna.

He lay in bed, sleepless, tossing, trying not to disturb Abby, who was soundly asleep beside him, and he couldn't get the speculation out of his mind. Perhaps, indeed, a gift from Johanna. When he had arrived at her house this afternoon, he hadn't simply barged in on her, he had rung the doorbell. She knew it was he and could have told him—before opening the door—that she wasn't dressed and he'd have to wait. She didn't do that, she let him in. She allowed him to have a hint of her, nude. She had, as it were, planted something to see if he would take it, as one tests a thief; left a lure, as one leaves a bit of bait for an animal. He wondered if he could have been right about that, or if he was imagining it; he wondered if it could have had anything to do with her calling him a prude.

He couldn't believe she could have come to such a conclusion except in her overwrought state. A prude—meaning what?—an overly modest man opposed to what he considers excesses? Yes, well, he was against her excessive frenzy for vengeance—there was an obscene lust in it, a sickness. But he certainly was not prudish about what might be exposed by Ben's so-called obscene pictures.

In the darkness, having come upon the distinction, he felt comforted. It was soothing to be lying here beside his sleeping wife; as he listened to her easy breathing, he too breathed easily again. If he had any amorphous disquiets about the distinction he had just made, he would not try to give them form, not tonight. Leave them out there in shadow; perhaps by tomorrow they would be gone.

Meanwhile, tonight, he knew he was no prude; he could make love to his wife in any way imaginable, enjoying it, and shocked by nothing they took joy in together. And he took particular pleasure in the unexpected.

Abby, partly in darkness and partly in moonlight, looked unexpectedly provocative tonight. Although she was altogether naked, the light and shadow made her seem half-clothed.

He touched her lightly, his hand on the curve between her breast and buttock. It was the deepest curve, the most satisfying in its voluptuousness, it made the most sensuous sweep between a choice of pleasures. He moved his hand downward on the soft warm skin, then upward; either way the hand moved, it moved to felicity. He reached to her breast, and for a moment simply held it cupped in his hand. Then moving again, only on the breast, moving gently, feeling the nipple, firmer and firmer, touching it between two fingers as if they were his lips. She murmured. She was silent for a while, then murmured again, saying nothing, murmuring. He felt her hand move slowly. As she tried to find him in the darkness, he brought himself closer, turned her slightly to take her breast in his mouth. Suddenly she was all mouths and hunger, she was all over him, here, there, gone and returned. There were musky dampnesses in the air. From the sea, he thought at first. Then, routing the idea, he thought: from her, and from the woods. He didn't know why woods came to him, now, in the midst of this, but it was indeed woods, deep ones where men go hunting, and women hunt as well. And he was on the verge of entering, where there were dangerous wild things, boars and blood and the unknown. And as he entered his wife, he entered the damp, the wooded darkness.

The weather messages didn't make sense. He and Herbstmann spent the first hour of the morning in Schotley's office, where the meteorological reports were, trying to figure them out. No matter where the communications came from—three from Tokyo, one each from Hong Kong, Nagasaki and an unidentified plane—they were discrepant with whatever the actual weather of the time had been. When reliable observer reports described the weather as being sunny and clear, it didn't make sense for the Japanese to be reporting they were in the midst of a heavy downpour. The words of the weather messages didn't, therefore, have anything to do with the weather, that was obvious, but what they actually had to do with none of the ciphers could tell.

To Tad the outlook was bleak. He was irritable. "We're stuck with an old cipher."

"We may not need a new one," Schotley said. He was certain that just the other side of the bad weather there had to be a rainbow. "Maybe we can find a new application for the old one."

"Thanks," Tad said. He preferred Herbstmann's Calamity Jane to Schotley's Pollyanna. "Let's see what we
can get out of the Red Machine—Herbstmann can do
that. And let's dig out the old gray-file codes. Anything from Ushikawa?"

"No, I don't think so," Schotley replied. "He called
yesterday when you were out. I think he merely
checked in with Fellows."

"Let's send him to the Dai Nippon Club and the
Muchisoki teahouse. Jap newspapers—weather reports
continued, of course. And want ads. Stuff for sale—
wellsprings and eardrums."

"Wellsprings and what?"

"Never mind." It bothered Schotley when Tad asked
them to look for phantoms. It bothered all of them. It
was hard enough, digging out the real things. The men
were bright, all right; they knew what they read. They
could identify a fact and they were pretty good at
spotting an outright lie. What they couldn't do was
see something when nothing was there; they had no
fear of apparitions, so couldn't believe in them. They
were well-satisfied young officers who had never been
hungry for food or family. When Tad hired a stringer,
outside the office, he knew he had a good possibility if
the man had starved a little. Better yet, if he had been
cheated by somebody. Of course, the best of all was a
man who had been cheated by everybody.

He left the two of them and walked down the corridor. He heard the new boy, Fellows, whistling in his
tiny cubicle across the hall. A half-hour later, when
he was sitting at his desk, Tad thought he was still
hearing the whistle sound, but it had changed. It was
no longer continuous. Little short squeakings, then it
would stop; short, then stop again. The cleaning woman, he supposed, with her complaining bucket handle.
It annoyed him, and he was soon going to be running
some very faint recordings; he wondered if he should
ask her to come back later. Getting up from his desk,
he opened the door and looked down the hallway. She
was at the far end. No squeaking noise. The only

sound she made was the whish-whoosh of the wet mop on the linoleum floor. He closed the door again.

The sound was outdoors, just the other side of his window, Opening the sash, he leaned on the sill, stood motionless, listening. Nothing out there.

He heard it behind him. He turned quickly. It was here—somewhere here—right in this room.

One of his file drawers was ever so slightly open. The noise came from the file. He yanked the drawer open.

The animal jumped out. It was an ugly cat, gray-brown, a wide-faced tom, dirty and mangy with an evil green in its eyes and a sick mouth torn slightly away from its teeth so that its mucus made a dark wetness on its fur. It was a nightmare cat, out of dirty cellars and wet alleyways.

But the main horror of it was what it wore around its neck. A ribbon, a lovely pink ribbon of shiny satin, a birthday-present ribbon, a ribbon for valentines; tied to it, a tiny, white, deckle-edged gift card.

Tad reached for it. The cat scurried, frightened, needing someplace to hide. Finding none, it started for the window. Tad moved quickly, blocking the animal's way. The cat retreated. Back into the farthest corner of the room it crouched, tried to diminish itself, to pull itself inward, into the smallest pocket of its diseased skin. Its eyes looked up at him with green malice.

Tad stood there, not moving. He didn't want to touch the cankered thing. But the card around its neck, the message . . . He took one step toward the beast. It curled its unclean lips back and made a hissing sound. He took another step. The creature stirred as if to run, then shook a little and was still. Another hiss.

He lunged for it and felt the claw, the rip. The cat was gone and he after it. Both hands on it now as it snagged and tore his hand, tore at the air, then at his hand again. Tad tore too, at the ribbon, and dropped the animal. It started scurrying again, a maddened thing, back, forth, across the room, up on the file, onto the desk, then, leaping, out the window, and was gone.

He looked at the scratches on his hand. He squeezed them, made them bleed to cleanse them, then squeezed again as if he enjoyed the pain of sanitizing himself of the ugliness.

Then he read the card: *You should guard your office better, my friend. I leave you this beast as a sentry. Please don't get rid of him—he's better protection than you've got. When the cat's away . . .*

The son of a bitch. Jerrold. The plaguing gadfly son of a bitch. He hurried to his files. He slammed open one drawer after another. None resisted; no locks. He felt a murderous heat. Rushing out of his office, he yelled Schotley's name. He tore open the lieutenant's door. The younger man jumped up in alarm. Herbstmann retreated from the other side of the desk, his face whitening.

"Locks!" Tad shouted. "Goddamn it—locks!"

"What?"

"I told you—locks!"

"They're ordered. Requisitioned."

"I told you last week, didn't I? I told you not to wait! I told you to go and get them yourself! I told you, didn't I?"

"They didn't have them! I went—they didn't have them!"

"You stupid little turd! You—!"

He stopped, midsentence, appalled at himself. He twisted his head away from them as if he couldn't stand the horrified looks on their faces. When he turned back, Herbstmann was edging toward the door.

"Wait a minute," he said. The ensign paused. Then, mortifying himself, "Since you heard me behave like a shit, I want you to hear me apologize for it. I'm sorry, Schotley."

He walked back toward his office. What he wanted now was to be alone and occupying the smallest space imaginable, smaller, meaner than the cat. What he wanted was to be alone somewhere, in a dark alley.

What he got was Jerrold.

The man stood there, in the middle of his office, staring at the door as Tad entered, an aghast look on his face. "I didn't mean that to happen—so help me, I didn't."

Tad said nothing. He couldn't bear to talk to him or face him, or anybody. He walked to the window and stood looking out, seeing nothing. Strange, he thought, the first thing I ever say to Jerrold when I see him is *go away*, and I can't even say that to him.

"I'm sorry, Thaddeus," the man was whispering, with genuine contrition. "I am—you have to believe me—I am most terribly sorry."

"Where were you?" Quietly.

"Right out there. The hallway—the entrance to the john. I heard every bit of it. When you were buggering about with that bloody cat, I almost pissed with laughing, and now I could cry."

Surprisingly without rancor, "What do you want?"

"Well, what I *wanted* was to heckle you and harass you and make you pay attention to me. But what I want now is to leave what I've got for you and quietly slip away."

"All right—leave it."

Wryly, "I had a pert little line all ready for you."

"What's the line?"

" 'Nice weather we're having.' "

Most of Tad was still busy castigating himself, so he only heard the important word, marginally. He turned a little. "What did you say?"

Jerrold pointed past Tad to the brilliant sunlight. "Coming down heavily, isn't it? Should have six or seven inches by nightfall. The children will love it for Christmas."

The man had pulled him back to his job. " 'Jingle Bells,' " Tad said.

"What? Oh, rather. We don't sing it in England."

"What do you know about it?"

The Englishman was enjoying himself. "I'll swap you."

"Nothing, except it's a fake. In reports we use the word 'obfuscatory.' "

"Then you do know."

"But I don't know what it's concealing," the commander said. "When weather information is so blatantly inaccurate, they obviously mean for us to pick it up. Then what . . . ?"

He didn't finish the sentence. The thought struck him just as, clearly, it struck Jerrold. Tad was telling him things. Speaking openly to him, giving him information. Nothing of any importance, certainly; in fact, merely divulging what he did *not* know. But even that, when one clearly outlines the compass and measure of one's ignorance, could be a useful intelligence. The man was finally getting to him; it was lucky he had caught himself.

"Go on," Jerrold said softly.

"That's it."

"Well, I'll go on, then." He was absorbed and concentrated. "You've got it right, of course. They know you're picking them up—they mean you to. Every day a weather idiocy—until you call it nonsense, and the hell with it. Then one day you'll hear another piece of nonsense—*higashi no kaze ame.*"

"What's that mean?"

"East wind, rain."

"And that?"

Jerrold paused. "Are you going to pay me for this?"

Tad had come this far and couldn't stop. "You were right about the *Enterprise.*"

"Yes." He said it factually, not gloating. "I'll be right about this, too. If I'm not, don't give me a penny."

"How much?"

"I told you—your price."

"What does 'East wind, rain' mean?"

"I think it means 'War with the United States is imminent—get rid of your codes and papers.' "

"When do they start getting rid of codes and papers?"

"I don't know." He grinned. "We'll just have to wait for East wind, rain, won't we?"

"And I'll pay you when it happens."

Jerrold held his hands wide in a giving gesture.

"I'm in no swivet for my money—I trust you, Thaddeus." Unhurriedly, seeming to feel a new easiness with the commander, Jerrold walked to the edge of Tad's desk. "Now, I want you to stop being so edgy, Thaddeus, and sit down. And I'm going to sit down, too. And this time I'm going to give you a piece of information that you can check immediately. The minute I tell it to you. Would you like to hear it?"

"Go ahead."

"A short while ago, your people lost track of three Jap battleships—you knew about that."

"Yes."

"I have another development. Two carrier divisions—not one carrier, but two—not carriers alone, but divisions—*two Japanese carrier divisions* have disappeared from sight."

Tad tightened. "Is that true?"

"Absolutely."

"Missing for how long?"

"I'm not sure. Certainly since Friday, maybe longer." The Englishman's long face eased and rounded; his smile was beatific. "Time enough to come heaving into sight, what? Hello, Hawaii—*moshi, moshi, koi, koi!*"

"I take it that means aloha, in Japanese."

Jerrold nodded, chortling with glee.

What incongruities their vocation brought about, Tad thought. Here was a man telling him about the deployment of two massive seaborne armaments. If it was true that they had somehow slipped away from American surveillance, somewhere on the high seas a threatening thunderhead might be coming down on them. War might happen at any time. Tonight. And Jerrold, because he had performed his work astutely, irrespective of the disaster the information might signify, was tickled. Moreover, by the canons that judged his competency in this business, he had a right to be.

"You're certain of your information?" Tad asked.

"I trust my source without question."

"That's not what I asked."

"So will you."

"Trust your source?"

"Yes. You can check it this very minute," he responded confidently. "And if it's not as I say, you don't have to pay me."

"All right," he said. "What's your source?"

"Your desk."

Tad was confused. "Mine?"

Jerrold pointed to Tad's In tray. "Third from the bottom."

Tad rooted to the bottom of the pile. It was a four-page report from Schotley, dated Friday, November 28. The third item in the summary started, "Further to the Manila tracking of Japanese capital ships, please be advised . . ." It was cagily written so as to conceal the use of any private codes and ciphers; no mention of any specific agents or operatives was made, no reference to Rory Boyle. But there was no mistaking Schotley's smug certainty that he had accurate information. More important, there was no mistaking that Schotley was no longer going to be frightened about doing something unauthorized; the significance of the information warranted not only his taking a chance, but putting it in writing, for the record.

And the most grisly aspect: Tad had not even read the report. True, there were extenuations. The weekend had seen a death and a funeral. He was a man shaken by a grief and by a quickening of uncertainties in himself he thought he had long ago put to rest. His stomach hurt and his temper was frazzled. But he had never been incompetent.

He knew about incompetencies like this. Records of great import buried under piles of trivia; urgent memoranda sent to the wrong department; messages garbled, directives ignored, the wrong people sent to the wrong place at the wrong time, secret documents mimeographed and sent exposedly through channels and then, by the most disinterested default, unread by anybody.

Unread, like this one. He felt sick. He could sense how ashen he looked. Reaching into his desk, he brought out the voucher book. "I'll write a receipt for your money. You can sign it and take it to Herbstmann. He'll collect it and give you the cash." He started to write and stopped. "How much do you want?"

"As I said before—whatever it's worth."

"The Navy can't afford that much," he said. "Just give me a figure."

"There wasn't much time spent. A couple hundred will do."

He finished making out the voucher and handed it to Jerrold. The Englishman studied the slip of paper with the utmost care. He smiled wistfully and tore it up. "I can do better than that," he said.

Drearily, "I gave you what you asked for."

"What I've *been* asking for, Thaddeus, is a bloody sight more than that. And I've been offering more, too."

"I know."

"No, you don't know, you bumhole idiot! I've been offering friendship. And until today I thought I'd be getting the better of the bargain. But to have a look at your deathly face, I think you need a friend a ruddy sight more than I do."

Not looking at him, "That may well be."

Jerrold's head twisted and turned restively. "Do you have a drink in this wretched place?"

"No, I'm sorry."

The Englishman licked his lips elaborately. "I'll pretend I'm having another one. I've had two already. *Sake kofun*—know what that means?"

"No, I don't."

"Means I've got a *sake* hard-on. Enough drink for a boy, not enough for a man. Sufficient only for masturbation." Except that he was more disheveled than usual, he didn't look at all drunk; if anything, more grimly aware. "I've taken to drinking a bit earlier in the day than I used to. I'm forty-six years old, Thaddeus—tomorrow I dye my hair. Point is, I'm getting tired of collecting experiences—there are hundreds of them I'd like to give away. I've traveled rich, but mostly I've traveled mean. I know every dirty pigsty, every cathouse and outhouse, every wormy water closet in the world. I've had crabs in Rangoon and clap in Calcutta. There's too much world, Thaddeus, too goddamn much world to get sick in. And there's too much spite—from the tight-eyed waiters who won't give a table for two to a single person, to the kids at the depot who piss on your luggage. There are too many cold rooms, Thaddeus. And I'm scared."

He stopped talking and waited, seeming to want Tad to take it up from there. All he got was silence. He'd been looking away from the commander as he spoke, now he turned to face him. He smiled wanly. "I'm not such an ugly bastard as that cat trick would illustrate."

"Are you sure?"

"No, please—don't say that. I'm sorry about the cat. It was desperation. Don't say that."

A glimpse of the man struck him, a faint glimmering that had never entered Tad's head. And Jerrold seemed to guess. "I know what you're thinking," the Englishman said. "That I'm a fag." He was motionless, not an eyelash fluttering, as he waited for Tad's comment. When none came, he prodded. "Am I right?"

"Yes."

"Well, I'm not." His glance was steady. "I've been up and down that gravel—but it never worked. So I gave it up. Oh, long ago. The last time was a wonder out of heaven—a cherub. You've seen him in a hundred Renaissance paintings. He was the most loving, the sweetest— There wasn't a bone of cruelty in him. He was the ingenuous one—the total purity, in every room of the house. Except the bedroom. And there —holy mother—he made Krafft-Ebing seem like A. A. Milne. Yet it all played as naturally as running brooks. Softly, with a kind of innocence. He was the only person I've ever known who had no hatred in him—none—and I loved him very much. Except that the sick ferment, that son-of-a-bitching yeast was missing, that nasty little agitation between the sexes— I'm convinced it's the urge to kill—it just wasn't there. If you think of fucking as the life force—Christ, think of all the murder in it. Well, if it's not there, no matter how much sweet-love-be-gentle *is* there, it doesn't matter a shit. I've had women who've given it to me—the murder rage, I mean—women I've detested, mind you—and I could see myself spending endless days with them. Nights, anyway. But that boy, that guileless, fawn-faced boy—whom I loved so dearly—two weeks and he was unbearable. It was torturous to realize that I was unworthy of simple, Christ-given gentleness. And I was terrified at how much cruelty I might need. I couldn't stand it. So one morning, in broad daylight just like this, I beat him bloody and tried to kill him, and wanted to die . . . That was the last time I had it with a male. I don't intend having it again. I get my women when I need them, and have done with them. But not a friend in the lot . . . Christ, I need a friend, Thaddeus."

Tad was touched. And confused by his own susceptibility. He couldn't understand how the Englishman had managed to burrow through all the hard rock of his contempt and touch a tender spot, a compassion he never imagined himself feeling for the man. A bid for friendship. How unpredictable that he should find himself considering it. Yet, not so unpredictable: he could not recall, not once in memory, having turned away from an outstretched hand. And hell knew, his own hand had often gone empty. Even now.

He was on the verge of doing something, he didn't know what, saying something—perhaps simply offering to meet Jerrold later, for a drink—when he stopped himself. Whatever his compassions, whatever his own needs for companionship, he had to remember that the man was a liar, a traitor, a corrupt conniver shrewdly on the take, a cruel, diseased-cat man, not to be trusted.

"You did that very well, Jerrold."

The Englishman took the rejection without flinching. After a bit: "Self-righteous little bleeder, aren't you?"

"I suppose."

"So fucking incorruptible, aren't you? Let Him hang up there—don't throw the bugger a vinegar crumb."

"The analogy's not altogether exact."

"No, and you're not altogether incorruptible, are you?" he said viciously. "Where the hell were you?"

"When?"

"You know bloody well when. At the meetings of the grand jury, that's when."

"I wasn't called."

"Neither was I—but I was there."

"On whose side?"

"On the side of whatever they asked me."

"And you testified?" Tad asked.

"No, they didn't call me, I told you. And they didn't call you, did they? Nor the Winter women. Why do you suppose that was?"

Tad moved cautiously. "I don't know. Do you?"

Snapping, "Because they got touted off, that's why."

". . . By whom?"

"By whom? Don't pull my birdie, lad. By Kley, that's whom!"

He didn't reply for an instant. He mustn't lie, but he must be wary. "Kley was outside this case. He had no authority in it."

"Then why was he there?"

Perhaps he was misunderstanding the man, Tad thought. "Kley was where?"

"Where you weren't. Where the Winters weren't. At the grand jury sessions."

"When?"

"All day Saturday. Most of Sunday. Busy as a beagle."

"You're a liar."

Jerrold stopped talking. He stared. Then he lay his hand lightly on the In tray, where Tad had returned Schotley's report. "Well, there won't be a written report on it. But it'll be easy enough to find out, won't it? If you've got the gut to face the old man with it."

The Englishman started for the door. When he got to it, he turned and said, with practiced affability, "Too bad about the friendship, Thaddeus. But as the old tart said to the dangler—no hard feelings."

He heard the man's footfalls slowly receding down the corridor. Beware the impulse to telephone, he warned himself; don't blurt. On the other hand, don't delay too long. If you don't talk to Kley within, say, the next twenty-four hours, the energy will be vitiated. And whatever urgency there may be in what you know or suspect or dread may all dribble away into the files.

There was the possibility, as there was always the possibility, that Jerrold had lied, that Kley had not, in fact, attended the grand jury sessions. After having advised them—subtly instructed them would be more nearly true—to stay away, his presence would have been, at best, senescent meddling; at worst, a subversion of good faith. He couldn't bring himself to say betrayal because, in the cant of the trade, it was an absolute without extenuation. And perhaps there had indeed been some extenuation for the man's being there.

He had warned himself he might dissipate his resolution to beard Kley with the question; now he found himself doing it. Making excuses for the man even before he charged him with anything.

He called Kley's office. Wally Blackburn answered the admiral's phone. "Well, it's a rocky day," he whined. "Won't tomorrow do?"

"No—today," Tad said simply.

"I'll get back to you late in the afternoon."

"Tell me now, Wally, or I'll come right over."

The silence meant surprise or annoyance, or both. "Well, he's got a small hole at four-thirty."

"I'll be in the hole." He hung up.

Be calculated, he told himself. The old man is wily, don't tip your hand and don't make charges. Discuss your official business first—carefully, with facts, all you have, whatever you can pull together. Say as little as you can, imply with silence, keep your secrets. Don't deny too readily, don't put him off with negatives; they last longer than positives, they're indelible. What is most dangerous about them is that they quicken vigilance. Positives, on the other hand, lull suspicion, they beguile confidence, they seduce. Say yes, say it a lot, nod often, affirm.

He went to work, briefing himself on whatever had happened in the last few days. He scoured every report, every memorandum, voucher, scrap and snippet in his tray. A little after four o'clock he came to a scribbled note from Fellows.

It said: *Ushikawa called to say that over the weekend, on two occasions, each one lasting about three hours, black smoke was seen to be coming out of the chimney of the Japanese consulate. He wondered if you knew what it meant."*

It could mean they were burning up files and codes. It could mean that the East wind, rain signal had already been given. It could mean they were already too late.

"It's excellent work, Thaddeus—I must say it *is* excellent work." Kley was roseate. His congratulations couldn't be synthetic, they came too ebulliently, they made his office too small for the length of his stride and the expansiveness of his gesture. "I think it's remarkable what you get in that little tin shack of yours, with those three little ninnies and only a handful of stringers. How many stringers have you got?"

"On regular pay—six, I think."

"Remarkable." His appreciation was crescent. Tad watched it dilating, breath by breath, like a circus balloon. "And the *really* remarkable thing about it is just that. You got that information about the carriers by the use of only one or two people—right? And over here it probably cost us the work of a dozen men to get the same stuff."

To get the same stuff; they already had it. Tad's information was stale. The balloon had burst. But there was always the chance the shrewd old man was lying —for what reason, Tad couldn't guess. He might be trying to weaken him for a killing chore. He was often up to that trick: it was aye and aye and aye, then unexpectedly nay, put the commander in irons. "You already have the information?" Tad asked edgily.

"Oh, yes, my boy. Known about the carriers for days."

"You mean you've found them?"

"Oh, no—we've known they're lost." He chuckled. "It's delicious, isn't it?"

Delicious. He had smiled and used the very same word when Tad had told him the three Japanese battleships were missing. Tad couldn't guess why the tracking gaps were so delectable to him. This one seemed even more titillating than the other. The old man said, in his merriment, "Don't be distressed about it, my boy." The same charming condescension to the not-too-quick-witted son.

The admiral must have seen him bridle. "Now, Thaddeus, my lad, don't think I'm disparaging your work—I'm not. Hell, there's a high-ranking Intelligence officer—a lieutenant commander with all the men and tracking junk he's ever asked for—and *he* doesn't know where the damn carriers are either. You know who I'm talking about—it's Layton, of course. Two whole aircraft carrier divisions—where are they? He *mislaid* them!"

The old man laughed too loud; there was something wrong with it. Some hidden joke, perhaps, on Tad himself; the tumbler he drank from would spring a leak. "I think I've skipped something," he said.

Quickly, compunctiously, "Oh, I'm sorry, Thaddeus —I'm not laughing at *you,* for God's sake. It's a private joke—don't think about it—a private joke."

"It won't be private if two Jap carrier divisions come rounding Diamond Head."

A scream this time, a paroxysm of laughter. The old man's face went purple with it. He sat down but couldn't remain seated—the hilarity rocked the chair —he got up and stumbled to the window sill, convulsed, dying of it.

"You've hit it!" he gasped. Then, amid coughs and wheezes, "You've hit it! As if you were in the room— you've hit it!"

Tad waited. After a bit, the spell subsided. "That's exactly what Kimmel said," the old man spluttered. " 'Do you mean to say that they could be rounding Diamond Head and you wouldn't know it?' That's what he said to Layton and Layton shit."

"Don't you?"

"Shit? Hell, no." He was graver now. "And Kimmel doesn't, either. Nothing's coming around Diamond Head, boy—nothing. If Kimmel thought there was one little risk of that, do you think he'd keep battlewagons in the Harbor? All choked up behind a bottleneck channel where they can't move their bows or their bowels? You think he'd have given up Halsey's *Enterprise* and the planes? You think he'd given up the *Lexington?*"

The *Lexington* was the last remaining aircraft carrier in Pearl. "Is the *Lexington* gone too?"

"No, but it's bound to go, Thaddeus—we don't need it here."

On the verge of questioning Kley's self-assurance, he pulled back. He must keep his resolution in mind: the smile, the nod of soft agreement. "You're probably right." Slowly, testing to see how much the old man knew, "You're certainly right at the present moment. But there could be a change in the weather."

The reference to the weather meant nothing to Kley except confusion.

"Weather? What change is that?"

"East wind, rain."

"What the hell does that mean?"

He didn't know. He couldn't even pretend that he did. Slowly, now. "It's one of their codes."

"You've cracked it?"

"We think so, yes."

"Well?"

"When they flash the weather signal, East wind, rain, it means diplomatic relations with the United States are broken off—burn all codes and papers."

"Where'd you get that?"

"Jerrold."

"Then it's bullshit."

"Oh, I wouldn't say so."

"Wolf, wolf."

"The last time, there *was* a wolf."

Recalling Jerrold's *Enterprise* prediction made the old man waver. When he spoke, it was a bluster, too loud to carry real conviction. "If you got it from Jerrold, I tell you it's bullshit. You wait and see—nothing'll happen, nothing'll come of it."

"Something already has."

"What?"

"Over the weekend, they've been burning stuff at the consulate."

He had broken through. Kley gave him a quick glance, blinked once, suffered an instant of indecision, then went to the phone and called Blackburn.

"Who's doing the consulate?" he muttered. Listening a moment, he nodded once. "Bring in his stuff—up through last night." He hung up and turned to Tad. "Wally will clear the air."

Tad rather doubted it. Wally had a great knack for oversimplification. He took a genuinely complex problem and reduced it to kindergarten terms. Troubled heads were gratified by them. But when he went away, Wally had the promotion and the problem was still unsolved. Ben used to hate him; he said Wally sold more tickets than he had seats. Tad didn't like him very much either. The man suggested wrong tissues in the wrong places; an adenoidal mind. And he was overweight and always eating. He came in, this time, carrying a handful of blanched almonds and a manila folder. Chewing, he offered to share the late-afternoon provender.

Kley shoved it away. "Nuuanu Avenue. Who's on it?"

"Fushima inside and Carolyn McKuen across the street."

"And the phone line?"

Wally's head, more alert than usual, twisted birdlike to Kley, to Tad, then back to Kley again. "It's all right, Wally. Tad knows about the line."

Tad did. It was a tap the Navy shared with the FBI. He had heard that the Mutual Telephone Company, having gotten wind of it, had ordered it removed. Apparently it was still there.

"What happened over there this weekend?" Kley asked.

"Happened?" Wally looked puzzled. "Nothing happened."

"Lots of smoke was reported coming out of the consul's chimney," the admiral continued.

"Oh, that." Wally shuffled through his folder and came out with a typed sheet. "Yes—here it is. They were having a *maru yaki*."

"What's that?"

"A barbecue."

"A barbecue—indoors?"

"Oh, yes—they have them occasionally. It was quite a party."

"It happened twice," Tad said quietly. "Did they have two barbecues?"

"No," said Wally. "One burning to cook and one to clean."

"What did they burn?"

"Well, it was really Jap-Hawaiian. They had roast pig and a good deal of fish. They used corn husks, banana leaves, lots of coconut stuff, that fiber—what's it called—"

"Never mind." Kley shook a hand at him. "Did they burn any paper?"

"Not that I know of. No report on it anyway." Suddenly something occurred to him. He stopped. A shrewd look came to his face; shrewd and cautious. "You're not thinking of the other thing, are you?"

"What other thing?" Kley said.

"Well . . ." Blackburn was again reluctant. He had to have permission to go where he needed to go.

"Go on, go on." Kley's patience was wearing thin. "What other thing?"

"East wind, rain," Wally said confidentially.

Tad could feel his face flush with embarrassment. Tad had brought Kley two items of information; both stale. Kley knew everything; no wonder he was condescending. But . . . a strange thing. The old man said to Blackburn, with a touch of asperity, "You also knew about East wind, rain?"

"Oh, yes," Wally said. "Known it for days."

"Why the hell didn't you tell me?"

"I did, Admiral. End of last week. The report's in your tray."

It was Tad's turn. He exploded with laughter. He couldn't help it, and he couldn't stop. No matter how stormy the admiral's look was, it threw no cloud over his enjoyment of the moment.

But it didn't last. The enjoyment turned grim. There was the irony under his fingernails: Jerrold might have picked up the East wind, rain information right here, from Kley's own office; and Kley, when he had heard of it for the first time, had scoffed at it for the very reason that it had come from Jerrold; and unless Tad had brought it to the old man by *way* of Jerrold, the admiral would still be ignorant—of important information in his own tray.

Round and round, the spy business, spreading its social disease back upon itself. All that work, all that blood, that bad blood pouring through the bureaucratic trays, the In files and the Out, the memoranda through channels, nothing more important than anything else, everything losing its significance with neglect and the passage of time. Nobody taking the time to look at it, or not daring to; and those who looked not daring to select the trivial from the vital, for fear of making the wrong selection. Anybody who was rash fool enough to dare, like himself, might find he floundered into the wrong choice; he had come up with inaccurate information or spring-trap stuff designed to confuse and encourage another wrong decision, or intelligence so obsolete that its bearer was stigmatized as someone too inconsiderable to be kept up to date. The safest procedure was Wally's: do the work quietly, take nobody into your confidence, get the information, write it down so you've protected yourself, then bury it.

"Oh, yes, sir," Wally said, "it's been there three or

four days. Here, sir, I'll leave my copy in the folder."
He was talking through his mouthful of half-chewed
white almonds.

"Get out, you pig," Kley said.

When Wally left, the admiral had the good grace to
laugh. "See that? It's been treated as if it doesn't matter a damn. And you know what? It *doesn't* matter a
damn."

"I don't think you mean that."

"I don't?" He reached onto his desk, picked up the
manila folder Wally had left, and, without opening to
read it, handed the whole thing to Tad. "Here. I
haven't read a word of that—and no harm's been
done. The sky's still up and the earth's still down. No
shots have been fired. Nobody has blown a single
belch across the Pacific. So, just to prove I do mean it,
I won't read a word of that—and you can tear it up."

Tad held the folder, doing nothing with it. The old
man was making a silly, grandstand gesture, with an
empty deception at the heart of it: he could easily get
another copy from Blackburn.

"Go on, man—tear it up," the admiral said.

Silently, Tad put the folder back on the desk.

"No guts," said Kley.

"There's going to be a war, Admiral."

"You're paranoiac."

"That's what you told me to be."

"Selectively, my boy, selectively. Don't, for God's
sake, be suspicious of everybody."

"That's what paranoia is. By definition."

"Then let me tell you, by definition, there's nothing to be paranoiac about, by definition, because
there's not going to be any war, by definition."

"By whose definition?"

"Mine!" Kley flared. "Whose definition do you need
—the Japs'?"

"Yes—exactly."

"The paranoiac can't believe anybody but his ene-
mies!"

Tad mused over it. "That's probably true."

"All right, then—I'll give it to you straight from

the Japs—there won't be any war." He was poised now, ready for attack. "And you want to know why they won't wage war against us? *Because they know they're stupid!* They wouldn't bet their know-how against ours in a million years! They don't even trust their Intelligence! Because they know that even their Intelligence is stupid!" He didn't stop his diatribe to take credit, as he usually would, for his pun. "How many million spies have they got? Why, they've got these little islands crawling with those miserable yellow worms and their black cameras. The goddamn consulate alone— How many have *we* got in the embassy in Tokyo—a dozen, two dozen? How many have *they* got in their dirty little buildings at the consulate—over two hundred accredited employees and God knows how many in the kimono. And what do they get out of them? Monkey piss. Not a goddamn thing that they can't buy on a dollar's worth of postcards. Everything we've got here—it's wide open and free. They can look at it, they can diagram it, they can take pictures of it, they can smuggle it out in their jockstraps. We are exactly what we are—and they're too damn stupid to understand it. And you want to know why they're stupid? Because they can't think *straight,* only slanty. If we are what we pretend to be, then we've got to be what we're not, because they are what they pretend to be when they're not what they're not. Now, what does that *mean*—how goddamn mixed up can they get? Well, they can get so mixed up that they get scared—of themselves!"

He halted only momentarily, long enough to bring his voice down to a quieter level of seriousness. "And that's the second reason they won't go to war against us—because they're cowards. Oh, they've got plenty of courage when they're up against a fat-bellied, weak-headed cretin like China that doesn't know its muscle from its asshole. But they know they don't have the guts to go at *us.* Because they can't go the distance. They've got no money, they've got no credit, they're hungry, their supply lines are spread over half of Asia, their factories are made of rice paper and so are their houses! A Fourth of July fizgig will blow 'em to pieces." He paused and raised a lecturing finger. "But those are all practical reasons. There's another reason that scares the hell out of them and it's part of what they are—something in their sick kind of mysticism. It's called *yojin suru tatsunootoshigo*—and it means 'beware of the sea horse.' That's us—the most terrifying monster of them all—roaring up out of the sea—the one that never lost a war."

His emotion had run down now; he was carefully adjusting his voice to the pragmatic problem. "So they'll shout and stay hot for a while, but ultimately they'll cool off, the yellow fever will calm down, and they'll meekly sit down to a bargaining table like the short little people they are." He reached to the far corner of his desk and picked up the morning and late-afternoon newspapers. He spoke with quiet persuasiveness. "I'm of course not the only one who says this, Thaddeus. Please note what I've circled in blue pencil. This is datelined Tokyo, December 2. *'A government spokesman announced officially today that Washington negotiations will continue, and said that Japan was still hopeful of working out a peace formula.'* " He smiled benignly. "Well, of course they are. Here's another one. *'Japan Gives Two Weeks More to Negotiations.'* Excellent—but that's what they said last week, isn't it? And here's another one says the *Wall Street Journal* carried a front page survey that concluded *'economically Japan is living on borrowed time.'* Look at this: *'Kurusu has no alternative but to negotiate a quick settlement.'* And he will, Thaddeus —take my word, he will."

He tossed the newspapers back on the desk and carelessly threw Blackburn's folder into his In tray.

The man's self-certainty was too rock-bound for Tad to alter it by even so much as a hesitation of doubt. The admiral blue-penciled circles around the articles he wanted to believe, he searched for news that would fortify his position, he quested for any argument that would justify the conclusion he had already reached. Even if it was an argument he would ordinarily ridicule. Take the mythical one, for example. Here was a practical, hard-headed man talking about the thought processes of a practical, hard-headed nation—and quoting a mystical terror of sea horses. Anything was grist to his partisan mill, all the biases and predilections and warped prejudgments, all the bigotries he could adduce to make his position impregnable.

And he, T. Thaddeus Clarke, was, in his own way, doing exactly the same. Doing it daily in his work. If he was to get anything done, as an Intelligence investigator, he had to have a starting point, a hypothesis; there couldn't be such a thing as a tabula rasa; an open mind was an empty one—spies had stolen its secrets. And it was always the same hypothesis, no other was tenable: there *is* an enemy. Peacetime, wartime, anytime—there is an enemy. This could not be questioned as a provisional conjecture, it had to be accepted: fact. It was modified only by where you were stationed. If you were in the Atlantic, the enemy was Germany; in the Pacific, Japan. By the Intelligence that was deductive, going from the general to the particular, if Japan was our enemy, so was every Japanese, no matter where he might be. And since the United States had won every war in its history, its enemy was always inferior; ergo, the Japanese were an inferior people—smaller, more stupid, uglier, physically and spiritually yellow.

But contempt alone did not bring about a war. Terror was needed. Terror and contempt, what an anomalous amalgam, one emotion seemingly incompatible with the other. And because Kley could only feel disdain for the little Oriental, and not one quiver of apprehension, the amalgam was incomplete. Well, Tad thought somberly, he himself could supply the other emotion. He did not consider the Japanese inferior in any way; he had no contempt for them. But he was candidly frightened; he heard the threat of thunder in every silence. And it occurred to him dismally that he and the admiral were each supplying an emotion that, if combined, would make the deadly amalgam.

Kley was straightening the position of his desk clock although it needed no straightening. He was finished, the meeting was over. But Tad didn't leave. There was the grand jury matter. He had a bizarre image of himself becalmed in a dangerous harbor, every fathom mined. If he didn't get out, any moment his craft would be detonated. Then why didn't he simply go, make a run for the nearest exit? Certainly he had effected nothing by his report on the Jap carriers and East wind, rain, but he hadn't actually been hurt; had simply come off as behind-time, slightly ineffectual. If he stayed, however . . .

Kley was restless. "Is there something else?"

"Yes, there is."

"Well?"

"What did you say to the grand jury?"

Kley went to steel. "What?"

"You attended the grand jury sessions."

Snapping, "Is that a question or a statement?"

"I was told you were there."

"You were told wrong, Commander. I was indeed at the courthouse, yes. But I did not attend any grand jury session. Both times I was there, I was in an anteroom with one of the assistants to the district attorney."

"Doing what?"

He could see the old man on the verge of rushing forward, into the challenge. But then, reckoning more closely, Kley eased back. He even pretended geniality. "I don't have to answer your questions, Thaddeus, but I will. I was there as an amicus curiae."

"Whose friend at court?"

Measuredly, "Only the court's friend, my boy—that's what the phrase means."

"You were a friend of the court—in an anteroom?"

"It was as close as I dared to get."

"Apparently as close as you needed to get."

Kley's blandness didn't hide the threat. "Now look, Thaddeus, I don't think it'll serve your purpose to drop little stools of insinuation all over the place."

Tad envied the man's calm; his own was gone. "You kept us from going down there—Johanna, Abby —Ben himself. You lulled us into believing justice would be done—at least Tokan would be indicted. We weren't needed. Nobody was needed. Then, for Christ sake, what were *you* doing there?"

Still unruffled. "I think you'd better go, Commander."

"Go and do what? Find out?"

"As you like."

The old man had thrown the challenge and Tad had to take it. He turned quickly to depart.

"Wait a minute," Kley said.

As he turned to face the admiral, the latter's eyes were blinking more rapidly than before, but there was no faltering in the man. "I'm going to tell you what I did there. I simply let it be known—no more than this—I let it be known to the assistant that I was not speaking for the Navy, but it was my personal opinion that there had been a just quittance between the two men, since both of them had been injured. And I felt that to protract the affair would work hardship on everybody."

"You son of a bitch!"

"You will apologize for that as soon as I tell you something else." Then he said, with the malice of a curse, "Ben Winter was a pervert."

I'm feeling what Johanna must have felt, Tad told himself; the ungovernable impulse to claw at something; at this old man's patrician face. "Do you believe that, Admiral?"

"Yes, I do."

"And so, by putting an end to the Tokan business, you were saving the family—all of us—from the filth we'd be dragged through."

"That's right."

"In addition to whatever else I called you—you're a liar."

"Retract that!"

"No. If you weren't lying, you'd put me on report for calling you these names, wouldn't you?"

"I may still do it!"

"No, you won't, Admiral. Because you want this hushed up. Not for the family's sake. But for some other reason. I'm going to find out what that is."

Almost without animus, Kley said, "I wouldn't advise that, Thaddeus."

"I'm not inclined to take your advice. Nor do I have to, since this is a family matter and has nothing to do with the Navy."

Uninflectedly, "It has to do with the Navy."

The admiral glanced at the bank of files on the far side of the room, then, inexplicably, at the couch nearby. He seemed suddenly weary, as if he didn't want to have to proceed with the subject at hand, but would rather lie down. The couch must, in fact, have seemed inviting to him. It had a plump white bed pillow at one end, and a blue service blanket at the other. It was well known that the old man frequently worked late and napped often. He smiled at Tad, cheerlessly, seeming to sense that the younger man had guessed at his impulse to escape. But he didn't escape. He heavily turned from the couch, crossed the room and opened the top drawer of one of the files. Even then his purpose seemed unsettled. His movements slowed, he couldn't find the papers he was after, his hands ruffled aimlessly through the folders. At last he found what he was looking for, a red Fabrikoid envelope held together with a tie string. Not opening the envelope, he dawdled at the string. He was a fatigued old man who had ceded too much and was reluctant to go on with a bad bargain.

Finally he spoke: "There's a Jap information conduit we haven't been able to plug up. We don't know exactly where it ends—whether it's Jap Navy or diplomatic or Third Bureau. We have a better idea where it starts. Honolulu, possibly—Hilo, more likely. It's called the Purple Code—it's come up twice in one of the ciphers. But we don't know what's going *out* on it. We don't even know *how* it's going out. It may be telegraphic in a code that doesn't look like one; it may be a private wireless, a special machine, anything. It could be working from a dinky little sampan out there, or off the top of a mountain. In any event, we think Tokan's got something to do with it."

Tad felt a wave of resentment. Exiled to an office outside the Yard, he now had another item in the series of exclusions that galled him. "Why wasn't I told about this, Admiral?"

"Because it's not your project. It's not even your branch—it's Communications."

It was a contorted joke. No locks on the doors to bar the enemy, but locks between the services, branches, departments, sections, desks, to bar one's colleagues. Where it wasn't motivated by suspicion, it was plain jealousy, the self-centered protection of prerogatives, the miserly garnering of credits toward personal advancement. And the farce of it was: gaping leaks spouted jets of "secret" information everywhere. What information one could catch was a vagary of chance, utterly unpredictable. For example, when would he have heard about the Purple Code, if ever, were it not for his threat to go out on the inquiry, on his own?

Kley had managed, at last, to untie the string on the envelope. He withdrew a number of sheets of paper, all uniform, all carefully typewritten, a dossier compiled by the department, perhaps, or a single agent's report. The old man did not read from the sheets; seemed to be selecting carefully so as to reveal as little as necessary. "There's nothing we know about the man for certain. Even his name—Kano Tokan— it's not typically Japanese. Nothing about him can be absolutely authenticated—not where he comes from, not what he's doing here, not even what he *claims* to be doing here. He has a Jap government employment card, but he has no status with the Japanese consulate, and that's odd because they've given cover to every damn keyhole peeper who's asked for one. But Tokan has no cover. He claimed to have been a scientist—a volcanologist—he wrote a Japanese monograph on the subject of plutonism versus neptunism. Some obsolete nonsense about whether the earth was born in fire or in water. Well, that seemed like eyewash, and just as we were about to write him off as a science fake, we're told he's written a classic book on a mythological interpretation of geology. It's called *Born in Fire,* and it's all about volcanoes and how salamanders live in burning coals and how real life can start in lava that's still warm. Well, then—all right, he's a scientist—but suddenly we hear he's an importer. But is he? Yes and no. Books, art objects, scientific equipment and materials. Not very much of it and only token quantities of it for sale. Then where does the stuff go? Where does *he* go? He disappears every once in a while, totally disappears. We know he can fly a plane—he's got a Piper Cub and we've seen his papers. But where is it, where does he take off, where does he land? We picked him up once, on the Big Island—tracked him, I mean. Followed him to a little town outside of Hilo, then up into the foothills. And lost him. In a few days, he came down carrying bits of rock and lava and little sackfuls of cinder and ash. The same afternoon, he was tracked to a teahouse in Japtown. Two men saw him go in, nobody ever saw him come out. Toward sundown, a lot of that rock and lava—maybe all the stuff he brought down from the mountain—was found in a trash can outside the teahouse."

He smiled with what seemed as much bewilderment as it was embarrassment, restored the sheets to the Fabrikoid envelope, carefully tied the string, and put the envelope back in his file. "Now," he said, "what do you make of it?"

"Nothing," Tad said. "I don't see any relationship of anything to anything. Lava rock—scientist—Purple Code—salamanders—I don't see any starting point. Not even a justifiable suspicion that the man's been *doing* anything. All you've got is a complexity."

"A complexity that seems so deliberately confusing that there's a suspicion of mischief." Kley was continuing to illustrate the validity of one of his favorite opinions. "It's precisely in the Japanese character. They think it's smart to be complex—well, it's dumb. If they were doing something simple, we wouldn't notice it. But they can't trust themselves to do something simple. It's think and double-think and quadruple-think—in the hope they'll lose us on the way. And what happens? *They* get lost. And we catch the little bastards—in their own goddamn little maze. And that's where we'll find Tokan."

The contempt again. As if Kley were, as he once described himself, as simple as an egg. He enjoyed the same complicated rope-tic game as they did, twisting in his connivances and contrivances, getting lost in his own labyrinths, warily turning every corner to confront the enemy stranger, frequently himself.

The old man concluded quietly, "So you see, Thaddeus . . ."

"That we have to let him go?"

"Yes, until we know what the hell he's up to."

"I would like to be assigned to him."

The old man weighed it. "I can't do that, Thaddeus."

"Why not?"

"Your motives aren't altogether . . . pure."

"No, that's right. I hate the bastard."

"Then you're no good for it. We don't want him hurt. We're not out to get him for an atrocity attack, Thaddeus. Only for information."

Trying to keep the challenge out of his voice, "I'll go for him anyway. On my own time."

"No, you won't, Mister," Kley replied. There was no edge in his voice, he had no need for sharpness; he was in command. "You're under orders not to."

"Admiral—"

"I can put it in writing. Will that be necessary?"

Tad's hands went cold; there was sweat on them. He was being told it was now a Navy matter, and only that. Had he not been given the confidential information, had he himself not demanded it, he would still have had some freedom to consider the affair a personal one, a family affair. But now his superior officer had locked him in. Tad wondered if the shrewd old bastard hadn't maneuvered all of it, hadn't enticed him into a port he could blockade. However he had gotten there, he was being reminded he couldn't move, he was not a free agent; he needn't upbraid himself for being timid or praise himself for being bold. Choice was out of his hands; he was under orders. He couldn't make his own decision.

And, blessedly, he didn't have to. For, as Johanna might have put it, Poppa had said no.

"No, sir," he said. "That won't be necessary."

"At twilight," Abby said, "I can be had by anybody."

She was standing at the railing of the terrace, looking down at the mauve channel and, beyond it, the last swaths of scarlet and vermilion where the sea became the horizon. Dinner had been early, the dishes were already cleared away. Only one cup remained on the table, Tad's. He drank the last drop in it and studied the grounds.

"By anybody," Abby continued. "Men who wear fountain pens in their outside breast pockets or use toothpicks in restaurants or put feathers in their hatbands or ketchup on their eggs."

"If you prefer that kind, I'm afraid I don't qualify."

"Not preference, really," she said. "But anything at twilight."

"I think I qualify for 'anything.'"

As he got up and moved behind her, she didn't turn but kept looking at the sunset. He pressed himself to her back so that he could feel the hardness of her shoulder blades against his chest and the softness of her buttocks against his loins; it was oddly gratifying, these opposite textures of pleasure, and he held her tightly, bringing his arms to the front of her, folding them on her belly.

"Touch me," she said.

He raised his left hand to her breast. "It's seven o'clock."

"If seven's a magic number, I'm feeling it," she said.

"So am I."

"I'm feeling you feeling it."

"Pure imagination," he said.

"No, it's a hard fact," she replied. "What's your right hand doing?"

"Not letting my left hand know."

"Is it telling anyone else?"

With his right hand, he reached under the waistband of her skirt. The band was too tight, then miraculously it wasn't. He touched one mound of softness, then a smaller one.

"I'll meet you somewhere," she said, and went indoors.

One moment passed another and still he didn't follow her. He was looking down at the Harbor; that is, he thought he was looking down at it until he realized he wasn't seeing anything, hadn't noticed ship, sea or shore. There was nothing between him and the horizon and, for the moment, nothing inside him either. The instant she had gone, the desire had gone with her. He had not felt well all through dinner. Not stomach ache, not head, nothing you could throw a pill at; not a palpable pain, only a botheration.

The benignity of having Kley take decision out of his hands—decision and the responsibility for action and potential culpability for failure—had turned into a doubtful blessing. If wars are to be fought successfully, they had been told at Annapolis, obedience was the first postulate: let your superiors make the decisions . . . But there were other wars. And whatever unruly spirit he had to battle within himself—was Kley to fight that for him too? Making decisions was the daily work of a man's mind and will, and self-respect was the paycheck. How much of the paycheck could he turn over to the head of the family? How badly did he need the family's support? Who was supporting whom? How long, for Christ sake, would he have to go on battling his goddamn unfamilied childhood?

Then, when Abby went to the railing and he could see her figure outlined against the sunset, another disturbing image had struck him. Holding her, in that moment of excitement, she was her mother. A glimpse of Johanna, the flurry of gauze and flesh against the light, the breasts in silhouette . . . And now, standing here alone at the edge of the terrace, a flush of guilt. The daughter in the bed, the mother naked . . . Again, the decision not made, the action blunted . . .

It was dark. He could barely see the ocean any more. How long have I been out here, he wondered, and what is she thinking? He turned to go in and saw her leaning against the jamb of the open door. She was naked, and he had no notion how long she had been there. Seeing her, he turned slowly and went back to the railing. After a while, she stood quietly beside him, not too close.

"Where did the man go?" she said.

"I don't know, love." He saw her shiver a little in her nakedness. "You'll catch cold out here."

"Then come and warm me."

Slowly she came closer to him, and he wasn't sure whether she wanted the warmth of love or the heat of it. She touched his cheek. "Come and lie on top of me," she said.

"I . . . don't think so."

"Don't do anything. Just lie."

"I'd want to do something, and not be able."

She didn't say it with irritation; in fact, tenderly: "What's eating you?"

He winced at the expression, however gently it was said. Not because it was a tired question but because it was too literal. Eating me? The rat, the rodent terror that eats the cowardly flesh. But then, if he were to confess it, what would he say if she asked what he was afraid of?

"It's nothing, darling. Just the gut—not much, a little."

The convenient lie. He suspected she didn't believe him, but there were certain truce lies that had to be accepted—time out for illness—and she accepted it. In a few minutes, he saw the light go on in the bedroom and he heard the radio playing softly. She would be reading now . . .

What's eating you? No, not a stomach pain. He wondered what name could be given to an ulcer of the soul. It was a permeative low infection of the spirit: dread. Not even fear, nothing so clearly focused, nothing manageable with rebuke. It was as if his muscles weren't muscles and his brain not meant for thinking.

I am a coward, he thought.

No, it was too horrifying—and the charge was unjust. He had done nothing to be ashamed of. He had refused to join Johanna's vendetta because he thought it was an ill-considered one, bound to harm everybody. And he had stood up to Kley until the last ditch; until, in fact, he had been ordered away. He must stop chastising himself for being relieved at not having to charge into battle. It was not his decision to make; it was the way of the armed forces, the perverse answer to the military conundrum. Safety in the services, it was called; just follow orders and you're snug on the hearth. And to someone who had grown up in strange houses, who had spent his childhood awakening in the night of frightening bedrooms, the snugness of the hearth was not to be denigrated. And, considering how little he had started with and how hard he had toiled, he was entitled to a modicum of snugness.

Then be happy with it, he told himself. You needn't be a rebel hero. Or a hero of any kind. Contrary to every catchword, the Navy does not survive on heroism but on order. The people who issue and those who execute. An echo from Annapolis parroted in his mind:

"*And what,*" inquired the ensign, "*is the order of the day?*"

"*The order,*" said the captain, "*is obey, obey, obey!*"

Well, he was obedient, and he had the snug hearth for his reward. If he had aches he could not diagnose, so had everybody else. If he had been a love-rejected child, he was not a love-rejected man. He rebuked himself for weeping in a lonely child's country. Stop looking back; look out there, at the beauty of the Harbor.

It was indeed beautiful. Down, down, a thousand feet below, the ships lay still in the starlight. How clean, how fastidious, how innocent they looked. He knew what monsters of murder they were; how their distance from their quarry lent them blamelessness; how even the *sound* of death rarely came back to the killer behemoths; how they could slay and still sail coolly into the chill sea, and slay again. But nighttime, now, with the wind so soft and the distance so far, how guiltless they looked. He loved them, and they were one of the compensations for doing what he did for a living, and for being what he was. He yearned toward them and longed to go to sea in one of them, to have his own command. And he had been twice told, as he himself had told Ben: you're too valuable where you are. Perhaps, if there's a war . . .

He hadn't noticed how late it was. The light in the bedroom was out, the radio had gone to quiet. Abby would be asleep by now, and it was time for him to go to bed.

The phone rang.

He hurried indoors, trying to catch it before it awakened Abby with its second ring. He whispered hello as softly as he could. The voice he heard was on the edge of sounding familiar, but he could barely understand the words. Then he recognized the asthmatic wheeze.

"You'd better get here," Karli said in his muffled voice. "Or something could happen to her."

"To whom?"

"Mrs. Winter." Then quickly, to make it clear, "Your mother-in-law."

"Happen? How?"

"She's in Japtown. She shouldn't be here."

"Where in Japtown?"

The phone clicked. For a moment, he thought of calling back, to get more information, but he knew it would be useless—he probably wouldn't be able to get at the man; if he did, Karli wouldn't add even one more syllable of intelligence.

Tad felt a flare of rankling anger. If Johanna was in trouble, she had brought it on herself. Anyway, what the hell could he do about it? He had no idea what sort of trouble it might be or where he could find her. Japtown was not big, but you just didn't go parading into Japtown, shouting where's Johanna?

Besides, he was under orders: hands off. That was his excuse—no, it was his *reason*—for doing nothing. Which was what he was doing: totally immobilized. He couldn't make himself start undressing, and he couldn't make himself leave the house. Yet he knew he would have to reach a decision, and he knew equally well that no matter what his decision turned out to be, he would be sorry for it. Kley stayed in his mind. The only course of action he was permitted was: go to bed.

He entered the dark bedroom. He could tell by Abby's breathing she was asleep. Soon he too would be asleep, no need for decision, the day mercifully at an end. He started to unbutton his shirt. Just as he was about to take it off . . .

What if Johanna was really in danger?

He stood there, doing nothing for a moment. Rebuttoning his shirt, he started out of the bedroom.

Eleven

ON TUESDAY NIGHT, when Tad departed, Johanna was certain he had left something behind, a material thing, an object on a table, perhaps, tangible. She thought at first it might be a pipe; men were always leaving pipes. But she knew well enough that he didn't smoke, and if he did, he would never leave a sign of it behind him, not so much as an ash. As she went to bed, she reflected that it might not be anything concrete he had forgotten to take with him, but a scent. That too was unlikely, however, for she recalled that he never smelled of shaving lotion, he had no addiction to peppermints or wintergreens, no inclination to savory soaps, nothing to leave an essence she could identify. Yet, all through the night, whenever she awakened, which was often, some evanescence clung to her, and she sensed his presence like a musk.

In the morning she knew what it was. He had left the odor of doubt in the air. It was an anesthetizing vapor, not only subduing her painful need for revenge but threatening to lull her into a deadly sleep. All day she languished in the miasma of it, as if locked in the garage with the motor running, waiting for the final drowsiness to overcome her.

Only once, in the middle of the day, did any emotion awaken. She saw a small boy, on an island somewhere, jump out of a dinghy with a pail of dead fish in his hand and run, screaming a joyous triumph into the house.

"Ben—dammit—don't bring those stinking things into the living room."

And, remembering, she began to cry. Tears: what a waning of the spirit. Where had all her hot rage gone, the great fury that could have fulminated through the mountains; how had it been devitalized to this feebleness of tears? Better to have no emotion at all than the self-pity of grief.

Then, toward evening, something happened. The *Star Bulletin* arrived. There was, of course, nothing in it. The Tokan case was over. No loose threads to catch up, no afterthoughts, no backward glances of any kind. Nothing more would be done. A boy would lie, unavenged, in a sandy Hawaiian grave. The grievers could go on grieving; they could neither add nor subtract anything to the weight of matters; tears were light on the scales of justice.

Only rage mattered. Not the kind she had experienced yesterday, the hot madness that boiled the blood and addled the mind, making muscles quiver ineffectually.

Only cold fury. The kind that makes a woman dress slowly and with care.

She parked her car on Beretania Street, the other side of the Stream, and walked the long distance into the darker part of the city. Hurrying, she caught a glimpse of herself in a store window and realized her gait would give her away; she didn't move like a tourist. Abandoning the long-stepped, purposive stride, she took to stopping aimlessly from time to time, looking into the open doorways of shops still open at night, and at the action pictures in the display case outside the Chinese movie theater—a traveling lady making a haphazard night of it.

When she turned toward the wharves on Maunakea Street, the faces became more Oriental and the street lamps fewer. A number of turns and she was in still darker places. Now she was on a side street, a dim one, where the last store alight was a tattoo parlor. Through its window, in dismal illumination, she saw a bare-armed American sailor being needle-painted by an elderly Chinaman. It occurred to her how discrepant it was for the scholarly-looking old Asian gentleman to be pricking a teen-aged Yankee with *Chuck loves Millie* or *Anchor's Aweigh*. Past the tattoo parlor, when she rounded the corner, the street became narrow. Abruptly, in her mind, she was back in Tokyo, the wrong side of the Ginza, as Oscar used to say, twisting her way in a frightening webwork.

It looked so different tonight from that early evening when Jerrold had brought her here. Yet she was certain, despite the devious route the Englishman had taken her, that she hadn't forgotten it, hadn't lost her way. And Nishi's camera shop should be easy to find, for it was open at night; it had been open on the evening Jerrold had introduced her to the Japanese, the only lighted store on this dark street. If this indeed was the street. But there was no sign of the shop, no glimmer of light out of any store window, and no other illumination, either, down the whole length of the narrow thoroughfare.

It was getting chilly and she was apprehensive in the darkness. Any moment, she suspected, she would feel the dread of unseen presences, of lurking things. But as her eyes began to pick objects out of the blackness, she became more and more convinced she had come to the right place. Distinctly she recalled the two herb shops, side by side, the tea-importing store, the empty, boarded-up building that had once been a garage. But then, by these landmarks, at the end of the street, on the other side, less than a hundred yards away, there should be the Nishi store. And there wasn't. All she saw was a wall of blackness.

She started toward the wall. Not half the distance away, she caught a hint of what it was. Not a fixed wall but a corrugated metal gate, its ridges horizontal. She had seen many such closures on storefronts in Paris. The night safety door, let down in the evening, rolled up in the morning.

Still across the street, she saw the small white sign. It would be a night message of some sort; information in case of emergency. She hastened to it. A foot square perhaps, cardboard, tacked to the wooden doorframe, the little placard was lettered in English and Japanese. But the letters were too small and there was not light enough. She reached into her purse, pulled out her cigarette lighter and snapped it aflame. NOTICE, the English words said, G. NISHI & SON—OUT OF BUSINESS.

As simple as that.

She smiled grimly. What had she any right to expect? Tokan-san had certainly not promised it would be easy. Out of business. Gone. Paid off and sent away, halfway across the Pacific, likely, en route home.

She had better be en route home herself. She shivered at her own foolishness. How naïvely she had approached the whole enterprise, as if simple action carried its own guarantee of accomplishment. She had had such contempt for her own inertia that she had broken out into a flurry of busy-ness. She felt her folly like a rash all over her body. Go home, she told herself, sit down and think at least one headache's worth, think it through, go home.

She walked to the opposite end of the street, not the way she had come. As she turned the corner, she found herself treading on old lava rubblestones, the kind she thought had entirely disappeared from the streets of the city. There was a flickering street lamp here, an obsolete one, gas fired, guttering like candlelight. It cast shadows, then snatched them back again, quick flares of brightness, gone, returned. She walked carefully; the paving was rutted and uneven. The night stillness was a tactual thing, it had materiality, close and uncomfortable, like something too tight to wear.

Suddenly, rending it, a crack of sound, a cannonade like machine gun fire . . . and stillness again.

She stopped, she didn't move.

Again the sound, seeming to reverse itself. She knew what it was: the metal gate, being lifted, then dropped again.

Turning, she ran back toward the corner. Within one step of it, she pulled herself to a halt and hung back in the shadow. Holding her breath, as if it would make her smaller to do so, safer against detection, she peered down the dark street, toward the entrance of the camera store.

Two men. One of them, Nishi. He was bending to lock the metal gate. The other one smoked a cigarette through a holder so long that it made the glow seem to have no relation to the smoker. He was an elephantine man, enormous in height and girth, and she thought of a *sumo* wrestler she had seen in Osaka.

Nishi straightened up and they started to walk. They were coming in her direction; her heart began to pound. This was what she had come for, she reminded herself, to see Nishi, and here he was. But she had come to see him alone, a man behind a counter, or in a back room where they might talk of bracelets and money and what arrangements could be made. She had not come to see him in the presence of a *sumo* mountain, on a nighttime street.

They were coming closer. Run, she told herself. But she was afraid her footsteps would be heard.

Their voices were nearer now. The enormous man was doing most of the talking. She hung back against the building, praying they would cross the street and not turn the corner.

Nishi murmured something and she couldn't understand his muffled Japanese, but his companion spoke clearly and was thanking him for something. His voice, unexpectedly delicate for a man so large, flowed sweetly, like *ame uta,* rain song.

Closer.

Silent now, they approached the corner. But they didn't turn it, they crossed the street. Her tension let up, she allowed herself a deeper breath. As they got farther and farther away, she felt how inappropriate it was for her to be feeling a release that was in direct proportion to the distance from her quarry. She was forgoing the very encounter she had come for. All because she was so uncertain: she articulated to herself no specific plan, no strategy of any kind.

She forced herself to make one. She would follow them, she decided, hanging close to Nishi until some time, whatever time it might be, that he went home. She could handle him better at home. If his wife was there, the woman might be a help rather than a hindrance, for Johanna would have familial things to say, she would fall back on what wives feel about their husbands, and mothers about their children; she would search out the Japanese way of it. She would talk of honor and justice, how they had to be weighed only in terms of equitable revenge. She would demonstrate that she, as much as they, had a regard for Tokan's dignity, but that *chu* had to be balanced against *giri,* the greater obligation against the lesser; that pain had to be measured against pain, its depth and its duration and the number of people who felt it. She would know how to talk to them; she had learned how and she had a talent for it. Money was not the only thing she had to rely on, although she would not hesitate to use it. There would be vivid expressions of sentiment and, perhaps most potent of all, family self-respect, the *jisonshin* that Nishi would want to display in front of his wife so that she would be proud of him and not turn her eyes down, to "the low-moving things."

Johanna slipped out of the shadow. They were almost a block away. She mustn't get too close, but she would have to hurry to keep them in sight. Walking rapidly, she experienced a thrill of pleasure at her own motion.

She was proud, too, of something else. Nearly always, when she was faced with a task, the plan refused to precede the action but presented itself only—as it had tonight—when she was in the midst of the undertaking. Sometimes the plan came too late, when the emergency was over, and she would reproach herself with might-have-beens. But she needn't scold herself tonight, for on this occasion, she had caught herself just in time; had made herself stop, collect her resources, and construct a scheme. And it was a good scheme too, she was pleased with it; it was simple to the edge of artistry and it was, best of all, within the scope of her talents.

She had shortened the distance between her and the men, just far enough away to see them. Her step was surer now, she almost felt she knew where she was

going; and she had confidence that she would lose
sight of neither the men nor her course of action.

Then she lost them. For a whole block—and not an
altogether dark one either; there was a street lamp in
it—she saw no sign of them nor did she hear their
voices. But as she turned the third corner, they were
there.

This time they were not walking. They stood halfway down the block, in front of a dimly lighted building, talking in quiet tones, seeming undecided whether
to go in. The looming edifice looked like a mistake,
somehow, unaccountably out of its appropriate atmosphere. Its façade, a false one, towered over the
others in the street. It had no windows and its portal
was like the *torii* gate to a Shinto shrine, a lovely
curved lintel extending past the heavy-timbered door-
posts. Hanging from each end of the gracefully curved
crossbeam, a stone lantern cast flickerings on intricate
woodwork, gold leaf and vermilion. Everything was
wrong with it; the wrong country and the wrong
neighborhood; too large for the buildings surrounding
it, too chromatic and too vivid. Yet the arched
portico had such a lift of wings, the lintel turned so
subtly skyward, all the lines shimmered so tentatively
in the air, that old temples came to Johanna's mind,
with nostalgic remembrances of tinkling wind chimes
and tiny bells as delicate as if they were not real but
tuned only to her fantasy.

A large door opened, a spill of light cast the men's
shadows on the pavement, they entered, and the street
was dark and empty again.

For an inconsidered moment she had the impulse to
follow them indoors. She didn't, but set her mind into a
new frame: waiting. Whatever they were doing inside,
whatever prayers, whatever offerings they were laying
on altars, couldn't take too long. But she did have one
misgiving. If there was another doorway to the place,
if Nishi didn't depart the way he entered, she would
lose him.

Slipping out of the shadows, she hurried to the portal.
The lanterns showed no other doorway on the front of

the building, nor any alleyways on either side. But if the building went straight through to the next street, there might be another doorway in the rear. However, if she took the time to go around the corner to investigate, they might come out the front way and depart while she was gone. Even so, if she ran, going and returning, she would still catch sight of them.

She started to run, then stopped herself: some eye might be gazing out a blind window; some ear might hear the racing footsteps. Softly.

The shrine did not go through to the back street. The block was solidly built up, without alleys or courtyards. Where the temple might have gone through—but didn't—there were a dry-goods store and a doll shop with kimono-clad marionettes in the window and huge silken *ayatsuri* puppets.

Hastening back as silently as possible, she looked down the street at the portal. Out of breath, she turned one direction, then the other. No sign, not anywhere, that the men had come out of the building; the street was as deserted as before.

But the emptiness did not last. There was a sound. Not ahead of her, where the shrine was, but behind her; it was there, no question about it, with the impact of dread certainty, and she knew she was being followed. With mounting terror, she didn't dare look back for fear her very glance would make her pursuer more real, more menacing. At last, deriding herself as a quaking jelly, she turned to stare into the darkness. There was nobody.

But the incident warned her to find some hiding place, out of view. She found one, a dark alcove across from the temple, a square recess made between the plate-glass windows of a travel agency, where she could hang back, waiting and unseen. But waiting came hard to Johanna, she hated it. She invented word games she could play alone, she tried to puzzle herself with numbers. What she wanted more than anything was a cigarette; she didn't dare light one.

She heard a cough. She was sure of it. A wheezing cough.

As quickly as caution would allow, she edged to the outside corner of the alcove. Looking through the right angle made by two plates of window glass toward the corner from which she had most recently come, she thought she saw a shadow move. Then, stillness. Worried about being seen, she was about to slip back into the depth of the alcove when she heard the cough again, rasping, asthmatic, a choking sound.

But it was night illusion, she told herself. A wind had come sweeping in from the sea, a winter wind, noisier than usual. She could have been totally mistaken about the shadow; the street lamp flickered and flung dark presentiments everywhere; the shadow wasn't real. Perhaps, she reconsidered as the silence held, the cough had not been real as well.

She had a more sobering worry. She had been here a long time, over an hour, she would have guessed, waiting, and the men had not emerged from the temple. The alarm struck her that they had indeed departed in the few minutes it had taken her to go around the block, and they had hurried out of sight before her return. She had botched it. Yet, she couldn't believe it had happened in such a short time.

She had to find out. Against all her better judgment, against her best-laid scheme to stand apart until Nishi went home, she determined to go inside the building.

She darted across the street. Approaching the huge door, she hoped it would not be locked, that she wouldn't have to ring a bell and clang to the world that she was putting in an appearance. On the other hand, if the place was a temple— She had known a Shinto shrine, in Kobe, the doors of which were never locked.

It was open. But it was not a temple. It was a crematorium.

The first perception was incense, an odor to dispel odors, acrid and sharp as an assault, a purifier that hung a sickly taint on the air. Out of this redolence— was it balsam or aloes or the camphor laurel she used to smell in the teahouses?—light came. Not much light, only nebulas from the low-glowing embers in the charcoal-burning braziers at the four corners of the large room. The unsteady rays played on the paneling of the room, gravures of bronze. One wall was a bronze screen through which, barely discernible, the two steel ovens were at rest now, their doors open, their coke fires banked low.

As Johanna's eyes became accustomed to the dimness, she saw that, as well as being a crematorium, the place was a general mortuary. Two catafalques were placed side by side in the center of the room, the platforms low, barely a foot off the floor. She thought, at first glance, that they were both empty, but in a moment she noticed the dark-gray casket on the far one, to the right. The flames from the nearest brazier threw flutterings of light upon it, like silk banners, across the dead woman's face; it was an old face, not as serene as death is said to be. The only movement in the room, except for the light, was the slow rocking of the old man. He sat on the floor, one hand in his lap, the other clinging to the edge of the cheap little coffin. He made a low mumble as he rocked. Johanna wondered if the old man knew he was crying, whether he would call it by that word; perhaps it was only a memory of heartache, its presence faded. He will be permitted by the ritual to cry only for tonight, Johanna remembered; tomorrow, when the coffin is interred, he must cry no more. The man moved his hand on the casket, touched the rice bowl he was sending with her, touched the household knife, the branch from the *sakaki* tree, and whispered something to the dead woman, reminding her perhaps not to forget to take things with her. Then he went to rocking again.

There was nobody else in the room. No Nishi, no enormous man.

Walking to the rear of the crematorium, she came upon an archway that led into a narrow arcade. As she was about to enter it, a youngish man came out of the shadows. He wore a black robe that imitated priestly ones, with a fine satin collar embroidered with peacocks and reeds. He would be, as Mitsu once told her, the *kaso-otoko,* the cremation man. He looked sleepy and apologetic. Bowing more deeply than an American's status demanded in such a place, he told her in English that he hadn't heard her enter. Was there, as he put it, a matter for him to do?

She murmured Nishi's name. He looked at her blankly and she repeated it. When he still looked puzzled, she thought he might not understand English, except for the rote questions he had asked, and she spoke to him in Japanese. The cremation man thought about it; no, he didn't know any man by the name of Nishi, nor had any such man visited the crematorium this evening, nor a fat man either. She would not have believed his bewilderment if it had not been accompanied by his stricken expression. He was punctiliously Japanese and, having been unable to answer a question that properly related to his own domain, he had been caught in a failure; his humiliation was not only abject, it was genuine. Elaborately she went through the observance of taking the blame upon herself, gave him the opportunity of a conclusive bow or two, and turned her back to him. As she was departing, the onslaught of the incense hadn't eased and the heat of the room was suffocating. She would be glad to breathe the fresh air again.

The wind was even higher than before. She could hear it rustling somewhere in trees she couldn't see.

She didn't see the mammoth either. One instant he wasn't there; the next, he came hulking out of the shadows toward her. It was more an embrace than an attack, a huge arm around her, loving the breath out of her body. She felt herself crushed against the enormity of his cumbrous grossness, the sponginess of his fat giving way to her body and finally not giving way at all.

She tried to cry out, but his hand was on her, not on her mouth, but on the back of her neck, and her pain couldn't give voice. The fingers held the agony at the base of her head, gripped it, ground the punishment into the bone until the hurt itself was gone. Nothing came in its place. A flare of light, perhaps, nothing more. And when the flare was gone, only darkness.

She smelled the incense, stronger than before. Then she heard the sound. The cough. Much closer now, as close as if it were her own. Perhaps it was indeed her own, so private was it, and there was no one else in the room who could be doing it, and no one to tell her whose it was.

The couch she was lying on was too soft; it made turning difficult. Her head ached. More accurately, her neck, in the back, at the start of her hairline. Without getting up, she looked around the room. It was small and cramped, with too much furniture and all of it too heavy, a collector's room, full of bric-a-brac, ivories, cloisonnés, boxes of marquetry and brass, and tiny lamps with colored bulbs in them, palest amber, beads hanging from the shades.

She was worried about being there and thought about getting up. She wondered if she could. Without arising, she tried her body, moving her arms, her legs, turning a little. The ache wasn't general, only in her head, not much worse than a hangover, she told herself, nothing to make her feel so miserable.

She heard the cough again. Not hers. There was a faint stir beyond the doorway, in the next room. She had been wrong about being alone. The cough turned into a wheeze, the same sound she had heard in the street.

She could barely descry the figure now. It was bent over in some awful way—it might not even be human, she thought, there was no face to it, no head, only a darkness like a shawl, hooding the top of the creature, whatever it was. Now she saw the fumes and smelled the incense again, stronger than before. Tincture of benzoin, she said, and she had remembrances of children inhaling the stuff to alleviate the huskiness of sore throats and laryngitis.

The shawl was lifted and she saw the man. He was middle aged and cadaverously thin. His face was wreathed with the sweat-steam from the hot basin. Sitting on a high stool, leaning over the sideboard, he coughed more gaspingly now and she thought he was strangling. The coughing stopped and he spat into a gray cloth that he set on the sideboard beside the basin. The shawl was not a shawl but a great brown towel with which he wiped his perspiring face and neck, then his thinning gray hair.

He saw that she was awake and he muttered something. A door opened somewhere behind him, cutting an oblong of light, and Tad appeared. He was carrying a tray with coffee cups and a pot on it.

"Is she all right?" he said to the man. Then, realizing she was conscious, "Are you all right?"

"I think so," she replied. "What happened?"

"I don't know." He pointed. "This is Karli—he phoned me. When I arrived, you were already here."

Her head was still a confusion. "How did I get here?"

Tad turned to Karli. "Go on—tell her." The man started to move away; he had no inclination to talk. "Go on."

Karli changed his mind and spoke. "I saw the big man. When he left, I tried to pull you out of it, but you wouldn't wake up. So I started to carry you—well, I didn't get very far—I began to lose my breath. I left you in an entryway on Pauahi Street, went across the Stream to Lono's taxi stand and told Lono you were a friend, you were drunk. Then we went back and picked you up and Lono helped me get you up the stairs. You just lay there—you didn't move."

"The big man," Tad asked. "Who was he?"

"I don't know." Karli went back into the darker area, lifted a teakettle and poured more hot water into the basin. Then he got up on the high stool again and sat close to the sideboard. As he did, Tad explained, "He has asthma."

Karli said, "I'm taking a breather." She gathered it was an oft-repeated expression, meant for humor. It sounded ghoulish. Then, more to himself than to anyone else, and entirely without complaint, "I'm not supposed to be out at night. Night air is dangerous."

"You're sure you don't know who the big man was?" Tad asked again.

Karli's voice was a monotone. "How many times do I have to tell you. I don't know anything."

"You knew enough to save her life."

Karli spoke with quiet finality. "Give her some coffee and then you better go, the both of you."

His words sounded Mainland, from anywhere in America, she thought. But, despite the rasp of his ailment, his voice had a lilt to it, a little singsong of the Islands. It wasn't only his illness that made his cheeks sink haggardly, it was the width of his cheekbones; there was a breadth of Asia in them.

Tad had placed the tray on the table beside her. She was sitting straight and not minding it too much. Looking up, her eyes thanked him for the coffee. She wanted to thank him for being there, more deeply than she could say right now, and she hoped her face was conveying it. Possibly it was; he was looking so closely at her that she had the feeling he was searching out her words.

"Drink it," he said.

The coffee was thick Kona and she welcomed the strength of it. She could feel it, by the mouthful, reviving her. Consuming it slowly, she decided not to let Karli rush her too summarily toward dismissal time. The man might be able to tell her where to find Nishi. Now that the latter knew she was following him, her plan to talk to him at home would be useless; he wouldn't be there, he'd be impossible to track, unless someone helped her.

By the time she was finished with her coffee, Karli was finished giving himself his "breather." She knew it would be useless to be oblique with him. "I was looking for Nishi," she said.

"I know." That was all he would give. He turned away.

"I have to find him," she pleaded.

Tad took a step closer to her. "You want to get killed? Give it up."

"Good advice," Karli muttered.

Doggedly, "I'm going to find him somewhere." She had to convince them she wouldn't turn back. "I'm more likely to get killed if I don't know where I'm going."

"You had Nishi tonight," Karli said. "Why did you leave?"

"The crematorium?" she said. "When I got inside, he wasn't there."

"Yes, he was." Having said too much, Karli busied himself. He folded the towel and put it neatly on top of the sideboard. As he started to carry the basin toward the kitchen, she stopped him. "Please—where is he?"

He continued toward the kitchen door. She took a few steps after him. There was a whirling in her head; she might fall. "Please," she repeated.

He turned, more because he sensed her infirmity than in response to her plea. His hand reached to steady her. "Go home. Are you dumb? Go home."

Tad was on the other side of her, ready to support her. "Come on," he said quietly.

"No." She narrowly withdrew herself from both of them. She didn't want them propping her up. All she needed was a word of information. "Is he still there?" Karli seemed, for only a flash, to be hesitating; she pursued the advantage. "Just tell me and I won't bother you any more."

He said, "The back of the crematorium connects with the back of the doll store."

His eyes wavered. She saw he was frightened, had said all he dared to say, was sorry he had told her anything. He walked into the kitchen and she had the sense he wouldn't come out until after they had gone. She turned to look at Tad. His eyes were steady. Whatever his thoughts, they were altogether his own; he looked imperturbable. She put the palms of both hands to her forehead and made her mind up: I won't get dizzy again. Then, one final fleeting glance at Tad and she started toward the door.

She had no idea where she was going, wasn't even aware of the stairs that led from Karli's apartment down into the tiny courtyard. She could hear Tad's footsteps on each tread, behind her. Now, outdoors, he went around her and, a step ahead, pointed to his car. "Come on," he said. "I'll drive you home."

"I have my own car," she said. Then, in a jumble,

"And I want to thank you for tonight. But I won't need—"

"Where's your car? I'll drive you to it."

"Please—I'm not going to use it now. I'm not going home—I'm walking—I—"

"You don't even know where you are."

She felt a wave of humiliation. Ready to do anything, prepared for nothing. He was right: she had no inkling whether she was blocks or miles from the crematorium.

He saw her shiver. "You don't know, do you?"

"Then tell me."

"No—it's idiot. Haven't you been warned?" His voice was sharp. Then, with definition, he pointed to the car. "Get in."

She said no more. Turning away from him, she started across the paved courtyard to the rounded archway that opened into the street. The arch was farther than the night pictured it. She didn't hear him start the car; there was no sound of it. Just as she arrived at the arch, she heard him call, not too loudly, "Wait."

She kept on going, without him. She heard him walking behind her, then running to catch up. By the time she got to the darkness under the archway, he was beside her.

The cremation man's befuddlement was so ingenuous that they were convinced he was telling the truth. Trying to understand what they were talking about, and comprehending nothing, he pulled his black satin robe tightly around himself; the disturbance the two Americans were making was an embarrassment to his body. He reiterated that he had not seen the two men Johanna described; as to the door that led into the doll shop, they could see for themselves that no such door existed.

His face was lined with distress. He pointed to the dead woman in the casket and the old man, mourning her. "Please," he said, "not to make a noisiness for the dead."

Johanna couldn't tell whether Tad was believing him. As to herself, something about the man's physical immobility baffled her. "Why don't you move?" she asked.

A flutter, nothing more; the man's hand behind his back.

Tad shoved him sidewards.

The wall behind the Japanese was no different from any other stretch of wall; a bronze panel, chased like the others, with an abstract design of pine branches, needles and cones. It wasn't a door, it had no doorknob, plate, no handle of any kind.

Tad saw it first: the keyhole.

The man was moving now. Tad grabbed him. "Where's the key?"

She thought the Japanese was complying. He reached under his robe to his trouser pocket. But it wasn't a key: a knife. She heard him mutter, *korosu* it sounded like, a killing word. She started to back away, but Tad was at him. The knife clattered to the tile floor, she pounced on it. The mourning old man half arose, in terror, and leaned across the coffin to save it from desecration. The other two were twisted with one another, writhing, entangled, until suddenly Tad had him. He pulled at the arm, yanked it backward and the man's body forward. He bent him down and down so that his head, inch by inch, was closer to the lighted brazier.

"The key," Tad said.

He pushed the face still nearer, only inches from the fire. "The key." Still closer. The head in the brazier now. The black hair, fallen forward, burning.

A cry of terror. *"Kame,"* he groaned. *"Kukyona."*

"An urn," she translated. "An empty urn."

"Where?" Tad prodded the man.

"Let him up," Johanna said. "Let him up."

He pulled the man to his feet. Again the yanking of the robe, the snatching for respectability, the quaking.

Tad tightened his grip. "Where?"

The man pointed to the low corbel that made a shelf along the wall. A number of burial urns, ceramic, damascene, porcelain, stood on the corbel, on display. He was pointing to the first one.

Johanna hurried and brought it down. As she was lifting the lid off, the Japanese moved, startled, murmuring no, no. But it was too late. She had already turned the jar over onto her hand, and the ashes, still warm from the oven, wafting downward, spilled over her. With an outcry, she put the urn back and brushed the dusty gray mortality off her hands and clothes. The cremation man began to whimper, shaking; the other one, he kept saying, he had told her the second one, not the first, the second, the second, and what would the bereaved ones do?

The second urn had the key. As she started with it toward the door, Tad still didn't let the man go. "The knife," he said. In dealing with the urn, she had dropped it. Now, picking it up from the floor, she handed it to Tad. He held the point of the blade to the back of the man's neck and gestured for Johanna to open the door.

She swung the bronze door outward. The Japanese made a soft sound, more a sigh than a sob, but as Tad pointed for him to precede them through the doorway, he let out a pitifully strangled cry and hung back. The knife urged him forward. Tad followed him into a narrow hallway; Johanna was behind them.

The hallway was pitch-dark. At the end of it, the doll shop opened outward, long and narrow, its windows facing on the back street. The store too was dark. The only light came from the Venetian-blinded windows, thin horizontal lines of white moonlight making chalk stripes across the shelves. Only dolls.

Dolls of all kinds, puppets, dummy figures of wax and straw, sewn ones and painted ones, tiny ones no larger than the thumb, and life-sized, lifelike creatures frozen in the midst of a word, with life at the tip of the tongue.

But no human being. Other than the three of them, nobody in the darkness. No Nishi, no mammoth man, not a breath, not a motion.

As Johanna turned, her elbow struck a Kabuki figure. It moved. One hand upward, one foot off the ground. It began to sing, a high macabre whine, a mechanical grief and ecstasy. It was too awful, too harrowing, and she wanted to turn it off. As she looked

for a way to stop it, as she touched its body, it started
to topple over. Trying to catch it, she was unable to,
and the Kabuki figure fell.

It fell where the moonlight came more brightly
through the blinds, onto the floor. Beside the human
body. Johanna couldn't tell whether the new sound she
heard was the Kabuki's or her own, adding to the
abhorrence.

Tad hurried to the blinds and pulled them up. The
light showed the thing more clearly now. It was Nishi.
He was slit from breastbone to loin, a straight, clean,
vertical line. Because he was a potbellied man, his en-
trails hung out in a single round mass, like a reddish
melon. There was a slit, around his throat, but not too
deep, a ritual one.

The ride was quiet. Tad asked Johanna where her
car was parked, whether his open window bothered her,
whether the door on her side was locked. She tried to
light a cigarette with the car's cigar lighter but it was
broken, so she used her pocket lighter. It had been
Oscar's, used for pipe smoking, and it sprang a huge
flame. They both made innocuous observations about
it. The rest was privacy and pensiveness.

She was surprised at how unperturbed she felt. It
was that thing about seeing death, no matter how hor-
rible, that makes a finality, dulling a certain commo-
tion of the spirit, settling it. She had felt that way when
Oscar had died of leukemia, the sense that agonies
have limits, the rack stops stretching, the crucifixion
ends. With Ben, however—the ravening rage unap-
peased—it had been a different story.

Different from Nishi in every way except that they
were both suicides. The Japanese wouldn't have called
it that, of course, for there was ignominy in Occidental
self-destruction, even sin; hara-kiri was no such thing.
It had dignity, it was the noble seppuku that would bring
Nishi honor among his family and friends, and would
shrive his soul. How inequitable it was that her son,
who had led such a radiant life, should have gone to a
failure's death, while this corrupt, this meretricious

man should have taken a seppuku glory to his grave.
How unjust geography was, to make such a difference.

But the important similarity: behind both self-de-
structions, the destroying evil, Tokan. How strangely
attractive malignancy could seem. It could, as in Tokan's case, wear the garment of an even requital, the
justifiable pound of flesh. And the man himself, if she
had met him in quiet days, would have seemed to her a
clear-eyed, cultivated artist or scholar, a man of infinite
charm. Had their paths crossed in Tokyo, for example,
she would have befriended him happily, envying the
generations in him, the centuries, the millennia of
poetry that had gentled him. And here she hated him.
Tokan, the suicide-maker.

She heard Tad's voice: "Is that the way it's always
done?"

Bringing herself back, "What?"

"Hara-kiri," he replied. "I've never seen it before."

"You still haven't."

The realization had been just that sudden.

It hadn't been hara-kiri, not at all. Murder.

She had said the words even before she knew their
meaning. They came out of something deep below her
consciousness, altogether contrary to what she had been
thinking. And as she uttered the statement, she felt
absolutely certain that the unconsidered judgment was
truer than the considered one.

"You think he didn't kill himself?" Tad asked.

"He was murdered."

"But the knife was there, in his hand."

"He didn't use it." How satisfying it was that there
was nothing blurred to her, not one detail was cryptic.
"Hara-kiri is nothing to be ashamed of—not to them.
It's a holy ceremony, it's a devotion. A man performs it
like a sacrament—openly—possibly with a friend. By a
noble act, he acknowledges his disgrace, and, as he does,
he comes out of the shadow of shame. He's in the light
again. It's his last pride—he doesn't have to hide any
more. He's doing a beautiful thing—he doesn't have to
do it sneakily, behind a locked door, in the darkness."

He didn't respond. She suspected he was impressed

by what she had said, yet, for some reason, had not come to the same conclusion. "You think I'm not making sense."

"Yes, I do," he said quietly. "But sense hasn't anything to do with it."

"With what?"

"Killing one's self."

With a pang she knew he wasn't talking about Nishi, but Ben. She could pretend she didn't know her son was in his mind. It would be painful to talk to him about Ben; they would have had to see the boy differently, and she didn't want any more to speculate about; where Ben was concerned, too much of her was unresolved. Yet, she was drawn, she couldn't resist. "It was the most logical thing for Ben to do," she said.

"I can't believe you think that."

"I do."

"You think that was all there was to Ben? Just balls?"

"I didn't say that!" What a bastard he was to put it so crassly, she thought. As if he needed to confront her with her ugly judgment. Or was he confronting his own? If the same horror had happened to this man, would he have killed himself? "If it had happened to you . . ."

"I wouldn't have killed myself."

She wondered if he was telling the truth, or if he even knew whether he was. "Well, then, you must have limitless resources."

"Just perversity."

He was tossing it off flippantly. But it occurred to her he meant it: perversity as a life force; the spite of an orphan: I'll live as a grudge against the world.

She said quietly, "It doesn't matter what gives you the sense you can cope. You may think you've got a brain that'll see you through, or the best tennis arm in the Club, or you look great in tight clothes—it doesn't matter. Anything you can rely on—predictably—that'll give you some power over the lousy unpredictabilities. And I thought Ben had it. God, he was so smart, he didn't have to *think;* he could have guessed his way through. And charming enough to smile his way through. And he never had to pretend about loving—it

came naturally. So I would have thought, when he lost
his testicles—my God, people have lost their *sight* and
just went right on to the next item on the agenda. And
the thing that's too terrible about his death is that he—
Ben, of all people—didn't think he had enough left . . .
And if he didn't think so, he had no alternative, did
he?"

"Yes, he did."

"What alternative?"

"Tomorrow."

"Tomorrow's not an alternative—it's just more of
the same."

"Oh, no. Tomorrow there could always be something else. Something, somebody." Then, almost to
himself, "But I guess it would be hard to sell tomorrow
to a rich kid."

"What in the world can that mean?"

"If you've had the best of it, and some of it's taken
away, things can only get progressively worse. But if
you grow up poor—with nothing—there's always tomorrow. There's *only* that."

To live for, she felt sure he meant. For the first time,
she had a glimpse of a paradox in the man. She had
never seen anything but the dour side of him, nor had
she imagined there was another side to see: he was a
dyspeptic, in fact as well as manner. His rectitude had
bespoken an apprehension of some higher power around
him, as if he were always wary of getting caught by an
unjust Disciplinarian. He lived, she had always thought,
on the shadow side of the moon, and it was eye-open-
ing now to hear him speak of brighter phases.

Even more damning, she had thought of him as a
frightened man. But he wasn't, he was still fighting.
She could draw the new conclusion not simply because
he had come to her assistance tonight, had reached
for a man who had a knife in his hand, but because she
was quite sure his decision to come had not been impulsive. He had had to fight something through, she
conjectured, possibly some answerability to rules, duties
to dockets, or to a complex, conniving old man who
had made it clear to all of them that they were to let

the hue and cry fade away. Yes, still fighting, not comforting himself with an extenuation and a drink. Still tilting at the deadliest dragon-serpent, the inside one, fire and fang.

How late it was for her to have stumbled onto this new insight into the man. And, paradoxically, as she saw another side of him, instead of knowing him more, she knew him less. As a particularized perception of the man became clear, the whole view of him became obscure; he was suddenly more mysterious than he had been; she wanted to know more about him. Inevitably there must be other darknesses in him, and they intrigued her. Why was tradition so important to him, why did he need to keep things so steadfastly in place? The hunt, for example, why had he been so outspoken against women joining it? Was he so uncertain of his masculinity? Was he, as she had accused him of being, a prude in bed? Or was he, as she had often speculated from Abby's look of creature contentment, ruttishly satisfying? She suspected there were enough ergs of sexual energy in the man . . . and to spare.

The thought struck her, she had been speculating about him as if he were a stranger. As if he weren't a member of the family, her daughter's husband; as if she had felt someone staring at her—someone at the bar in the Club, for example—and had turned to look into the wanting face of an attractive male. A wanting face, what an odd expression, wanting him to want her. The fantasy that he was a stranger, an excitement of rubbing too close to someone in a dark place . . .

She felt a quickening. I must be blushing, of all things; I'm glad it's dark and he can't notice. We must talk of other things, impersonal ones. Better still, of things that restate the orderly familial ones.

"I hope Abby won't be worried," she said.

"She won't be," he replied quietly. "She'll be asleep."

They said no more until they arrived at Beretania Street. There was no need for him to get out of the car and she was surprised that he did. Yet, in the darkness of the chilly damp night, and with no street lights to speak of, she was glad for his chivalry in walking her to her car. She unlocked the door and got in. He waved and she did too. Then he said something that, over the start of the motor, she couldn't hear. He came around to the other side of the car, next to her, and opened her door.

"Are you all right?" he asked. "Shall I follow you all the way?"

"Oh, no—I'm fine," she whispered.

There was a silence. He didn't go, nor did he shut the door. She made a movement to do so. "I can't think of . . ." She stopped and started again. "I haven't thought of a way to thank you."

"There's time."

"Yes . . . I'm glad of that."

"Good night."

"Good night."

She pulled the door to shut it, not seeing where his hand was. With a muffled cry of pain, he yanked it away, rubbed it a little, as if he were rubbing away a stain.

"Oh, God," she said.

"It's all right." To reassure her: "Just barely—not much."

"Oh, your hand," she cried, "oh, your poor hand!"

Unthinking, she took it to her lips, she kissed it.

She wished he would say something again, say anything, make a bad joke, say good night, or simply go. But he stood there. She must refer to her clumsiness, her stupidity, must at least manage a smile. She tried.

He tried too.

Neither of them accomplished it.

The door was closed now. She had no idea, finally, whether she had closed it or he had. She pressed the gas pedal so that the motor might take the moment away from both of them. She was glad to be rid of it.

But driving away along the dark streets, the moment wasn't entirely gone for her. She kept clinging to it.

She must, she told herself, stop thinking of him. Not that they were actually thoughts. Senses, mostly, without perceptions. Memories so compounded of incidents that had and hadn't happened—how could she call them memories? How could she call them anything, since they were so vague and formless, so mixed with curiosity and anxiety, with panic and pleasure?

Whatever they were, she had to get rid of them. Think of something else. But what, in this stillness of night, driving through it, would have the power to take its place? Then something did happen to take its place. A reverie.

It's happening right this minute, Johanna thought. Now. If it doesn't go away, she will have to stop the car.

She sees the dead man, Nishi, his belly open, the melon of blood. Then, Tokan's face, full of questioning wonder, the brow washed of worry, he is putting an offering on the household altar, a bloody offering, and he is delivered of an incriminating eye. His face comes closer, through the windshield, someone holds a gun, his face explodes, not ugly, a picture seen through a different glass, horror as beauty, beauty as retribution, pulling the trigger on a Jap. She has never used that expression for a Japanese. Like pulling the trigger, it gives her pleasure.

But the car is swerving. She must stop.

She stops the car to rid her mind of the reverie. When she does, the image of her son-in-law returns. She puts the car in gear again and drives more carefully.

Twelve

HE ARRIVED HOME in the interval between darkness and dawn, in the edge of light, a time that always suggested surveillance to him, somebody watching him through one-way windows, as animals are watched in experiments. He usually found himself doing things more cautiously at that hour; he too was watching.

As he got out of the car, he saw a glittering object on the seat. Johanna's cigarette lighter. It gave him a dart of pleasure that she had left something behind, betraying she hadn't altogether gone. Gazing at it, not touching it, he decided to leave it there as a reminder to return it to her. But it occurred to him that Abby might use the car and see it. He didn't explore what difference that would make. For the moment, he wasn't ready to decide how much he was going to tell Abby about the evening's happenings. He might tell her nothing.

Picking up the lighter, he shoved it into his trouser pocket. The hand that put it there was the injured one, it throbbed a little. Out of the garage, in the dim dawnlight, as he was walking up the path to the front of the house, he looked at the bruise. It was on the knuckles of two fingers, had bled hardly at all and was barely noticeable. He had no difficulty working his fingers; the hand would give him no trouble. He could still feel her mouth on it.

He unlocked the front door. The living room was in total darkness except, through the terrace windows, seaward, he could see the magenta onset of the sunrise. He stood in the middle of the room wondering if Abby was awake. She wasn't, he concluded, or she'd have heard him and called. So as not to disturb her, he undressed in the living room. He had never done that before and felt furtively ridiculous. Old cartoons came to mind of Jiggs sneaking home in darkness, his shoes in hand, smugly certain he is undetected, only to be assailed by Maggie's rolling pin.

Naked now, his sense of the preposterous increasing, he carried his clothes into the bedroom, tiptoeing as carefully as if the room might be booby-trapped. The curtains were drawn and the room was dark; he didn't see her, wasn't even sure she was in bed. All he knew was the warmth; the bedroom was always warmer than the rest of the house. Even on chilly winter nights there was always a lingering remembrance of Hawaiian summer.

Suddenly something changed. Through the crack between the curtains, the dawnlight, like a surprise of fortune, altered the room. It wasn't bright, just enough to light Abby as she lay naked and asleep. She was lying, almost precariously, at the very edge of the bed, one arm hanging down toward the floor, the other spread across Tad's pillow. One leg was straight, the other was bent wide and easily. With the chiaroscuro of the room more to the dark side, her belly was in shadow; there was a highlight on her legs, but the inside of her thighs was in darkness. The only thing that was in vivid light, the event that the sunrise created, was her bosom. One of her breasts was in the dimness, the other was silhouetted against a corona of light. Her breasts seemed as soft as the light was soft, and as beautiful as it was transitory, for any moment the light would change. For this caught breath of time, the nipple was perfect, erect and fully formed, and glowing in the one ray of morning. As she breathed, her bosom barely lifted, only enough to bear witness that in her sleeping nakedness she was pulsingly alive and vulnerable.

Rapt, he didn't stir, he gazed at her. Then, slowly, studying her body every step of the way, he moved around the bed and stood over her. The light was spreading a little, undressing more and more of her. Her whole bosom was now revealed, and there was no longer darkness between her thighs. Whatever wantings he had ever had for her, none was like this. He could feel it, a surge, a mounting fervor in his blood, like hot quicksilver, here and gone, a joyous agony in his arms, his legs, belly, anus, and suddenly they were all nothing, and his penis was everything. Moving close to her, he took hold of himself and gently touched his penis to her breast. Nothing about her changed; her breathing was as steady as before. Her softness against his hardness was as if she were the love-making one, she was bringing herself to him, the caress was hers. And as he touched her nipple, rubbing it gently, then more firmly, it was a sweet lunacy he could hardly bear.

Her eyes flickered and opened. For an instant, he couldn't tell whether there was fright in them. He heard her murmur something and couldn't tell what that was either. He knelt on the floor, reached with his hand for her other breast. Now the sound she made was clear. "Please . . . no."

She was, he could see, just barely awake. He didn't stop what he was doing; wouldn't stop, he told himself, until she knew what it was.

"Please . . . no," she said again.

Continue, he said, don't hesitate, continue. In a while, arousing, she would want him, she was bound to get caught by what had taken hold of him, they would get caught in it together.

"Stop," she said. "I'm still asleep."

He started to kiss her, her breast now, her belly. Whatever paradise of a dream she was wandering in, he would lead her to a realer one. Her nipple in his mouth, his tongue at it.

"Stop," she said. "Won't you please stop?"

He put his hand on the inside of her thigh, stroking her, searching her. Only her voice was telling him to cease, her body wasn't. She was moist, her moisture was for him, he thought, or for the thing in the dream, it didn't matter, it was all one, and his now. He touched the wetness with his fingers, with his whole hand.

"Stop."

He was on top of her. She moved this time, as if to prevent him, but when she saw he wouldn't hold back, he felt her thighs opening. Then he went at her savagely for wanting her and for her not wanting him. And when she screamed louder than he had ever heard her, he thought for an instant she was in pain. But still he pursued whatever it was he pursued when he was making love, whatever he was running to capture, whatever he was running to elude, the enemy, the friend, the love, the parent, the home, the shelter against loneliness, the thing or the ghost of it, until the end had come and he was altogether spent. Then he lay beside her, wet, and still unsatisfied. And he wondered if there would ever be any comings and goings that would help him catch or be caught, and leave him finally at peace.

They were sitting at breakfast and Abby hadn't asked him where he had been last night. She was quieter than usual, as though she were hiding something specific; not a vague reticence, but a carefully defined puzzle to which she alone had the answer. He wondered if what she was concealing was her awareness he had slipped away in the night and come back, early dawn. He didn't know how to find out and didn't know whether he wanted to, and felt strange.

What was even more strange: he didn't know what her mood was. She had done something unusual last night, afterward; had silently turned away from him and silently gone to sleep. Not a word. And this morning, a tacit astonishment between them. Abby, the sensible, the predictable one, whom he thought he knew: he could tell nothing about her today, whether she had enjoyed last night's love-making or been offended by his refusal to give her any choice, or whether she too didn't know how she felt, or whether she did know and simply wanted to keep it all to herself.

"What's that?" she asked.

He didn't know what she was referring to. She put the toast dish down, then the percolator. She reached and almost touched the bruised hand. "How did that happen?"

He had no idea he could say it so casually. "I don't know. I noticed it in the shower. I must have banged it in the night."

"Among other things."

He looked at her quickly. Her eyes were bright with pleasure, yet confused. She was smiling, and not smiling. Something he had never seen in her, some perplexity was happening: a private sensuality she wanted to make into a stealthy thing, he imagined, something she didn't quite approve of, yet liked, something she might want to understand better, yet might be afraid of spoiling. Mostly, he suspected, something she wanted to make into a mischief, a delicious bawdry, perhaps.

"Whatever got into you?" she said. "Into me, I mean."

There was a risk he might spoil it for her, so he held back. He must let her have it her own way, somehow. Smiling, trying not to invade her concealment, he couldn't help patting her behind. Damn, he rebuked himself; the most trivial goddamn thing to do. Then he realized how much more common sense she had than he did; she nodded, understanding his embarrassment.

When he was ready to leave, she saw him to the door. She stood there, close to him, her bathrobe barely open. She let it fall still farther open. "Stay home," she said quietly. As he hesitated, she ran her hand down the outside of his leg, then down the inside. "Stay home."

"I can't," he said. "I've got to get the war started."

She looked at him obliquely. He couldn't believe he had said such egregious nonsense. What war, and what would he ever have to do with starting it? Or ending it, or preventing it, or effecting one word in the history of it?

"Stay home," she repeated. "You don't want to play war and I don't want to play teacher. I want to play fuck-fuck."

"It sounds hyphenated."

"It's supposed to be."

It was a joke, but there was seriousness; not quite a rebuke—almost. He almost stayed. But he didn't.

As he opened the door of his car, he reached into his pocket for his keys and could feel the smooth cold roundness of Johanna's lighter. He had the impulse to rush back into the house and tell Abby where he had spent last night's hours of darkness. He felt certain that if he didn't—and if she spoke to Johanna today— she would surely find out. But perhaps she mightn't . . .

With a reckless excitement he couldn't understand in himself, he decided not to go back into the house . . . Let whatever happens happen, he said.

"Are you all bonkers?" Jerrold screamed at him. "Have you bloody Americans gone completely out of your bloody heads?"

"I'm sure we didn't do that to you," Tad said, trying to calm him. He hoped nobody had seen the English-man come into his office. The man looked terrible. "Can I get you something? Are you in pain?"

"What the hell do you think? They didn't kiss me, Taddy-boy."

He stood stiffly, uncertainly, trying not to move too much, like a man held together with darning thread. The bandages that were actually visible, those on his face and head, didn't cover all the mutilation. His fore-head was gashed, one eye was a raw laceration, the fingers of his left hand were brown and green.

"You stupid bastards," he yelled, "you arrogant stu-pid bastards!"

"Why do you blame it on us? You say they were Japanese."

"I didn't say they were Japanese—I said Oriental. They could have been Chinese—Korean—anything."

"Come on, Jerrold. You'd have known."

"How, you bloody cretin—how? The room was dark —no bigger than your desk—no window."

"Voices."

"For Jesus' sake, look at my head. You think I was tuned into voices? And what the hell point are you mak-ing? They could have been Japanese and still been sent by that mother bleeder."

As neutrally as possible, "What mother bleeder are you talking about?"

"You know goddamn well."

"No."

For the first time he spoke with restraint. "Kley."

"Kley doesn't send three Orientals out to mangle Hugh Jerrold. Kley doesn't need anything Hugh Jerrold can give him." Then with devastating calm, "Kley has total contempt for Hugh Jerrold."

"Don't talk to me about Kley's contempt. He'll use anybody, contempt or not. He'll go down on a syphilitic whore if he can get a word of information out of her."

"Meaning you?"

An outcry: "I didn't *have* any information!" His body was shaking. "They kept asking me questions about Tokan and where he went when he disappeared for days at a time."

"Well—where?"

"I don't know!" he said desperately. "If I knew, you think I'd look like this? What the hell kind of hero do you think I am?"

"Then who knows?"

"Ben—ask Ben!" He started to laugh, but no pleasure in it, only bitterness, frustration. "It's so naïve. Here we are in the most complex business in the world —and all our processes are so fucking naïve! Nobody knows what anybody knows. What did Ben know? Did he *know* what he knew? When he first met Tokan, was he interested in the man's art objects—or his secrets—or his wife? And why did he want a transfer? You know what I suspect? I suspect that kid was on the verge of The Big Discovery and he didn't *know* he was on the verge! I suspect he wanted to be transferred for no other reason than Muna—to take the trouble out of her life. So there's the nasty joke: a silly sentimental kid on the edge of the big secret and he mucks it up for love. What's our trade worth? All these exciting, intricate, formidably mysterious problems—what happens to them? The kids and the idiots get hold of them, and all the brandy and champagne gets watered down to soda pop."

"Who is Tokan?"

"Why don't you hit me, you bastard? Why be subtle? Just hit me—the way your Jap bleeders did! And maybe you'll get the answer to the *other* question!"

"What other question?"

"Why don't you hit me? Don't be fancy with me, Thaddeus—hit me!"

"What other question?"

"The Purple Code!"

He couldn't be fancy even if he wanted to, Tad realized, for he didn't, in fact, know anything about the Purple Code. "What is it?"

"Don't lie in your scrags, old boy. You know damn well what it is."

"I give you my word—I do not."

Jerrold looked at him a long time. Then, believing, "Oh, Christ," he said softly. "Wouldn't it be funny if it doesn't exist? Wouldn't it be funny if the Japs were pulling our dinguses? Wouldn't it be the laugh circus of all time if they were throwing all this shit into all the airwaves and ciphers and codes, and into all the locked safes and security boxes and diplomatic pouches and double-bolted dispatch cases? Wouldn't it be the great big music-hall-water-closet-turds-and-jakes joke-of-the-world?" This time he didn't even try to laugh; the irony was too caustic. The distress of it caught up with him. "But it couldn't happen," he said soberly. "You know why it couldn't happen? Because nobody in the business could pull a joke like that. I've never met a spy with a sense of humor—I dare you to name one."

"You."

It surprised Jerrold and his misery was mitigated; he was touched. "Well, thank you for that, old sod—except I'm not what you'd call a good spy, am I?" He was somber now, and still. His rage, his fireworks had fizzed away; his badly maimed face wasn't flexible for anything. He was dead tired. "I'm going to get away," he said, almost inaudibly.

"From what?"

"Here—Honolulu—everything."

"Where are you going?"

"Doesn't much matter."

"Then why leave?"

Jerrold spoke with utter simplicity; he'd suddenly lost his appetite for drama. "Because if I stay, I'm going to get killed." The faintest flicker of irony returned. "And the doltish thing is—I'm not worth killing. I don't know anything that has to be hushed up. My connections no longer talk to me because I haven't got a bob to pay 'em. Even when I do get something, nobody believes me. I'm hiding nothing. I've got no secrets and I'm a danger to nobody. I'm not worth a bullet. Yet I am absolutely certain—because there isn't one man on either side who knows the value of one goddamn thing—that if I stay here I will be killed."

"Then you'd better go."

"Oh, I'm going. And I'm not waiting for the Clipper. I can get a ride on a sampan to Kona. There's a charter boat from there. If I leave in an hour, I can make all the connections. There's only one problem."

"How much?"

"A hundred dollars?"

Tad's wallet contained seventy-four dollars. He kept the four ones and handed Jerrold the rest. "It's all I've got."

"You could give me the rest out of petty cash."

"It's not mine."

The Englishman's face was filled with wonderment and envy. "You had no hesitation in saying that, did you?"

"No."

"How does it feel to be so ruddy certain about following a rule? Crikey, if I could be certain about any bloody rule that's ever been written—!" There was no mockery in it. All aching envy, fully exposed. Then, "I'm going to reimburse you for this money right now. It's a very valuable warning. Take care. You Americans are going to catch it this time. You're parading right into your first lost war. I don't know where the opening attack will be—maybe it'll start everywhere at once. But there will be an attack, my boyo—and wherever it happens, the little yellow monkeys and the big white Krauts are going to grind you up and make sausage stuffing out of you. Maybe out of all of us. So take to the brush, lad!"

Tad heard himself being sarcastically superior, taking the aloof official position, high Navy. "All data accounted for," he said.

The Englishman slapped him. Clean, hard, across the face, with the full force of his one good hand. Apoplectically, "You smug—!" He couldn't make an articulate sentence. "You goddamn smug Americans! You know what smugness is, you know what it is? It's pus—it's corruption!" An echo of his voice seemed to strike back at him. His laughter returned. "Oh, Christ, listen to the pot—the pot shrieking at the bloody kettle. Talk about corruption—oh, Christ, talk about corruption—!"

He laughed his way agonizedly out of the room. In a minute, Tad saw him through the window, a wounded, limping man, laughing bizarrely, weaving this way and that, not certain where he was going, making his way on foot toward the main highway.

He could still feel Jerrold's slap. Curiously, he had had no impulse to retaliate; he bore no grudge for the insult. On the contrary, some unaccountable beatitude seemed to have ensued from the shock. He could feel it in his head, his innards, a cleansing of some sort. It was as if the blow had shaken things loose inside him, had torn malignant adhesions away from his vitals. He was not quite sure what had happened to him, but, whatever it was, he was grateful to the Englishman.

And it entered his mind, with a twinge, that Jerrold had gone possibly forever, and Tad would miss him. Making no attempt to analyze how he could be fond of a man whom he held in such low regard, he was grateful that he could feel the freakish affection. It gave him the warm sense that he had come upon a new emotional power within himself, a more catholic talent for friendliness than he had ever suspected he had. And it made him sad that it had come after the man had departed.

But perhaps he hadn't departed. One must never believe Jerrold, never believe anything he said. Having proclaimed his departure, the Englishman might actually have gone, never to be seen again; on the other hand, he might, just as likely, show up next Tuesday. He might, indeed, not have gone at all.

And if gone, gone only for Tokan.

Tad grinned. It wouldn't surprise him even a little if the man had again perpetrated one of his hoaxes, a practical joke, the hostile riposte, the counterattack for the beating he had suffered.

Without having any evidence to adduce to the argument, Tad was convinced he was right—Jerrold was going for the big prize, for Tokan.

As so many others had done and were doing. Ben, to begin with, one way or another; then Kley and his operatives; and, of course, Johanna. He had a nagging regret that he couldn't add his own name to the list. Last night couldn't really be accounted as a going-for-Tokan; he had merely gone to the assistance of a member of his family, in a state of emergency. He had not, technically speaking, disobeyed Kley's orders to keep away from the man. Nor did he intend to disobey.

Still, as he thought of the others: Ben, tilting at the real Tokan, only to be sidetracked by some romantic windmill; Jerrold, going for the grand prize; Kley, snaking his way toward Tokan through all the intricacies of the codes . . . and Johanna . . . He felt that excluding himself from the quest might be, in some way he couldn't fully comprehend, a default for which he would not forgive himself.

Tad stood on the doorstep and couldn't bring himself to enter his own house. He dreaded it. He dreaded the confrontation no matter how it came: she could hold back the question until dinner was over, even until they were in bed, or she could immediately blurt it out. "I spoke to Johanna today. Why didn't you tell me you spent the night with her?"

"Abby—Christ—you can hardly say I 'spent the night' with your mother."

"Whatever you call it, why didn't you tell me?"

Why didn't he, in fact? How could he have kept the erratic secret all through the day, fondling it as he fondled the cigarette lighter next to his thigh? What irrational compulsion . . . ?

He unlocked the door and let himself in. He could

see her on the terrace, setting the table. She was wearing a muumuu, loose-fitting, lightweight, taking the late-afternoon breeze, a drift of flowers.

"Is that you, darling?"

The same words as usual, the same lilt of voice; nothing different. Of course nothing would be different; what had he really expected? Abby, in a rage, charging the foyer like an express train, wheels grinding with sparks? No, she would do it coolly—later—as casually as an afterthought: "Oh, by the way, I was talking to Johanna . . ."

He walked out onto the terrace. There was a lovely scent: plumeria and new-mown grass, and Abby, fresh from the shower. And the table, beautiful. Hot rolls and cold dolphin with dill-and-caper mayonnaise, and papaya to begin with; he loved it all, to hell with conscience and gastritis.

She kissed him and put a tall stem's worth of cold vermouth in his hand. They asked each other about having nice days, and she said nothing about her mother.

Then, "Why didn't you tell me . . . ?" she started.

He stopped swallowing for an instant. "About what?"

"Nishi."

So that was the way it was going to come. By stages. "What about him?" he said.

"He committed hara-kiri."

"How did you hear that?"

"His little boy wasn't in school today. They sent a message."

Of course. The little boy. He'd altogether forgotten about meeting Nishi, with the child, that Sunday afternoon of the Donald Duck.

"Yes, terrible, isn't it?" he said guardedly. "What else did you hear?"

"Well, that was certainly enough," she replied. "So he couldn't stand it. If he'd only gone to testify . . . They can't really endure it, you know—being ashamed—they can't bear it. I guess he was a bastard in many ways—cruel, certainly—pinching those kids—punishing them in mean little ways. Yet, when a man kills himself . . ."

While she wasn't stricken with any sense of tragedy, she was disturbed through dinner, and she ate absent-mindedly. Usually she was the more talkative, but tonight it was he who made the conversation sounds and frequently found himself having to repeat things. It's not Nishi who's on her mind, he told himself, it's Johanna. If only he could bring himself to blurt it all at once: I was with your mother last night. Instead, "Have you talked to Johanna today?" he asked.

"Yes."

"What did she say?"

"About what?"

It occurred to him what she was doing: gentle torture. She would keep him on the tenterhooks of not knowing. She would harry him, quietly, until he shouted the confession.

"About Nishi—didn't she say anything about Nishi?"

"Not a word," she replied. "Isn't that weird? She merely said she had heard it on the radio—and that was all. Not another word."

"She . . . heard it on the radio?"

"Yes."

"And that's all she said?"

"Yes."

Could it possibly be that Johanna . . . ? He must move even more circumspectly now. "What does she do with herself?" he asked.

"How do you mean?"

"Well, how does she spend her time?"

"She's been reading a lot."

"Hasn't she gone out?"

"I asked her that and she was so peculiar." Abby sounded baffled. " 'Why are you questioning me?' she said. She was very touchy."

He wanted a cigarette. He had stopped smoking years ago and now he badly wanted a cigarette.

She had lied. Johanna had lied. Not too overtly, but in a worse way, by omission. To her own daughter, she had not mentioned that she had gone through a night's darkness with her daughter's husband. She had kept their secret. Without any prearranged plan between them, without so much as a word, they had conspired with one another, they had tacitly agreed to share the blame, whatever blame might fall, for having done something awry, for having committed an act together that was not at all unsanctioned, yet was too oblique to be confessed. Only ten minutes ago there was nothing wrong with what they had done together; now, not having spoken of it, it was illicit.

And perversely exciting. How tantalizing it felt, at such a distance, to be having this ferment with Johanna. And he was certain she had to be feeling it too.

He didn't know what to do with himself. He tried to fall back on whatever was commonplace, whatever was routine. He helped Abby with the dishes. The dinner had brought her back to herself and she was chattering. This time it was he who was abstracted. If she asked a question, he was slow to answer. If there was a pause in the unbalanced colloquy, the best he could fill it with was a neutrality. He missed a number of cues for laughing. He was elsewhere.

As Abby was putting things away, he drifted back to the terrace. It was dusk. The ships were lighting up, some of them; the Navy Yard lamps on the *makai* side were already bright; on the *mauka* side, still dark.

He didn't actually make a conscious decision. He simply found himself doing what he would have had to do if he *had* made a decision. Walking quietly into the bedroom, he changed from his uniform trousers into civilian ones, and he selected a lightweight sports coat, brown herringbone. Briefly, he debated whether to carry a gun. Deciding he would not want to use it but might need to show it, he opened his handkerchief drawer and rooted to the back. The automatic, he noted, was empty. He loaded it and tucked it into his inside breast pocket and glanced at himself in the mirror. The bulge would not be so conspicuous, he decided, if he didn't button his coat but allowed it to hang more loosely. Even then, he could feel the gun tightly against his chest and he hated the closeness of it; it made him feel not more secure, but less. As he was about to leave the bedroom, Abby entered.

"Well, holy—" she said. "What are you all dressed up for?"

"You won't make a face if I tell you?"

"You've got to work?"

"Yes."

"I will make a face. I'll freeze ugly."

He moved closer to her but did not touch her. "If anybody calls, you don't know where I am. Even if it's Kley."

Her face shadowed. "Really?"

"Yes."

"Does that mean . . . anything?"

He tried to say something of circumstance, yet vague. "It's just a matter of . . . first priority."

"That's flannel, isn't it?"

Apologetically, "Yes."

"Why? . . . Is it dangerous?"

"Well, not really."

She heard the reservation and moved near, to embrace him. She felt the gun. "It is, isn't it?"

He hated responding to the word. He made a show of scoffing at it. "Me—in something dangerous? I have a clerical position."

She was too bright to be taken in by fatuities, or to let him get away with them. "I don't mind your being inane, Thaddeus. I just don't like your being dauntless. I know you very well, darling. I know all the pitched battles you fight—even some of the little skirmishes. And I know how brave you are. And you *are* that, brave. But what I cherish most is that little spot of cowardice in you. It'll keep you safe. I cherish that above everything else."

"It's bigger than a little spot."

"You're closer to it than I am. Up close everything looks bigger."

As he was putting his keys and driver's license into his pocket, she caught sight of his bruised hand and started to touch it. She's going to kiss it, he thought, and he snatched it away, not wanting her any more deeply degraded by the duplicity. She saw the reflexive movement and misconstrued it. "Does it hurt?"

"A little. Not much."

Shortly thereafter, he departed. As he got into the car, he tried to calm his stir of expectancy. But then he let the excitement gather, enjoying it. He was going to see Johanna. He was going for Tokan. The two things, in some unbridled way, belonged to each other.

Thirteen

NOT A WORD between them. Not the briefest telephone call to tell her he was coming, yet Johanna knew, she knew for certain, without a quiver of doubt, that Tad would be back. Toward late afternoon, she expected he already would have been there. It puzzled her that he wasn't. As the sun started to set, she knew he would arrive before dinner, any minute, and she carefully considered how to dress.

She must, indeed, be more cautious in what clothes she wore tonight, she warned herself. No more heedless nightgowns, no reckless inattentions to a man's presence; she no longer had madness to excuse such thoughtlessness. She was a calculated woman now, not even slightly off balance any more. She must remember that if clothes can entice, they can also set limits—and limits with her son-in-law must clearly be defined. He was to be her ally against Tokan, nothing more; if indeed she could intrigue him into being even that. Clandestine though such a relationship must be—for his sake more than her own—that was the totality of it. Not one breath more. The man was forbidden, taboo. There were mountains, the Hawaiians said, that must never be scaled, for they will boil at the heart and the hot evil will flow down the mountainside. Thinking of her son-in-law that way was a depravity, born of desolation; stop it. She had had only one drink.

She dressed in a two-piece beige cotton suit, with a white cotton blouse; she buttoned her jacket almost to the neck. She had another drink and very little dinner, and it was dark. He hadn't come.

Well, she had imagined it all. The simple fact was: there had been no communication. They had made no appointment, no rendezvous, they hadn't said a word; no message. But she had thought there *had* been a message. A silent one, through Abby, as clear, as

261

direct, as unambiguous as if they had spoken face to face and made an assignation. The lie, through Abby, was the truth to each other. Then why had he refused to respond to it?

She had misconstrued the silences between them. The quiet moment in the courtyard outside Karli's house, the moment when she had hurt his hand, and this whole day of silence. It was a failing of hers. She was always disappointing herself by assuming rich promises in silence. If she ever asked Oscar for something and he didn't say no, she always assumed his stillness meant yes. When she was a child, after her first unhappy year at school, her parents promised her a most special present, something they assured her she would love.

"I know what it is," she had said. "You're going to take me out of school, and when you move to Europe, you'll take me with you."

Silence. When the birthday came, she was registered again in the boarding school and they left her for another year. The actual present was a huge life-sized toy, a lovely, warm, cuddly stuffed sheepdog—somebody, they said, she could take to bed with her. She was too old to take toys to bed and too young to have stopped crying, but she had indeed stopped, years ago. So, instead of tears, she stabbed the sheepdog with a scissors and threw handfuls of its stuffing out the dormitory window, into a rainy night.

But that was childhood credulousness. She should, by now, in her forties, have learned the lesson, don't walk so hopefully in other people's silences. But she'd go bumbling into the darkness, barking her shins against unimagined rejections.

If he didn't come, it would be worse than rejecting her; he would be rejecting the whole Tokan business. Leaving her alone to deal with a man who was unquestionably—at least unquestionably in her mind— a murderer. And since there was violence in it, she knew that if the time came when she might have to meet it with violence of her own, she would almost certainly not have it to give. She was not equal to any of it; not alone.

So she would, after all, have to take herself out of action. She would have to deal with her rage passively, in solitude. Take it to bed with her at night, like the sheepdog, and stick scissors into it. She would wind up hagridden by herself, learning to hate yellow people, sticking pins into slant-eyed effigies. She would drink a lot, nursing her ineffectual wrath in alcohol, an anger-shriveled female homunculus preserved in a martini.

Tad arrived at 8:30.

As she let him in, he said, "I came to return your lighter."

She didn't mind his needing pretenses; she felt enkindled. "Oh, do you have it? I wondered where I left it."

"In the car."

She turned away from the door and, as she entered the living room, she felt him close behind her. When she looked at him again, he was reaching into his pocket for the lighter. It wasn't, apparently, there. He tried another pocket, then the rest. It wasn't in any of them. He smiled in a way that left him, somehow, less concealed. "I had it in my hand, driving over. I must have left it on the seat."

She said nothing. They simply stood there, only half glancing at each other.

He said, "You didn't say anything to Abby."

"Nor did you."

"No."

We're both trying to say as little as possible, she thought, and succeeding very well.

"I'm going to try to find Tokan," he said.

"Are you?" He was waiting for her to continue. "Where will you look?"

"The most obvious place," he said. "Where he lives." He paused. "Do you think you could tell me where that is?"

"I'm not sure," she said. "I had to be guided there."

Was he, after all, going to exclude her from the search? Or was he simply giving her choices? "But I'm sure I could find it," she offered.

"Do you want to come?"

"Yes, I do."

"Can you come now?"

"Yes."

She left him and went back into the bedroom for a lightweight coat. It would be chilly; the nights were getting windy. As she was buttoning the coat, the word *kaaluna* came to her mind. It was Hawaiian and it meant sailing against the wind; more idiomatically, a recklessness with nature.

Nothing about Tokan's garden had changed, yet it seemed, tonight, altogether different. It was not, she told herself, because last time she had come alone and this time, with Tad. He looked at her, sensing her disorientation, asking if they had come to the right place. Certain she was not lost, she nodded, yet she was vaguely disturbed at not knowing what had changed. Perhaps nothing, perhaps only the light. A few nights later in the phases of the moon might make all the difference. The stone lanterns were the same. So were the gray and golden carp, barely disturbing the motionless and silent pool, so was the gravel underfoot, the same ominous crunch.

Perhaps that was the difference. The sound last time was not, on reconsideration, ominous. She had been expected—invited, in fact, and guided there with bowing courtesies; the noise underfoot had been neutral. Tonight's sound was a warning.

She was frightened. Tad's presence, contrary to her expectation, made her frightened all the more. She wondered why, wondered if a man's presence increased the possibility of challenge, perhaps provoked it, whereas a woman alone merely invoked inquiry. No, the situation itself had become more dangerous. Last time, under that earlier phase of the moon, she had walked this gravel path to meet a man who had avenged injury with injury. Under tonight's phase, she was walking toward a murderer. Perhaps even an institutional one, backed by power and patriotism and respectability. He was, at the least, an assassin of careful circumstance, with practiced virtuosity and dexterous allies. How rashly they had come, she thought.

And suddenly they were there. Twenty feet before they arrived at his door, it opened. Out of the doorway an oblong of yellow light, like a golden carpet, was spread on the gravel path. There was no one on the threshold, only the glow, and there was no sound.

Then they heard the voice. Tokan's. "Come in—please come in."

They walked into the illumination, up the steps, then into the darkness of the entryway. Johanna heard a movement behind the door, then had a glimpse of the middle-aged woman who had guided her those nights ago. She was a flickering white kimono, then gone, that quickly, Johanna couldn't tell where—outdoors, perhaps, into the darkness.

Tokan stood in the middle of the room. Before, she had seen him in American clothes, but now he was dressed in a *hakama,* a divided skirt so closely pleated that it seemed to be made of fine chains of silver. His kimono shaded from gray to deepest brown, and on it he wore a delicately stitched family crest, an embroidery. As he moved, his costume had a hundred lights in it; it was extraordinarily beautiful. Even in Japan she had not seen such attire, and she had the feeling he had unpacked it from under layers of heritage, to try to make new wonders out of old ceremonies.

He didn't wait for Tad to be introduced. He inclined his head a little and whispered, "Mr. Clarke," then, correcting himself and inclining his head again as if to acknowledge a second introduction, "Commander Clarke." Before either visitor had a chance to speak, possibly to put them at their ease, he spoke again. His voice was muted and respectful; it was deeply grave. "You have come to arrest me," he said.

She couldn't have answered. Tad did. She heard him trying for meticulousness, keeping everything straight, everything in order. "I wouldn't have put it that way," he said. "We're not police officers. But, yes—that's what we're here for."

With utmost politeness—an apology altogether genuine—Tokan said, "Would you give me your gun, please?"

Johanna saw Tad tighten. The Japanese said quickly, "Forgive me for saying that. I have put you in the awkward position of having to prove how brave you are. I should not have done that."

Like ritual dancing—swiftly, adroitly—he was across the room. He reached upward—not even at Tad, it seemed—upward, toward the ceiling. Then a step or two backward, a short bow, a little outcry of apology, a touch on Tad's shoulder—not more than a touch—and the gun was in Tokan's hand. Deftly he broke it open, deposited the cartridges into one hand, the automatic in the other, and moved back to Tad again. As if ashamed to be in possession of something that did not belong to him—made untidy by it—he returned the gun.

Almost in self-rebuke, "Please do not be embarrassed," he said. "Mrs. Winter—Commander Clarke—please sit down." When he saw they were not about to be seated, he hastened to fill the discomfiting pause. "If it will make things easier, let me say quickly—I *want* you to arrest me."

What she saw in his face was totally incomprehensible. A look of compassion, she thought for an instant, humane, wounded, the pitying eyes of one who is sharing an affliction. Then, fleeting, she had the sense that his pain was private, all his own. And that he was enjoying it.

Because she was the first to sit, she was the one to whom he addressed himself. He had drawn back a little; whatever expression she thought she had seen was no longer there. His politeness had returned, he was lacquered again.

"I am sorry you were harmed last night," he said. "But your being there was a surprise, and hurting you was not part of the plan."

"I understand," she said. "Only killing Nishi."

He didn't blink. "Not even that. We were—shall we say—inducing him to seppuku. It could have been done gracefully—in a mortuary, a fitting and ceremonial place. But then, with your arrival, it had to be hurried—and bungled a little, I'm afraid."

"In fact, it had to be done *for* him."

Reluctantly, "Yes." Then, hastily, "But that is between us, I hope. His wife and children think it was seppuku. Their grief is tempered by the dignity. So, at the end, Nishi received far better than he gave. He certainly did not deserve to leave his family with such a noble picture of himself."

"You would have to believe that, wouldn't you?" Tad said.

"I do believe it—he betrayed me. Twice. The first time, for a garnet bracelet. The second time— You see, he agreed to leave the city and not come back. When no indictment was brought against me, he felt he could return to his family. He knew very well it was against our agreement."

"It was unforgivable, wasn't it?—his wanting to be with his family," Johanna said.

"Forgiveness has nothing to do with anything." He took no umbrage at her remark, "I forgive him. I forgive myself. I forgive everyone for having human feelings. Starting with your son, and ending with me, we are—what is the expression—'frail giants'—to be feared and to be forgiven. But what has that to do with Nishi's *haji?*"

"Guilt, you mean?"

"No. *Haji* does not mean guilt—it means shame."

"Ultimately the same."

"Not at all," the Japanese said. "Guilt is vanity."

"Vanity, my God!"

Tokan seemed barely to note the disparagement. "Yes, vanity. You Americans say to yourself, 'I know when I am guilty—my conscience tells me so.' It is called—by self-identity—a guilty conscience. But it is you who are speaking to yourself—and one of you can be very easily mistaken. Or misled. Or bribed by a comfortable feeling—or a bracelet. You have all sorts of ways to give yourselves the benefit of the doubt. You say to yourselves, 'There's another way of looking at it'; you say 'extenuating circumstance'; you say 'justifica-

tion'; you say 'the quality of mercy is not strained.'
And when you have found the most soothing expression, you find not only that your punishment is mitigated, but you weren't even guilty in the first place. You
can then, without damage to your vanity—which you
call conscience—fall in love with yourselves all over
again. The guilt is gone." He paused a moment. Then:
"But *shame* will not permit that. Shame does not come
from the judgment of yourself; it is the judgment you
see in the eyes of others. Your friends tell it to you,
your neighbors, the people who work beside you. Your
wife, your parents, even your children tell you. Oh,
not necessarily in words; we are more polite than that.
Not even in our actions. Nobody ever stops inclining
the head or opening the door or giving the mouth of
welcome. Only the eyes change. The warm eyes of a
daughter turn cold as winter. The lively eyes of an old
friend become glazed with death. Shame is in the eyes
of the world. There is no escaping it. There is no argument that will alter it, because, except for the law,
charges are rarely made. No plea will gentle it because
there is rarely a spoken verdict. So ultimately you must
pronounce the verdict upon yourself, you release your
friends of it, you release them from the pain of performing continuous acts of cruelty upon you. You have
done them all a most profound kindness—you are a
man of generosity and courage and nobility. And if you
perform the action upon yourself with grace, you redress a grievance, you restore the balance of the world,
you create a small poem."

"And Nishi refused . . ."

"Yes."

"So you murdered him."

He looked at her, puzzled, seemingly disappointed
in her: she had not understood enough of what he had
said: "You think that is why I told you I want to be
arrested?"

"Isn't it?"

"Oh, no." His disappointment in her apparently justified, he turned away a little. His voice was unsteady.
"A more terrible reason."

The terrible reason came unexpectedly to her mind. Apparently Tad thought the same; they exchanged a quick glance. Tokan had killed his wife.

"Where is Muna?" Johanna asked.

He made a painful effort to smile. "No, I did not kill her."

"Where is she?"

"She has run away."

"Where?"

He didn't respond. At last, tormentedly, "I don't know." He started to speak softly, with great difficulty, seeming uncertain how much of the pain he could handle in words, uncertain even of the chronology of events that had led him to his unhappiness. "I said 'more terrible,' and it is. A Japanese man does not speak of loving his wife. It is an idea too open and too closed. Whatever I felt for her, it was the instant I saw her. Her family—most of the Japanese in Honolulu—came from Hiroshima. They came here to work in the fields, because that's what they did in Hiroshima. I met her first—there—in her native town. It is a kinder place than Tokyo. I always found life sweeter there. I loved Hiroshima very much. You see, it is easy to say 'love' about a place—not so easy about a woman. So, everything I found in her was what I found in Hiroshima— simplicity and sweetness and the sense she would always be as she was when I first saw her." Now, as he managed to distance himself from his memories, they came more readily. "One day I met your son. He came to my shop, ostensibly to look at curios. Actually, he was trying to betray some information from me. He was interested in the Purple Code. He suspected I knew something about it." He turned to Tad. "Do you also suspect it?"

Tad answered with a question. *"Do* you know something about it?"

"If I say I do not, you will not believe me, will you?"

"Since you were the one to mention the Purple Code —no, I won't believe you."

"Ben did . . . finally."

"I doubt that very much."

"Did he ever tell you anything about it?" Tokan inquired quietly. Tad hesitated too long for a lie to have been convincing. The American's silence gave the Japanese the answer he expected; he nodded. "If he hadn't believed me, wouldn't he have spoken to you about it?"

It was a plausible point and Tad again delayed, but this time he recovered quickly. "There was an obvious reason why Ben might not want to tell anybody anything—until he was certain, and until he had to."

Muna, the obvious reason, her name unspoken, was like a presence in the room. Tad had struck a wounding blow; the man slowly inclined his head, in deference to a worthy opponent. "You are a bright man, Commander—and without subterfuge. I appreciate that. Your brother-in-law was not so sincere as you are. From the beginning, he was full of little tricks. He came to me babbling about old scrolls and inkstone boxes. But I was not offended—his naïveté amused me. So I played with him, I flattered the young man. I complimented him on his Japanese—and one evening I brought him home with me. I don't know why I did it—it was an impulse—I rarely brought visitors home with me. But I liked him. And that very first evening, I should have been forewarned. No matter how much more naïve Americans are about the art of love, they are far more sophisticated in the art of flirtation. And it started instantly. When I first presented my wife to him—I don't know what glance he gave her—she behaved in a way that seemed strange to me. For one thing, she did not leave the room, as she should have, immediately after the introduction. I had never seen her loiter in the presence of a guest. Certainly I had never had occasion to send her out of the room; I could not imagine I would ever have to. But that night I did. And when he departed—it was already evening—I saw her walking along the pathway where she knew he would have to see her. And she was not wearing a kimono, but an American dress.

"One night, on a pretext of having to show me a valuable curio he had come upon, he arrived at my house uninvited. I was of course polite to him. But then a shocking thing happened. My wife, also uninvited, entered the room. And although I am certain they did not speak a single word to each other, I am equally certain they had their first meeting—somewhere —however briefly—that night.

"A perturbing thing happened to me in the next few weeks. I stopped being a Japanese man, I became an American husband. I did not warn her and I did not rebuke her, not even by a glance. I certainly did not command her to account for every hour of her day. I kept my suspicions, my jealousy, my heartache, all to myself. And because I was too proud, possibly too frightened, to say what I felt, they both became more bold, even blatant. She would disappear for hours at a time, occasionally at night. She began to hide little keepsakes that I knew he must have bought for her; she even—" he paused, to deal with the humiliation—"began to smell of scents I had never noticed before."

An outcry: "If only they had been more circumspect! If they had allowed me to pretend that the falseness was all in my mind—! But they would not allow me to pretend anything, because they themselves were past pretending. There is a wanton honesty about love, even when it is most dishonest. It is a candor that celebrates cruelty to others. They exposed their love, like an obscene insult. Even my friends became aware of it . . . And then Nishi brought me the pictures . . . So there was no pretending any more—not in them and not in me—and I read my shame everywhere.

"So I mutilated him and told myself it was a fitting justice. Even the Japanese newspaper said it was a fitting justice. But I knew it was not. It was despicable— it was what we Japanese call the justice of bedbugs. It was American justice. It did nothing. It certainly did not redress an imbalance in the world. The earth still tips. And nothing I have ever done—nothing I will ever do —can bring me comfort again. Every day I live, I will dwindle with shame!"

It was a cry of such self-loathing, his voice made a tumult in the room. He shook with it. After a while he spoke with deathly calm. "The terrible irony is that there was never any doubt in my mind what I had to do. My duty was clear, it was always clear. I was required, as a man who had to resolve the dilemma of faithlessness, to kill them both; and then, as a man already dead, to put the same knife to myself.

"But we have become Westernized, some of us. We have begun to speak of love in other ways than we can ever really know, we speak of living as if it had a virtue in itself. We are losing courage and finding extenuations. We have begun to talk about guilt, which is a coward's morality, and we are learning to live with shame."

He was silent. He was viewing the aftermath of a catastrophe; a hurricane, its wreckage. "After your son came out of the hospital, he telephoned her, but she did not go and see him. I took this as a good omen, and I made what you might call an 'adjustment.' That is, as long as my wife continued to stay with me, I adjusted myself to the fact that she despised me. I was learning, as you see, to live without pride, and I might ultimately have mastered the craft of it—if your son had not killed himself. On the day Muna read about his death in the newspapers, she screamed so terribly that I thought her voice would shatter the universe. Japanese women do not scream like that. Then she disappeared. I thought perhaps she might have returned to Hiroshima. Then I thought she too went down to the sea and threw herself into it . . . I do not know . . . I hope, Hiroshima . . . In the last few days, I have bathed myself countless times and I have rinsed my mouth and prepared myself for the knife. But I cannot do it. I am no better than Nishi. I have come to the final cowardice: life itself is more important than my station in it. You cannot know how tormenting that is to me. All the clean air has been sucked out of the world and I breathe only the vapors of contempt. Even my government has contempt for me. As soon as all this news became known, I was told I was no longer useful. When you have worked for the government in Japan and it will no longer have you, you no longer have yourself. In America, if you stop being a civil servant, you can start to be something else. In Japan, when the government door is closed, no other door is open. Contempt. Shame and contempt."

He turned away from them and opened two doors of a narrow cupboard. The knife he held was long, its blade gleaming, its hilt inlaid with dull brass and rubbed wood.

"This has never been used," he said. "It has not even, as we say, cut the petal of a chrysanthemum. It is a fine knife—it is too good for me. I am not worthy of myself, only of the punishment by others. By . . . Americans."

It was the definitive mortification. "It is kind of you to come to me," he concluded. "If you wait until I change into a less Oriental costume, I will join you."

Johanna barely nodded. Tad made no movement and said nothing. Tokan bowed deeply and left the room. His movement made a soft rustling of satin. Then even that was gone. They did not hear him in the next room, heard not the slightest sound of the man changing his clothes.

Tad was studying the objects in the room, the beautiful figurines of old ceramic, the books bound in rubbed vellums and hand-painted silks. She wondered, watching him, if he was really seeing the art objects he was looking at, the books he touched. His mind could not, she was certain, be so deeply occupied with physically embodied things. Hers wasn't.

Hers was full of marvel at how, at last, this thing had settled itself, and so appropriately. She marveled too at how unaccountably she pitied the man in the next room. There must be something wrong with her, something irremediably romantic, if she could allow herself such a swing from all-consuming rage to such a rueful compassion for someone who had caused the death of two people, one of them her own son. She was allowing herself to be moved by old affections—for Japan, for Mitsu, for bygone happinesses she lamented; she was being swayed by an abstract sympathy for a different way of life. She was making room in her mind for distinctions: in the mind, for justice; in the muscles, for balance; in the eye, for beauty. And she was an easy mark for a man who might also be seeking distinctions, a man who could descry every nuance of his own cowardice, who could convict himself with such self-loathing. His very self-abasement was in her eyes a kind of honesty, a merciless honesty so soul-shriving that he had come out of the torment almost cleansed; only seppuku could have cleansed him to whiter purity. It was a Japanese absolution; she could not imagine it as American. The concept of *station*—she had quite forgotten this—had a different meaning. In the West it entailed a view of self-worth, its illimitable promise, the hope for the heights of glory; in the East it included a view of one's worthlessness, and the abyss. With suicide as salvation. But for this tragic man, too smitten with life . . . unattainable.

There was a change in the atmosphere of the room. She couldn't tell what it was. Nor had it just this moment started; she had the sense she had been subliminally aware of it moments ago. At first she thought it was a new scent, fresher than she had noted when they had entered the house. But now it was an almost imperceptible movement in the room, only an air current, perhaps. She saw what it was. The curtain had been stirring only lightly before; now it billowed from the open window, came to rest and returned, billowing again. It *was* a change; there had been no draft through the room before.

Even before she investigated, she knew. So did Tad.

"Tokan!" he called.

A moment.

No answer.

He ran through the open doorway and Johanna hurried after him.

Tokan's bedroom was empty. His *hakama* lay on the floor, his sandals, his kimono. The room was in a disarray of haste. One of the French windows was open, and the bamboo shade, stirring in the breeze, made hardly a sound.

Like Ben, he had gone into his bedroom to get dressed; like Ben, through a back door, he had dis-

appeared. How gullible they had been. In a police report, it would never have been believed, certainly not
a second happening of a similar kind. In a detective
fable, in an annal of espionage, real or fictional, in
an operative's memorandum, it would never be given
even a single point for credulity, but would have been
judged a camouflage for something sinisterly concealed.
How could Johanna, as a newspaper person, or Tad,
as an Intelligence officer, dare to write: I was taken
in by the human factor, by the heartache of the man,
by his shame, by his frailty, by mine, by the frailty
of all of us, of giants. How absurd. Giants, indeed.

Fourteen

"**W**HY DO YOU BRING others into it?" Karli said querulously. "Why the hell do you do that?"

He was referring to himself, of course, but he was also referring to Johanna. They stood in the recess of the restaurant where Karli always secreted himself, and the man, in a sweat of anxiety, hated them being there, especially Tad's companion.

"Besides," he continued, his whine getting more plaintive, "I don't *know* where he went."

"You *can* know, Karli." Tad was patient but persistent. He had set his mind on a deliberate tactic with the man: calm, immovable tenacity. "And you *will* know. We won't rush you—we'll wait until you do." Then, thinking of Kley, "Because none of us wants to go to the police."

At the mention of police, Karli began to have more trouble with his breathing. It wasn't, Tad conjectured, the man's fear of the police themselves—he probably had nothing to hide from them—it was more likely his terror of exposure to others, whoever they might be. When he had a breath to spare, Karli said sullenly, "I thought I had a choice—I could help you or not, the way I wanted. But that's not true, is it? In the end, if you people want something, I have to give it."

"I'm sorry."

"Another lie." Then, rankling, he looked at Johanna. "Do you need the whole world in on this?"

"I'll put her in a taxi. It'll be just you and me."

"Not here," Karli said. "I'll go home."

"I'll meet you there."

Karli reached for his jacket on a hook behind him. He pulled a gray scarf out of the pocket and started to wrap it around his head as a protection against the night air. Then he made a brusque gesture for them to disappear; he didn't want to leave in their company.

As they got into the car, Tad could feel Johanna's unspoken questions piling up. But she didn't unburden herself of them until they arrived at the taxi stand. When she spoke, she had, surprisingly, no cavil in her voice. She was asking a direct, uncomplicated question and seemed to promise not to judge the answer. "You're not shutting me out of this, are you?"

"No, I'm not."

"Are you sure?"

"Yes. I'll be back later."

"And if you're not . . . ?"

"I will be," he assured her. "And don't worry about me."

"If you're not back, I'll call the police."

"No please don't do that."

"I will call them." It was not a threat. She simply meant she would not take chances with his safety; nothing more.

When her taxi was gone, he made a U-turn and drove toward Karli's place. He resented the time it would take to cross through Chinatown, with Tokan getting farther and farther away, so he pushed the car to its top speed. When he got into the courtyard, he parked as he had done the night before, not far from Karli's steps. He hurried into the dark passageway and ran upstairs.

The door was open. Karli was taking a breather. He was seated on the high stool, against the sideboard, his head covered with the towel, his face inclined forward over the hot water in the basin. Except for the fact that there were no noisy snufflings, no labored inhalations of breath, his breather was no different this time from the last. He didn't move, however, not even when Tad called his name. He was dead. It required a tug at the man's body to lift his head out of the still-steaming water. A gush of the yellow liquid came out of his mouth, and small bubbles, out of his nose. Perhaps he had scalded to death, Tad thought, or his heart had stopped beating in the midst of the treatment; most likely, his head had been held under the surface of the water and he had drowned in the shallow basin. Whatever, he would no longer have to flee from the dangerous night air.

Behind him, Tad thought he heard a door open and close. He stepped back into the dark kitchen, away from the sound, and waited. It seemed a long time, and the stir was not followed by any other. He came out of the darkness, went to the doorway, opened the door and stepped aside. Nothing. He inched his way onto the landing at the top of the stairs. He looked down the flight of steps and saw nobody.

Then a hurrying sound, shuffling. It was down below, in the courtyard. He could hear the footsteps, a rush of them. He couldn't decide whether or not to go down the steps. But he couldn't remain here unless, at whatever disclosure of himself, he called the police. Slowly he descended the staircase.

The courtyard was silent. The single post lamp threw more shadows than light. There was no sign of anybody. But he thought of all kinds of perils—someone lurking under the archway, someone hiding in the car, or the car itself as a danger, brakeless or converted into a fireball.

Even though the distance to the car was short, he dreaded crossing to it. Tread by tread he approached the vehicle. Nothing happened. No gunshot, no *himo* around his neck garroting him, no figure darting out of the blackness. He opened the car door and stood back. Nobody in it. Nothing unusual. Even Johanna's lighter, intact, on the front seat.

Then he saw the paper. A white sheet, folded, tucked up against the windshield. Carefully, not yet getting into the car, he lifted the paper out and held it. He had an impulse to get into the car and read it, but he was not yet altogether secure about enclosing himself. Reaching in, he flipped on the headlights. Then he stepped toward the beams and, by their illumination, read the meticulously handwritten note:

My dear Commander Clarke,
    This evening, everything I told you was true, except that I would come with you. That, unfortunately, I

had to lie about. For which I ask you to forgive me. A man is entitled to his revenge, and I have deprived you of yours. This I so deeply regret that I cannot bring myself to beg the least merciful remission.

Yet, you must understand. I could not allow myself to be turned over to the law and its petty processes. I cannot die by a rope, nor can I linger forever in a place where iron bars make shadows across my brighter memories, where my whole life is spent adding the small sums of my hateful selves.

So I am a fugitive.

From this day, every knife I see will be a reminder of my cowardice; every day I live will be a sin. It is said that one prayer will wipe away ten thousand sins and that one cry suffices for a compassionate salvation. I have, in some way, made a confusion: my ten thousand cries will not wipe away my single sin. As to prayer, I am too old in the world to believe in it.

What I need now is an enemy stronger than myself. So I beg you not to forsake me: be my enemy. Do not stop; remain steadfast in your hostility, nurture your malice. You may be a kinder enemy to me than I have been a friend to myself.

Come after me. If you do, I warn you I will not make it easy for you in any way; I am sure you would not want me to insult you by doing so. But I promise —whatever the outcome—you will not regret having accepted the challenge.

> *Yours most respectfully,*
> *Kano Tokan*

He finished reading the letter, folded it, and tucked it into the inside pocket of his coat. Slowly he walked back to the car door and opened it. But still he did not get in. Abstractedly, thinking of what he had just read, he reached for the cigarette lighter, held it in his hand for a moment, then dropped it into his trouser pocket. At last he got into the car.

Sitting there, he did not know what the next step might be. The letter was too bizarre. Tokan's heartbreak had unbalanced the man. He was bereft of reason . . . or possessed of too much of it. Possessed—yes, that was the word. It was a word Tad was beginning to understand; he could feel something of possession overtaking him. It had to do with Johanna, of course, but it also had to do with this man. Possession.

No, he must not think of it that way. He must not view this quest as being, in any form, an aberration. For Johanna, it might be: going for Tokan was going for revenge. For himself, it was to vindicate Commander Clarke, the officer, to find the meaning of the Purple Code, the meaning of himself as a man of courage, with talent at his job. Those were good, old-fashioned, rational, commonsensical reasons for going on a quest; they were reasons worth the risk.

So—now—to the common sense of it: what was the next step? Without Karli, he had no inkling where or how to begin the search for Tokan. He had no agents, no stringers, no informants deployed in that direction, none at all. He knew nobody who could supply him with even one smattering of information about Tokan.

Except Kley.

He debated whether to go through the main gate or one of the rear ones. If he went to the rear, the guard might not know him. He'd have to furnish identification and his entrance and departure would be put on the report. At the main gate, however, where he might be lucky enough to be recognized, the guard might neglect to write him down.

Deciding on the main, he drove up to it, waved and started through. The light flashed and the guard came running. Tad stopped and rolled his window down. He spoke as casually as possible. "I'm going to Radio, North."

"Identity, sir."

"Commander Clarke," Tad replied. "Intelligence Auxiliary—Special Section."

Nothing changed in the guard's face. He was waiting, vigilant. Tad, annoyed at having to root for his identification, moved too abruptly and the guard tightened. Then suddenly the man relaxed. "Oh, yes," he said. "Schotley's department, right?"

He smiled wryly at the guard's thinking Schotley was his superior. "That's right."

"Didn't know you out of uniform, sir." His flashlight went off, the man drifted back to his post, making no move to write anything, and Tad rode through.

He drove the whole distance toward Radio, North, not stopping to make the turn toward Kley's building. All around him he could feel the looming grays, the superstructures of the warships, the overhang of the signal tower, the ominous pendency of the derricks. The smell of the sea was tangier here than on the playtime beaches of Kailua and Waikiki, brinier, as if the blood of battles were already in it, and the sweat and gunpowder.

Radio, North was at the end of the road, a small, low building, partly tin, corrugated. In case anybody saw him, he would have to pretend to go inside, make some sort of busywork in the Files Room, then come out the back way, in the dark. He rooted in his pocket for his keys and, walking toward the main entrance, jangled them a little; if anyone was looking, he wanted his behavior to seem routine and innocuous.

His old key to the front door didn't fit; they had changed the locks. Well, he thought with mixed feelings, at least in this building, unlike his own, a regime of vigilance had begun.

But it meant he would have to move more circumspectly, not making ostentatious little clatterings with keys. He looked in both directions and quietly slipped out of the lamplight, into the dark. Starting toward the end of the building, he crossed the concrete walk. As he turned the corner to enter the dirt street behind the building, he stopped and slid back again, into the shadow. Two shore patrolmen were walking toward him, going to barracks. He let them pass. When they made a diagonal crossing, away from him, he hastened onto the rutted dirt.

Every night noise was helpful to him. From somewhere, the screech of a winch, the hiss of steam, the turning of a derrick. Farther away, working through the night, riveters and chippers were beating a tattoo;

hammers clanged at protesting steel. Elsewhere, a porthole slammed open; somebody cursed, somebody laughed; he heard the squeezed trill of an accordion.

He was at one of the back doors of Kley's building. It was locked; the other back door was locked as well. If they were locking rear entrances, he thought discouragedly, his chance of getting in the front was minimal. But there was no predicting the capriciousness of security; the front door was not only unlocked but wide open, as if someone had started to air the place, and had forgotten. His luck didn't hold. Walking along the dark corridor, feeling for doorways with his hand, counting each one, he stopped at the fourth—and the door was tight. He tried the only three of his keys that might fit, but none of them turned anything. Then, the twist-tumbler skeleton; it wouldn't even go in.

If the lock was a simple one and not flagship regulation, he might be able to pick it. He had a combination pocketknife, with a number of blades and gadgets, and he might also have a paper clip. What he needed mostly was light, and he hadn't any. Then he remembered Johanna's lighter.

A light here would be dangerous, he knew, but there was nobody; both ends of the hallway, deserted. He flicked the light, bent over and peered. No good: the lock was special issue.

The sound was like a gunshot. The front door, caught by the wind, blew shut. Not daring to take a chance that it had been merely wind, he hurried still farther away from the front door, made the turn in the hallway, and entered the men's room. The instant he got inside, the inspired memory struck him. Kley's private bathroom backed onto the plumbing of the public one. And he remembered, too, from having seen the work being done, that what had been originally the men's-room cleaning cupboard had been preempted by Kley as his own clothes closet. There would be two doors, one this side, one in the old man's office.

He twisted the wheel of the lighter, held the flame steady, flashed its light on sinks, on urinals, and there it was, the narrow door. The lock was an ordinary old-fashioned warded one, without tumblers, only bolt, ward and keyhole. Even a key was unnecessary. Pushing his weight against the door, he inserted the thinnest knife blade, and the bolt slipped back. He extinguished the lighter and entered the darkness. Coats, hanging things, were all around him, brushing against his face. He groped for the knob on the other side and, finding it on his left, shoved the clothes hangers to the right. The wire made a scraping sound on the metal rod and he was motionless a moment, awaiting an eventuality. None happened. If this too was a warded lock, it would not be as easy to open as the other one had been. No need to; the door was unlocked.

It was a different room, entering it from this direction and in darkness. He had an impulse to try the lighter again, but he couldn't remember where the window was, and he didn't want to flash where someone might see. If he walked slowly, he told himself, he would be able to piece it all together. The window should be to his left, but since there was no light coming through it, he wasn't sure. Kley's desk, straight ahead, at right angles to the opposite wall. Yes, he could feel the edge of it. To the left, a visitor's chair, behind which, a few feet back, the other entrance leading by way of his ensign's office, to the outer hall. Where were the files, to the right of the doorway? No, that would be Kley's couch. Then the files had to be on the wall immediately adjoining the closet door, directly behind Tad and to his right. He turned, felt for the files in the dark, and was rewarded by the cold corner of metal.

He moved meticulously, stretching his arms out to feel the width of the steel cabinets. He remembered distinctly that the admiral had opened a top drawer, but there were four banks of files, and he couldn't recall whether it was the first or second bank. He flicked the cigarette lighter and flashed it on the title labels. The first bank was marked A-M and the second, N-Z. Thinking Tokan, he opened the second. He flashed the fluttering light across the file folders and envelopes, back and forth. No Tokan. It occurred to

him, abruptly, that Tokan might be the man's given
name; his surname, Kano. He closed the drawer and
opened the top one in the left bank.

There was no Kano, but there was a Kanoshima. And
it was on a red Fabrikoid envelope. Excited, he
snatched the envelope and laid it on top of the steel
cabinet. Inside, there were two folders; one of them
contained the sheets Kley had held in his hand. The
other one contained pictures of the man, snapshots,
one of Tokan leaving the Japanese consulate building,
another coming down the gangplank of the *Tatsuta
Maru*. No question about his identity. And pages of
data, in addition to the typed ones in the first folder;
also, a couple of holograph letters, a diagram of Tokan's house, pond and gardens, together with copies of
passports and visas, some going many years back.

For an instant, Tad had an impulse to take the envelope and hurry away, but even if it were safe, it
wouldn't be necessary. All he needed was a description
of the places the man might go to, perhaps only the
one place Kley had mentioned, somewhere near Hilo.
He read, he skimmed quickly. The fluid in the lighter
was running out, the flame was flickering badly now.
No other name than Hilo came off the page, not one.
Then: Palao. And now that he saw it once, the name
was there again, and still once more, with references to
woods, mountains, wilderness. The lighter went out.

The arm came from the darkness. It was around
his throat, a grappling arm, with something hard, a
tough, painful hard thing at his back, and he was
strangling.

"No!" he tried to say and, gasping, again, trying,
without any sound being made. He flipped the wheel
on the cigarette lighter. Dead. He flipped it once more,
the desperate hope, and it came alight again. He held
it against the bare arm that was strangling him. The
man cried in pain, and Tad was free, choking for
breath.

The electricity came on, overhead, blind white. He
was face to face with his assailant. Kley.

"You lunatic!" the admiral said. "You stupid, insubordinate lunatic!"

His thin gray hair was disheveled, his shirt was partly out of his trousers; the old man had been asleep on the couch.

He reached for the red envelope. "Give me that!" he cried.

Tad handed it to him. The normally suave old man had lost all his urbanity, he shook with outrage. Throwing the envelope on his desk, he rubbed his burned forearm, tried to bring his shaking voice under control, and couldn't.

"You don't do anything properly, do you? You don't know how to handle *anything,* do you? Do you? You don't know how to listen or take orders or look after your job or your own damn good! Do you?"

Tad was absolutely still.

The admiral, forcibly and by deliberation, took deep breaths. They helped him bring himself under control. In a moment, he was himself again; if anything, more unremittingly cold than Tad had ever seen him. "You're under hack," he said.

Not confined to quarters, but under hack; Tad had never heard an officer's arrest spoken in such humiliating terms. The old man was leaving no insult unspoken. "You're relieved of duties and restricted to limits," he added.

"What limits?"

"Your domicile."

Well, Tad thought grimly, at least I'm not thrown in the brig. And of course he knew why: Kley wanted to do it as quietly as possible. He could have one tiny retort's worth of revenge. Playing on the old man's penchant for duplicity, he said, "Would you like me to give it out that I'm sick, sir?"

"Get out."

Tad walked to his car. When he got into it, he couldn't move. His hands clutched the wheel as tightly as rigor mortis. His gut had a knife in it.

Under arrest.

He had never failed anything, never. He had slaved in order not to fail. And never—not an examination, not a seamanship trial, not an inspection, never. He had never been put on report, never been disciplined.

Under arrest. He didn't know how he could stand it. He would have to break out, some way or other he would have to break out. What a demented notion—break out. Why? What for? There was nothing to break out from—it wasn't as though he would be in jail, in a brig—he would simply be at home. Break out? Why did he think "break out"?

Why hadn't he broken out before?

If he had wanted the sea, why had he been content with Kley's "You're needed here"? Why hadn't he done as Ben had done—simply pushed past authority for a transfer? Why had he needed to stay here? What hearthstone of familiarity—(strange houses are frightening!)—did he hunger for? How long could he go on clinging to whatever place would allow him to form comfortable habits, see the same people every day, give him an illusion that he belonged with them, and he was home? When would he stop searching for a father, for cast-off surrogates, foster parents, paternal admirals, when would he stop picking pockets in the park? When would he break out?

He had to go for Tokan.

He had no alternative, really. Whatever motion had begun in him was past control now; it could not be arrested. If he acceded to the arrest, he would wind up like Tokan, filled with self-contempt. If Tokan needed social approval in order to survive, Tad needed self-approval. And he couldn't survive, frightened of the substitute poppas he had had and those he couldn't have, truckling to the institutional family, sucking up to the Navy tit, crying love me, shelter me, shelter me! Well, in one ironic sentence, Kley had given him the definitive shelter—jailed at home.

Break out.

Go for Tokan.

He had to. And he would.

It was an obsession now, a compulsion forward, into

whatever place the motion took him, into whatever action.

Suddenly he felt exhilarated. Felt, for the first time in his adult life, as if he had no public designation of any kind, not a Navy man, not an officer. Only a private name, his own. He did not have to answer to anybody; or more precisely, if he had to, he wouldn't. He had no number, he had no encoded desk or section. And, his private identity notwithstanding, he felt like an anonymous man, wearing the anonymous clothes that would make it impossible for anyone to sew stripes on him, labeling him a certain kind of man, a Navy kind, an officer kind, a commander kind. He no longer—at least not tonight—had a uniform. He need no longer strain against its confinements. Arrested, he was free.

It was frightening. It occurred to him that most people in the world lived in this same freedom, unfettered by the shackles of authority, free in a world of choices. Free to starve, free to be homeless, free to die of loneliness.

Frightening.

And euphoric.

It had a touch of madness in it.

Fifteen

WHEN TAD ARRIVED, considerably after nine o'clock, Johanna was not surprised at seeing him, but surprised at what he wore. She had last seen him in a sports jacket, nut-brown herringbone, with tan-colored trousers and brown shoes, and a shirt and tie that might have been blue or gray, all sedately assembled. Now he wore scrubby clothes, indeterminate-colored poplin trousers stuffed into laced-up field boots, a collarless knit shirt, and a hunting coat that seemed all pockets, something her father used to call a fowling jacket. Slung over his shoulders was the most shapeless, the most disreputable-looking rucksack she had ever seen.

She was about to make a flippancy but saw he would give no encouragement to it. The rifle he was carrying he carefully stood up against the wall beside the door, then he turned to face her. His speech was swifter than she had ever heard it, more abrupt, as if he were on troublesome maneuvers, talking to an incompetent subordinate.

"The man can be anywhere," he said. "But there's not much real choice—Palao, then. It's near Hilo—I don't know how far—never heard of it. He's got a plane—his own, a Piper Cub. If he's good at it, he can fly it by night and even land at night—the place must be familiar to him, and there's bright moon out there. At any rate, I'm going to Hilo—there's a night steamer leaves in an hour—do you want to come?"

His tone was, somehow, forbidding; she couldn't tell why. If he was angry, it was something she had no knowledge of, and she couldn't guess at it. She pointed to his gun. "It's hunt time, is it?"

"Yes." He seemed irritated with the obvious. "Do you want to come?"

"A night boat?"

"Yes—it lands in the morning—I don't know what time—early, I think."

"Abby . . ."

His irritability was mounting. "I've told her I'll be away for a few days. I didn't say why. I left her the car."

"How did you get here?"

"Christ."

She was silent. So was he. Then: "I'm sorry. Shouldn't I have asked about Abby?"

"By cab—I got here by cab," he said. He looked at his watch. "If you don't want to come . . ."

She wanted desperately to come and couldn't understand why she put off saying so. It wasn't only that there was something prohibitory about him; it was worse than that, brutal. Yet, had she ever thought of him as an easy, affable fellow? Did she, because of some qualm she herself had, need him to be gracious and well-mannered for this enterprise; did it have to be a Sunday-morning hunt, with ale at the landmarks and Pimm's Cup back at the Club?

"I want to come—you know that."

"Then why the hell don't you say so?"

"Do you have to be a bastard?"

"I'm sorry—I'm under hack."

She had heard the word before, of course, but didn't understand it out of context, coming so suddenly. "Under . . . ?"

"It's an old-fashioned word. It means—"

"I know what it means."

She saw it now: his tension. The nerves, bone splinters through the flesh. "But why?" she asked.

"I raided Kley's files—he caught me."

"Oh, God." She could see him suffering, and making anger of it. "Does Abby . . . ?"

He lashed. "Christ, what the hell difference whether she knows! No, she doesn't!" All at once, he was different; seemed to realize he was letting her have all of it, the vexation, the ache, keeping none for himself. "I'm sorry, Johanna." After a bit, he went on. "The peculiar thing—what I can't handle yet—when he first restricted me to limits—I was—it was wonderful, I was exhilarated. It was as if I had asked for it, I had *wanted* it—and it was *given* to me!" His worry became quieter, darker. "And now it's suddenly too much to have."

He was more distressed than he wanted her to see, but she saw enough of it. "Under hack for how long?"

"He didn't say."

"Where?"

"At home." He smiled bitterly. "Kley's got one of Wally Blackburn's stringers watching our house. Christ, you'd think he'd at least give me enough credit not to put an idiot on me—in an Auburn convertible I've seen a dozen times—!"

"How did you get out?"

"The most obvious way—the back door. Down the hill, through the brush. If anybody asks for me, Abby'll say I'm in bed with the flu."

She was silent. Then, softly, "I think you better go home."

Abruptly, his anger was back; he twisted to her. "You haven't heard a goddamn thing I've said! I'm going for Tokan—I've got to do it!"

"Don't yell at me!"

Remorsefully, reproaching himself, "Oh, Jesus."

There was no reason for what happened, nothing graceful about it either, no logical progression from one tenderness to another; they were simply clinging to each other. He held her crushingly tight, as if he wanted to hold himself that way; and the ache was what she needed for the moment, the more pain the better she could stand it. And the kissing had trouble in it too, the pleasure coming only through the hurt.

It had happened. An uneventful event. It had simply happened.

They were apart, then, not looking at one another, trying to make sense of an excitement that felt like an affliction.

Quietly, "Please go home, Tad," she said.

Before, when protesting that he had to go for Tokan,

his vehemence had made his determination seem suspect. But now he spoke with deliberation. "No . . . I'm going for him."

"Don't. You can't—it's an arrest. You can't."

He had a strange expression, part wonder, the rest indefinable. "Yes. I know I can't—and yet I'm going to do it."

"It may be exciting—for the moment—but you won't like what's happening to you."

"What *is?*"

"I don't know—disorder."

"Yes." Putting a word to it, even so inconclusive a word, seemed to steady him. "Like a riot in the street . . ."

"You're frightened . . . aren't you?"

"Yes . . . but I like it." Altogether controlled now, he said, "Will you come with me?"

She made a small, almost imperceptible gesture to the place in the room where they had clung to one another. "After that? . . . I couldn't."

"If I promise I won't come near you?"

"What good is that? . . . I'd come near you."

"If we both promise."

She laughed wanly at the oversimplification. "Make a pact—prick our fingers—write in blood."

"Don't make fun of it."

Quietly, gently, "It could only be funny."

"I wish you were coming," he said.

He started for the door and she stopped him. "Is it possible . . . ?"

He turned. "We would simply have to make it possible."

" 'Simply,' you said."

He didn't speak for a moment, knowing he didn't have to.

"What time is the boat, did you say?" she asked.

"I didn't—but we'd better get there separately. There are plenty of cabins—it's not the season—you won't have to call first." Easier with himself now, he was warm and simple. "I'm glad you're coming."

She didn't want him to say anything soft, anything

intimate, for she was still unprotected against him. "Please talk *things* for a minute," she said. "I'm not quite steady yet . . . What do I carry with me? You're carrying a gun, I see."

"Yes."

"I'll carry one too."

Then he said, surprisingly, "I'd rather you didn't."

"Why? It's a hunt, isn't it?"

Her voice had suddenly turned to ice. She needed nothing more to steady herself; she had found the perfect thing.

He didn't respond immediately. She could see the misgiving in him, the tightening of the jaw. "We're not going to kill him, Johanna."

"If I can, I will."

"No. That's not what we're going for—we're going to bring him back."

She turned slowly to him. He was worrisome to her. She could tell, in a word, why she was going on the hunt. His reasons would be more complex, she reflected; perhaps he didn't know them at all; perhaps they were reasons she shouldn't trust. "Why are you going, Tad?"

She was going to be disappointed, she thought; he was going to put her off with a glibness. But he didn't, he surprised her. He started to talk, stopped, started again. It was difficult for him, but he was trying, painfully trying. "I—there isn't any reason—and maybe that's the reason. Something—I've got to let something happen—instead of *making* it happen. I've got to trust that something . . . All my life—reasoning—calculating—keeping myself in order—and suddenly I'm frightened I can't handle disorder. And I have to be able to handle that too. The riot in the street—if it's against something in my mind—a family I never . . ." He couldn't finish the sentence, couldn't handle it verbally. She could see he had gone deeper than he had intended. He surfaced now and tried to handle more tractable things. "There are rational reasons too—good, sound, practical ones. Going for Tokan—that's part of my work, part of what I have to do. I think he goes up there—

up the mountain—not for any lava rocks, not for any of that scientific hocus-pocus—I think he's got something up there. A monitoring station maybe—a listening device or a sending one, both perhaps—wireless—I don't know—a crypto-gadget of some kind. I want to find it, I want to bring it back—and I want to bring him back too."

"Arrest him?"

"Yes."

"And sweat things out of him."

"I wouldn't be the one to do that."

"But it would be done, wouldn't it?"

"I have to say it again—I wouldn't be the one." Her attitude was puzzling to him. "You're suddenly very sensitive for him, aren't you?"

She heard the hint of aspersion and it bothered her a little. "Why are *you* carrying a gun?"

"For protection—self-defense—no more than that."

"If I say I'm carrying it for the same reason . . .?"

"You'll be lying."

She knew he was right and slowly nodded her agreement. "What do I do, then?"

"Carry it empty, if you like."

"Empty?" She almost laughed. "What good is that?"

"Confidence."

"Not much confidence when I've got no bullets."

There was an impasse. At last, he broke it. "If I know you're going out to kill an animal, and the animal happens to be a man, it's murder, Johanna. I can't go that way."

"All right," she said quietly. "I'll carry it empty."

The truce was not altogether amicable; there was an uncertain bristling of arms, somewhere. She could see he delayed going because he wanted to ameliorate things in some way. He struck upon a triviality. "By the way—your lighter." He poked into his pocket and handed it to her. "I'm afraid it's dry."

She smiled. "That's all right—I'll fill it."

Still, he didn't go. Then, suddenly, he reached, retrieved his rifle and opened the door. *"Bon voyage,"* he said.

"Good hunting."

When he was gone, she didn't immediately move to change her clothes. She remained motionless. Her promise to carry an unloaded gun perturbed her; how could she have let herself agree to such a meaningless thing? It was not only preposterous, it was a hypocrisy. He would shut his eyes to whatever they might do to a captured Japanese, whatever variation on the rack and wheel, to get a scrap of military gossip out of him. But a good clean shot between the eyes . . . Or even in the back . . . A clean revenge. Tad would be willing to degrade the old Biblical rectitude of it—and the Japanese redressing of imbalances—with covert bruises and bad blood. Carrying an empty rifle—it wasn't the risk she minded; somehow she felt she would be safe with Tad. But capturing the man to torture him—it suggested an interminable immorality, the kind we perpetrate on one another every day, that never ceases; there was no finite poetry in it. Whereas, to kill Tokan . . .

But she had promised, and she would go through with it. Opening Oscar's gun cabinet, she selected the lightest rifle, still too heavy, the one she had carried on the boar hunt. She broke it open to make sure it was free of cartridges. It was. She leaned it against the wall, near the door. She noted, with the sense of a follower, that she had rested her gun precisely where his had been.

Then she went into the bedroom and changed. A lightweight jersey cardigan, jodhpurs, boots and all, and not so much as a glance at herself in the mirror. She put some money into her concealed pocket, two handkerchiefs, a tube of colorless lip salve against the weather. Weather: it would be cold at night. She would carry a sweater. Somewhere, she couldn't remember where, there was something Ben used as a yannigan bag. She had no idea what a yannigan was, but the bag was the perfect thing, if she could find it; canvas, beat up, nondescript and as disreputable-looking as Tad's. She found it. Into its maw she stuffed the heavy sweater, more handkerchiefs, toothbrush and toothpaste, a cake of soap, aspirins, extra underwear, her refilled cigarette lighter, cigarettes, a sheathed hunting knife, and a miscellany of trivia.

She looked around the bedroom and, noting the disarray that always follows packing, had no impulse whatever to neaten things up. The room was curiously not her own. But she did have one chore she couldn't avoid, a task she dreaded. Calling Abby. She lifted the phone.

"Oh, hey," her daughter said. "I was about to call you."

A few more words, both ways. No mention of Tad, either way. Palaver.

"I thought I'd run away for a few days," Johanna said.

"Run away?"

"Get some sun. Lie on a beach. Waste money."

"Good idea. Where will you go?"

"I don't know—and I don't want to tell. Hiding. Kona or Hilo or maybe Kauai."

"Oh, not Kauai, this time of year—you'll get flooded. Hey, why don't you try the new hotel—what's the name of it?—the Naniloa."

"I might—I just might," she said.

More palaver. Then the click.

How effortless it had been. A lie so untroubled, so painless in the telling and so painful in the aftermath. And it had a right to be painful—she was running off with her daughter's husband. What a stupid way to label it—and what a shoddy expression, "running off" —she wasn't doing that with anybody. She was simply going, with her son-in-law, on an obligatory expedition, to bring back a criminal, to discharge a debt to herself and to her dead son. And "running off" was not a way to describe it. Luckily, she had been forewarned; she had kissed the man, and some guardian spirit had uttered the word: beware. And beware was precisely what she was going to be. Nothing more would happen.

Nothing. No matter how she thought of him as an ally, from now on she must also think of him as someone to be guarded against, a potential adversary. An enemy. Whatever plans they had together, whatever pacts they made, she would make with her eyes wide and her fingers crossed . . . Nothing.

She was ready to go now. She turned the light out in the bathroom; then, after closing the closet door and the bureau drawers, she extinguished the bedroom lights. The living room also looked vaguely disarrayed but she thought, the hell with it. She pulled down all the shades, went to the door and picked up her rifle. Without any speculation one way or another, she went back to the gun cabinet, opened the middle drawer, drew out the box of cartridges and loaded the gun. She carefully set the safety and departed.

There is no white like the white of a steamer pleasure-bound, she thought, as if some corruption in landlocked toil sullied the colors of daily existence, and sea idleness alone could cleanse them. The night steamer to Hilo was as clean white as a holiday, and Johanna felt it. As she walked up the festooned gangplank— night on the sea and the lights of the boat twinkling— she thought what a mocking joke it was for her to be enjoying this festive spirit. Here she was, death bound, her own or someone else's, her insides fouled with a profane rage, enjoying the sweet innocence of a pleasure boat. Enjoying, worse, the easy gaieties, the balloons blowing and popping, the streamers lifting on the gusts of laughter, the ukulele band and its singer serenading everybody's sweet Leilani.

"That guy sings it better than Bing," the first Mainlander said.

"That *is* Bing, you goofball—it's a Victrola record."

They laughed at the first man and he laughed louder than the others. Only on holidays, she thought, do people enjoy being laughed at.

The gaiety subsided as the ship put out to sea; then silence. No more than the sound of the motors could be heard, nothing of wave or motion in the water.

Johanna sat in her stateroom and smoked. It wasn't really a stateroom, although her ticket said it was, but a tiny cabin, the best available at so late a booking. Any moment it would get stifling in here if she didn't stop smoking, she told herself; and the porthole was stuck.

She looked at her ticket. Mrs. Norton, it said, a name out of college, a teacher of journalism. She wondered what name Tad had taken, if he had thought to take a fictitious one. And she wondered where he was. She hadn't seen him board, had made a point not to look for him. But now she speculated where he might be, this deck or another, fore or aft, far or close.

What if he hadn't come? It was a renegade thought, a petty spite. She put it in a class with a hundred little vandalisms she played against herself. In the early days of her marriage, whenever she was giving a dinner party, always she had the same assault of self-disparagement. At the very last moment, when everything was spotless, the table perfectly set, the flowers arranged, the ice in the ice bucket, she would tell herself nobody would show up.

"The obvious thing is," Oscar would say, "you don't want them to come."

Maybe she still didn't. If there were terrors in a dinner party, what terrors here?

The cabin *was* stifling. She looked at the ashtray and couldn't believe she had smoked four cigarettes. Tugging at the porthole once more, she swore at it. Then she dumped the butts into the toilet and walked out on deck.

The two people standing at the rail were middle-aged. The man nodded uncertainly, the woman smiled with a sweet reticence. Reluctant to intrude, Johanna whispered a politeness and started to move away, but suddenly she didn't want to be alone. She murmured something about how beautiful the night was and they took it as a personal compliment.

"You're our next-door neighbor," the woman said shyly.

Johanna pointed. "Is that yours?"

"No, the other side of you," the man said.

He was quiet-faced and his clothes had nothing aloha about them. One generation earlier, he could be taken for a missionary. He might still be, she thought, for he had the selfless, responsible mien of someone who was looking after God's well-being. And the wife, in her long-outmoded pongee three-piece suit, seemed even more sedate than her husband.

"We're terribly excited," she said. "We're going to live there."

"Hilo?"

"Yes," the woman responded. "My husband's going to be vice-principal of a new school."

The second wave of missionaries, Johanna thought. Religion was the first R, then came the other three. Suddenly they were in the midst of a discussion about enlightenment, and the man was saying he had less interest in intellect than he had in intellectual manners. Quailing at the thought that this was preface to a dissertation, Johanna observed that the water was as still as earth and the prow seemed to be making a furrow in it.

"That's nicely put," his relieved wife said quickly.

She shook their hands and wished them luck, then ascended the companionway to the upper deck. She thought, at first, it was deserted, then saw the strollers, forward, ambling in and out of the darkness. She could have had the aft part of the deck all to herself, but she found herself seeking the proximity of others. Glancing as inconspicuously as possible into one face, then another, she knew she wasn't looking for strangers but hoping to catch sight of him, even if they had decided not to recognize one another.

He wasn't there. She tried another deck. When she had walked herself tired, the capricious thought that he might not be on board became not so flighty any longer. He might have been delayed by an emergency, and missed the boat. For example, Kley, having discovered that he was on the loose, might have apprehended him. Or he might—a humiliating simplicity—have changed his mind. There it was again, the flowers arranged, the ice in the bucket ...

She went to bed.

Certain she wouldn't sleep, she lay in her bunk, in darkness, smoking. She had determined, slumber or no slumber, that this would be her last cigarette of the night. Just as she extinguished it and put the ashtray away, she heard the sounds from the next cabin. She heard the schoolman's voice first, then the moaning of the wife. The woman's in pain, Johanna thought, then realized, in pleasure. Her outcries came louder and faster and, through the thin bulkhead, she heard the pounding and shaking of the bunk, and the man's voice, raised, in an unintelligible absurdity that trumpeted and yowled.

Suddenly the woman's voice, "Say that word," she cried. "Say it—say the word."

His voice changed now to a laugh, a hideous sound, a mockery, more cruelty than love-making.

She yelled, pleaded, "Say the word—say it—oh, please!"

The man stopped shouting. He said something, a whisper, too soft to be heard, then the next sound was a wail of thank you from the woman, one wail after another, thank you, thank you.

What ridiculous abracadabra had he uttered, Johanna wondered, what verbal Spanish fly? She couldn't imagine the man speaking an obscene word, yet what other kind would have sprung the sedate pongee lady out of her trap of incorruptible respectability? It need not necessarily have been something obscene; simply any word that was aphrodisiacal to her. Wouldn't it have been strange, and bitterly disappointing, if the term was "pavement," or "binomial theorem" or "Radio Corporation of America"? Something dirty, like that. As to herself, Johanna thought the word "divulge" was the filthiest in the language. But it excited no orgasm.

She thought how perverse love was, and wondered if there couldn't have been another mode for procreating the species, if that was absolutely necessary. Perhaps the so-called necessity was itself a perversity, an ungovernable compulsion of the Creator. A sick illusion that He must. If that was so, then all the rest had to be an illusion as well, and virulent perversity, together with perversion itself, had to be the price paid for perpetrating the falsehood. Love-making as Lie. How apt that, in English, the word "lie," as well as meaning falsehood, meant to be in a recumbent position. She wondered, vaguely, if she did it standing up, would she take the falsehood out of fucking? . . . She really ought to have another cigarette.

A bathrobe and another cigarette and, with it, she walked out on deck. Again, up the companionway. This time the upper deck was indeed deserted. Only one man, the farthest end of the boat, sleepless like herself, his arms resting on the rail, his eyes looking out to sea. Except for the fact that she knew him to be Tad, she wondered what else made him so singular-looking.

He turned. Slowly, he started toward her, a passenger seemingly at leisure, no more momentous than that, ambling along the promenade of a pleasure boat, in the balm of a sea breeze, by moonlight. Understood or not that they were to act like strangers on shipboard, he was clearly coming toward her. Unaccountably—how schoolgirl-giddy I am, she thought—her heart began to race. But it would be nothing—he would merely pass by, no more than that: good evening, lovely evening, shipboard courtesies.

But he didn't. He stopped.

"In the morning," he said in an undertone, "when we go ashore, I'll have to rent a car. I don't think it's a good idea for you to be with me. It'll take me about an hour. I'll pick you up at the pier. Is that all right?"

"Of course."

That was it. Not even "lovely evening." He kept on walking.

Her heart still went faster than necessary. She didn't know whether to stay at the rail or go inside. She had a yearning to be with him. She heard the pongee woman, she heard herself: say the word.

Remembering her resolution, she had a fit of disgust with herself. No say-the-word about it; the word is no. But—ruefully—that might be the most aphrodisiacal word of all. She would have to find another.

Sixteen

ONE SUNDAY, years ago, when Tad first came to the Islands, he decided to go hunting alone rather than with a Quarterdeck Club party, so he came to the Hilo side instead of going to Kona. On that occasion, he walked to the outskirts of town, where the saddle road began, and rented a dilapidated Willys from an old Islander.

Today, the Islander was still there. His business had enlarged by now; newer cars and two small Caterpillar tractors and a front-end loader, all for rent. But the Islander hadn't changed. He was a white-haired, hoary man, lean and handsome, with all his strength intact and more cheeriness than his wide grin could accommodate. He exaggerated his *da kine* speech as a goodwill way of ingratiating himself; he was a canny business man.

"What kine da kine?" he asked.

"A four-wheel drive," Tad said. "I'm going up the mountain."

The man pointed to a Willys. Tad could have sworn it was the same one he had driven years ago. He offered the comment, as tactfully as possible, that the car seemed a bit on the venerable side.

"I old, you young. Who stronger?"

Tad spoke admiringly of the man's muscles but suggested that senectitude wasn't always a correlative of great strength.

"Car all make begin," the man said.

Tad didn't understand. The man explained that it had been repaired inside and out, and added, "New belly, new balls."

Smiling, Tad recalled to the man that the last time he had used the vehicle, he had been so slowed down that he hadn't returned until nightfall.

"Oh, now fast," the man assured him. "You ride so too fast you catch *kualele* before da watah."

Again he needed a translation. The man obliged with a longer version. What he meant, Tad finally understood, was that the car would go so fast he would catch the falling star before it struck the sea. That was fast enough; he took the Willys.

As he turned the key in the ignition, Tad leaned out the window. "What's the best road to Palao?" he asked.

He thought the man hadn't heard him over the noise of the motor. "Palao," he repeated. "What road?"

The Islander's good humor was gone. "Away road," he said quietly. He pointed back toward the harbor and away from the mountains.

Tad tried to restore the good humor. "I can't go away—I have to go there. Is it better to go by way of Kilauea, or through the valley?"

The man's face was stony. Moreover, his *da kine* speech, previously playful and almost incomprehensible, was now stolidly clear. "Is nothing in Palao. Only dead *heiau*."

That was it. A *heiau*. He was resentful of Mainlanders who had desecrated the ruins of an antiquity, a temple, perhaps, or an immemorial burial ground.

"I'm not really going *to* Palao," Tad explained. "I'm going through it."

But the Islander was silent. An old censure was in his eyes, an old malice, without forgiveness. Slowly the man turned away.

Tad drove back toward the harbor, the bay front where he had told Johanna to meet him. He didn't remember the town too well. Much of it had changed since he had last been here and, not finding old landmarks, he strayed. He saw the snow on the sharp pinnacle of Mauna Kea in a place where the mountain had no right to be, then the rose light of morning in the other direction, on Mauna Loa, changing the white snow to coral, and north confused with south. How the tall chimneys of the sugar mill got into his route he couldn't tell, nor the freight train high on the trestle, its black smoke sucked down into the gorge, nor—only a few minutes later, it seemed—the lofty waterfall dropping its tattered white ribbons into the turbulent black pool.

It was not finding the banyan saplings that had confused him, he realized; they were nearly full-grown trees now, their aerial shoots taking possession of the Drive, shading and sheltering it. Having circled his way back, he at last came within view of the bay. The trade wind was whipping up whitecaps and there were rustling rumors in the palm and pandanus trees. The sailboats were whiter than the whitecaps and the sampans were bluer than the sea, and he thought how irreconcilable this romantic idyll was with his errand of violence. Sweet Leilani, heavenly flower, didn't go with blood and bile.

He didn't see Johanna on the pier, and since he was nearly a half-hour late—it was nearly ten o'clock—he wondered if she had gone to look for him. Then he saw her. She looked twenty-five, and she was the only woman he had ever met who made the flare of worn, dun-colored jodhpurs a sexual insinuation. She was loaded with encumbrances. She carried Ben's old hunting bag, her rifle, a heavy sweater, dingy and abraded, and two huge brown-paper bags, with a brand-new Thermos sticking out of one of them. She had fabricated it well, he thought, the picture of the disorganized tourist, ardent for anything and properly equipped for nothing.

Pretending picnic noises, she got in and stowed her gear on the back seat.

"Been shopping?" he said.

"Hardware store and the Seaview Deluxe Lunchroom," she said. "You want some coffee?"

"Not yet, thanks," he said. "I'd like to get out of town."

They rode in silence. They didn't mention the loveliness of the morning, nor the star-filled night they had spent on the steamer, nor having spoken at the railing. He had a sense they had made a pact to erect silence as a wall to protect them from each other. It seemed impenetrable to him, and palpable as rock.

The road, winding slowly upward, was through a tangle of trees now, fern trees and ohias and, here and there, a koa. Yet, the rise was so gradual that the only sign they were scaling a mountain was the slow disappearance of the palms and the sight of cedar and cypress. But there was one distinct difference, and a strange one—the air. Strange not only because it was cooler, despite the fully risen sun that should have made it warmer, but because there was a new message in the wind, a puzzling scent too unfamiliar to be understood.

They were at the top of the Kilauea mountain, at the rim of the volcano, on a moonscape of gray ash and black lava, in a desolate waste that had once been flame. Below, to the right of them, they could see Halemaumau, the crater within the crater, fury within fury. It was the most fulminating dragon of them all, the youngest, breathing smoke, fuming because it was no longer on fire. There was smoke everywhere on the mountain, there were many dragons. This, then, was the message of the wind, warning of sulphur and damnation. Why the message was incomprehensible was because up here, at the volcanic summit, there was an ambiguity of birth and death. These mountains were infants, newborn from the sea. Why then did this skyscape seem so devastated, so like perdition? If this was new life, there was also the wrath of terminal havoc in it. A nest of ugly dragons, seething with hatred, their feverish throats sickening with hellfire. It was awesome, it was terrifying and . . .

. . . It was not the right direction. The road ended and, beyond, where the forest thickened, the mountain did not rise, but started downward again, returning to the sea.

He pulled a map out of his rucksack. After studying it, he pointed to a notation. "This thing is wrong," he said.

Johanna glanced at it. "It looks like an old one," she said. "I got a new one at the gas station." She picked it out of one of the paper bags, and they perused it together.

"Yours doesn't even have Palao on it," he noted.

"Maybe it's not there any more."

"We'll go through the valley."

They descended and went the other way, through bright grasslands, long reaches of cultivated cane fields past one sugar mill, then another, all in the foothills of Mauna Loa. It didn't seem possible, because this was tranquil farm and meadow country, that they could be at the base of a mountain moored so deeply in the sea that it was greater than Everest, and that the core of it could summon, from the earth's firebox, the final holocaust. They rode peacefully at its quiet foot, the trade wind blowing a sweet zephyr through the valley.

"Did you say coffee?" Tad asked.

"Black, with one sugar per cup."

"Is that the way you take it?"

"No," she said. "You do."

He paused, to consider her having made the observation. "And you?"

"It's a good way," she replied.

"If you're hungry, I've got some dehydrated stuff in my rucksack." It was Navy issue—experimental—he had been given a supply of it months ago. "It's not bad—got a slightly meaty taste—sort of like hardtack."

"I bought some sandwiches," she said.

"Egg salad."

"Of course."

He laughed. It was the family joke on Johanna. Egg salad, delicious on a picnic, inedible at any other time . . . Were they on a picnic, then?

The foothills changed. The breeze died, the early afternoon sun started to zero in on them, scorching, and there were no more cane fields. It was all bunch grass now, dense turf at first, then scrub and deadwood. There would be a reason for the deadwood, he thought, and soon they came upon it.

Lava. Old desolations of it, black tongues of the

residue, some smooth, some jagged and spiny, dead remnants of a hot molten cascade, now cold and disintegrating into dry cinder and pumice. The road had been worsening as they drove upward. Long miles ago, the macadam had slipped away, then the single-laned gravel track had turned to a cracked and rutted trail. Finally, no pathway at all.

It wasn't the lava that had obstructed the roadway, it was the forest. There had been wasteland and wasteland and, for at least thirty miles, only wasteland. Then, unpredictably, turning a shoulder of the mountain, they had come to a dense growth of trees and underbrush, to the onset of bamboo, wild cane, great ferns, ohia.

And there had been no hint of Palao. For hours they had passed no crossroad they could have missed, no sign to direct them in any other upward direction than the one they had been traveling; they had passed no town or village, not the meanest little settlement.

It was dispiriting. The very first lap of the journey and he couldn't even find the starting landmark. What had made him think—if Kley's men had followed Tokan's trail and failed to run him down—that he would succeed? And with less data and briefing than the others were bound to have had. It was ingenuousness, and he sensed he had only seen the first hint of its consequences.

At the next turn in the road, Tad switched the ignition off. He put the key in his pocket. "This is it," he said.

"This is what?"

He pointed into the woods. "It's somewhere in there."

"Palao?"

He heard the doubt in her voice. "It has to be," he said. He pointed to the map. "We've been following this exact road. Every turn of it has corresponded."

"Except that the whole road should have been twenty miles to the south."

He felt she was rebuking him for the inaccuracy of his map. He tried to smile. "Yes—except." He pointed to a series of tiny dots on the map. "That dotted line goes straight in there, then it stops. And see those letters? Palao."

Her skepticism was increasing. He would stop dealing with it, he decided. It was midafternoon and he was hot. He needed to get out of the car and in motion, not by wheels but by muscles. A mile or so, according to the diagram, couldn't take him forever.

"Sit there," he said. "I'll be back." He opened the car door.

"It's not a town, it's a jungle."

He heard it. Not skepticism purely; more like alarm.

"I've been in a jungle before," he answered evenly. "So have you."

He got out, shut the door and started away. Hearing her door open and close, he didn't turn back to look, but he could feel her hurrying behind him.

"We may as well take our stuff," she said.

He turned. She was carrying all of it, his rucksack as well as her own gear. She must have seen him start to take everything from her. She straightened and simply looked at him. Then she quickly emptied her paper sacks, reorganizing, so that all she needed to carry was the yannigan bag and her rifle. As he strapped up his rucksack, she slung her bag over her shoulder.

They entered the forest.

The major trouble with woodlands was certainly not, as he and Johanna almost immediately agreed, the bathroom problems. They were managing them quite well, he thought, with Kleenex and leaves and a whole jungle full of privacy. The major problem was directions. His compass, because of the mountain's interference, was erratic—there seemed to be more quarters than north, south, east and west. And unless you know exactly where you're going, he reminded himself, any direction is as good as any other direction. Except a circular one. There's panic in circles. No matter how wide the diameter of a circle may be, it ultimately seems to be getting narrower and narrower, and at last you face the terror-stricken inevitability that you are tracking yourself, and closing in.

He mentioned the thought to Johanna, thinking to make a joke of it, but she caught the gravity rather than the humor and offered, not at all captiously, that it should have been easy for them to follow the map's relatively simple straight line. But he pointed out that what little sunlight filtered through the trees came from almost directly overhead; there weren't any shadows.

Then they smelled the smoke. They couldn't determine where it was coming from; no matter how they turned, it seemed to have emanated from a place behind them. Yet it hadn't been there all along, it was a presence that had just happened.

Suddenly Johanna pointed. "There!"

It was the tiniest wisp of smoke. When it vanished in the high greenery, they walked carefully, hoping to get closer. Another wisp and, unmistakably, the scent was stronger. They kept walking.

Abruptly, it was gone. Not the faintest wraith, and the scent had cleared.

Simultaneously they gestured to each other to be still, to wait, to disturb nothing in the atmosphere. When they had paused a long, incalculable time, they decided they had no alternative than to go forward in the direction they had been moving.

"Listen," she said.

He listened and heard nothing. He moved only a step, his foot made a crunch in dead leaves, and she turned, startled. The instant he paused, he too heard the sound.

A chopping noise. Just once, not repeated.

He nodded to her. They hesitated.

The sound. Then, again and again, at slow intervals, but more or less regular now.

Unmistakably, they had the right direction. Almost right angles, to the left. They walked toward it. No question that they were getting closer; the sound was louder. Then it stopped. They waited.

Chop. They continued onward. Chop.

Right there, Tad would have guessed, the other side of the bamboo thicket. Moving more quickly, they advanced through it. The ground was soggy underfoot, but not a marsh; it wasn't difficult.

The forest opened. The sunlight in the clearing was tawny golden, the ground looked like a lion skin.

Nobody was there. Not a soul, and the chopping sound had ceased.

It wasn't a large open space; he could have thrown a stone across it. The *heiau* was not exactly in the center of it, nor was it exactly a *heiau* any longer. The ruined old temple had been converted into a dwelling of some sort. On top of the foundation of old black lava stones, a hut had been built, strung together with sennit rope and overlaid with pandanus and coconut leaves. Coconut was the surprising thing, this altitude. Not that they were more than a thousand feet up, but he had never seen so many palms so high above the sea; the clearing, circled with them. Nor had he seen them so still. All the winds of the island had ceased; everything in the clearing, quiescent, in a lull. Whatever was visible had come to a conclusion, caught in a museum, behind glass.

Chop.

They looked up. There he was. Someone, not altogether discernible, high in one of the palms, the other side of the trunk. Chop, a palm branch fell. Chop, a cluster of yellow-green coconuts.

Then Tad saw him clearly. He had a *pahi ka* in his hand, a cane knife, a long machete. The way he held it in the air, it seemed poised to strike, without warning, at anything. Staring down at them, he didn't stir. He threw the cane knife down. It fell somewhere, into brush. Quickly he started down the tree. He wore nothing but a *malo,* tied around his waist and drawn up under his crotch, no belt around the tree to keep him from falling, no spikes on his feet to drive a foothold into the bark. Unaided, hand under hand, foot under foot, he floated down from the branches.

On the ground, he quickly found the cane knife and

held it, again poised in the air, ready to strike. He didn't move, simply stared at them. He was twenty, perhaps, or older. He had the purest Hawaiian face Tad had ever seen, not the blurred outlines of the mixed bloods, but the discreteness of feature, every line distinct. He was beautiful and, because he was obviously frightened, he seemed dangerous.

Before anybody said anything, there was a sound from the *heiau* and a girl came hurrying out. Younger than the other, perhaps a year or two, she was not really beautiful, not of face, but her body was lithe and altogether naked, and all of her was alive at once, as if created out of a single supple material, a yielding softness, without any intractable articulation of bone. She was a liquid thing, of melting amber.

Seeing the boy's stillness, she stopped. She saw what he was seeing, the intruders, and knew how naked she was. She ran quickly back into the *heiau*. Almost at once, the older man appeared at the doorway.

He didn't move for a moment. In the shadow, he was a blur. Then he stepped out into the clearing.

"Yes," he said quietly, talking to the girl inside. "*Haoles.*"

The girl had apparently called them by that name, but the older man too was a *haole,* as Caucasian as Tad was. But beyond his recognizability as a white man, all the rest was unidentifiable; he seemed, somehow, jungle-born. For one thing, he walked in a feral way, simianly, as if he was not altogether comfortable in the upright position. As he advanced slowly toward them, he tiptoed unevenly, tentatively testing the ground, suspicious of it.

Ten feet away, he stopped. His skin, in this healthful sunlight, had no right to be so sickly sallow, Tad thought, and he wondered why his rimless spectacles were attached to his head by means of black elastic. Now the man turned his face a little, sideways, as if specifically to answer the question of the elastic, and Tad saw the earless side of him, the long dark slit where an ear should have been. He seemed to derive a pleasure, showing it. The man's eyes were small, and when he smiled they disappeared. His frown had had less cruelty in it.

Pointing in the direction from which they came. "Your car?" he asked. "Not so's it could be anybody else's."

His voice seemed deliberately too quiet; making the listener strain to hear him evened the disadvantage. "Yours?" he repeated, insisting on an answer.

He made Tad's skin crawl. And Johanna was, clearly, trying to hide her apprehension. Uncertain whether they themselves were in any jeopardy, Tad rather doubted it. He felt less secure about the car. "Yes, it's ours," he said. "We rented it."

"Mm," the man said. He turned from Tad to Johanna, appraising her. He seemed to be taking the measure of all her dimensions, and when he glanced indolently toward the *heiau,* Tad thought he was comparing her to the naked girl. Slowly he looked at Tad and his eyes blinked like a lizard's.

"Gorpy's my name," he said. "It don't matter about the first one—Gorpy's enough."

His demand that they identify themselves was clear, there would be no avoiding it. "My name is Ames," Tad said. He paused, trying to decide what to call Johanna. Gorpy would be the kind to lay hands on anything unclaimed. "This is my wife."

The young man with the machete was approaching measuredly. When he had come within earshot but not yet part of the group, he stopped. Gorpy, not looking at him but seeming to sense he was there, waved vaguely in his direction. "This, my coconut boy."

He made the introduction as if he had used a proper name. "Inside there, that's Kaora. They have it with each other. Ain't married, but they have it."

Gratuitous information; nobody had asked for it. He seemed to take pleasure in saying it—as an affront. And to express his disdain for the goatish natives. Sensing this, Tad wondered why, if he disapproved, he was allowing her to run naked in his presence.

The sociabilities were over. Gorpy's voice lost its furriness. "What you doin' here?"

"Hunting."

"Bullwaddy."

Tad let the insult sit, didn't touch it. Johanna was studiedly ladylike. "Oh, but we are."

Gorpy looked at her with unspoken derision. "Runnin' away from somebody?" he asked. His manner was elaborately casual. "Or after?"

Tad tried to use silence against the man. But perhaps Johanna's method was better. Her pretended vacuousness, her silly trill seemed convincing. "He's out for wild sheep, I'm out for boar." Then, giggling, "Or is it the other way around?"

She had gone one step too far. Lazily the man shifted his pelvis forward. "Don't shit me, lady."

He was quietly annoyed, and he was mean. With a slow, precise movement, he pointed up the mountain, into the wilderness. "He's up there." His loose mouth tightened. "Now, let me tell you. Toward end of summer, two guys went up there after him—and lost him. One of 'em came down with a hundred and four fever, near croaked. Just a month ago a guy went up and into the jungle and got sucked into the swamp, almost didn't get out—came down here lookin' like a mud pie and stinkin' like shit." He took his time, waiting for everything to register. Then: "You won't get him without I help you."

The man was too clearly a crud, Tad thought—nobody to turn your back on. He had to be lying in one way or another, possibly in everything. He was certainly not to be trusted in a deal.

Gorpy obviously saw Tad's hesitation. The man shrugged. He had had his say and was finished with them. Turning away, he moved to the edge of the clearing. Standing against the trunk of a coconut palm, he opened his fly and urinated. While he was doing it, the girl came out of the *heiau*. She wore a muumuu now, swirls of amber, like her skin. She looked at the coconut boy and then at Gorpy, pissing. Taking courage to glance at the strangers for only a flash of eyes, she said something in Hawaiian. The boy didn't answer.

Johanna moved slowly, a few feet away from them. Tad followed.

"You think he knows where he is?" she said.

"Perhaps."

"What do you suppose he wants?"

"Our guns, maybe." He took a firmer grip on his rifle and saw her do the same. "More likely, the car."

Gorpy shook himself and unhurriedly buttoned up as he approached them. "You sure you want to go up after him?" As they said nothing, he continued, "Let me tell you, nothin's easy up there. It's jungle. There's scorpions and poisonous white centipedes that looks as innocent as peppermints. There's a kind of boar that feeds on *oliana* root—he'll attack anything movin' that's bigger than a rat. There's ticks that'll burrow under yer skin and in twelve hours the blood's comin' out of yer eyes . . . And there's him." He paused, watching them between slits of eyes. "But if you want to go—you ready to make a deal?"

Tad nodded. "Ready to listen."

The man looked up at the mountain. "I'll tell you how to make yer way."

"In return for?"

"Damn little." He seemed to be making an attempt to loosen up. "A little company. It's lonely here, with them two niggers."

The crawly feeling again. "What's company?"

"Come 'ere, I'll show you."

Gorpy led the way to the other side of the *heiau*. There, in the shelter of the lava rocks, protected against the wind, a small fire glowed in a shallow *imu*. Suspended from an arch of metal across the fire pit, an earthen pot contained a stew of sorts. The gusts of smoke that issued from the wood embers and mingled with the steamy vapors from the pot had little in common with the gray wisps they had seen in the woodland. Those were a nameless smutch in the atmosphere; these were a deliciousness that made the mouth water.

"It's wild goat," Gorpy said, "with pineapple and coconut in it. Mango too, and I think it's got some papaya, whatever was left from breakfast. I ain't got a lot of pots, so I have to throw everything in together. I never know whether it's gonna be scrumptious or pukey." He lifted the huge ladle and tasted it. "Oh, yeah, there's poi in it. I hate poi, but it does a do in my bowels."

Tad still had no inkling what their payment in the bargain would have to be. Certainly if the man told them anything about Tokan, eating Gorpy's food wouldn't even the score, their obligation would be greater. But Gorpy was already being his own version of a charming host, brushing the cooking debris out of the way, throwing dry pandanus leaves on the fire to get rid of the smoke, directing Kaora and the coconut boy to serve them.

They sat on a low platform of lava boulders, carefully hewn and matched, and Tad imagined some ritual having been performed here; a priest, an elderly *kahuna*, a sorcerer making magic against the forest evil. As Kaora brought scooped-out gourds and was about to ladle the stew into them, Gorpy muttered something and the girl looked frightened. She set the gourds down and hastened inside. For quite a while, nothing else occurred and the meal seemed, because of some unknown crisis, to have been postponed. Gorpy shouted. The words were, Tad assumed, meant to be Hawaiian but they sounded pidgin. The boy came running outdoors. He had a black-brown pottery jug in one hand and three glazed terra-cotta cups in the other. He set the objects down on the ledge, beside Gorpy. The latter said, with unctuous charm, "Ever drink *okolehao?*"

Tad had tasted it on a couple of occasions. It was a noxious liquor made of ti root. He tried to sound noncommittal. "Yes, I've tasted it."

Gorpy leered. "He don't favor it. How 'bout you, lady?"

"It's not my favorite either."

The man laughed as if he had heard a lecherous

joke. "You'll favor *this,* I betcha. It ain't just boogie blood, it's got ginger in it and guava juice." He poured the pink liquor into two cups and set them down on the platform. "Go on—taste it."

When he saw them hesitate, he squinted unpleasantly. "Don't trust me, do you?" Pouring the third cup, he drank it down in one gulp. As the liquor dribbled down his chin, he looked at them triumphantly. Then, when he still saw them hesitate, he grabbed each of the two full cups and drank them both. Immediately thereupon, he refilled all three cups and watched them with animal vigilance.

Tad's reluctance to taste the stuff was augmented now by a repugnance against drinking from any cup that the unsavory man had put to his slobbering mouth. Overcoming his queasiness, he lifted one of them to his lips.

The stuff was ambrosial. It had a bouquet almost floral, it was bitter and sweet, it was strong and mellow.

Johanna took a sip. Her eyes met Tad's, and when Gorpy saw the exchange, he crowed. "See? Wha'd I tell you? You can drink this hooch and get piss-potty drunk and wake up in the mornin' with nothin' bangin' in yer head, no pain at all, like you been suckin' momma-milk all night."

They finished their cups and each had another and suddenly the man didn't seem quite so detestable. The stew was like venison, peppery hot, with a pleasant aftertaste of pungent spices that puzzled the palate. They had another drink, and the man was saying, "Why you wanta go up there for? Whyn't you stay a while?"

Tad wasn't drunk, only a bit blurry. He wasn't sure he understood what the man meant. Johanna seemed less unclear than he was; her eyes were on the alert.

"Stay here?" Tad asked.

"Yeah—here." There was a hint of desperation in Gorpy's eagerness. "You c'n try it."

"Try what?" Johanna's voice was almost inaudible.

"Livin'!" He laughed, clearly attempting to recapture his earlier joviality, its freedom. But the constraint was evident.

It was his own liquor fuzziness, Tad thought, that brought the edge of peril so close; the man was being friendly, that was all, inviting them to stay, perhaps for a short time, perhaps for a long one. But when he looked at Johanna, he saw the same disquiet.

Gorpy, noting that neither of his guests had expressed any outright derision of his offer, seized what he took to be his advantage. His voice rose. "Yes— livin'! People always talkin' about eatin' off the earth. Well, here's the place to do it. Never was more eatin' to be had, or better. All kinds. Goat and wild pig and mountain sheep. Wood beans and crazy okra and the sweetest young onions that don't leave nothin' on yer breath. And fruit—by Christ, compared to this, the land of Eden only had one apple and that one stuck in the man's throat. Why, you c'n live here like the first day of the world!"

The desperation in the man was more lawless now, a frenzy of it. Then, unexpectedly, his voice softened. "I'm askin' nothin' from you," he said.

Tad started carefully. "Well, it's a very kind offer . . ."

Hearing the hint of refusal, Gorpy increased the urgency. "You won't even need no car," he said. "See there? Out there—past the bamboo—I got a mule." Tad looked and had a glimpse of the animal, browsing on a tether. "Once a week, I go down to Komohana. I pick up flour and sugar and terlet paper and, sometimes, soap. I listen to the radio awhile and pick up a newspaper—you won't be all cut off from the world. Look—I got a newspaper—a fresh one."

He ran inside the *heiau* and came out, waving it. It was last evening's *Star Bulletin*. One of the headlines made a point that seemed to Gorpy to be the clincher. He tapped it vigorously with the back of his hand. "Look at that. Look at what it says there. '*Hull Sees No Prospect of Japan Accord.*' Sure he don't be-

cause there ain't gonna be no accord. Gonna be a goddamn war. Them Jap niggers is gonna blow the shit
out of us. But not me, goddamn it, not up here—not
us! We're gonna sit on this mountain and we're gonna
eat oursel's sick and drink oursel's silly, and we're gonna rut oursel's into the goddamn ground!"

Rut. The one word said it.

He restrained himself, realizing he had let it slip. He
had said—too soon—what he most needed to say.
Taking a step backward, he changed the subject,
pointing to the foundation stones. "You know what
this was? A *heiau*. You know what a *heiau* is?"

Tad was thinking: ways of departure. "Yes, I know
what a *heiau* is."

Johanna nodded reservedly.

"Have some more drink," Gorpy said.

Tad reached for his rucksack and rifle. "You were
going to tell us which way, up the mountain."

Gorpy didn't raise his voice. "You ain't goin' yet."
The man drained his cup. When he started to move,
Tad saw him lean even farther forward than before,
and realized how drunk he was. He might not, therefore, be too dangerous. But just as Johanna too began
to move, Gorpy called out in his unintelligible Hawaiian. The girl came first. Behind her, the coconut
boy, with his cane knife in his hand. The threat of
force was shrill, yet frighteningly quiet, with something demented in it.

Feeling new strength, with the coconut boy's machete at the ready, Gorpy could afford to be his ingratiating self again. "We was havin' such a good time
—why're we wreckin' it? Come on—let's enjoy oursel's." He fixed on Tad. "See that girl, Kaora? She's got
the nicest pair of brown nubies you ever seen. How'd you
like to show her yer big cock?" He tried to outwait
the stillness, hoping somebody would say something.
"Go on—don't be ashame. She's seen cock before.
She's seen his'n and mine. Many's the time. She's had
me in her mouth and every other goddamn place. Go
on—show her yer cock."

Again he tried to outwait the silence. At last he turned to Johanna. "You see that coconut boy? How'd you like him down on you? He does it good. I've had him lots of times. Real good."

"You filthy bastard," Johanna said.

He didn't seem to take offense. "Don't say 'filthy,' lady. I pay for everything. I give 'em all they got. I give 'em food and drink—and a little extra in their drink that makes 'em think the world is crazy-nice instead of crazy-terrible. They love me for it—they have to love me for it. So we all fuck oursel's and nobody complains. That's the way in nature, everything fucks everything. And they ain't so innocent, them two. They ain't man and wife, them two. You know what they are? They're brother and sister. Yes, sir, same father, same mother, hundred percent. They got a word for it that makes it all okay, makes it all fine and dandy—they call it *puna ponoi*. To me it's just plain poon. Nothin's no nicer than it seems. Christ, them Hawaiian folk down Hilo way, they tried to get me out of the *heiau*—said it's holy. Holy, my ass. You know what they used to do here in them olden times? Them old-time folks—they slit throats and drank blood. They killed children and et their bellies. They plucked the feathers outta birds—not dead birds, live ones—chirpin' in their pain—and they made capes out of 'em. Yessir, everybody fucks everybody . . . How 'bout it, lady—how 'bout we have a look at your bare titties?"

He started toward her and reached for the button at her throat. Tad twisted him away, and when the man called for the boy, Tad hit Gorpy once, then again. Suddenly the boy's knife was in the air. He heard Johanna's voice and threw himself out of reach. He felt the wind of it and saw the boy coming at him again. Again he whirled away, but the older man was up, reaching for him. Gorpy grappled with him, took him into a tight clutch and muttered to the boy. The knife was now behind Tad, he knew it, and couldn't move away.

The gunshot.

The boy's arm was all blood and the knife was at his feet.

Johanna let her rifle down.

Tad looked at her, then at Gorpy, then at the boy bleeding on the ground. Turning to the *haole* man, Tad said, "Take care of him."

The Hawaiian girl was on the ground beside her brother, making murmurs, crying, trembling.

Tad saw the stunned look on Johanna's face. She was staring at the bleeding boy, so staggered by what she had done to him that she had let the rifle slip out of her hands, onto the ground.

"Come on," Tad said.

She went one way, then another, looking for her canvas bag. Finding it, she started to follow him.

"Don't forget your gun." He pointed.

He could see that she only heard the fact of what he said, didn't hear the black resentment over the loaded gun and the betrayal it stood for. Nor did she hear his confusion: the loaded gun had saved his life.

He waited for her to retrieve it, then went ahead of her, out of the clearing, upward into the mountain.

It had to be sundown, he thought, but he couldn't tell, for the light in here was baffling. The woods were deeper now, darker, more unruly, with rampant vines and a rankness of ferns that smothered everything. The sunlight could not invade, except an occasional sword-point of it, stabbing into the ground. And the ground, while it should have become drier as they moved upward on the mountain, was getting soft and wet, sometimes so boggy that it slowed them down.

Slowed them down. Worrisome, how much more intensely he was feeling the pressure of time. Distances that had to be covered. First, from the clearing, from Gorpy and his two companions, from a machete that could cut its way through bamboo and canebrake faster than he and Johanna could ever travel; from rifle slugs, perhaps, that knew their way through fern bush

and ohia trees. Strange, he had heard no sound of any
of them. Stranger still that it had not occurred to Tad,
not once when the decision had to be made, to go the
other way, backward, toward the car and the certainty of escape from them, instead of forward into
unpredictable perils. Point was, he realized, no decision *was* made, none was possible. From the moment
he had started on this wayward enterprise, there were
no further determinations to be made, except forward
and deeper into the wilderness.

Toward Tokan. That was the second distance, the
important one. Enlarging the distance from Gorpy,
from fear; and diminishing the distance toward Tokan, toward self-justifications of a hundred kinds—or,
perhaps, explicably only when the end was accomplished, no more than one. Whatever it might be—
toward Tokan.

All he could guess about the man's whereabouts
was: upward. Toward the peak of Mauna Loa, somewhere, upward.

The climb was getting steeper now, more difficult,
and the ground was soggier, sucking at his endurance.
He felt sure that Johanna was even more fatigued than
he was, but he had heard not a sound of weakness or
complaint. He admired her forbearance all the more because he knew she was following his lead without any
profound confidence that he knew where he was
going. Well, he admitted it, he didn't know. So, upward.

Widening the pathway, he whacked at the bamboo
with his short hunting knife, wishing he had hold of the
coconut boy's machete. He rebuked himself: how stu-
pidly unprepared they were for this trek. As if they
were indeed—egg salad sandwiches remembered—going on a picnic. How cocksurely American, starting on
a war, unready for it, certain the Lord would provide,
Fortune's Favorite, banners and bugles, the great ad-
venture. He was disgusted with himself. Hacking harder
with the blunted and now almost useless knife, he split
the handle. In a temper, he looked at the three parts;
the knife was unfixable, he tossed it away.

She was a good many yards behind him. "May I use your knife?" he called.

She had stopped walking. Perhaps she was listening to something else, or in a daze. She didn't answer. He repeated the question.

"Oh, yes," she said quickly. But she didn't reach into her bag to find it. He wondered if she was all right, but didn't ask. "Could we stop for a while?" she said.

He nodded. Always, in his mind's eye, she had a smooth, unwrinkled face; now, fatigue put furrows in it. Reaching into his rucksack, he yanked at his canteen. "You want some water?" He walked back and handed it to her.

She smiled gratefully and, just before drinking, shook the thing. "Not much in it."

"Go on—drink it."

She merely moistened her lips and returned it to him. There was still a little water left, and he was about to lift the container to his mouth when, thinking better of it, he screwed the cap back on.

"I thought you said there'd be water up here," she said.

Her first complaint. Although he had expected it sooner, he was annoyed when it happened. "Look at that." He kicked irritably at the wet ground. "Wouldn't you say there's water up here, somewhere?"

"I don't know."

Studied vagueness, he thought. Embracing ignorance to avoid her share in the chore of thinking. It provoked him. "Well, you should know—you've written about it."

She looked at him blankly. "I've written about what?"

She couldn't have forgotten; she was pretending. "One of your Oddities," he said. "You wrote a column on it."

"I don't think I did."

His annoyance growing: "Living off the jungle—finding food and water, coconut milk, gourds, cactuses."

He thought her empty stare was an affectation, but suddenly he realized she was bothered by the lapse of memory. "Scary," she said. "I can't remember at all. I must have copied it out of a book." Then, wryly, not at all enjoying the thought, "You take it from one printed page and put it on another. It's manual—it barely goes through the mind. And now—all at once—there's a fact I can use, I can do some *living* with it, and it's gone."

He didn't think it was that regrettable; she was making too much of it. He had seen her often, dramatizing, making a social game of a thing like this, bereaved by the death of a neuron. Her mind always did things too easily, he thought; like Ben's, it was quick at the job. He envied it. Add to his envy, he was often nettled by her head pride. As he was now. "Tut, tut," he clucked in mock sympathy. "The Brain Lady flunked her memory quiz."

"Don't be a creep."

He *felt* like a creep; it was an inane, petty thing for him to have said. He realized why he had. It wasn't the Oddities column he had been talking about, bickering with her because she had forgotten it; not any more than she had been caviling at him because he had failed to provide water. They were quarreling over the lie. About the loaded gun. It was on her mind just as it was on his. She was waiting for him to charge her with breaking a promise, with an outright betrayal of trust. And disturbed because he hadn't brought it up. Good, let it disturb her, let it gall her.

"You wanted my knife," she said.

Handing it to him, she put the sheath back in her bag. He hefted the knife, then took a swipe at a *kamani* branch. The blade was sharp. Assuming she would follow, he went onward through the bamboo thicket. They didn't talk.

Sunset always comes more quickly in the tropics, but darkness was never as swift as this. One moment they were in movement, in semilight; the next, they were beneath a black mantle, flung by conjury. What made it most like black magic was his certainty there was a moon and there were stars tonight, but the jungle growth overhead barred all of it.

Some way or other, in utter sightlessness, they made a clearing for themselves. They could barely tell what was underfoot, only that it seemed reasonably dry, with a ground cover of low-growing verdure. Johanna selected the place, and he quoted something about women liking imaginary grasses; when she asked what it meant, he didn't know. The grasses here were not imaginary; they were a soft bladelike herbage that clung to one's clothes. The prickles were not unpleasant and they made a matting so thick that no damp penetrated.

Johanna was already lying in it. He chose a spot, a safe arm's length away, and let himself down on the ground. Covering his rucksack with a layer of the grassy stuff, he lay his head on it. His fatigue throbbed. He could feel it, like a liquid pressure in every blood vessel, trying to pour out of his skin. He lay there, very still. He listened to the complex murmur of the night, trying to separate its sounds.

Her voice in the darkness: "When are you going to talk about it?"

Enjoying her disquiet: "Talk about what?"

"You know damn well what. The gun."

"No need to talk about it. If it's bothering you— good."

"It's not bothering me."

"Then go to sleep."

"You were wrong."

"*I* was wrong? You were the one who lied."

"You were still wrong."

"Then you should be feeling fine. Go to sleep."

"You were wrong—"

"Jesus!"

"—to make me promise not to load it."

"But you did promise."

"If I hadn't loaded it, you'd be dead."

"You knew that only *after* the lie."

She went right on without confronting what he had

said. "You didn't see the boy behind you. If my gun had been empty, he'd have hacked you to death. But instead of saying thanks, you tie yourself into your strait jacket. Christ, you're self-righteous!"

"You lied!"

"And rigid!"

He knew that's what she thought of him, had always known it. It stung, the more so because it might be true. He spoke without vindictiveness, trying to be even-tempered. "All right, I'm rigid. Let's see how flexible you are. It doesn't bother you that you betrayed me—but something *is* bothering you. What is it? That you betrayed yourself?"

"I didn't!"

Holding to his quiet: "I think you did. You're an honest woman, Johanna—you don't lie. You don't have to—you're so smart that it's not necessary. You can *brain* your way out of most of your dilemmas. Well, you didn't this time—you lied. You betrayed your mind. Isn't that what bothers you?"

She took a long time answering. "Yes," she said softly.

He had set the trap and she had walked right into it. He asked the question without crowing, as gently as he could. "Do you mean it bothers you that you betrayed yourself but not that you betrayed somebody else?"

He could practically hear her mind thinking it through. "You're sounding like Tokan." Her disturbance was going deeper. "True to myself, false to others. Guilty conscience—no shame."

"It's awful pat, but . . ."

"It's worse than pat—it's not true."

"No, it's not true, generally. But this time . . ."

She didn't say anything for a long while. She was having trouble with it. At last, with genuine feeling, "I'm sorry I lied to you, Thaddeus."

"Well," he said, almost to himself, "the way we started on this trip, we can't be too finicky about the truth, can we?"

"You're trying to let me off easy," she said. Then, with an edge of pride, "I don't need that—I can take care of myself."

"Yes . . . I'm sure you can."

He had the sense, without glancing in her direction, that she was sitting up, wanting to discuss it further. But he wanted to think it through on his own. He felt he had come off better in the argument, without deserving to do so. He had been unfair; worse, sophistic. There was a simple fact: by lying, she had saved his life—and he had made her apologize for it. But how could he be right and not deserve to be right—and how could she be wrong and yet, justifiably, have so much more humanity on her side? Maybe *he* was the one who was brain-proud; so distrustful of the deepest feelings, the potentially hurtful ones, that they had to be reasoned into a too disciplined order. After a moment, he wanted to say that to her, but she had already, he was sure, turned away from the whole thing. Perhaps she was asleep.

The wilderness noises seemed more subdued than before, more tranquil. The faint falling of leaves somewhere, a flutter in the brush, an animal, likely, scudding from one darkness to another. The cry of a distant bird, a quiver in the trees.

Tokan, during their argument, had been with them for a moment tonight, in spirit. He wondered now how close he was in person.

He heard a scream. It sounded human at first, but when he heard it the second time, he supposed it was a bird. A myna bird, perhaps, mocking at the softness of the forest sound, vandalously tearing it. Again. This time, different, a terrifying screech. Like the agonized outcry of a woman.

Seventeen

SHE THOUGHT OF waking him up. Not because she resented his sleeping soundly while she couldn't catch a wink but because she suspected something was moving in the underbrush. Not something, someone. A short while back, she had thought she heard the chopping sound, the same one, the cane knife cutting at branches. When she first imagined the noise, it had chilled her. If it had gone on, she would have awakened Tad. But it stopped. In its place another image came: the boy, wounded, bleeding on the ground. But soon that image also faded.

The sound she heard now was not in her imagination, it was a quite real rustling noise. She told herself, for the sake of solace, that it had to be an animal. Any conjecture that the stir was human had to come from the duplicities of the night, not to be trusted. Jungle forebodings.

Matter of fact, she wasn't sure she had heard *any* sound. Perhaps what really prompted her to think of waking him was that she didn't want to have all this night to herself, it was too vast.

Nor did she want to think of wounding the coconut boy. Why did she have to be acquitted of it? If she hadn't pulled the trigger, Tad would have been killed. Then why this guilt that needed absolution?

Because she *felt* no guilt.

Not one flutter of remorse. She had seen him raise the machete and had lifted the gun without even taking aim. It was a new experience, not even sighting the target, and being so certain of purpose that bang, the boy's arm was blood. She had never known such certitude. When the smoke had cleared, she had looked at the boy bleeding on the ground and she hadn't started to shake. No ladylike vapors, no regrets. On the contrary, an upward surge, some excitement too pleasurable to show openly, something she had to hide, stolen. A new energy in herself, a mettle in emergency, a muscle responding without flabbiness, a power to act that transcended reason: no need to consult the brain. The brain—perhaps Tad was right—that had made her unwarrantably proud. And this action of muscle, more than mind, had given her an excitement so seductive that it had to be private, like the unwonted pleasures of the bed.

But was she deriving pleasure in violence itself? She had come into the wilderness to kill a man—but that was to revenge a son murdered, to exorcise the torture of his memory. It was a quest in a primitive place for a primitive justice. But the shooting of the boy . . . had she so quickly come upon a jungle excitement? And what might be the price of it?

She heard the sound again. This time she couldn't identify it at all, not even as a chopping noise. More frightening than before.

That might be the price of the jungle pleasure, then. The jungle terror. The nameless noises in immeasurable darkness. No less real because they were nameless, no less terrifying. More.

The sound. Closer still. She heard the snapping of some dry thing, a twig perhaps. Then the footstep, unmistakably a footstep.

The first glimpse she had of the creature was the eyes. There hadn't seemed to be enough light to see anything at all, yet the eyes shone. Two burning glows, shimmering with flame as if lighted by a fire within the creature's head. Now that the animal saw her, it was still. So still that she might have been able to identify it if there had been moon enough, or stars. But all she could tell of the animal was that it was slight and delicate; whether it was beautiful or not, it made a beauty where it stood. Although Johanna had the sense it would do her no harm, she was vaguely alarmed by it, and tried not to understand—for fear of losing the feeling—why her dread of the thing made it so much more beautiful. As it stayed, as she got used to it, as she got over the feeling of being frightened, it did indeed start to seem not so rare a creature as she had imagined, a wild goat, perhaps, and no longer so breathtakingly beautiful. So she reached down, found a pebble and threw it to make a disturbance in the brush. The creature slipped away.

She thought about the thing for a while, regretting its departure. Soon, the regret too was gone and in its place, a languorous peace. There was no chill in the air, but it was cool, blessedly cool. Then, with the passing of the night, the breeze changed. It might be an eastern one now, she thought, with the balmy promise of sunrise in it.

Feeling herself getting drowsy, she could hear Tad breathing even more deeply than before. A need got into her, she wanted to touch him, to run her hand over his body, and wondered whether she could do it without awakening him. It would be especially pleasurable, she thought, if she could touch him everywhere and feel him respond to her touch, yet not arouse him. Did she mean "not arouse"? No; what she didn't want to do was awaken him. She wondered how much satisfaction she could get out of the night without having to pay for it.

Slowly, very slowly, she put her hand out. Without daring as yet to extend her arm full length, she thought: what if his hand is also moving in the darkness? What if it touches mine? The thought stopped her. Bringing her hand back, she turned away from him.

She awakened in the dawn and thought how mild the air was, unusually warm considering how high they were, above the foothills. Turning quickly, she looked at Tad. He was vaguely stirring, but still asleep. She too would be sleeping, she thought, if it weren't for the prickliness of the sedge. More briery than sedge, it seemed to her; perhaps she was lying in thistles of some kind, or a bed of nettles. The expression had an archaic twist of condign judgment in it, a bed of nettles, a minor retribution of the fates.

Minor or not, the sting was annoying, getting more bothersome all the time. Especially the barb in her left ankle—it had not stopped itching and had started to feel hot. Then the jab, like a needle, sinking deep.

She yanked at the pant leg of her jodhpurs and pulled downward on the heavy sock. By the faint morning light, all she could see of the lower mark was the red spot made by a drop of blood; but the other mark was clearer. She could see the second insect, for it was larger than the other, engorged with her blood, red-black underneath her skin.

She felt the scream in her throat, and stopped it. She had seen ticks before, she reminded herself, many times, and not all of them brought deadly fevers. And every one of the vermin could be dug out, every miserable one of them; she had done it herself for how many hunting dogs? But none as big and bellied with blood as this one, none so monstrous, and the other one was also starting to enlarge. She would have to get rid of them. But she had a terrifying recollection of how, on one occasion, they were dislodged from a dog's skin, and she hoped Tad knew another method.

She mustn't panic, she told herself, she must awaken him quietly and ask for help. She might even be able to do it herself; no need to play the flap-elbowed lady, shivery over an insect.

She felt it on the other foot. Tearing up the other jodhpur leg, she saw them, a cluster of them, as large as her thumbnail; her ankle running with blood.

She screamed.

"What?" He awakened. He looked and all he saw was blood. "What is it?"

"Ticks."

He was up now. He reached for the bloody leg. Carefully, he started to press the flesh around the largest of the insects.

"No!" She tried to wrest her leg away.

"Hold still."

"No—no!"

"Goddamn it, hold still!"

She yanked away and fled. Not knowing where to go, she ran one direction, then another.

"Wait!" he yelled.

She heard him closer, then closer still, then his clutching hand on her arm, restraining her. Again, she tried to run, but he held her tighter.

"Stop it, you can die of those things!" he shouted. "We've got to get at them!"

Out of control, "What—what?"

"Get rid of them."

"No."

"Stop it!"

"How—oh God, how?"

His voice was quieter, a little. "I don't know—we haven't anything to do it with."

She dreaded asking. "What would you need?"

"Kerosene," he said. "Or gasoline—they'll come out if you soak them with it."

If he knew that much he would probably know the other method; it made her shudder. "There's another way," she said.

"I know."

"I won't be able to stand it."

"Yes, you will."

"No—think of something else."

"I don't know anything else."

"Oh, Christ." Then, shaking, "You want my lighter?"

"No—a cigarette. Light one."

She didn't do anything about it. He made an impatient gesture. Patting at her pockets, she found nothing in them. She remembered emptying everything into the canvas bag last night. Pointing to the place where she had slept, "It's over there," she said.

He hurried back to where she had pointed and she followed him. When he got to the sedge clearing, he saw her bag and reached for it. About to lift it from the ground, his hand pulled back. Simultaneously she muttered, "Watch out."

The ground was crawling with them. They were streaming out of a wooden burl of decay, a wet-brown parade of them, no larger than mites, all moving in one direction, all over her bag and into it. It was the food in there, she thought, or a special dark dampness they had made for themselves.

He stood there indecisively, not knowing how to deal with the verminous invasion. He reached for the bag again.

"Don't!" she said.

His movement stopped. "Get away."

She didn't move. He hurried into the thickness of trees and came back quickly with a length of green bamboo. Angrily, seeming to enjoy the ferocity of it, he beat at the bag and beat at it. He paid no heed to the rifle sticking out of it.

"Careful," she said, "that gun might go off."

He didn't stop his fierce whipping at the thing. With every slash of the bamboo, he took a breath and made the same savage noise.

Both her ankles were hurting now, and one of them was hot.

He threw the bamboo down. The bag was free of insects, at least the outside of it was. Cautiously avoiding the open end, he grabbed the bottom, lifted the whole thing high off the ground, wheeled away from the verminous spot, turned the bag upside down and let all its contents fall out of it.

The remainder of the food was a loss. The whole mass was covered with insects, covered solid, like chocolate icing on a cake. So were the odds and ends of things, the handkerchiefs, the tube of lip pomade, the toothbrush, toothpaste, all covered with the crawling things. And there were a few of them on the package of cigarettes, one single tick on the cigarette lighter. He lifted the cigarette packet and blew them off; as he picked up the lighter, the creature couldn't hold to the slippery metal and fell away.

He handed both objects to her. She withdrew a cigarette and returned the package to him. Flipping up the cap of the lighter, she tried to twist the incised wheel, but her hand shook and nothing happened, there was no flame. He took the thing from her, snapped out a light, and she dragged deep at the cigarette. He led her away from the place, a good distance away to another clearing, a clean one, free of nettles. At the edge of the clearing, he pointed to a strong eucalyptus sapling and told her to stand at it and, with both hands, hold tightly to its trunk. She put the cigarette in her mouth and took hold of the tree. Kneeling, he reached down to her feet, pulled one sock off, then the other, and rolled up her pant legs. He arose again and took the cigarette out of her mouth.

"Hold onto the tree as tight as you can," he said. "Try not to move."

"Oh, Jesus,"

He blew the ash off the cigarette. As he touched her flesh with it, she felt the pain, so hot that it was cold. And he held it there, he held it. She started to move, to scream, and restrained herself.

"One out," he said.

He started on another. This one was worse. "Bloody bastard," he said.

Oh Christ, oh Christ, oh Christ, won't it ever be over, she asked, and suddenly it was going faster, one after another, with a tide of painlessness, a receding wave of absence, as if she were going to faint, yet she wasn't fainting, an engulfing flood of nothingness, all pain gone with it, all awareness. Yet, she *was* aware of something, her eyes as open as they had been a moment ago, seeing the gray-green bark of the eucalyptus, hearing the soft soughing in the trees, the sound of Tad's breathing and his occasional curse, or murmur of conquest over the small wretchedness. But . . . nullity, a sense of insubstantiality, nothing existing, herself least of all, her flesh burning.

Then it was over.

Precipitately, just as he rose from his kneeling position on the ground, her own existence returned to her. And with the reawakening of awareness, she knew a terrible thing.

It was not over.

She could feel the bite and burn of the creatures all over her body. For the first time since the ordeal had begun, she made a sobbing sound, a choke of it.

He saw the pain in her face, sensed the horror. "Where?"

"All over me."

"Show me—where."

She unbuttoned her sweater and saw the marks, as he did. There were three of them across her middle, and she couldn't face the dismay of how many more there might be.

"Get undressed," he said. When she hesitated, he had no patience. "Go on!"

She took off her sweater and jodhpurs and stood in her underwear. There was another one on the inside of her thigh halfway up from the knee, a huge one, so bursting with blood that she thought she could pick him off with her fingertips. But Tad stopped her for fear part of the poisonous thing would remain inside. He burned it out quickly and two others more slowly, since they were bedded into the flesh more deeply. This time she couldn't stop the outcries, yet she knew the pains were nothing compared to what would come in the next moment.

"My breast," she said.

He stopped and looked at her. He pointed to her brassiere. It wasn't modesty that made her cry she wouldn't, it was plain terror that if there were any on her, she simply couldn't stand it. He didn't let her make or not make the decision. He put the half-burned cigarette down on a ledge of rock, then moved quickly behind her. He reached for her brassiere and undid it. In an instant, it was on the ground and he was standing in front of her, looking at her breasts. Free of the clothing now, a driplet of blood coursed downward from one of them. As he reached for the cigarette, he heard her moan.

"I can't—I can't!" she said.

He blew the ash, then slowly brought the red tip toward the skin.

"Oh, God."

Then, brutally swift, to speed the thing and have it done, he touched the fire tip to her bosom. As, reflexively, she started to move, he held the breast firmly and pushed the fire deeper. He held and held. Slowly, backward, the bloody thing crawled out.

There were no more.

She stood there, unable to believe there weren't any more, unable to relate the pain of the burnings that she still felt to the relief that it was over. She began to shake. She shook and she wept and laughed and kept shaking and not knowing how she could keep from shaking herself to pieces.

"Stop it," he said.

"I can't—oh, help me!"

"Stop it! Johanna, stop it!"

"Stop me—stop me!"

He clutched at her, he took her into his arms. She shook and she ached and nothing that she was belonged to her, and she was more terrified now than she had been before. She could feel him gripping her, holding her in a vise, trying to pull her together. And she thought it would never happen. Then, moment by quaking moment, she began to return to herself, and to him, to his closeness, to the rough coercion of him against her naked body. At last, more clearly as her mind returned to her, she could feel a hundred textures, all of them surrounding her, hard textures and soft ones, warm clothes and the coldness of buttons against her bare skin, and the metal of a belt buckle and the softness and hardness of his lips against hers, then on her breast, and the feeling of wetness as he took her in his mouth.

"No—don't!" she cried. "No!"

But her trembling was different now. Opposite, in fact, not the trembling of falling apart, but of all her parts coming together, in a great accession of wanting.

"No—please—no!"

He didn't hear her, couldn't. And if he had heard and stopped what he was doing, she knew she could not have stood it.

There was an expression in old Hawaiian, *ahi wela maka'u,* and it meant something between fire love and fire terror. It referred to the story of the heartsick young girl who fell so deeply in love with one of the lesser gods of the volcanoes that she threw herself into a crater of blazing, boiling lava. Luckily, Pele, the supreme goddess of all fire pits, forgave the girl her folly, and she lived to love a cooler fellow.

Johanna, now fully dressed but still lying beside Tad on the leafy ground of the wilderness, felt as if she had just come out of the burning pit, and wondered if she'd be forgiven her foolishness. The baffling thing, the painfully baffling thing, was that she didn't know whether she wanted to be forgiven. There was in the plea for exculpation the implicit promise—explicit too —that one would go and sin no more, and she was not yet ready to make such a pact with righteousness. The moment with Tad had had in it too much of what she had hungered for; how could she say she would be able to abstain from it another time? Maudlin as the *ahi wela maka'u* myth might be, there had been a lovely terror in the fiery experience, and she was still too close to the elation of it to pledge it out of her life. If there was obscenity, there were also the flames to cleanse the obscenity—it had been a purifying conflagration—and she could now permit herself the cooler pleasure of lying on damp leaves in a woodland quiet. And if the irony in guilty pleasure was that it was ultimately not pleasurable, she would not get caught in such a mockery; she would enjoy it. For the first time in years—long years, beyond memory— she had enjoyed with hedonistic exhilaration the insolence to her own morality. Perhaps she had mistaken who she was; perhaps, all these years, decorating herself with all the blue ribbons of respectability, she would have been happier with a red letter on her breast, where the insect had bitten and the man had sucked. She was feeling, for the moment, volatile, satisfied, shallow-brained, frivolous, a bit trashy, and the hell with everything.

She wanted, now, for him to make love to her again, and wondered if it was time, if she dared reach for him. But before she could touch him, she heard his voice. It was too sober for touching, she realized; it had distances in it.

"We're even," he said.

She knew he was referring to the broken promises—hers about the gun, his about not exciting her. He was such an adder and subtracter, she thought; always searching for the sum of things. It had not occurred to her to score one breach against another, not only because they were unlike but because neither of them had ever believed his promise in the first place. Or could it be that he had believed it, had made himself believe it; that he was a man who needed to shore up his belief in his integrity with a falsehood here and there? If that was so, perhaps he was now having a bad time of it.

"Don't blame yourself," she said.

"Well, you're certainly not to blame." An indeterminate waiting. "I never meant that promise, not a word of it."

Good, she thought, he *wasn't* lying to himself, at least no longer. "When you made the promise—did you know you were lying?"

". . . No."

"Will we go on, do you suppose—telling lies now and confessing them later?"

"Or not confessing them at all."

"Yes."

He made a vague gesture, referring to their present state, lying beside one another. "Is this really what we came here for?"

She thought awhile. "No."

"Is that another lie you'll have to confess to later?"

"No." She spoke slowly, trying to be sure of what she was saying. "I may have wanted you. But what I came here for was Tokan."

"Wanting, the condition—hunting, the act."

"Exactly."

"Are you sure it wasn't the other way around?"

"I'm positive," she said.

A vague uneasiness wormed inside her: she wasn't positive. If it started as a certainty that Tokan was the quest, not illicit love-making, it was not altogether a certainty any more. The most she could say was that her motive was no longer single; her impulses were now too confused with one another. Why couldn't it have stayed clear, with only one single incitement drawing at her energy instead of plural ones, inextricable from each other, the wires crossed, short-circuiting, perhaps fouling energy at the source.

"How about you?" she asked. "Aren't you positive?"

"No." Then he added with a wry smile, "I can't be positive when there's so much that's negative."

He was only playing with words, she told herself; she mustn't take it as meaning overmuch. But the word he had used, whether he had put any deep significance into it, was indeed "negative." What guilt he must be feeling about having made love to her. And charging himself with infidelity might not be the full measure of his self-incrimination; he was probably beset with a more heinous offense: fornicating with his wife's mother and therefore, by the lengthening of the accusatory finger, with his own. Incest and original sin and adultery—if her estimate of the man was at all accurate, there was no saying to what lengths of *mea culpa* he would go. Carrying her with him.

Damn him for ruining it so quickly, for returning so homingly to the cold Puritanism from which they had both sprung. Couldn't it have waited another day, another afternoon, another hour? Couldn't it, if only while they were in this wilderness, not have returned at all?

Perhaps Tokan was right. Only shame was an effectual way to make order among the frail giants. And, in the end, probably the only endurable way. Not the guilty conscience. Yet, as between shame and conscience, Tokan-san, you were wrong; conscience is not the easier way. It was the assassin of joy; it made man a murderer of his happier self. But shame in the eyes of others—that was, at least, bearable. And here, in this secret jungle, where there were no others to condemn them, where they had no fear of public obloquy, they could have managed to make love and, perhaps for an idyllic moment, even fall in love.

The idyll did not beguile her for long. She knew its flaw. They might make love without the shame of others, but fall in love? They would have their own shame, one with another. They had carried it with them, like mementos of a respectable world, as men carry images of their wives into whorehouses.

Damn him for giving something and taking it away so soon, damn his Puritan additions and subtractions.

She had to get away from him, at least for a little while. Rising from the ground, she pretended to stretch against the morning sun. Slowly, almost aimlessly, she pushed her way into the deeper woods. She heard him calling after her. She wasn't sure whether he was telling her to be careful or reminding her that they had to get on with finding the man they had come for, and she had the acrid thought that murder would have to wait.

She didn't feel well. The cigarette burns on her body, which she had scarcely been conscious of during lovemaking and immediately after, now smarted; her head felt heavy and hot. Damn the ticks, damn the man. It would be a good thing to get off and be alone with herself, if she could also be alone without herself. What a mess I am, she said, and how Johanna Winter deserves to be alone with Johanna Winter! If only they could stand each other. Well, if she had been able to endure herself, she would long ago have gone back to the Mainland.

She couldn't tell what distance she had walked or how long she had been away from him. She hadn't meant to go too far, but her head was dizzier now and she had no sense of time or place. But she could see that the terrain had changed. The ferns were wilder, more arrogantly green, the vines were greedier. Most of the eucalyptus trees were gone, so were the banyans and ohias. Here, the struggle between the trees and the ravening undergrowth was deathly. Green murder was in everything—the sword ferns and staghorn ferns and itchferns, the funguses that bracketed the gaunt bamboos, reaching high for light and breath, the koas wrapping serpentine branches around everything, even around their own trunks, strangling themselves with their embrace. All uncanny, and feverish, as her head was feverish.

And all so deludingly still. No wind, not a breeze stirring, not a leaf falling; the only motion, her own. Starting to be apprehensive, she decided to go back. She turned, she doubled on her track, or thought she doubled on it. But something, she told herself hazily, had altered, she could not name what it was. Woods had no right to change, she said, straight lines had no right to turn to crooked ones, paths she had never traversed had no right to present themselves as familiar. She was stumbling and unsteady.

And she was blundering. Well, she wouldn't let it worry her; there were things one did. The jungle principle: if you can't retrace your steps to the place where you were last certain of the pathway back, seek higher places, a ridge if you can find one, look for the overview; avoid the valleys, the water courses—that was the cardinal canon—for the vegetation is denser there, the ground marshy, the passage hard to make.

Reiterating old advices made her calm. Clinging to her composure, steadying her wobbly knees, she reminded herself that blundering was not a fatal thing; in the very first hour of this trip, they had mistakenly gone toward Kilauea instead of away from it, yet they had found their right track. But the disquiet returned. Two people going in a mistaken direction have merely missed a landmark; one person is lost.

Lost is panic. She could have sworn she had been moving, as she had cautioned herself to move, in an ascending direction. And if she was, it could not have happened. But it did.

There had been no warning of the swamp. One instant she was on solid earth, albeit damp; the next, she was in it. One foot slipped beyond control, then the other. She routed her alarm; she was not in so deeply that she couldn't extricate herself. All she had to do was move backward a bit, to the drier place she had just started from, and she would be out of it. But the dry place was gone, had gone somewhere into her dizziness, and she was now deeper in the morass. She called out, but nothing happened, nobody came, and she could feel the suck now, under her, could feel the pull of the thing, the swallowing, engulfing mouth of mud. Trying to use her torso as a lever, she writhed and flung her arms upward as if to strike through the treetops, at the sky. But it only made her sink the worse, and the ooze was over her boottops now. Once more she reached, this time not for an unattainable heaven but for a nearer objective, the stalk of a vine. Slime made it difficult to hold, but she pulled at it and yanked. A stronger one came with it and suddenly another, a tough, unyielding creeper branch. She strained and tugged to lift herself out of the brown muck . . . and there was hard earth under her.

Lying on the ground, gasping, she tried to make one breath catch up with another. Her head was a massive throbbing ache and her skin was ablaze. She hoped it was the exertion, not the tick fever, but resting didn't cool her, and there wasn't even the relief of sweat. No, it couldn't be the fever, it couldn't have happened so quickly, except why couldn't it, what did she know of it? She knew this much: she wouldn't *let* it be, wouldn't give in to any fever nonsense, to any blood-battened, blood-fattened little monsters that . . . Oh God, she couldn't just lie here.

She tried to get up, half made it, then fell back again, gasping for breath. Weirdnesses assaulted her, wild primroses and galley slaves out of old novels and bits of *Lohengrin* and she couldn't sweat. She heard somebody say all things were reasonable, and she believed it, she saw her father frying porgies in a pan, she had to learn how to crack her knuckles and swim the whole length of it and conjugate *venire* and how to tell croup from common cold and she knew she couldn't manage any of it. She would never dissect earthworms, never, and frogs were out of the question because she was a soprano who couldn't sing high C and therefore bound to fail.

She was sweating. She sat on the ground in a prison of green wilderness and her skin poured perspiration

into her hair, her clothes, down her forehead and into
her eyes, off her chin and out of her fingertips, and
she luxuriated in the clean, cool wetness of herself.

For a while, she had no inkling where she was or
how she had come there. Thinking of Tad, she tried
to imagine how long she had been away from him.
Not for long, she thought, for what sunlight filtered
through the trees suggested morning light; there was
something fresh as lavender in it.

How strange that everything was so still. One should
hear murmurings and whisperings in a woodland, she
thought, of leaves and animals, of insects whirring
and buzzing. Something was wrong here: there could
not be such tranquility in so much growing, there had
to be some turbulent mutterings. But none.

A shriek. Shocking as the sound was, and beauty-
less—twisting the air out of shape—it relieved her to
hear it. She had worried whether she was losing her
hearing or developing some preposterously mystical
sense about the stillness, and now there was an ugliness to make things normal. She wondered what bird
it was. A wild parrot, perhaps, or a macaw if there
were any in these woods, or a myna bird. The sound
again, and she had had enough of it.

She was hungry. She was more than hungry, the
emptiness inside her was a piercing attack. She would
have to find Tad, and food, or live on the jungle. Everything sprang alive at once, the whole memory in an
exploding brilliance like rockets, everything, every Odd-
ity she had ever written about wild foods in wild
places, every wild guava and strawberry, every native
avocado and breadfruit, all the wild bananas and coconuts and papayas and mangoes and *panini* cactuses,
and the edible *lauhala* and mountain apple and passion fruit.

Unsteady, but not feeling ill, she was on her feet.
She would go foraging, she decided, and make the wilderness feed her aching stomach. She started to look,
first, for the ripe and fallen things. That was the way
she had started the advice in her column, as she remem-

bered it now: don't start by climbing when all you have to do is stoop.

A miracle happened.

She found something that had not simply fallen from a tree, it had been cooked. It lay there, a neatly appetizing thing, wrapped in a bamboo leaf. Picking it up, she slowly, carefully unwound the wrapper. All at once, in a burst of memory, she identified the luscious aroma of the white thing.

It was a rice cake. Ginger, soy, other spices she had long forgotten. She couldn't wait to eat it. Sweet yet pungent, it was delicious. She chewed it ravenously, the delicate glutinous confection, and by the third bite it was gone. Regretfully, she tossed the bamboo leaf away.

Where it fell, she saw the second one. Not far from where the first had been, perhaps only ten feet.

Then the third. Also ten feet away. The thought struck her, hot and cold. They had not been accidentally dropped, these Japanese rice cakes, they had been placed there, in a deliberate line upward, up the mountain. They were pointing a direction.

Her throat tightened. Tokan, up there, leading the way, challenging.

She saw a movement in the woods.

It stopped, it moved again. Then the figure came toward her, only a vague form, behind leaves, behind bamboo. Terrified, she could not move, she couldn't stir a foot. She couldn't run toward it, nor run away.

Eighteen

TAD SAW THE BOAR just within range of his rifle. Spotting him first in ground cover of jungle creeper, he now watched him move, his snout nervous from one root to another, until he found his food between the trunks of two sandalwood trees. The beast stood there, forelegs spread, complaining at his provender, snuffling so loud Tad could hear him as he fed.

Lifting the gun, he sighted the animal meticulously, there was no rush. He put his finger on the trigger, started the slow pressure, and stopped. He wasn't hunting hogs this day, but other quarry, and firing at one might bring the other at his back, just as he himself was at the back of the wild boar. A gunshot would have been a stupid blunder, he warned himself. No matter what Gorpy had said about the beasts attacking at sight, there was no danger from this one; the animal had clearly caught no sign of him.

He watched the hog finish gorging, saw him throw his head up and snort repulsively at the empty air. How ugly he was, how mean his tusks were, how symbolic that he had to gore from earth to earth, coming under his prey to wound it, then butchering it on the ground. Tad saw a low stir in the distant brush. The boar saw it too, and was gone.

He hoped Johanna was nowhere near it. She hadn't taken her rifle with her which meant she hadn't intended to go far. Why was she away so long, then?

She wanted time, away from him. She was angry and had a right to be. How bumbling he had been to express his regret so openly, especially since he had felt less of it than he had shown. He realized, with distaste, that he had fallen back on the old fraud that the pleasure had all been his own and, therefore, so was the blame; he had gotten her into it, hence he was the one

who must fulfill some binding covenant of atonement.
But she had no such covenant to fulfill. The old
words, like "seducing" and "taking advantage,"
strange how they left the woman out; only the man
had done it. She was not only excluded from the
pleasure, but even from the guilt; as if she were not
strong enough to bear the burden of it. In what oblique
ways we diminish them, he thought; like the rule he
had tried to get passed at the Club: women barred
from the hunt.

When she returned, there would be stables to clear.
Together they would say that together they had hungered and found each other and made love. He had not
raped her and she had not lain passive but had come
to him, *at* him, a wolverine, panting and wanting and
shrieking all the branches bare. Yes, they would both
have to say it: there had to be some honesty, even in
falsity. As to regret, that was for quiet places, later,
where the linen was white, not here with the ticks
and the wild boars.

And myna birds. Hearing the screech again, he
cursed, hating the violence and mockery of the sound.
But when the sound was repeated, he didn't try to
shut his ears to it, he listened carefully.

It wasn't the myna the second time. The bird's voice
always mocked the human one, but this cry had no
mockery in it. The distress in it was true, it was imperative. And it might be Johanna.

He started to go. A few steps and he halted. What if it
were not Johanna, and he departed from this place.
She, returning and not finding him, would not know
where to move. They could either be locked into immobility or lost from each other. But then, there was
the boar, and he had visions of her, gunless, cornered
by the beast. Or by Tokan.

He moved quickly. Knowing that if the sound was
not repeated, he'd never be able to locate where it had
come from, he warned himself that the foolhardy mode
of search in wilderness was always circular, so he
thrashed in a straight line upward. But the straight

line led him to thicker and thicker underbrush, almost impassable now, through vines and the tendrils of great trees and ferns the like of which he had never imagined, their fronds covered with gluey hairs that bit and stung, clinging to his skin.

He wished his arms were freer than they were; it bothered him to be carrying both guns. And here, with the start of swampland underfoot, he would need whatever grasping power he had. He walked more slowly now—wary, wary—forswearing the straight line. It was wandering time, any direction at all, searching for her and not daring to call her name. For if Tokan was there . . .

What then? The hunt was all to the Japanese, especially if he caught them unaware. He would gun them down, one shot apiece, no problem in this wilderness. But what if it were the other way around, if Tad had a bead on the Oriental? He'd merely wound the man, that's all he needed to do. He was a good enough marksman, in good light and without too much obstruction, to wing his quarry or hobble him. He was not a murderer. Besides, he needed the man alive. There was information to be gathered, talk to be snatched out of a living throat, not a dead one. There were wind messages and ships lost at sea and codes, lurid purple ones; killing the man would derive none of it.

Johanna was the one to worry about. She would kill him; she had said as much. And she had the violence in her. He had heard her scream in love-making; her passion, even in an embrace, had vengeance in it. Besides, she was a good shot, probably a surer one than he himself was. The Japanese man would fare better with Tad at his back than Johanna. She could commit murder, no doubt of it, and go to trial and uncomplainingly take her punishment.

He couldn't let her do it—not to Tokan, not to herself. He thought of emptying her rifle, but there were dangers in that. What if she came upon the boar, or it upon her? Well, that was no worry really, not if he stayed close to her, his gun in hand. But what about

Tokan himself? Again, if he stayed close to protect her . . . Besides, Tokan was precisely the whole matter: he could not let her commit murder.

He looked at her rifle, paused an instant. Then he did it. Cracking it, he emptied the magazine of its cartridges. Hefting them in his hand a moment, he at last let them drop and, with the toe of his boot, ground them into the muck.

As he looked up, he heard the sound behind him. Turning quickly, he saw the quiver of leaves, like aspens showing another color to the wind. Whatever the thing was, it was hiding behind the tree. And animals don't use tree trunks for the purpose.

He lowered himself a little, behind a brake of gorse. Quietly as he could, he dropped Johanna's gun and released the safety on his own. Never had the sound seemed so loud. His heart was also too noisy, the man would hear it. Yet, it didn't matter, he told himself, for clearly the Japanese had seen him or wouldn't have gone behind the tree. It was waiting time. Everything seemed to be waiting, even the jungle.

The man moved. Just a tremor at first, then low across the ground, and away, as if for better cover.

Tad raised his gun. He had a good shot now, even if the moving thing was blurred.

Then he saw her, Johanna. Fleeing from him.

"Stop!" he yelled. "It's all right—stop!"

She turned. She was a wild thing glazed into stillness. Then she ran toward him, making sounds that were the catchings of breath and the chokings of relief, ran in a twisting path downward, past scrub and canebrake, until she was right before him.

"If I'd had a gun, I'd have had you!" She was laughing with dismay.

He pointed to his rifle. "I almost let go."

"Oh, murder."

"Yes."

"I thought Tokan . . ." She still hadn't caught her breath. "I thought . . ."

"I thought you were too."

They started to laugh at the absurdity, the perilous

absurdity of tenderfeet, and he thought of naval war games and maneuvers with subs sinking their own destroyers, of the terrible wardroom joke of Blue Takes Blue; always the laughter, but the ignominy too, as there was now.

"We'll have to stay together," he said. "Please—from now on—don't go far."

"I won't." She smiled. "Do you have my rifle?"

He didn't answer.

"You forgot it?" she said.

"No." He hurried back to the gorse brake, picked up the empty gun and handed it to her. She barely glanced at it. She had something else on her mind. "Look," she said, and held her hand out.

The thing was squashed. All he could identify was a large leaf, wrinkled but still green, wrapped around something of uncertain shape. Excitedly, she peeled the leaf away and he saw the white confection.

"What is it?"

"Rice cake. It's Japanese." Then, quickly, "Come with me."

Perhaps twenty paces away, she pointed to the ground. He saw another one. Indicating where she had found the first, the one she had eaten, she said, "They were almost equidistant from each other. They weren't merely dropped. He put them there."

She said it as a statement of fact, not asking an opinion, nor was he inclined to offer one since it seemed indisputable: the confections had been carefully placed there, they had been cooked and carried; they were not wild, of the jungle.

Making a sudden movement of her head, she bent toward the rice cake. She was devouring it. Seeing his bemused glance, she said self-consciously, "I'm famished."

"What if he put something in it?"

"What do you mean—poison?" She laughed at how unlikely it was, but she didn't finish the cake. "I'm still hungry," she said. "Could you save anything out of my knapsack?"

"I didn't try. You wouldn't have eaten it after having those slimy things all over it."

"No, I guess not."

"I thought of saving some of your other stuff—there was some underwear and handkerchiefs—but those little bastards are so tiny, you'd never be sure . . ."

"It's all right," she said.

"But if you want us to go back . . ."

She looked at the path Tokan had indicated with his rice cakes. He realized she was thinking, as he was, not to waste time. Reaching into his own bag, he dug around for the dehydrated food. As he was doing it, he saw her pick something up from the ground and work it over in her hand. "What's that?" he asked.

She extended her hand. The thing she held was round and walnut-sized, the color of a dried-up lime. "It's a guava, I think." She pulled at the skin with her teeth and exposed the fruit, pale lavender-pink, with a pungent scent. Tickling it with her tongue, "It's strange," she said. "They were probably planted and abandoned—how many years ago?" She was chewing at it. "It's sweet and sort of—uh—sexy. Nice. Have one."

The ground was covered with them. He ate one. It was, as she said, sweet, but it had the other taste too, indeterminable, a musky aliveness, more animal than fruit. He ate more and more of them; so did Johanna. They would have a bite of the hardtack, which tasted like bacon flavored chalk, then follow it quickly with guava. They were laughing at the incongruity of eating something too manufactured and dead with a garnish too wild and alive, and they were making nonsensic symbols about not knowing which they needed mc trying to outdo each other in ponderous silliness. so noisily enjoying themselves that they totally the man up there, waiting in the wilderness.

Then they heard the myna bird.

Not that it had anything to do with the they told themselves; only that they had bee moment of warm-hearted concord betweer of surprise in their friendliness, even of beauty, and the ugly bird noise had mocked and insulted them.

Irritably, "I heard that damn thing in the night," he said.

"You couldn't have. Myna birds are silent at night."

"That cruddy thing was noisy."

They looked at one another, thought about it a moment, then tacitly let it go; both of them could have been mistaken.

As they started to move upward where the rice cakes had directed them, she paused and looked back at the little clearing where they had been. He thought, and was touched by the thought: she's sentimental about these few minutes we've just had. But he was wrong. She was regretting the loss of the bag.

"You weren't even able to save the Thermos?" she asked. "We could use it for water."

"If you want to go back—"

"No, the hell with it."

He heard the annoyance but decided it would pass. On the contrary. As he made his way ahead of her, there was the irritation again. "You're going the wrong way."

"I'll get back to his damn little rice cakes." He pointed to the wet earth. "I'm trying to avoid the swamp."

"You can't avoid it."

"What then—walk through it?" He was losing his temper. "I'm sure *he* didn't."

He heard himself defending the pathway he had chosen as if it were dry; there was no such, it was simply a choice of sludges. But he did stay as close to the edge of the swamp as he could. She was right—the only trail upward seemed to lead that way. And yes, one step to the left and they would be mired, and sucked into it. Nor were the forward more reassuring; each foot was a decision. It was going through the thicknesses; sometimes they needed by needle thorns, sometimes glued by things from a gray-green vine that clung to no letup in the rankness. There will be a clearing a hundred steps from now, he would tell himself, but two hours later the jungle was thicker than before.

They weren't speaking any more. Their annoyance with each other was now worsened by the moil of movement. And Tad had a disquieting illusion. Although there were signs of animals all about them, tracks and spoor and nesting places, and sometimes they caught glimpses of them—a mongoose, a white-tailed deer, a mountain goat—he began to feel that the most animal thing about him was the jungle itself, its green malignancy. It seemed to grow as he watched it, encircling to suffocate, angrily advancing all around, never still, every leaf enlarging before his eyes, every limb thickening in his grip.

About to share the unpleasant image with Johanna, he saw she was hard at it, handling her own. And no longer working out her irritation on him, but diverting it against the jungle. He had returned her hunting knife to her, and she was using it. She lay an angry hand on everything. She swore and spat and whacked irascibly at things that needed no cutting, slashing them before they slashed at her. This was the way she fought the whine and wince in herself, he thought, and he speculated why she went to such extremes to do it; she couldn't make the mouth of self-pity if she tried. He began to think she was stronger than he was, muscularly tougher and more durable, and she would carry this cross better than he would, when suddenly she stopped, as if someone had beaten her.

"I can't stand the smell," she said.

He had been noticing it only the last mile or so. It had seemed no stronger than an unpleasant insinuation at first, hardly an insult to the nostrils. But it had been growing worse. And now that they had stopped moving, it was an assault, a terrible fetor, disgusting and unescapable, abusing all the air. It was unclear where it came from; seemingly, it was everywhere, a reek of excrement and unimaginable putrefaction.

There was something horrifyingly wrong about the place. It was a new world, these islands, newly thrust up from the sea, yet this swamp seemed old, full of ancient carboniferous damps, rank odors that said this place was not meant to be as it was, and was dying in a blunder of decay.

Seeing that Johanna, as motionless as he, was caught in the same gloom, he forced himself forward. And there, as they moved out of one forest entanglement and were not yet twisted into another, they came upon the stinking morass.

It was hideous. Near the border of the swamp, no more than a dozen feet from the edge, there was what seemed to be a whitish windrow. At first glance, it looked like a wavelet of bleached leaves, then, closer, like a narrow spume of scum. But it was alive, at least part of it was alive, wriggling in small tortures, squirming, trying to twitch itself free. But it wasn't one large thing, it was thousands of small ones, quivering animals, each no larger than a thumb, white, as slimy as pus, each trying to extricate itself from the death and disintegration of the others. You could tell the live ones not only by the motion of the repulsive things but by their paleness. The dead were turning dark brown and green, already assuming the colors of the swamp ooze; their decay was the stench. The live ones were, in their way, an even more disgusting horror. Aside from their sickly whiteness and their desperate writhing to free themselves from the rot, they had no other definition. They were not fish or tadpoles or maggots or slugs, yet they were all of them. They had no fins or tails or heads, yet they made a forward motion, shaking, twitching, convulsing themselves out of the ooze, trying to contort themselves onto the shore.

He heard a sickly, guttural sound from Johanna and abruptly she moved away.

But he couldn't stir. He was fixed to the view of the abhorrent thing. Something made him keep on looking, something insisted that he see it all, to watch the mucous creatures squirm from death's muck to the nearest dry land. What forced them to do it? he asked. What coerced the blind and headless things to torture themselves to safety, how did they sense there was safety for them anywhere, how could they distinguish one covert from another, how could they be so certain they might not be better off with the brown and green ones, perishing in the slime? They were wet things, wet slippery things in a wet warm place; how could they dare a dry one? The desperation for a dry haven and the brainless, eyeless squirming for it—was this, then, the beginning of things, the beginning of awareness, of courage? Did the creature, in some nameless, mindless way, dream of itself as something better than the brown green dead ones—a brown pig, perhaps, snuffling for worms like what it itself used to be; or an upright animal, clambering in trees? Aspiring perhaps to a navy-blue suit with brass buttons?

How ludicrous if it all came down to nothing more than a yearning for a dry place. And what paradox did it stand for that he was a sailor, loving the sea, yearning to go back to the wet? What aboriginal home in the deep was he longing for? There must be something more profoundly wrong with himself than he imagined if he, while all life was struggling so achingly for the shore, kept nudging himself into swampy wildernesses like this. Exiling himself, if only momentarily, from the clean and dry and sunlit streets—and the electrified offices—back into the damp and fetid pathlessness of the jungle. What was he trying to live over again?

He looked around and couldn't see Johanna. Then he heard her. She had resumed her whacking at the wilderness. When he got close, he saw she was no longer preoccupied with the white, squirming things. There was a glitter of excitement in her eyes. She pointed straight ahead.

He saw no difference in the look of things; the same trees, vines, thickets. She took a few steps forward and, with the barrel of her gun, pointed up at the branch of the ironwood tree. It was head high and had been cut by a sharp thing, a hunting knife or an ax, and it hung, a crippled limb. He indicated her knife. "Did you do it?"

"No."

It was too sharp, too clean for an animal to have cut

it, and too high. Yet, there was something fundamentally wrong in assuming it was the way Tokan had gone. "It's downhill," he said.

"Why do you assume it's uphill all the way?"

"Because that's all I got from Kley's papers," he said. "And Gorpy kept pointing to the mountain."

"Maybe they're both wrong."

"Then we've got nothing to go by."

She pointed to the cut limb. "Except Tokan himself."

There was going to be a real altercation, and he knew it could not be prevented. But something did prevent it.

The myna bird. The sound told them which way to go—Johanna's way, downhill. As they both, without thought, took the bird's cry as the unquestioned authority, Tad felt a chill.

It was not a bird's call. It was the call of a man, and it had been a man in the night, as well. A man mocking the bird—and mocking them. Leading them to where he was.

Tad felt his hand, the one that carried the rifle, go clammy. The weapon seemed, all at once, useless, insufficient for what it was meant to do. He felt more impotent than frightened; whatever action he might take would be not enough, or too slow, or in the wrong direction. He had the haphazard image that his gun was as empty as Johanna's, someone had robbed him of all his cartridges, so that whatever he did with his weapon would make no difference, he would be pulling the trigger on emptiness.

But why was the awareness that the bird call was false more upsetting than the appearance of the rice cakes? In both instances, the man was leading them to where he was. What, then, was the difference?

He heard the bird call again. The mockery.

That was the difference. The man's derision was a boast. It bespoke his superiority. It said that, although he could, he would not have to flee farther ahead than a bird's cry. He was the one who was blowing the hunting call, not they.

Tad was not the hunter any longer; the hunted. Starting to feel the difference between one and the other, he told himself it would be better not to think of it; simply to get on with the hunt.

He looked at Johanna. There was no need to say anything. Her face was drawn with gravity.

He struck out strongly past the broken branch and followed where the myna sound had directed him. The path did indeed lead downward quite a way, through rougher terrain than before, and his memory of the Kley information told him that this pathway was trickery; there would be disaster at the end of it. He kept a longer distance between himself and Johanna; if only he could lengthen the distance between himself and the thing that was overtaking him: fear.

He had to face it at last. That was the difference between the hunter and the hunted. They had lost the advantage of the pursuer over the pursued. The lust to kill or capture is the big edge over the terror of being slain. No matter how dangerous to the hunter the chase might be, his edge over his quarry was what made a sport of it. It allowed pauses for laughter and refreshment, allowed the mind its leisure to speculate on how the hunt was justifiable or beautiful, how it benefited the very species it slew, how it ameliorated the hungers in the wild, how it rectified the wastefulness of nature, how it was written in the ordinances of natural selection.

But the hunted had no time for philosophy. Pursued, flight was its only pursuit. It had no time, no strength to spare. What strength there was in terror was, in every sense, fugitive; the rest was weakness. Weakness not only because flight is ultimately disabling, but for an even more elementary reason: flight is blind. It has no eyes in the back of its head.

That, Tad realized, was the mockery, the bird mockery, of this hunt. The Japanese man, ostensibly the pursued, had no eyes in the back of his head; yet *he* saw *them*, and *they* were blind. He knew the terrain; for him every step was a certainty. For them it was all ambush, all swamps and snares and deadfalls.

Suddenly it became clear to him why he and Johanna were able to stay on Tokan's trail although Kley's men had lost it. The Japanese was *allowing* them to stay on his trail. They would never have been able to keep track of him if he had not wanted them to do so. He was actually guiding them . . . to what heinous entrapment?

No, it would not do to think of it that way. Always, at some stage in an enterprise, there was the specter of failure in it. In a life-and-death enterprise, mortality was the specter—but only the specter, not necessarily the reality. He must get on with the hunt and not infect Johanna with his terrors.

"It looks like we're moving upward after all," she said.

He hadn't noticed, but it was true. Slowly, imperceptibly to him, they had been turning an angle at the base of an elevation, and now they were mounting. What was more unaccountable was that the forest had thinned and was more traversable than before, the matted undergrowth disappearing as they ascended. He imagined, to begin with, that a trail had long ago been hewn through this woodland, but he realized, gradually, as the trees became sparser and the undergrowth less luxuriant, that they were emerging from the jungle.

Sunlight came through, in mottled patches, then great swaths of gold across the greenery. In a little while, they were in the open and could see the sun—setting, he was sure; it must be afternoon.

Stopping to look at the full sky, he breathed deeply and lifted his head into the dry wind. It felt good. He turned to share the relief with her, but she was tense, saying, in effect, this was no time for a free breath; they were now more exposed than ever.

Not that they saw any sign of the man. The space was empty. But there were lava boulders here and there and, occasionally, a clump of dwarfish *hala* trees. He might be behind anything, at a distance, or close.

Thinking it better to stay within the edges of the wilderness as long as possible, they took a few steps

backward into the woods and continued upward. Now
the trek became even more puzzling. They were on a
saddle of the mountain, a narrow plateau tilting upward. Stretching alongside them was a field of exuberant, low-growing vegetation. Yet it didn't seem altogether wild, at least it had not always been wild.
Whatever might have been cultivated had long gone
to seed, rank and stunted now. Perhaps there had been
a sugar canebrake here, or pineapple fields. Certainly
taro, and, even though there didn't seem water enough,
volunteer plants still struggled out of the earth. But
what had happened to these fields, why had they been
desolated?

As they came around the curve of the mountain,
they had their answer. Wind and devastation and,
most terrible, lava, the gray death, distances of lava.

In these volcanic islands, he knew, all ravages were
possible. But this was a grotesque. The eruption had
played its whole repertory of havoc. It had thrown a
torrent of molten rock down the mountainside, leaving
behind every variety of ashen destruction. There were
wavy billows and ropy twistings of it. Some had col-
lected around verdure and mounded into slag heaps,
some had simply laid a fine deadly blanket over fallen
trees, and the outlines of branch and bark were still
visible like sculpturings in stone. Smooth tongues of
the stuff, shiny as polished granite, lay exposed against
ridges of talus and hummocks of cinder. And the blustering wind blew everywhere.

But the paradox: as if nature could not live with
its own ravage, the disaster had left islands of vegetation. In the midst of the black desert, there were oases
of lush herbage, low-growing *ohelo* bushes and island
juniper and cypress. In one place, out of a rocky gullet,
an enormous koa tree grew lushly against the sky. And
at a distance, a patch of wild taro grew on a memory of
moisture.

The wind was a punishment. They had no shelter
from it. They could no longer remain under the canopy
of trees, for they no longer had a choice; if they continued in their upward direction, they had to cross the

lava slope. Gusts of cinder cut into their faces, lacerating their skin, needling their eyes. Bent into the blowing grit, they made their way over one lava drift, descended into a black breach, climbed out of it and crossed another drift.

The second breach took them entirely unaware. It was a chasm. One moment they were scratching their way, on hands and knees, over slag and cinder and ash, the next moment they were on an eminence, moving toward the crevasse. It was wide, it was forbiddingly craggy, it was fathomlessly deep.

They could not believe they saw a bridge across it. Too bizarre out here, Tad thought, on this dust-racked mountainside, to imagine that anyone had spanned a bottomless gorge to travel from bleakness to bleakness. But when they came closer, he realized it had not always been a bleakness. There had indeed been taro fields here, before the devastation, and homes and farming people. And the wooden bridge had had more trestles then, had been sunk firmly into more solid earth, and had given less heed to the howling wind. Now the bridge sighed with the blustering of every gust. At the foot of it, they heard its creaking complaint, old wood against dried old wood, like a decrepit rocking chair threatening to fall apart.

There was a redoubtable beauty here, in every half-tone of destruction, along the jagged cliffs, the cruel escarpment, deep down into the gray abyss. And the only way to the end of this was from one perdition to another, across the bridge, across the bottomless canyon.

She didn't ask him what he was thinking, she simply tried to pull him away. "No," she said.

He pointed across. "It only goes one way."

"Let it."

"*He* went across," he said, pretending to misunderstand her. "It's strong enough."

"I don't mean that—you know it."

"What, then? Go back?"

She hesitated an instant too long, and he started

for the bridge. "Wait!" she cried. "He's just on the other side. You'll be a pigeon. One rifle shot!"

"He's had the chance before." He pointed to their exposure on the waste of lava. "He's got it now."

"He hasn't got the range now—and you can run for cover. But if you cross—if you go closer—!" Her voice was getting wild. "Don't go!"

He couldn't believe it; Johanna, hysterical. She'd be sorry for it tomorrow; he was sorry now. Hurrying away from her, he scrambled low, ten feet from the bridge. But she was after him. "I won't let you!" she cried. "I won't!"

She grabbed at his sleeve, then threw her arms around him. "Let go!" he said.

"I won't!"

He tried to pull himself out of her grasp, but she had a frenzied strength. "For Christ sake!"

"I won't! I won't!"

One of his arms was free and as she reached for him again, he hit her. She fell back, more stunned than hurt, and again was at him. But now he was away.

He could feel the loose planking underfoot. The timbers gave too much; he wished he were lighter than he was. Run low, he warned himself, keep your body in a crouch; low is better than fast.

"No—no!" she called.

He heard her behind him. He stopped and twisted his head to look. She was already on the bridge.

"Stay back!" he yelled.

It was as stupid, he knew, as her telling him not to go. Yet, "Stay back!"

She was gaining on him, not crouching as she ran, heedlessly rushing toward him in an upright position. "Get down!" She was crazy. "Get down!"

She stopped an instant, dead still, then understood. She crouched and ran again.

One-third of the way, and no rifle fire. The only sound, the wind. The bridge swung, it swayed. The danger isn't only guns, he thought, it's howling gale as well.

Nearly halfway now, and still no rifle fire.

Almost as if the man had measured, the first shot came, halfway. Another shot. It was so close, the last one; the next shot would do it. Oh, murder, what a foolish ending, what a makeshift self-sacrifice. Pigeon, she had said.

Another shot. No closer to the mark, no farther away.

He'll do it the next time, he thought; he won't miss me now.

The fourth. Still no closer, still no farther away. As if the marksman had carefully measured every distance from the mark. Then the hunted knew what the hunter was doing. Using the running target as sporting game. Torture. Tantalizing with close ones, enjoying the quarry's torment.

Another shot.

Still another. Six. All patterned in a circle, a halo of gunfire around the running prey.

His lungs bursting, Tad made it: the foot of the bridge. Still scrambling low, he hurried for the brush as Johanna came gasping toward him. "That monster," she muttered. "What's he doing?"

He didn't answer. Lying in the scrub, catching his breath, he pulled her back so she wouldn't be so directly in the line of fire. Panting, she lay beside him.

At odds with his body, his muscles, which should have relaxed with the running, were wire-drawn. It was weirdly painful, feeling them so fatigued and tense at the same time. If he could have a moment of release, he thought, if he could simply shut his eyes for a spell . . .

He had an unquestionable premonition. A presence. The man was there.

Sitting bolt upright, he looked behind him. He saw nothing. Then his eyes moved upward. The man was on the ridge above them, standing there, as still as stone. He was gazing down at them. The slant of sunlight caught only half his face, and what was visible had no expression in it.

When he realized he was seen, the Japanese did

nothing, simply waited a moment. Then he raised his arm a little, gently. It could have been a salutation, or it could have been a beckoning: come.

It was the most beautiful stream Tad had ever seen, and it made an exquisite music. It murmured of simple things, of spring freshets that emptied into it, of white snows on Mauna Loa. They followed it upward, hypnotized by the sound of it, as if it were bringing them reports of past happiness And promises.

For moments—hardly more than flashes—Tad would forget that he was stalking quarry. He suspected Johanna also forgot. It puzzled him that they could be so close to destroying or being destroyed and yet lose track of it, if only for a flicker of time. He considered whether the man had done this to him, whether he had worked a spell, an Eastern magic that would make the end a sweet one, tender as this stream, as quietly perfect. He considered too whether this was the beauty, this the composure that comes to people who know they are about to die and make their peace with it. Did the murderer turn angel before the noose trap was sprung? He could not reconcile the gentleness of this place and his feeling for it with the brutality of the hunt. Yet, hunters were always talking about the peace and serenity of wilderness. What did the discrepancy mean? Could beauty only be cherished as a discrepancy, could it be described so facilely, only as a function of conflict, a release from terror?

The release didn't last all day. Toward late afternoon, the rapacious jungle moved in again, the vines reached up to snatch them, the stickers and nettles clung. But the stream stayed with them, broadening as they ascended, getting wilder, colder, turning from time to time to whirlpools and to falls.

Slowly they began to feel another change in the terrain. The mountain too, like the wilderness, was closing in on them. Heretofore they had had only one shoulder of it to deal with. Now, two. They were making their way upward in a valley that kept narrowing as they moved. Mile by mile, the pocket between mountainside and brook on the one hand and steep escarpment on the other became more constrained.

Then they saw him again.

The cliff was precipitous on the other side of the stream, straight up. Once more, he stood on a high place, a shelf of headland, waiting. Nothing else, simply standing there, attendant on a cliffside, the mauve-gray mountain behind him.

Reflexively, Tad raised his rifle. If he had taken a sighted aim, he surely would have had him. But he didn't wait, he didn't get an eye bead on the man, just sighted with his fingers. Only half-raising his gun, he took an off-wrist shot.

He wasn't sure he had missed. For a flash, he thought he saw a change in the man's posture, no more than a twitch, perhaps, or a quick startlement, then the relaxed recovery. But perhaps it had been an illusion; nothing else gave evidence he had been hit. The man, without a change in his flowing rhythms, turned gracefully away, and was gone.

Tad twisted to Johanna just in time to see her lower her gun. He had the racing thought: she has pulled the trigger and found her rifle empty. But he had heard no sound, no click.

"You were too fast," she said, "and I was too slow."

It had been such an easy, standstill shot, and he had muffed it on a reckless swing. And Johanna . . . if, one breath sooner, she had pulled the trigger—and if her gun had been loaded—the man would be dead. He was right to have emptied her gun; she'd have shot for the kill.

The disturbing realization: he too had shot for the kill!

At the critical moment, when there was no time to think of Purple Code or East wind, rain, or to weigh such imponderables as justice and survival and murder, he had simply raised his gun and fired. Not, as he had solemnly resolved, at an arm or a leg, but as he was taught to do, at the animal's vital center, the gut. If he were cocksure about his marksmanship, he might even have gone for the dot between the eyes. One target or another, he had aimed to kill. Aimed badly, as it happened, and now he was eating at himself, nagging to know whether the failure pleased or distressed him.

"You're a better shot than that," she was saying quietly. "How'd you miss him?"

"You said the reason." He was irritable.

"What did I say?"

"Too fast." His annoyance was mounting.

"Or too unwilling."

"Go to hell."

He didn't know he was going to say it. Oddly, she didn't mind. She touched him gently, then said something about moving on.

Moving on would soon seem impossible. They were at the base of a jagged volcanic rift. The walls were getting steeper. The floor of the fault was craggy, and each boulder was a conglomerate mass of black cinder. Often they lost footing and fell forward on the scabrous stuff. Tad's hands began to feel it—scraped raw from abrasion—and he suspected Johanna's would be worse. Only the presence of the stream gave them any comfort; it ran cold and pure, and they used it for cleansing themselves and for drink and antiseptic. But it had ceased being a sweet brooklet. It rushed frenziedly and made a frightening turbulence. Somewhere, ahead, it boomed like cannon.

They came to the headwater. It was not the tallest waterfall Tad had ever seen, but it was the angriest. Three waters collided with one another at the top, none of them friendly. The cataract made a twofold roar, the one at waters meeting on the summit, then the thunderclap when the torrent plummeted into the whirlpool below. Although it was twilight and the sun was splashing reds and golds across the sky, the cascade caught hardly a tint. It was a forbidding noncolor, icy and resentful, born of a volcano's blazing and freezing rages.

They stood there and stared at the ominous sight, the

collapse of an element. The cataract seemed so vindictive, bent on deserting the past and destroying the future.

There was another dismay. The cascade was a terminus. Here, where the water fell, the two shoulders of the canyon came together. The waterfall was the juncture of the fault. They had come to the end of a blind alley.

They looked upward. Steep mountain faces on both sides, precipices straight up, sharp, stark, uncompromising. Johanna raised her hand to it. "Could anybody have climbed that?"

"He must have."

"Or else we came too far."

It had occurred to him, but he felt sure they hadn't. Nothing they had come upon had suggested another pathway up the mountain; there had been no slit, neither to the right nor left of them, no ravine or gully, not the slightest defile of any kind.

He pointed to where the late-afternoon shadow stopped, just a few feet to the right of the cascade. The fading rays of sunlight caught the hillside, etched the ledges. "There," he said. "If he did climb it, he went up there."

"It's straight up."

"And wet." He knew it might get wetter as they ascended, the falls widened at the top. Perhaps there was a better place to climb, or perhaps Tokan had his own technique for it. But if this was the end of the canyon and there was no other trailway upward, it made decision easy.

"Shall we try it?" she said.

"Not 'we.' "

Her voice was not sarcastic. "What do I do while you're trying—urge you onward?"

He hesitated. There was no time for argument. The sun would disappear too quickly, he feared, and leave them hanging up there, in the dark. But if they waited until tomorrow, what might happen? The man was unpredictable . . .

"You think we can make it before dark?" she asked.

His own qualm. "Yes, I think so."

They were carrying too much by hand and would need the use of all their limbs. Her sole burden, in addition to the knife that hung in its sheath from her belt, was her rifle; he had gun and rucksack. He lifted the flap of his canvas bag and looked inside. There was some dry food left, the water canteen, a cartridge case, and some smaller odds and ends of things. He stowed what he could in his trouser and jacket pockets and tossed the rucksack away. Then he refilled the canteen with water and undid the buckle of his belt. Slipping the strap of the canteen over his belt, he was about to buckle himself up again when he got an idea about the rifles. "Slip both rifles behind my belt," he said. As she did it, he tightened his belt and snapped the buckle ends together. The guns were firm against his back, and when he got into his jacket again it made them firmer still. But he looked like an immobile hulk.

"Will you be able to move with those things?" she asked.

It wasn't easy, but he could do it. They started up in tandem, Tad going first. They had barely begun the ascent when it occurred to him that since they were not climbing with ropes, going single file presented an extra danger. If he slipped, he would drag her down with him. "Keep going your way," he said. "I'll move to the left."

The left turned out to have stonier footholds, the water having eroded the softer debris away, but it was wetter and more slippery. Either place, however, it was hand over hand and kicking ash and cinder away with the tip of the boot, every ascending step a wrench of muscle. If only his fingertips held out, he could make it; his fingertips and his palms. The grit, the sharpness of the rock edges, made him feel that every handhold was a clench on broken glass. And he had to keep warning himself against moving so much to the left, for a random surge of water might wash him down the cliff.

He heard her curse, then the splattering of rock. He

looked toward Johanna. Her left foot perched on a sill so narrow that she barely had a toehold on it, her right leg dangled midair; the lava had given way. Precariously, she hung there, her hands carrying most of her weight, her left foot starting to lose its insecure grip on the stone. Worse trouble, she could not, apparently, see where to reach with her free leg.

"Upward—to your right!" he shouted.

Her leg moved, treading on empty air, missing the slight outcrop of rock. "I can't see!" she cried. "I can't see!"

"Keep trying—it's higher—just a little higher."

"I can't!"

He saw the tension go out of her elbows; her handgrip was weakening. "Go on—higher—do it!"

Her right foot landed, and held. She pushed with it to take the strain off her arms. He prayed the rock wouldn't crumble under her foot. As he saw her summoning her strength, he realized the rock was firm.

"Now shift your hands," he called. "Can you shift your hands?"

She moved her right hand first, a few inches closer to the footing, then the left. Edging her way, inches at a time, she soon had a securer hold on the palisade. Almost instantly, she started upward again.

"Take a moment—catch your breath," he yelled.

But she couldn't—or wouldn't—hear him and continued her ascent.

The lava was getting more crumbly as they climbed. Every step had to be tested against the possibility that the foothold might collapse; every handhold meant cinders in the hands and in the eyes. If only there were a resting place . . .

There was. It was a ledge they hadn't suspected could be there. They pulled themselves upon it and lay there, breathing heavily, swallowing the air in gulps, trying to ignore the agonies in their limbs and backs, and the lacerations of their hands.

The respite was brief; then, upward again. The ascent was steeper now, with the beginning of a new hazard: the rocks were wet. The falls water seeped horizontally along the shelves of lava stone, and every handgrip was too rough with cinder and too slippery with water.

Glancing at Johanna, he saw her on a level with him, her face running with sweat, and filthy from the mountain rubble. But she didn't look at him, her clutch was always upward, and now she was a step higher on the precipice.

Looking downward, he hadn't realized they had come so high, nor could he see how they could get any higher. There were no longer any ledges to rest on; every step hereafter would be purely perpendicular. Moreover, he was climbing into increasing wetness; even Johanna, farther away from the torrent, was slowing down because of the increasing dampness of the footholds. But they kept going, both, foot and hand, foot and hand, toil by ache by toil.

Ping.

He didn't think of it as a rifle shot; too quiet. He hadn't, in fact, heard any gun report, only the crack in the stone perhaps ten feet above him. True, the sound of a gun would be muffled by the roaring boom of the cascade; still, the timbre was different. Besides, Johanna had not even exchanged a glance with him, so perhaps she considered it what it doubtless was: a stone flung by the falls, cracking against rock.

Ping.

Closer this time. And this time she heard it. Looking at him quickly, she stopped moving.

Ping.

Yes, a gunshot. What was he doing, the bastard?

Tad too stopped moving, as perplexed as he was alarmed, and sickened by the torturing sickness of the man, the perverted, sick tormentor. Why didn't he just shoot to kill instead of nicking at the mountainside, pot-shooting above every handhold, playing at a sadistic sport with . . .

Ping.

Everything at once. He started to move, heard another ping, Johanna's warning, felt the rock chips falling in his eyes, lost one handhold, then the other, grasped, clutched, fell.

He knew the aroma: a cigarette. He thought he himself might be smoking it, but he couldn't be doing that, he was asleep; besides, he hadn't smoked for years. It couldn't even be a cigarette, there was no glow in the darkness.

Then he saw the bud of flame and the smoke after it. He didn't say anything. Having no idea where he was, he would try to figure out if he was in a room. Although his leg ached—was it his leg—no, his ankle—although it ached, everything else was pleasant. He lay on something that yielded, something crunchy-soft, like cornflakes; the place was dry and the air was beatifically warm.

The bud of flame again, and he saw her face.

She was very beautiful, more beautiful than he had ever seen her. Then he remembered how dirty she had looked when he had last seen her, and he reflected on how she could have washed, and where—oh, yes, the stream, the waterfall. He was recalling more now, bits and pieces, then masses of remembrance.

She sensed he had awakened. "Are you any better?"

It seemed an odd question. "Better than what?"

"You don't remember?"

"I fell."

"Yes."

"What's this?" he asked. "This place."

"You walked into it," she replied. "You don't recall at all?"

"I walked—from where?"

"From the ledge—up there. You don't remember, do you?"

"No."

"I tried to carry you down. You wouldn't let me." Her smile was peculiar, he couldn't understand it. "There was something strange about you—for a while

I thought you had hurt your head—something bizarre —like a zombie. I knew you must be in pain, but *you* didn't seem to know it, so I guess you weren't. But your behavior—I told you to move, you moved; I told you to rest, you rested. Every step of the way, whatever I said, you did it. And you came down all by yourself. When we got on the ground, I led you in here. You seemed absolutely all right—not saying a word, but all right. Then suddenly—right there—you just seemed to fall apart, you collapsed. And you've been unconscious—I don't know—maybe a couple of hours."

He started to move and had to groan. He ached all over. But the big hurt was in his foot. "Am I crippled?"

"I don't know—I don't think so," she said. "How could you have come down the whole distance . . . ?" Her voice trailed off in the marvel of it.

It didn't seem possible he could have forgotten so much. He made himself sit up and look toward where her cigarette smoke was drifting. There was some light in that direction, blue, as if there might be moon out there. But there was little light anywhere else.

She answered his question. "It's—I don't know—a grotto, a cave of some sort. It's strange. I think the water wash may have done it, over the years." Then, "Reach out."

He reached and touched something, a wall. It was rough but unexpectedly warm. He asked her what it was.

"I can't tell," she said. "There may be hot lava in there, way inside that wall—who knows how far back?" Laughing, "The latest thing—radiant heating."

For the first time, he was conscious of the booming waterfall. "How far are we from that?"

"Not far," she answered. "Thirty, forty feet. We're practically under it."

He ran his hand through the pleasantly dry soft stuff on the ground. "What's this?"

"My first thought was, maybe guano of some sort—caves, you know, rats and bats."

"I hope you had a second thought."

"Look." She flicked her lighter flame. It was an agreeably crumbly mixture of black lava sand, dried ferns and cedar needles. It too was warm, as if it were alive and at work at being something else. Whatever it was trying to be, the seeming sentience of it gave him an unaccountable pleasure, oddly stirring. He played with the stuff a moment.

It was a shame, he thought, to drift away from this namelessly gratifying feeling, but that other phantom was in his mind. He tried to rid himself of it, but couldn't. "How about him?" he asked.

"Not another sign."

"He's up there."

"Yes." She held the silence, but he knew her mind wasn't quiet. "Why hasn't he killed us?"

"Not us—me." As he said it, he thought he had come upon the answer, the most obvious explanation possible. "He wants to keep me alive for the same reason I want to keep him alive. He thinks he'll get something out of me."

He smiled grimly. What an irony's in store for you, Tokan, he thought; I know nothing you can torture out of me—I've been entrusted with nothing.

"I don't think that's it at all." She didn't continue for a while. "I think it's more twisted than that. I keep thinking I'll never understand him, he's too convoluted —the Oriental mind, too complex. And yet, I wonder— maybe it's me. He may be very simple and I may be the convoluted one. I hate him—that hasn't changed. He maimed and killed my son—I'll always hate him. And I mean to kill him—that hasn't changed either. But hatred should be very pure to be . . . effective. It shouldn't be mixed up with other things."

"Like what?"

". . . Fascination." He could feel the churning of her thoughts. "The man is not insane. He's educated, he's shrewd, he is gifted with an extraordinary flair for self-preservation—he finds it impossible to kill himself when he knows that's what he's meant to do. And I suspect he has a hundred other talents as well. Then, if he's not insane, what is this insanity he's putting himself through—and us? What does he want of us, finally? What can we give him?" Deeply troubled, she stopped speaking. Finally, with difficulty, she resumed. "It's terrible for me to ask those questions, as if the answer to them is more important to me than killing the man. It isn't. It's just that I have to know about him. And yet, I have the feeling *he's* not complicating it—I am. It's probably simpler than I think. And it may turn out that way—simpler. It'll be like a Japanese poem—you expect meaning within meaning within meaning. And it's not there—it's a different thing. It's feeling within feeling within feeling." Then she said, almost to herself, "And elegant."

"Elegant?"

"Yes."

"He's that? Elegant?" He recapitulated in his mind all the uglinesses he knew of the man, the murder of Ben and Nishi and Karli Karli, and the uglinesses he had put them through, the ticks and the toil and even the hideous white creatures of the swamp, which seemed to be of Tokan's own devising. And he could not think of him as elegant. "You don't really think of him that way, do you?"

"Yes, I do."

"Won't you find it hard to kill him if he's elegant?"

"Harder than if he were a wild pig, yes."

He thought: how much better we understand each other than that wild-pig day, how much closer we have come; yet, how far apart we are in what we demand of living things. Paradoxically, he who had no intention of killing Tokan would have less qualm about doing so than Johanna would. For the man had abused his man-genius, had made a wild pig of himself. And was making pigs of them. That was the terrible thing about the hunt, he realized, the most terrible of all. He was gaining jungle courage, more than he had ever had of it, to fight the jungle fear the man had aroused in him. But losing something else, something perhaps more precious, he was pulling triggers on guns, self-preservatively perhaps, shooting to kill. And he thought, somewhat chaotically, of wild pigs . . .

"I have some bad news for you," she said.

He turned quickly.

"Oh, not desperate bad," she continued, with quick reassurance. "We've lost one of the guns."

"Lost—how?"

"When you fell, it dropped from your belt. I could see it in the pool—but I didn't dare leave you—and the water was carrying it downstream . . ."

"Whose?"

He hadn't meant to say the word so urgently. She looked puzzled. "Yours," she said.

His head ached and that was the reason, he told himself, he wasn't putting things together properly.

They were weaponless.

What did that mean? Even if they found a way of tracking the man, could they now really risk finding him? What foolishness could make him think, what foolishness had ever made him think they had any chance of . . . He could work it out—not tonight, tomorrow, maybe—when his head didn't ache.

She was touching him, gently, comfortingly. Perhaps she saw the stress in his face. If she did, he hoped she hadn't guessed about the gun—he wasn't ready, yet, to deal with it—he hoped she thought it was his leg that was bothering him.

She reached down and touched his ankle. "Does it hurt too much?"

"No."

"Can I do something for you?"

"No."

"Are you hungry? We've got some rations left."

"No, not hungry. Thanks."

He ran his hand over the sand beside him. It was smooth to the caress, and when he took a handful of it and let it sift through his fingers, it had a sensuous flow to it, like tepid water. He was trying to recall the feeling of pleasantness it had given him before, and he was recalling it. She saw him touching and touching it. "Can I do something . . . to comfort you?" she whispered.

She looked at him steadily, full of readiness. As he started to lean toward her, she was bent on making it easy for him, and she came most of the way. She took him in her arms and held him close to herself. Comfort, she had said, and that was what she was giving him. Then she kissed him and he could feel her breasts loose under her sweater. As he reached for them, she seemed to slip out of his grasp, and he felt her unbuttoning him and loosening everything, and her hand was on him.

Later, as they lay naked and quiet in the strange, soft, warm place, there was a rise of the moon and, for a brief while, the edge of the grotto shone in a silvery magic. It lighted her. How smooth her skin was; her cheekbone seemed so high, above the shadow, and her hair had such a shine. What a wonder of excitement she had been. They had had each other twice, one way and another, within an hour or so, the first time to his satisfaction, the second time to both; each time, tantalizing and incomprehensibly cruel with one another, yet gentle, so deeply gentle, as if love-making were an assault and a confession at the same time, as if it had to illustrate a confusion in themselves that it was imperative for both to understand.

Looking at her now, in moonlight, he had the feeling, as he had had since the first time he had laid eyes on Johanna, of her beauty—yet nobody, seeing a photograph of the woman, would call her beautiful. He thought he knew what her beauty was. It was the kind a woman hides, not consciously, of course, because it is a beauty born of pain and her secret ways of dealing with it; of courage when she isn't sure she has it; of the mind when she suspects her excessive pride in it may betray she values it at less than she pretends, because it fails to comfort her; of frailty and frailty and, ultimately, the strength to bear frailty itself.

He loved this woman and he loved her daughter, both. And he thought how awry it was that the world would say it was unlikely he could be true to each of them. This thought gave him pain, for, at the moment, he didn't consider it unlikely; the more pain because he knew that at some future time, not too far off, he too would consider it unlikely.

She was sound asleep. When she awakened, there would be no avoiding it, he would have to tell her the truth about the rifle. He would say it flatly, without extenuation, without trying to excuse himself in any way; I emptied your gun. We are weaponless. The hunt is over; we go back.

He couldn't do that. Nor, perhaps, would he have to. There might be, there had to be, some scheme he had not come upon, some contrivance so simple . . . It was always the simple things that were elusive.

Johanna would not agree with him, he knew, in his belief there was a simple solution to the Tokan dilemma. She had said as much: it had to be complex. After she had described her feelings for Tokan, he had speculated whether, between the savagery and tenderness of Johanna's love-making, she had been trying to say that savagery and tenderness had to be in it together, that loving and killing were parts of the same feeling she had for the Japanese man. It was as if she was trying to figure out how much of this murder journey of hers had been generated not in her head and heart, but in her gonads. And just as the thought had occurred to him, in the night, she had awakened and said the very word: "It takes a bit of bloodshed, doesn't it?"

"Love or hunting?"

"Both," she had said. "But I was thinking of love."

"Whether it 'takes' it or not, there *is* murder in it, isn't there?"

"Also the other way around," she said.

"Love in murder?"

She nodded. Then, smiling, as if to pretend to be playing with the talk, not meaning it. "Am I in love with Tokan?"

He joined the game and also smiled. "Oh, I think you can live without him."

"I wonder if I can." Her smile was fading.

"Live without your enemy?"

"Yes."

"You think you can't?"

"I don't know," she replied. "He's done something for me . . ."

"What?"

"Made me—I don't know exactly where I'm going when I say this—made me tough enough to stand myself."

It was another version of his jungle courage to fight jungle terror, he thought. "Well, toughness *is* everything, isn't it?"

She heard the irony. "It's a lot." An instant. "I used to think smarter was the most important thing. Wrong. Tougher."

"It's great for pig hunting."

She winced and turned quickly. "I don't mean that kind of toughness. How can you think I mean that?"

"What kind, then?"

"Toughness on myself."

"I thought you had enough of that," he said.

"Oh, no."

"When did he do that to you?"

"Up there. When you were lying on the ledge, unconscious. At first I said to myself, 'Move back—move away—there's a shadow to be safe in.' Then I realized you were not reviving, and might not. So I decided to carry you. Well, I knew I *couldn't* carry you down that steep place, with him up there splattering the rock with gunshot. But then I knew that 'could' or 'can' or 'shall I' hadn't a goddamn thing to do with anything, and I started to do it. The fact that you revived and could manage on your own—that turned out to be . . ." She paused, searching for the rest.

". . . of interest, but not important."

"Not important at the moment, no."

"And you give credit for that moment to Tokan."

"Well, he let me do it," she said.

"In fact, made you do it."

"Yes." With a hint of excitement. "Exactly."

"And you love him for it."

"Don't say it that way." She sounded injured. "Any-body can make any word sound asinine. 'Love' is an easy mark."

"I asked you a question—love him for it?"

"Somehow . . . yes." He said nothing in response. It seemed to bother her. "I said 'hate' a while ago, and 'love' now . . . You don't make that jump in your mind, do you?"

"Is it really a jump?" he said. "Love thine enemy?"

"I'm not talking about that kind. The implication of 'love thine enemy' is turn the other cheek. What I'm talking about is love thine enemy—"

"Enough to kill him," he said.

". . . Yes."

"I'm not sure I could kill him," he said. "But if I could, I don't think I could tell myself I love him while I'm doing it."

"Hm."

"You can?"

Barely audibly, "I don't know."

"There's another question that's probably more to the point," he said.

"Why doesn't he kill us?"

"Yes."

The question obsessed her just as it did him, he could see that. It will keep her awake all night, he said, she'll be demon-ridden. Then, amazingly, after not too long a silence, he heard her breathing deeply and, while the thought continued to plague him, she lay asleep.

He also had the other thought to plague him. How to tell her about the empty rifle? He worried the possibility of not telling her at all, but he knew it was a betrayal he couldn't perpetrate. Emptying the rifle had been difficult enough, but in some way justifiable, certainly since he could protect her with his own gun. But for her to venture forth with confidence in fire power she didn't have, at a time when he could no longer protect her . . . He couldn't.

Then the scheme occurred to him. Why need she venture forth at all? He could slip away and continue onward—by himself.

How he would do it he didn't know. But, then, this was nighttime; he didn't know lots of things, particularly how, unsteady on his feet as he was, he could pursue the man up the precipice he couldn't climb before, on two good legs. But daylight, when it came, would bring the answers, simple ones like the one he'd already come upon, to leave Johanna behind.

He felt peaceful. It surprised him how little of his mind he had given to the question: whether to go on at all? It had been only a passing thought, a quickly passing one. He was taking his newfound courage for granted, whatever its origin and whatever kind it was, and it gave him a feeling of satisfaction. Without worrying the thought, he wondered what springs of resourcefulness he had come upon that made him ignore the recklessness of going, hobbled and unarmed, after an armed and dangerous man. He must not linger too long on the doubt, he decided.

His headache had cleared. Only the pain in his foot hung on and that, he knew, he would have to bear. He had apparently borne it before, coming down from the ledge.

Suddenly a new thought occurred to him. A remembrance of something gone.

He had no stomach pain. He didn't recall what he had done with the chalk tablets, or even when he had last taken one. Days ago, perhaps . . . It seemed a distant, a separate, time; it seemed another person.

Something surged in him, something he welcomed and disliked, some feeling of the street brat, the guttersnipe, fearful, fearless, tough yet unarmed; a feeling he had never expected to recapture and had hoped never again to need. Well, it was back again.

He heard the sound of the myna bird. Don't be impatient, he said to the call, I'm coming, wait until daylight, I'll be there.

Nineteen

S HE HAD NEVER known such darkness. The moon had shifted to the other side of Mauna Loa and no light, not a ray of it, came through the opening of the grotto. So dark, in fact, that even sound seemed dimmed by it. The waterfall was farther away than she had remembered and, from moment to moment, she imagined she no longer heard a murmur of it. Certainly she heard no sound of Tad's breathing, although he could not be lying more than a few feet away.

Silent in the darkness, not moving, not wanting to awaken him, she thought how warm it was here, how soft under her body, how pleasant, how sheltered from the wind, the torrent, the crack of gunfire, the marauding of wild things. She was not such a romantic as to believe that even a week of such cavernous bliss would be endurable, but she yearned for another night of it, at least the prolongation of this one.

The word again came to her mind, love; in talking about Tokan, it had sounded asinine. Was any single syllable ever asked to carry a heavier millstone of meaning? If love had to bear the weight of only one night of love-making, how lightly it would sustain its burden. And how lightly it had. They had made love in a way she had never done before, as if all she was and all she had ever read in books, all she had heard from Mitou and seen in the geisha house, all her questionings, imaginings, yearnings had been thrown together in an omnium-gatherum of a love-making moment. She was in love with him last night, and he with her, and they had no other weight to carry. Not the burden of Abby, not their lifelong burdens of guilt, not their shame or embarrassment about the most secret places of their bodies, nor how to touch and kiss and play with one another, nor even notions of what made pleasure or pain.

They didn't even carry the burden of fear. The man they had set out to stalk was not, at least for one night, stalking them; he ceased, for the moment, to exist. He was in fact not a terror but someone who had made the joy a possibility. Another reason for being grateful to him. The reasons kept mounting.

She heard a sound. Thinking it might be Tad, she almost reached to touch him. But as she extended her hand, she heard the sound again and clearly it was elsewhere, not close. A snuffling sound. The last time she had heard such a noise, it had been a wounded boar. Tightening, she sat up.

Silence. Only the sound of water plummeting.

Listening, hearing nothing, she remembered the boar again, wounded and strangling for breath.

Another remembrance. A Japanese legend. There had been, somewhere in the mountain forests of Hokkaido, a magic boar. He had taken whatever form he desired, a tree on a hillside, a flying deer, a rivulet, a whispering wind, a silver bird. Every form delighted him and in every form he was happy. One day he made himself into a man and couldn't endure the heartache. But the most heartbreaking end of it was that, from that time onward, the boar could not bring himself to assume another form again. So he remained a wild pig, rooting in the earth, forever snuffling into his own ugliness.

She wondered and played with the wonder: was Tokan, the killer, really a wild boar who had taken on the guise of a man? Was this his last chance at elegance? Did he already know the end, the heartbreak?

The sound again. More perturbing now.

Idyllic as this grotto had seemed in the night, paradisiacal as it had felt only a few moments ago, it could be the abode of any number of wild things. Dangers she might not even hear. Scorpions, for example. Centipedes and millipedes, black-widow and blind-eyed spiders, tarantulas and murder ticks.

The sound was clearer now. Louder, more sustained.

Reaching, she scrounged in the darkness for her rifle. Finding it, she debated whether to awaken Tad; she could neither see nor hear him. She decided to let him sleep. Silently she got to her feet. Not moving, she waited. If only there were a ray of light, a single ray.

It occurred to her: beasts are afraid of fire. Setting her gun down softly, she reached into her pocket for her lighter. She moved a few steps deeper into the cave so that the flare of flame, behind him, would not disturb Tad.

The burst of fire and in it she saw something. Rather, she did not see what she expected would be there. No boar, but no man, either. Tad was not there.

It unsteadied her. She looked in all directions. Softly she whispered his name. Once more. Then, picking up her gun again, she tread warily toward the mouth of the cave. She stood there, not daring into the outer darkness. Yet, surprisingly, the darkness was not total. A band of light was splashed across the summit of the farther palisade, not white-blue moonlight but yellow, with a blood streak in it.

As she stood there, even as she watched, the dawning light was spreading. Nobody was there, nothing. Only the break of day and the thunder of the cataract.

Looking upward, her eyes slowly, ledge by ledge, scanned the precipice they had tried to scale. She couldn't believe he would have attempted it again, by night, with an injured leg. If only she could see a little better, if only there were a few more scintillas of light. She came fully outdoors and went over it again, surveying every crag of both escarpments, and when she saw no sign of him, she slowly returned to the grotto. Inside, pacing, she waited, not doubting he would be back, momentarily, from whatever mysterious place he had gone.

When the sound came again, she was certain it was nerves. She lighted a cigarette, and as she was about to close the lid on the lighter, a draft made the flame flicker. Not from the outside of the cave inward, but from the inside out. And the sound—there could be no question of it—was a wind, a gust of it, coming from somewhere deeper in the cave.

Carefully, studying her way along a wall of the grotto, she started back into the darkness. The ceiling was lower now, and the grotto was narrowing. She would come to the end quite soon, she realized, and not find the source of any wind. Yet, implausibly, the gust seemed to be getting sharper, stronger.

As if a switch had been thrown: a light. A sharp ray, white and trembling, with a million motes in it. Quickly now she advanced toward it. The grotto turned, twisted right angles to itself, and there it was. The ray, broken by ledges of rock. An opening in the cave. And suddenly she knew this was not a cave.

A lava tube. She had seen several of them, on sight-seeing trips one place or another. A tunnel where molten lava had flowed and continued to flow until the outside layer of it had hardened to rock; and when the molten stuff had finally flowed away, a tube of lava stone.

She crawled through the opening. The tunnel led upward, so steeply upward that she had to grasp jagged handholds, from time to time, and pause for breath. Now, coming to the final hundred feet or so, she wasn't sure she could do it. The ascent was steepening all the way, the holds were as rough as rusted nails and her hands were bleeding. Besides, her rifle, tucked into her belt, kept slipping, adding nuisance.

Twenty feet from the top, she inhaled deeply, pointed the barrel away from her, tossed the gun ahead and hoped it wouldn't go off. When it fell silently, she pulled herself upward, one tortured twist at a time.

She was out.

Out on a terrifying awesomeness. A wide reach of devil's brimstone gone to gray. Huge boulders of lava devastation, great expanses of it, all extending upward, upward to the crown of snow. She had never read of such a desolation, never heard of it, could not believe it existed, couldn't believe nature had ever had so mean a revenge, a retribution so frighteningly beautiful.

It had been a flaming requital at one time, but now it was freezing. The sky was cold, the wind was icy. No snuffling breeze up here, but a cruel tempest, all one direction, unchanging.

And nobody in sight. Nothing alive. Only rock and blowing pumice.

She stood there, stunned with wind and chill, frightened. She wasn't sure this place existed, or that she existed in it; she had come through hell to nowhere.

Then she saw the movement. Far. A man hobbling onward.

"Tad!"

He didn't hear her, kept on going.

"Tad!" she yelled. "Tad!"

He paused but didn't turn. He seemed, a man at this distance, like the picture of someone who hears spectral voices.

"Tad!"

He half-turned and, as she continued shouting, turned altogether. He saw her. Waving as he had waved when she had followed him across the canyon bridge. "Stay back!" he yelled. "Stay back!"

What a fool he was to think she could stay back now. She lifted her gun and hurried after him. She saw him quicken his pace, but she knew she would overtake him before long; his limp was hindering him. Hurrying, she saw herself reduce his lead, by a quarter at least, then half. If only her breath held out against the gale, she would quickly overtake him. She had to stop, finally, to cling to a rock, to breathe deeply. Sucking at the air, she realized why it was she was losing breath so painfully; the elevation had been too sharply upward, the atmosphere more rarefied with every foot of rise. Well, if it didn't slow him down, it wouldn't her, she told herself, and started upward again. She had barely taken her third step when she saw it.

The drops of blood.

His blood, she thought for an instant, Tad's. But it did not go straight upward as Tad was going, but obliquely to the right. She followed it. Another drop, another. No question of it. A second trail.

"Tad!" she called. He didn't turn. Her shout was desperate. "Tad! Look—look!"

He must have heard the tumult in her voice; perhaps he thought her in trouble. Turning, he squinted into the sun behind her and held his hand to his forehead.

"Blood!" she called. "Look—blood!"

As she saw him turn back, she didn't wait for him. Rushing, she followed the trail she had found. She could be mistaken: it might not be a man. It might after all be the very wild boar she thought she had heard in the cave, perhaps, it had been wounded; perhaps Tokan himself had wounded it.

But it might be their quarry. Tad's shot, the single shot he seemed to have missed with, could possibly have struck its mark. In any event, there was blood up here. The final trail, perhaps—the rice cakes, the myna bird, and blood. And it had to be tracked.

She forgot her breathlessness, forgot how icy cold it was. She felt certain she was on his footsteps now, knew it in her nerves, in her heartbeat, in her gun hand. She was a hunter again, in the wild, pursuing the live game, stalking the wounded prey. She was beast tracking beast, frightened, relaxed and tense at the same time, somewhat crazed, and exultantly alive. She knew only one thing—obsessively—that she herself must run the creature to earth, she must be the one to find it, to kill it.

Gasping, boiling with heat and cold in the freezing wind, she rushed, she ran onward. But something told her to stop. Some sense warned her to turn, some fright that came from nowhere.

She heard the sound, the gruff guttural noise, the outcry, then Tad hobbled behind a boulder. Running downward again, she was there before she knew she was.

He stood there.

Tokan.

He was walled in by the broken rampart of boulders. He had his rifle in his hand, but he wasn't raising it, wasn't even threatening to raise it. Blood came from a wound in his shoulder. His face was ashen gray, dirty with unkempt beard and grime. He was not elegant. He was a wounded animal, a deadly wild hog in a wild place.

Tad stood there facing him. He seemed unable to move.

She started to raise her rifle but couldn't do it. Just as she had a second thought, she saw Tokan throw his gun away.

Then the cry and he rushed forward. With his one good arm he reached, and his hand came down on Tad's face with a beast's onslaught, a claw. Tad lunged for the arm and twisted. The man kicked at his groin and kicked again, and as Tad cried out, Tokan grabbed him close, kicking and kicking at the groin. Then, abruptly, something so strange, so quick, she barely saw it happen, and Tad was thrown, lying on his back, Tokan throttling him.

Lifting her gun, she was afraid she would catch Tad with it. But then she saw him do something, saw Tad reach with his one free hand, reach into the wound with his fingers, with his fingernails, claw into the blood of it. Tokan shrieked but did not remove his throttling hands. Tad's claws dug deeper into the open gash, the blood ran, and suddenly the man was off.

Now they were standing, close, entangled, grappling, blood and bone together. She heard the crack. It had to be a bone that was cracking; no other sound could be the same. She ran forward in terror. "Oh, Christ!"

As they broke apart, she saw the dangling arm. It looked like the tree limb that had been cut, hung there nearly free of attachment, hung by flesh and skin alone, dangling. It was Tokan's arm. Broken by his own wrench, his own force reversing itself.

The man stood still, not falling. Mindless of his left arm, the bloody wounded one, he looked at the swaying one, quietly looked at it. She saw Tad move forward toward him once again, then stop. It wasn't necessary.

Yet, she thought, it might be. Tokan stirred again. With his left arm he reached into the folds of his clothes. He held the knife up, point raised, skyward. He tried to smile, or seemed to, then stepped forward.

Why didn't Tad move? She shouted the warning.

The knife was coming down. She raised her gun and pulled the trigger. Nothing happened. Oh, God, the gun is fouled, she said, and pulled again, and nothing.

The knife was down, but Tad had grabbed for it. Then, missing it, he stepped away.

In that instant, Tokan fell to his knees. At first, she thought: he's going to beg. Oh, no, please, she wanted to cry out, please don't beg. She started toward him.

The knife flashed downward. Kneeling in the ritual position, he sank the blade deep into his belly. Almost all the way, then indeed all the way, deep to the hilt of it, deep into himself. Then upward, downward, with a strength too impossible to believe, yanking at the knife, yanking again and, with a moan, pulling it out of himself. He raised the bloody blade now and pointed it backward, toward his throat. He almost did it, then strength failed. Again he tried, and couldn't.

His eyes looked up—not at Tad, but at her. His face was pitiful with need, with longing, with entreaty for her help. He extended the knife.

She knew what he wanted and knew she couldn't do it. The final step of the ritual, and she knew she had to fail him.

Suddenly she saw the whole chase, the whole stalking, the entire hunt as he had meant her to see it. She knew why he hadn't killed them, hadn't shot them down when the shooting had been easy. He needed to be brought to that last desperation from which there was no escape; no escape from them or from himself. He needed them to give him the courage, as the lesser of two terrors, to kill himself. Needed to be run to earth like a wounded boar; needed, most of all, an enemy. The enemy who would be the attendant friend to help him with his seppuku to complete what rites he might start upon himself, and might not have the strength to end; the enemy that would love him to death.

The pain on Tokan's face was no longer physical. But the agony in the eyes, the terrible supplication for the final grace, was more than she could bear. She started toward him.

"No," Tad murmured.

She didn't know what the word meant; whether it signified beware or do not kill him. It didn't matter. She continued forward.

When she got to him, she loosened his grip on the knife and took it from him. He raised his head as quietly, as gently as a child, as if he were lifting it for a kiss.

She was hardly aware she was doing it. She drew the knife across his throat.

She saw his lips move, but no sound issued from them. She would have guessed the words were *kino doku*. She recalled that it was as close to an expression of gratitude as the Japanese had. None of their words for "thank you" really expressed gratefulness, only shame. For having caused trouble in the world.

They found his shack, almost by chance, not more than a hundred yards away. It was this small lava-built house that he was homing to, this perverse romantic; here was where he had hoped to die, where he had hoped the ritual would take place. He had almost made it.

It was a strange house, more like a miniature temple, a shrine of growing things. He was, as Kley's papers had described him, a volcanologist. More accurately, a plutonist, an obsolete designation, a mystical one, something that had to do with igneous fusion, birth by fire in the center of the earth. Whatever studies he had made up here didn't seem to have much to do with explosions at the core of the earth but how things grow on the surface of it. In lava, particularly. A huge copper vat was strapped to the ceiling. Out of it, a dozen jets dripped water onto copper vessels containing samples of earth, all lava earth. From two of the vessels grasses grew, weak grasses barely managing to survive. But three bore flowers, two resembling hibiscus, the other, a pale mauve orchid. It was

the other containers that grew the wonders: strange
plants neither she nor Tad had ever seen before, almost
animal in their aliveness to the touch of the hand, like
much of the jungle; all very small, some with blue
leaves, not blue as flowers are blue but as gems are.
Others, with lavender leaves, all tremulously alive.

There was a shelf with a few books on it, another
shelf with a row of small bottles containing, they supposed, nutrients for the growing things. And a slight
platform from which, through a window, one had a
lovely, peaceful view of the snowy cap of Mauna Loa.
The platform, it seemed to her, when she mounted it,
gave the feeling of an altar. She imagined that this
was where he had meant to be.

Tad searched every crevice in the stone and every
splinter of wood. If he was looking for a wireless or a
decoding machine or a listening device, he found none.
There was no mechanism or implement of any kind,
no double-type machine, no deciphering manual, no
plotting map or diagram, nothing of any codes; neither
white nor yellow nor purple, he said almost to himself, and she didn't understand what the reference
meant. There was no sign that the man had been an
enemy agent, stringer, operative of any kind, no sign
at all.

Nor was there any sound up here, except the wind
outdoors and, indoors, the dropping of the tiny water
jets. Someone could have written a haiku about the
silence. There was no deeper meaning than that; no
meaning within meaning within meaning.

Outdoors again, she watched Tad search for a
weather device of some kind, and when she asked
him what it might look like, he didn't answer. He
smiled cryptically, and in a little while, again more to
himself than to her, said, "No East wind, rain."

She didn't understand that either. If he was referring to Japan, it was west of Hawaii, not east. Still, one
did think of it as the Orient, East.

He was barely listening. He had a grave look on his
face, troubled, but with a deep accomplishment under
it, the aspect of a man who has found that the impos-

sible is not impossible. And he murmured something
about his having had some rain, from the East.

Downhill is always easier than up, she realized, and
knowing the way is easier by far than blundering. Still,
it was unbelievable how quickly they came down
through the wilderness and arrived, in the afternoon,
at Gorpy's place.

Peculiarly, they had no apprehensions about the man
any more; they could deal with him, even with an
empty rifle. What made her sure they could deal with
him she didn't understand fully yet; she didn't need
to.

There was no necessity to deal with Gorpy. He was
gone. Everything was gone. The clearing was as still
as if it had been deserted years ago. It was pervaded
by an uncanny silence. There was no sign of damage,
no hint of violence, nothing of devastation. It was almost exactly as they remembered it, except no people.

Although it could only have been two days since
Gorpy and the Hawaiians had left, Johanna imagined
the wild things already closing in. She knew it couldn't
happen in so brief a time, yet there was the sense
that the jungle had waited long enough; the *pili* grass
was already growing at the foot of the *heiau*.

It occurred to both of them: the car would certainly
be gone. That might be the explanation for the deser-
tion by the young people; they had at last found a
means of travel. But, amazingly, the car was there.

By late afternoon, they had hired a quiet Filipino
man and his four-seater plane, and after he lifted it
from the burnt-down cane field, he started to point out
the landmarks of the Islands as if they were Mainland
tourists.

She recalled how they had come here, by the same
boat but separately, so that nobody would associate
them with each other. This time it had not occurred to
either of them to return without the other.

As they flew over the Pacific, she looked at her
clothes. How dirty they were, how torn. How her legs
and back ached; Tad's leg must be an agony to him.

But he showed no sign of it. His face wore a weariness and a thoughtful, disconsolate smile.

Without staring, she studied him as closely as she dared. He had managed to wash the blood of the struggle away, but he was still filthy, his hair matted, his clothes ripped and begrimed. Yet, she had never realized how romantic-looking he was, truly romantic in the sense that one could make an imaginary picture of the man and know that the reality would not lessen him. He was more than she had ever supposed he could be, for he was a man forever struggling with his sadder, weaker, lonelier self; he would never cease the struggle and, from time to time, he would score a victory, as he had on this occasion . . . She loved him.

She saw him look down at his hands. They were raw, as hers were, and swollen. Slowly his left hand reached for her right one. She took his, and held it. His clasp was tight and she tightened hers. It was painful, almost to the bone, but she hoped he wouldn't stop holding her. Then at last, as they were landing, he had to.

Johanna got out of the shower, toweled herself dry, brushed her teeth for the second time and decided she would have to do something about her hands. The cut on her right palm hadn't quite stopped bleeding, and her raw fingertips should really be attended to.

She went to the medicine chest, found gauzes and Band-Aids and adhesive tape. She had a decision to make: whether to put zinc ointment on the wounds, or iodine. The ointment would be slow and comforting; the iodine, quick and painful. She chose iodine. It stung more than she had anticipated, and for a moment she wished there had been someone who had made the other choice for her, someone to soothe the ache.

She had already made the bigger decision; surprisingly, it had been easier than zinc ointment versus iodine. She was leaving. The question was no longer whether she would depart, but how soon she could manage it. The last time it had taken days of choosing and pining and fretting, of poring over dusty books and keepsakes, memorabilia so old she could no longer identify their origin. Then she stacked everything all around her, boxes and suitcases and stuffed pillowcases, had made a barricade so impenetrable that she couldn't inch her way to the door.

This time, nothing; she would take nothing. She had gone to the other side of the universe with nearly nothing; had, in fact, when inner encumbrances were counted, carried more than she could bear. She would travel lighter now.

She would travel without the heaviest things: plans. Once, it would have been inconceivable to her to go back to the Mainland—permanently go back—without any notion of where she might live and work. But the unknown no longer had terrors for her. She didn't know what work she might do—some sort of writing, if possible, yet not an absolute condition of her happiness; but work itself, a positive necessity. She would look for many things at first, perhaps, and then not so many . . . and ultimately, one . . . No, the unknown could never be more frightening than coming out of the darkness of the lava tube . . .

The question was: when to go? If she could do it tonight, do it now . . . There would be no Clipper flight, however, nor even tomorrow or the next day. No steamer either, not on Saturday, except the charter boat from Kona. But even that was irregular, most Saturdays not at all.

She telephoned Kona. There was a boat that would be leaving tonight, at nine o'clock.

But it was already late afternoon and there would be no way to get to Kona. Unless, perhaps, the Filipino pilot was still at John Rodgers Airport. She telephoned and spoke to one man, then another. Nobody knew the pilot or his plane. A third man came to the phone and heard the strain in her voice. He said he would look for the pilot. Taking her number, he promised to call her back.

When she hung up, she didn't know whether to start

dressing or wait until she was sure she was going. Dress, she told herself, don't wait to go, start going.

For an instant, she couldn't move, except to tremble. Eccentrically, it made her smile, as if it were not a present trembling but a past one, the tremors of a person in a former time. But the trembling became worse. What if the man called back and said she had to leave within the hour—would she be able to do it? What if, worse, he said there was no way of getting her to Kona tonight? Would her resolve to depart stay strongly with her until a day when she *could* depart, or would it languish and die?

Goddamn it, Johanna. She started to dress, without tremor now, quickly but not hectically, with a quiet and deliberate purpose. She didn't hesitate over what to wear, didn't pick up anything and set it down, mislaid nothing, didn't drop so much as an eyebrow pencil.

How strange, she thought, that it had taken so long to come to this. What had she been afraid of? The starting over again? The starting over again of what? Of love, was that it, the search for it? The fear she would never find it again, or not be capable of it once more? Was she afraid of her own rage—against herself for not being equal to the emptiness, against the world for not filling it? Did she need the excuse of Ben's death to get revenge against her own existence? Whatever the quest was, whatever the riddle, how many deaths did one have to suffer before one heard the answer to it?

But after each death, there had been a new life. And now she had to go searching for another. And the question—whether she was ready for it, whether she had the courage for it—had a built-in lie. It suggested she had an alternative. She had none.

The telephone rang. It was the airport. They hadn't found the Filipino pilot, the man said. But if Mrs. Winter wanted so badly to get to Kona by nine o'clock, he himself, for a reasonable price, would see she got there.

She was ready, then.

She looked around. No memorabilia. Only her purse, her checkbook, some cash, some gloves to hide the gashes on her hands, some identification papers. When she got to the Mainland, she would write to the realtor, arranging all the details and asking if his office would, for a fee, take care of the disposal of her things.

There was one important thing to do.

Reaching for the phone, she dialed Abby's number. Oh, God, she said, I hope he doesn't answer the phone.

It was Abby's voice. "Mother, you're back!" How pleased she sounded.

As she explained to Abby that she was leaving, as she heard the wonder in her daughter's voice and the insistence that she would meet her mother at the airport to say good-by, Johanna caught a glimpse of herself: she was eating guavas in a woodland. So was he. How musky they taste; sexy, she had said, and sweet.

"Really, Mother? You really mean you're going back? For good and all?"

For good and all, what a perfect expression. "Yes, for good and all."

Abby said, "I feel so happy for you—and I ache."

The word hurt. She took a breath and then another; they didn't help. She said: you're old enough, Johanna, you're old enough to leave your children . . . both of them.

She said a loving thing; so did Abby. And they hung up.

As she left the telephone, she caught a glimpse of the jodhpurs she had worn. She picked them off the chair. They were torn and dirty. She must get rid of them. Wadding them up to throw them into the wastebasket, she wondered if she had left anything in the pockets. There was nothing except a long leaf, crumpled now and nearly altogether brown, a bamboo leaf. Then she saw, clinging to it, a few grains of rice. The rice cake he had left behind him, for a trail. Bemused, she followed the remembrance. Another ache. She had an impulse to keep the sad, disintegrating leaf and the white grains. Then she routed the notion; how cheerless it was to look at, falling apart so quickly. Without crumpling it any further, she let it slip from her fingers, into the wastepaper basket.

And she departed.

Twenty

SHORTLY BEFORE Johanna's telephone call, Abby was bandaging Tad's hands.

"Don't fuss over them," he said gently. "A few Band-Aids will do it."

"Oh, no," she said. "I'll put this white stuff on—they look so raw. My God, how did this ever happen?"

"I told you," he said quietly. Then he added to the story, nothing truer or more concrete than before, all vague things, about mountains and rough ascents. She didn't seem suspicious of his reticences; accepted them as Navy-Intelligence Confidential, and gave her attention to his wounds. He didn't want her distressed over him; he would have preferred taking care of his hands himself, or hiding them. But the tenderness in her voice moved him and he knew she had to do it for him. He touched his free hand to her hair. "Thank you," he said softly.

"I didn't know what to tell Kley," she said.

"When did he call?"

"This morning was the first time. The man in the Auburn didn't see you go out, so they assumed you were here. When Kley called, I hemmed and hawed about your having the flu and he didn't believe me. In about half an hour, the doorbell rang and there he was."

"What did he say?"

She didn't answer for a moment. Having difficulty, she replied at last, "You didn't tell me about the Auburn. I didn't know you were under arrest."

"House arrest."

"You know what Kley did? He went through every room!"

"Indignant."

She thought about it. "No, not really. He seemed —desperate."

"Desperate?"

"Yes." Then, after a long moment, her voice not altogether level, she returned to the former subject. "If he didn't send you on an assignment . . . where did you go?"

He knew she hadn't the remotest suspicion of Johanna; she couldn't in a million years—not Abby—have associated the two absences. Yet, she had readied herself to be hurt, without having achieved any invulnerability at all. "I can't tell you that," he said.

"Just tell me one thing." The question was hesitant. "Was there really a man? You said there was a man."

"Yes."

"And were you really trying to get something from him?"

"Yes."

"Did you get it?"

". . . Not what I expected," he responded. "But quite a lot."

She nodded and smiled a little. She was much relieved.

Then the telephone rang and he heard her speaking to Johanna.

It was just before nightfall. The battleships, below, nestling against the bosom of Ford Island, seemed white although he knew they were gray, seemed deserted although he knew there were thousands of men belowdecks. They were probably listening, as he had been listening, to the report of the afternoon's football game, Hawaii versus Williamette, the former having won; the score, 20 to 6. Men and officers were probably paying and collecting betting debts. He heard the orchestras of two of the ships, one playing, the other tuning up; there would be a musical contest of some sort tonight, he wasn't sure of the details, one band playing against another, perhaps a number of them. There would be lots of shore leaves and liberties and, later, the sleepy reeling back on board again.

With the darkness, the lights from the ships seemed

brighter now. It was a lovely sight, down there. It disturbed him a little that the *Lexington,* the last of the carriers, had gone; but that would probably be a good sign, as Kley had said, that they weren't needed here.

He looked at his watch. It was getting late and Abby was not yet back from the Rodgers Airport. If she didn't return soon, he would wait to dine with her later; he wasn't hungry anyway—and in a while he'd have to leave, to keep his appointment with Kley.

The admiral would have made the appointment earlier, he had said, but he didn't want to miss the last quarter of the game; then, immediately after it, he would be having an "important drink with an important admiral." Don't drive in, Kley had said, "I'll send a car."

How unexpectedly friendly he had sounded. As if he had entirely forgotten that he had put Tad under arrest, certainly as if he had forgiven everything. That, of course, meant he wanted something unorthodox from Tad, something perhaps "outside the normal formulations," as the old man had once put it; in a word, tricky.

Somewhat nervous, Tad had another look at his watch and made the decision. Before seeing Kley, he would write the letter.

He went downstairs to his study, and typed it, original and four copies, one of them for later delivery to Kley. The original copy went to Washington. *Dear Admiral Weybrandt,* it said. *This is my application for reassignment. I have an urgent need, as I once expressed to you, to go to sea. . . .* He wrote covering letters and signed all of them. Realizing, with a peaceful, quiet gratification, that he had done it at last, he put the Weybrandt letter into his pocket, took one final look at his watch, and knew it was time to go; the car would be arriving any moment. He checked his uniform to be sure everything was in order and lintless, and went outdoors.

The car was already there. He got in without saying anything to the driver, barely greeting him, and they went down the Aiea hills. At the foot, he asked the driver to stop at the mailbox; he got out and posted the Weybrandt letter and returned to the car.

They drove on and came to the main gate. There was a flattop truck ahead of them, with an enormous evergreen, a mountain pine, perhaps; it had not occurred to him that Christmas was so close at hand. Winter was in the air—Hawaiian winter, to be sure, but Yuletime nonetheless—and he thought of Mauna Loa with snow on its summit, and of Johanna going back to other snows. He must try not to think of that.

The car stopped outside the white building and Tad got out. Even though the place was the same and just as dark as when he had been there a few days ago, stealing information, the corridor now seemed altogether different. He couldn't tell why; an illusion, perhaps.

The anteroom of Kley's office was empty, and the only light in it was a weak one, a gooseneck lamp on one of the bare-topped desks. From inside the admiral's office, the sound of men's voices. Kley's was one of them. The other, faintly familiar, was not distinguishable, for it was pitched low. He knocked on the door.

"Come in."

Kley sat at his desk with an ostentatiously friendly expression on his face. Across from him sat Hugh Jerrold. The Englishman was bandaged from the beating he had taken a number of days ago; where there was no gauze or adhesive, his face was black and blue. He half arose from his chair with shy uncertainty, his discomposure plain.

But Kley was the hospitable naval host, piping Tad on board, happy to make a ceremony of it. "Welcome back, sluggard!" he said too companionably. "Been vacating, have you?"

Tad said how-are-you to both of them; then, filling the void, turned to Jerrold. "I thought you'd gone."

Kley made a jovial sound. "We wouldn't let him," he said. "Too valuable a man."

Jerrold had a quick, abashed look at Tad. His uneasiness growing, "I'm back in good graces."

"Well, if things change," Kley said, "we all have to change with them."

Tad said warily, "What has changed?"

Kley laughed professionally. "Well, my mind, for one thing. I thought those yellow bastards would never lift a finger against us. But Jerrold here—he's convinced me that they will."

"How has he done that?"

Kley turned to Jerrold. "Tell him what you've got."

Jerrold didn't respond immediately. There was some demurrer in the air. Tad couldn't interpret it. Not a word of my arrest, Tad thought, not a question where I've been. And the two of them together, the Admiral and the Procurer, the strange companions, each with his contempt for the other, the one denying it with a fool's caperings that misled nobody, the other plainly ashamed. How had it happened so quickly? he wondered. Don't be naïve, he told himself; someone had a commodity or spied a weakness; someone seized an opportunity. Opportunism is, by definition, a quick process; the door has to be opened at the first knock. So quickly . . . the blood of Kley's beating still not dry on Jerrold's face.

"Go on," Kley boomed cheerily at the Englishman. "Tell him what you got hold of."

"Well," Jerrold started disconcertedly, "the Purple Code *is* Japanese—they send stuff out on a machine. It's not a naval code, it's diplomatic—and we've cracked it."

"Who's 'we'?"

"Washington—Army—Navy—I'm not sure."

"When was it cracked?" Tad asked.

"Well over a year ago," Jerrold said.

Tad was stunned. "And we haven't heard about it?" Then, quietly, "What's been *in* it?"

"Everything. Tokyo's complete instructions on diplomatic negotiations—the near certainty that they're going to attack."

"I don't believe it!" Tad said.

Kley jumped in. "Neither did I," he said. "Fantastic, isn't it? Everything about it—incredible. You know

what Washington calls the operation? *Magic!* Honest
to God, that's what they call it—as if it's all a goddamn
fantasy! And Magic has built—Jerrold, how many machines?"

"I know of seven. Probably more."

Kley laughed. There was hysteria in it. "They've
built at least seven decoding machines to break the
Purple Code—and Hawaii doesn't have a single one
of them!"

"Who has them?" Tad asked.

"Everybody!" Kley shouted. "Washington—Manila
—Singapore—who else, Jerrold? London—even London's got one! That's how I heard about it!" Pointing
to Jerrold, "Through an Englishman! Imagine that—I
get American Intelligence reports—designed for American use—acquired through an American machine
—from an *Englishman!*"

Reservedly, Tad asked, "How do you account for
that?"

The question had the opposite effect from the one
Tad had expected. It somewhat tranquilized the old
man. "Well, it has its good side, actually. If we don't
get the reports, I think that's because Washington is
sure we don't *need* the reports . . . We're safe here."

Tad turned slowly to Jerrold. "Is that what you
found out?"

Jerrold shifted his weight uncomfortably. "Well, in a
way, yes."

"You were sure we weren't safe here," Tad continued.

"Well, he was guessing then," Kley said. "But now
it's increasingly clear—Hawaii's safe. If it weren't,
would Kimmel have sent the two carriers away? We'd
have needed them for protection, true? And why would
he leave the battlewagons bottled up in the Harbor?"

It made a sort of sense; yet Tad had queasy feelings
and he couldn't tell what caused them. Mostly, he suspected, it was Jerrold's uneasy eyes, his shiftiness, as
if he was holding something back—or, more likely,
not believing his own conclusions. He was puzzled by
what the Englishman's reservations might be.

"Jerrold," he said, trying to sound as quietly confidential as if Kley were not in the room, "you've changed your mind about this—and maybe you're right to change your mind. What I want to know is why you did."

Jerrold cleared his throat. "Well . . ." Then he stopped. He started over again. "Washington has made at least seven Purple decoding machines. They've given them out—world-wide. If they can make seven, they can make eight, nine, ten. They can easily make an extra one for Hawaii. Why didn't they? Unless, for some reason, they are certain Hawaii won't need it."

"Or unless they simply want Hawaii *not* to have it."

Tad had said it because he thought that was in Jerrold's mind; that was the Englishman's reservation. And for the split second it was in Tad's mind as well. He wasn't entirely sure where the thought would take him. He was not making any charge, merely following a logical possibility. But suddenly he realized that the logic had a formidable accusation in it.

Kley caught it. "What the hell do you mean by that?"

"I don't know," he said. He was floundering, trusting only the impulses of his mind, letting his intuitions carry him wherever they might. "What I mean—if a war *has* to start, and if a reluctant country is dragging its feet—and if some catastrophe *has* to happen—somewhere—!"

Kley interrupted apoplectically. "You mean we—right here—we're being set up for it?"

"Not actually set up, but—"

"That's traitorous! That's a goddamn traitorous thing to say!"

"I am not traitorous!" Tad retorted. "I'm merely asking why we don't have the machine!"

"Do you realize what you're saying? Do you realize that in these times—when fire power can destroy a whole city in a matter of minutes—you are saying somebody in the Navy Building, in the White House—somebody in our own government is purposely withholding information we need if we're to protect ourselves?"

Tad felt himself go bloodless. The man was right. What a sink of disillusionment, of suspicion, what a bog of cynicism he had fallen into that such a notion had crossed his mind. He was ashamed of himself; he suddenly felt weak with humiliation. "No, sir—I'm sorry—I don't believe that. I know it can't be true. And I have to confess—I don't understand the situation." The confession was genuine; he felt helpless with ignorance.

The tension subsided. Kley had long ago divested himself of the spuriously cheery manner. He now continued soberly. "Well, we're at the next step. If it's true the Japs are going to attack us, we have to know *when and where*. And we think we have a clue to it." He looked at Jerrold, giving him a sign to speak.

"East wind, rain," Jerrold said.

"Has that signal been given yet?" Tad asked.

"No—not yet," Jerrold replied.

Kley, deliberately, "But we think we know who's going to give it."

"Who?"

"Tokan."

He couldn't believe he had heard Kley accurately. He wondered if they could guess how icy his hands had turned.

"Tokan?"

"Yes." Kley nodded. "Because we think he has what may look like a weather station up there, somewhere —but it's really the message center of the Pacific."

He couldn't speak. Unready for this, prepared with no answer, he didn't know where to go. Stalling, "Is there a plan about this?"

"Yes, there is," Kley said. "I think your instincts about going for Tokan were absolutely right." Then, the magnanimous smile. "You see, I've even changed my mind about that, Thaddeus. And I'm sorry I didn't give you the papers you came for."

He reached into his file and brought out the red Fabrikoid envelope, the full dossier on Tokan. He handed it to Tad. "Here you are—I want you to read it."

"For what reason?" Tad asked. "What's the next step?"

"Jerrold wants to go up into those mountains—after Tokan," he answered. "And he wants you for a partner."

He's dead, he wanted to cry, Tokan is dead, he killed himself, or I did or Johanna did. The man who was supposed to have been a spy, but wasn't, is dead —all three of us, we killed Tokan. Perhaps he would have said those things if Jerrold weren't there. But he was no longer trading information with Jerrold, that was over; tomorrow, or next month's tomorrow, he would not even be trading it with Kley; he would be at sea. He was certain of it, in his bones.

There would, of course, be no going for Tokan, but this was not the time to say it. He didn't know what to do about the envelope, whether to take it or not. He wanted badly to read what was inside it, wanted to know all he could know about the man who had been a three-time murderer and who had died, by Eastern lights, nobly.

Kley shook the envelope at him. "Take it," the old man said. "When you've read it, I'd like you and Jerrold to go up after him. I don't care how you have to get it out of him—I don't care how far you have to take him—I don't care if you have to take him all the way." Then, when Tad still hadn't accepted the envelope, "Here, take it—take it."

Tad took the envelope.

When he got home, Abby was already in bed, but not asleep. He didn't turn the light on, nor did he start to get undressed.

"I saw Johanna off," she said.

"Did you?"

"Yes." A meditative moment. "I didn't think she'd ever do it. And suddenly she did."

"She had to—sooner or later."

"Yes, I suppose," she agreed. "She seemed so

strange—and kind of wonderful. A radiance . . . I don't know what it was—she looked so different from the last time we saw her."

Abby had said "we"—without a surmise that he had seen Johanna alone since Ben's funeral when they had seen Johanna together. His guess had been right. She suspected nothing, and there was the end of it. It was a relief, of course, yet . . . he wasn't quite ready for an ending . . . something forever regrettable . . .

Abby was having her own regrets. "As she got into the airplane she didn't look back . . . She didn't cry, but I did."

"I'm sorry."

"It's better for her, I guess," she said. "Ever since Ben died . . ."

He thought he heard her crying; perhaps he was wrong. In a moment, no sign of it. "Aren't you coming to bed?" she asked.

He rustled the papers inside the envelope. "I've got this stuff Kley gave me. I have to read it tonight."

"Tonight?" She sounded woebegone.

She wanted him badly, he knew that, but he couldn't, not yet, maybe not for a while. "I'm not over the trip," he said. "I ache." God knows it's true enough, he thought; all over. And some part of the ache he might never get rid of.

"Poor baby," she said. "Come to bed—I won't attack you."

"Later," he replied. "When I've read the stuff."

He took it into the living room and sat on the couch; under not too bright a light, he started to read. By what unrecognizable descriptions they had labeled the dead Japanese. Purloiner of documents, fake importer, fraudulent scientist, consular *persona non grata,* hugger-mugger man. It had nothing to do with the figure Tad had seen on the headland, beckoning him to come. The person who had described Tokan's disappearance into the woodland knew something of lava, perhaps, but nothing of despair and loneliness, he knew of mountains but not of magic. The report had nothing to do with the dead man.

When he had read it through, he went to bed. Abby barely heard him. She muttered something, dream murmurings, and nothing came of it.

Tomorrow, he would tell her about his application for reassignment. She would take it well, the Navy woman, but she would be in trouble with it; they both would. But she knew he loved her; he knew it too, deeply. He wondered if, as she got older, he would see her mother in her. He hoped he wouldn't, for he loved them both and wanted to continue to love them both—and separately; so he would need them separate in his mind, separate for the rest of his life; he was quite sure he would not be equal to two such women combined into one.

As he fell asleep, he had a picture of Johanna, running after him—on the bridge and on the mountain, high in the high cold, her empty rifle in her hand.

"Stay back!" he called.

He asked himself if he would always be wanting her to stay back or if, as the years went on, he would want to remember her coming closer and closer on the mountainside.

Toward dawn, unable to sleep, he got out of bed. He had had dreams. First, of Ben, talking to him in a language—Japanese, he assumed—that Tad did not understand. Then he saw Ben speaking softly to a girl, again in Japanese. His dream took for granted, without his ever having met her, that it was Muna Ben was talking to; she was lovely and delicate and she held her hands clasped in a gentle way. When he awakened, he kept thinking of her and wondering if she ever got back to her native city in Japan, the softly serene city Tokan had described, whatever its name was. He hoped she had indeed returned to the town again, and that she could be quiet there.

He had an impulse to awaken Abby, only to talk; he felt forlorn. But he didn't disturb her.

A little after seven in the morning, Tad made himself some coffee and, seeing that the sun had fully risen, he went out into the morning cool, onto the terrace. He drank his coffee there and looked down at the Harbor. The ships were beautiful and now, with his letter in the mail, closer than ever to his life.

Then he saw the plane.

He thought at first, because it was not altogether familiar, that it might be one of the new ones the Air Station had been expecting. Then he saw the shell. Actually saw it before he heard it; saw it fall and float and fall. Almost as an afterthought, the noise, the bombardment, the burst of flames; soon, the other planes, so many of them.

It can't be here, he said, it can't be.

It can't be anywhere, not anywhere.

He saw the first battleship go up in flames, then the second. Then another.

He started to cry.

The thought came to him—not comforting—simply a random thought: They now know where and when.

Going for Tokan would not be necessary.

ABOUT THE AUTHOR

N. RICHARD NASH is probably best known as a playwright. Both *The Rainmaker* and *See the Jaguar* have been produced all over the world, and *The Rainmaker* has been translated into over thirty languages. He was one of the group of playwrights who were responsible for changing the whole current of television drama. The movement is now called the Golden Age of Television, and Nash, Robert Alan Arthur, Gore Vidal, Paddy Chayefsky, and Horton Foote were its vanguard. Nash has also written many screenplays, including *The Rainmaker* and *Porgy and Bess*, and has taught philosophy and drama at Byrn Mawr, Haverford, Brandeis and the University of Pennsylvania. He is married to the former Katherine Copeland and has three children.

DON'T MISS
THESE CURRENT
Bantam Bestsellers

RELAX!
SIT DOWN
and Catch Up On Your Reading!

Bantam Book Catalog

Here's your up-to-the-minute listing of every book currently available from Bantam.

This easy-to-use catalog is divided into categories and contains over 1400 titles by your favorite authors.

So don't delay—take advantage of this special opportunity to increase your reading pleasure.

Just send us your name and address and 25¢ (to help defray postage and handling costs).

"The Fiction Sensation of the Year!"

"Against an exotic background and an atmosphere of sensuality...a compelling portrait filled with fascinating characters caught in a web of intrigue and violence..."
—**Sidney Sheldon, Author of The Other Side of Midnight**

"A totally absorbing book, with imagination and compassion skillfully blended with the background of reality."
—**Helen Van Slyke, Author of The Rich and the Righteous**

"A superb read...suspense that's nerve-tearing *and* believable...characters you care about."
—**John Jakes, Author of The Warrior**